Gabriel-Francois Coyer

The history of John Sobieski

King of Poland

Gabriel-Francois Coyer

The history of John Sobieski
King of Poland

ISBN/EAN: 9783742851154

Manufactured in Europe, USA, Canada, Australia, Japa

Cover: Foto ©Andreas Hilbeck / pixelio.de

Manufactured and distributed by brebook publishing software
(www.brebook.com)

Gabriel-Francois Coyer

The history of John Sobieski

THE

HISTORY

OF

JOHN SOBIESKI,

KING OF POLAND.

TRANSLATED

From the FRENCH of M. *L'ABBÉ* COYER.

LONDON:

Printed for A. MILLAR, in the Strand.
MDCCLXII.

His HIGHNESS

The PRINCE of BOUILLON.

DESCENDANT of a great King, you will find, in the History of his Life, a pattern of the virtues you aim at, and of which, at your age, it is sufficient, perhaps, to have only a faint idea. SOBIESKI was a Hero, before he was a King: and the heroism, to which he owed his elevation, must animate all who intend to do great things.

I am not ignorant, my Lord, that your own family can furnish you with models of every sort; and that the blood of the House of Lorrain, which flows also in your veins, was always

A 2   fruit-

fruitful in Heroes. I would enume-
rate the Princes of Lorrain and Bouillon, who have been the admiration
of Europe, if hiftory, and public monuments did not proclaim their praife.
Yet, without forgetting their glory, fix
your attention upon that of Sobiefki;
and you will learn by what actions
immortal fame is acquired among all
nations. You will acquire it yourfelf
by cultivating the qualities with which
nature has endued your mind. To
admire great men, and to ftudy
their characters, as you do, is beginning to imitate them.

I am, with great refpect,

Your Highnefs's moft humble

and moft obedient fervant,

C O Y E R.

PREFACE.

THE History of an hereditary and absolute King does not ordinarily interest our attention in so high a degree, as we naturally wish to have it interested in reading the actions of Governors of nations. To a King of this sort, whatever be his character, his people submit, as having by birth a right to command them; and they are not permitted to shew any marks of their discerning between good government and bad. If any convulsions happen, they are generally slight, and authority, in the end, subdues every thing. This monotony of passive obedience, which is beneficial under a good King, but ruinous under a bad one, fills the stage of history with cold, unanimated performers, who move and act under the direction of one principal actor; and this principal actor, being equally spiritless as he is void of fear, is himself incapable of interesting us in a lively manner.

But the case is not the same with an elective King, who is raised to the throne either by his virtues, or by force. If by the former, it makes a moving sight; if by the latter, he still engages our attention by surmounting obstacles;

obstacles; and when he is carried to the sum-
mit of power, he stands in perpetual need both
of prudence and activity to keep his feat.
The King, the law, and the nation, are three
powers incessantly endeavouring to weigh
down each other, and it is difficult to preserve the ballance between them. The nation, under the protection of the Law, thinks,
speaks, and acts with a liberty becoming
reasonable beings. The King, by either observing or violating the law, is approved or
thwarted, obeyed or disobeyed, and has a
peaceable or disturbed reign. Of this sort is
the History I now write; which presents us
with a Polish Noble, the famous *Sobieski,*
rising to the supreme power, and maintaining
himself in it, in times of confusion and distress. We shall see him acting in the Army,
the Senate, and the Diets; and I shall describe him with that truth of narration, which
it is in vain to look for in the history of an
absolute Monarch, who governs in the dark,
whereas the head of the republic of Poland acts
always openly. So that an Historian, without
being reduced to conjectures, and by this
means imposing upon posterity after having
first imposed upon himself, has nothing to do
but to chuse good memorials; and the two
which I have principally followed, seem to be
of this sort.

The military part is chiefly taken from the
manuscript of a French Officer in the Polish
service,

fervice, named *Dupont*, who being chief engineer of the artillery, and Captain of an independent company of two hundred dragoons, attended his Hero in his campaigns. He relates what he faw with his own eyes; and being neither a Pole by birth, nor a fubject of the Prince whofe actions he records, he was likely to be free both from national prejudices, and that blind adoration which perfons frequently pay to the mafter under whom they were born.

The political part, I am indebted for to the familiar letters of *Andrew Chryfoftom Zalufki*, a Bifhop, Senator, and Chancellor of *Poland*: three 'qualities which placed him in the very center of bufinefs. His letters were writ according as events happened, and intended to be feen neither by the public nor the Prince, but addreffed to private friends; and friendfhip knows no language but that of unreferved franknefs. They were put to the prefs long after the time of their being writ, when Sobiefki was no more, and his family did not wear the Crown. I find in them neither beauty of fentiment, nor elegance of ftyle, nor exactnefs of expreffion: all that I fought for was truth: and if, with this firm purpofe, and fuch guides, I have neverthelefs gone out of the way, we may tear all our Hiftories in pieces.

What

What remains to be obferved, is, that before I exhibit Sobiefki upon the ftage of Poland, I have given a fketch of Poland itfelf. This labour might well be called fuperfluous, if that kingdom was as well known as Germany or the Low-Countries. But without fuch a fhort defcription, the generality of readers would have had a very imperfect idea of many facts recorded in the Hiftory of Sobiefki, which relate to the foil, the manners, and the government of that country.

THE

ERRATA.

Page 19. Line 19. for *Palatine*, read *Palatinate*. P. 22. l. 3. for *fhal*, read *fhall*. P. 29. l. 5. for *diminifhes*, read *difmiffes*. P. 35. l. 23. for *Vizier*, read *Vifir*. P. 59. l. 17. for *thei rmanners*, read *their manners*. P. 89. l. 5 for *tbe*, read *foreign*. P. 90. l. 4. for *off*, read *of*. P. 111. l. 19. for *was*, read *is*. P. 141. l. 22. for *pointed*, read *and painted*. P. 174. l. 2. for *forrefts*, read *forefts*. P. 182. l. 19. for *Mandreofki*, read *Mondreofki*. P. 196. l. 16. for *continued*, read *contained*. P. 198. l. 16. for *entertainmentt*, read *entertainment*. P. 215. l. 10. for *Gulga*, read *Galga*. P. 216. l. 6. for *tb ediverfions*, read *tbe drverfions*. P. 226. l. 26. for *but is*, read *but it is*. P. 248. l. 19. for *eight*, read *eighth*. P. 264. l. 34. for *created*, read *erected*. P. 298. l. 15. for *extenfiv eas*, read *extenfive as*. P. 332. Note 2. for *(a)* read *(b)*. P. 336. l. 1. for *deftefted*, read *detefted*. P. 363. l. 16. dele *be*. P. 390. l. 16. for *en*, read *an*. P. 422. l. 22. for *tbe Empire of Poland*, read *tbe Empire and Poland*. P. 427. l. 9. for *which much*, read *which was much*. P. 449. l. 9. for *Moldovia*, read *Moldavia*. P. 475. l. 12. for *wealtb*, read *benefits*. P. 484. l. 29. for *bena*, read *bene*. P. 489. l. 12. for *intereft*, read *interefts*.

THE
HISTORY
OF
JOHN SOBIESKI
KING OF POLAND.

BOOK I.

A General Sketch of POLAND.

BEFORE the fixth century after Chrift, when the Poles were yet Sarmatians, they had no Kings, but lived without government in mountains and forefts, having no habitations but waggons; always meditating fome new invafion; bad troops for foot-fervice, but excellent cavalry *(a)*. It is fomething furprifing, that a barbarous people, without a leader, and without laws, fhould ftretch their empire from the Tanais to the Viftula, and from the Euxine Sea to the Baltic *(b)*: boundaries prodigioufly diftant from

(a) Tacit. Hift. lib. i. cap. 79.
(b) Pompon. Mela, de Situ Orbis, lib. i.

B   each

each other, and which they enlarged still further by the acquisition of Bohemia, Moravia, Silesia, Lusatia, Misnia, Mecklenburg, Pomerania, and the Marches of Brandenburg. The Romans, to whom so large a part of the world submitted, never penetrated into Sarmatia.

This historical paradox shews what can be done by strength of body, a habit of living hardly, a natural love of liberty, and a savage instinct, which supplies the place of Kings and laws. The Sarmatians were called robbers by civilized nations, who forgot that they themselves had begun in the same manner.

The Poles, who took this name about the middle of the sixth century, are far from having preserved entire the inheritance left them by their ancestors. 'Tis a long time since they lost Silesia, Lusatia, great part of Pomerania, Bohemia, and all that they possessed in Germany; and they have since lost Livonia, and the vast plains of the Ukraine. Many a great empire has, in like manner, sunk under its own weight.

About the year 550, *Leck* formed a design of civilizing the Sarmatians, though he was but a Sarmatian himself. He begun with cutting down trees, and erecting himself a dwelling. Other huts were soon raised round this model; the nation, hitherto erratic, became fixed; and Gnesna, the first city of Poland, took the place of a forest (*a*). The Sarmatians seem scarce to have known what eagles were, since we are told, that from their finding several nests of these birds in the trees which were cut down upon this occasion, the eagle came to be painted upon the Polish standards. But these fierce birds make their airies only upon the tops of high rocks, and Gnesna is situated in a plain.

(*a*) Martin. Cromer. de Orig. Pol. lib. i. c. 14.

Leck

Leck foon drew the eyes of his equals upon him, and by difplaying talents fit for government, as well as a&tion, he became their mafter, with the title of Duke, when he might as eafily have' af-. fumed that of King.

From the time of this leader, down to the prefent age, Poland has been fucceffively governed by other Dukes, by Vaivods, now called Palatines,. by Kings, Queens, and Queen-Regents, with the intervention of frequent interregna. Thefe laft have been little better than fo' many times of anarchy. The regents have always made themfelves hated. The few Queens there have been, have fcarce had time to fhew themfelves. The Vaivods have always been oppreffors. Among the Dukes and Kings, there have been fome great Princes ; the reft have been mere warriors or tyrants. Such will always be the fate, in a great meafure, of all the nations of the world; becaufe it is not the laws, but men, that govern.

In this long feries of ages, the Poles reckon four claffes of fovereigns. The heads of the three firft races, are *Leck*, *Piaft*, and *Jagellon*; the fourth, which begins with *Henry of Valois*, forms a clafs by itfelf, becaufe of the Crown's paffing from one family to another, without fixing in any. There are many fingularities in the fucceffion of thefe four claffes which are well worth being known.

In the year 750, the Poles had not yet examined the queftion, whether a woman might govern men. It had long before been decided in the Eaft, that women were born to obey. *Venda* however reigned in Poland, and reigned with glory. The Polifh hiftorians (*a*) relate (but are we obliged to believe them ?) that a German Prince named *Ritiger*, won

(*a*) Cromer. Dluglofs. Hift. Pol. lib. i.

by

by the charms of this unfeeling beauty, demanded her for his wife at the head of an army; that she offered him battle; that the German troops refused to fight in a love quarrel; that Ritiger killed himself, and that Venda threw herself into the Vistula, that she might no more disturb the peace of her subjects. Whatever becomes of the truth of this story, it is certain, that she would have done them greater service by continuing to govern them well.

From this time, the Salick law, or rather custom, of France, was adopted in Poland; for the two Queens that reigned there afterwards, Hedwigia in 1382, and Anne Jagellon in 1575, were advanced to the throne only by accepting the husbands which were appointed to support them in so exalted a station. Anne Jagellon was sixty years old when she was elected, but *Stephen Battori*, who married her to get the Crown, thought that a Queen was always young.

In former ages, other ways had been laid open to arrive at royalty. In 804, the Poles, being embarassed about the choice of a Governor, offered their Crown as a prize to the best runner; a practice antiently known in Greece, and which did not appear to them more singular than to annex the Crown to birth. It was won by an obscure youth, who took the name of *Lesko* II. The annals of that age say, that he retained, under the royal purple, the modesty and gentleness of his former fortune, and was fierce and audacious only when he (a) took the field against the enemies of the State.

Almost all the Poles maintain that their Crown has always been elective; but they are little interested in the decision of this question, because they enjoy the thing contended for. If it was

(a) Kadlubek. Hist. Pol. lib. i. epist. 4.

to

to be decided, by a feries of facts for fix or feven centuries, it would be given againft them, fince it can be fhewn, that, under the two firft claffes, the Crown conftantly paffed from fathers to children, except in cafes of the entire extinction of the reigning family. If the Poles had at this time a power of chufing their Princes, would they have elected children, whofe riper years might prove a curfe as eafily as a bleffing to their fubjects? It was much more natural to chufe perfons of experienced wifdom from the body of the Palatines. Would they have gone and taken a monk out of a cloyfter to fet him upon the throne, merely becaufe he was of the blood of *Piaft?* And yet this was the cafe of *Cafimir* I. the fon of a detefted father *Miecislaw* II. and of a mother ftill more execrable. Being left a widow, and Regent of the kingdom, fhe fled into France with her fon. The Polifh ambaffadors, who came, five years after, to offer him the Crown, found him in the habit of a monk in the abbey of Clugny, where he had taken the vows, and was in deacon's orders *(a).* The ambaffadors hefitated a little at this fight; they apprehended that his mind might be debafed by lying in afhes, and wearing a hair-fhirt; but reflecting that he was of the blood royal, and that any King was better than the interregnum which defolated the kingdom, they executed their commiffion. One obftacle was ftill in the way; Cafimir was bound by his vows, and the holy orders he had taken; but Pope Clement II. removed this difficulty, and the monk became a King.

It was not till the end of the fecond clafs, (an æra which fhall be taken notice of hereafter) that hereditary right was abolifhed to make way for election.

The form of government has alfo had its revolutions. In the time of *Leck* it was abfolute, per-

(a) Dluglofs. p. 208.

B 3

haps

haps too much fo; but the nation afterwards felt its own ftrength, fhook off the yoke of a fingle go-vernor, and divided the authority between twelve *Vaivods* or Generals, with a view to weaken it. But thefe Vaivods, who were exalted upon the ruins of one throne, collected its fhattered fragments, and formed them into twelve, which by their mutual collifions, fhook the very foundations of the ftate. The whole was now a fcene of rebellion, faction, oppreffion, and violence. The nation, amidft thefe dreadful agitations, regretted the government of a fingle perfon, without duly reflecting on what they had fuffered by it : but the more prudent part fought after a man fit to govern a free people, and to re-ftrain licentioufnefs without encroaching upon liber-ty. Such a one was at length found in the perfon of *Cracus*, who gave his name to the city of Cracow, which he founded in the beginning of the feventh century *(a)*.

The extinction of his pofterity after the firft ge-neration, put the fceptre again into the hands of the nation, who not knowing where to beftow it, had again recourfe to the Vaivods, who had been fo lately profcribed. Thefe laft compleated the dif-orders introduced by the firft, and the effect of this ill-formed ariftocracy, was nothing but weak-nefs and confufion. The Hungarians, who had long been under apprehenfions from Poland, now refolved upon its deftruction, and fpread terror on all fides by a fudden invafion. The Poles affem-bled, but could come to no refolution. The chiefs of the nation were hated and defpifed, the foldi-ers had no confidence in them, and the people was plunged in defpair. In the midft of this confu-fion, an obfcure man, of no credit, conceived a thought for faving his country; and drew the Hun-

(a) Dluglofs. Hift. Pol. lib. i. p. 50.

garians into a narrow paſs, where the greateſt part of them was cut off. Przemiſlas (that was his name). became in one day the idol of his countrymen : and that wild people, which had as yet no idea of any other title to the Crown but virtue, placed it upon the head of their deliverer, who wore it with equal glory and ſucceſs, by the name of Leſ- ko I. (a).

VIII. Cr tury.

This reſtoration of abſolute power did not laſt long without a freſh concuſſion. *Popiel* II. the fourth Duke from Przemiſlas, deſervedly drew upon himſelf, by his crimes, the ſcandal of being the laſt Prince of his family. He abandoned himſelf, without the leaſt remorſe, to a life of ſloth, to the moſt brutal debauchery, to treachery, cruelty, and poiſoning ; and his wife was ſtill more deteſtable than himſelf (b).

This Prince leaving no children, an interregnum, or rather the moſt ruinous anarchy, ſucceeded. The baſtards of the Ducal family on one ſide, and the twelve Palatines on the other, were employed in rending out of each other's hands the reins of government (c) ; and theſe two principal factions engendered a hundred more. Every individual flew to arms, and right was made to conſiſt in force only, courage in brutal fury, and ſafety in murder ; till the nation, weary of tearing itſelf in pieces, (a thing which it had not done in a more uncivilized ſtate) ſaw the neceſſity of taking ſpeedy refuge under the government of a ſingle perſon. The candidates met at Cruſwick, a village in Cujavia; where an inhabitant of that country received them in his ruſtic cott, entertained them with a frugal repaſt, and diſplayed a ſound judgment, an honeſt and humane heart, abilities ſuperior to his condi-

(a) Dlugloſs. Hiſt. Pol. lib. i. p. 61.
(b) Cromer. p. 38.   (c) Id. lib. ii. p. 39.

tion,

tion, a refolute mind, and a love for his country, which thefe madmen did not feel in their own breafts.   Ambitious men, who themfelves defpair of governing, chufe rather to fubmit to a third perfon, who has not entered into the competition, than to obey a rival.   In the prefent cafe, they determined in favour of virtue; and by this means, repaired in fome meafure, the mifchiefs they had oc-

IX. century.

cafioned by their contefts for the throne.   *Piaſt* therefore was chofen King.   The Polifh hiftorians will have it, that two angels were concerned in this event, though Poland had not at that time embraced Chriftianity.   What they relate of the good government of Piaſt, is fupported by better proofs.

The Princes of his family, who fucceeded one another, continually encreafed their authority, which even feemed to be more abfolute than ever under Bo-

X. century.

leflas I.   Till his time, the fovereigns of Poland had only the title of Duke.   Two powers, the Emperor and the Pope, were then contending for the right of making Kings.   If either of them had fuch a privilege, the Emperor's claim feems the faireft.   The diploma of royalty was ufually purchafed of him; and this cuftom has fubfifted a long time, as a fort of homage paid to the ancient grandeur of the Roman Empire.   But if we confider that nations are independent of each other, they themfelves only have a right to give titles to their chiefs.   The Pope mifcarried in his pretenfions; and it was the Emperor Otho III. who, refpecting the virtues of Boleflas, invefted him with the regal dignity, in his paffage through Poland (*a*).   One would fcarce imagine, that, with this inftrument of defpotifm, the firft King of Poland laid the foundations of a republic.   This hero, after having penetrated into

(*a*) Cromer. p. 53.

the

the heart of the empire, and extended his conquefts as far as the confluence of the Elbe and the Sala, where he erected three columns as monuments of his glory, after having twice fubdued Ruffia, begun at laft to think ferioufly; and confidering on one fide, that his enemies were fubdued, and on the other, his fubjects exhaufted and ruined, and their wounds ftill bleeding, had the humanity to weep over his victories. Hitherto he had reigned without a council; but he now created one, confifting of twelve perfons of diftinguifhed merit (*a*).

The nation, which had hitherto obeyed implicitly, now turning its eyes towards liberty, difcovered with pleafure the firft image of it; for this council might in time become a fenate. We have feen, that the Poles had long ago abolifhed monarchy to make way for twelve Vaivods; and this tranfient idea of a republic had never been entirely effaced. Though the Polifh Kings, after the reftoration of the old conftitution, had regularly fucceeded one another by hereditary right, yet there ftill remained a perfuafion, that there were circumftances in which the nation might refume the crown: and it exerted this right by depofing Mieciflaw III. XII. century, a cruel, knavifh, avaricious Prince, and an inventor of new impofitions upon the people. Inftances of this fort were repeated more than once. Uladiflas XIII. century, Lafkonogi, and Uladiflas Loketek, were forced to quit the throne; and Cafimir IV. would have had the fame fate, if he had not thought proper to change his conduct upon the remonftrances of his fubjects.

It muft be owned, however, to the honour of the Poles, that they have fcarce ever attempted to depofe any of their kings, but fuch as were incapable of wearing the crown, or wore it only to opprefs their fubjects; and that to deliver themfelves

(*a*) Cromer. p. 64.

they

they have never fhed any royal blood, not even that of Bolefſlas II. This tyrant, after the taking of Kiovia (a), fituated upon the weftern bank of the Boryfthenes, forgot his labours and his glory in the arms of the Ruffian women, and the army followed his example. As foon as the news reached Poland, the Polifh women, who had not feen their hufbands for eight years, married their flaves. The hufbands, upon this intelligence, without afking leave to be abfent, (for they did not hope to obtain it) returned home. The flaves had recourfe to flight, and the women to tears. The hufbands forgave the fault, becaufe there was a neceffity either of punifhing, or of forgiving them all. The King did not fhew the fame indulgence, but provoked by the defertion of his army, and forced to return to his dominions fooner than he intended, he returned with a rod of iron. He forced from the women the wretched produce of their proftitution, in order to be expofed in the fields; and by a ridiculous abufe of the fovereign power, forbad them to appear any where without a dog hanging at their breafts (b). After this, he let loofe his vengeance upon the hufbands, who had left their colours; confifcated the goods of the richer fort, and put the reft to death in frightful dungeons, or by ignominious public executions: he even abandoned himfelf to the moft extravagant debauchery, forgetting that it was the crime he punifhed; and filled up the meafure of his iniquities by affaffinating with his own hand Staniflas, bifhop of Cracow, at the altar. At laft,

---

(a) This city, which belongs once more to the Mufcovites, was at that time very populous and flourifhing; but is now poor, and fcarce contains between five and fix thoufand inhabitants. Whenever a Prince difcovers fuch alterations for the worfe in his dominions, he ought to enquire into their caufes, and prevent the fame ruin from extending, as it may eafily do, to other cities.

(b) Paftor ab Hirtemberg, p. 43.

the

the patience of his subjects was exhausted, but they contented themselves with banishing him.

A nation which has proceeded so far as to depose its kings, has nothing to do but to chuse its materials for erecting the edifice of liberty, and time will do the rest. The present conjuncture was favourable enough for such an undertaking, there being scarce any absolute sovereigns in Europe. The nobles in France, England, Sweden, Denmark, Italy, and Sicily, confined the authority of their princes within very narrow limits. The Spaniards have not to this day forgot the ancient form of inaugurating their kings. " We, who are as good " as you, make you our King, upon condition that " you will observe our laws; otherwise, not." The Poles too had laid some restraints upon the regal power; but this power being always ready to overleap its bounds, they still thought it too extensive; for their kings made war and peace at their own pleasure.

In the fourteenth century, Casimir the Great, being impatient to put an end to a long war, made a treaty of peace, which the enemy required to be ratified by all the estates of the realm. Being assembled for this purpose, they refused their concurrence; and from this time were convinced, that it was not impossible to establish a republic, and at the same time keep a king (a).

The foundations of this constitution were laid even before the death of Casimir, who having no son, proposed his nephew, Lewis, King of Hungary, for his successor. The Poles gave their consent, but it was upon such conditions as laid heavy fetters upon absolute power. They had attempted more than once to lessen it by rebellion, but they now attacked it by treaty. Their new ruler ex-

(a) Dluglofs. p. 1038.

empted

empted them from all contributions, and gave up an eftablifhed cuftom, by which the nation defrayed the charges of the court in all journies. He engaged alfo to repay his fubjects all the expences he was forced to be at, and even all the damages they fhould fuftain in any war which he undertook againft the neighbouring powers (a). No conditions are thought burdenfome, when a crown is to be obtained.

XIV. century.   Upon thefe terms, Lewis gained his point ; and his fubjects farther obtained, that public offices and employments fhould be given for life ; that all ftrangers fhould be excluded from them ; and that the government of forts and caftles fhould be no longer conferred upon fuch nobles as were fupcrior to the reft of that body, and had too much influence in the kingdom by means of their birth (b). Lewis, who poffeffed two kingdoms, chofe rather to refide in Hungary, where he commanded with abfolute fway, than in Poland, where his fubjects were employed in making laws ; and fent the Duke of Oppelen thither to govern in his name. The Poles refented this appointment of a foreign governor as an affront to their nation, which implied that it had no ftatefmen of its own ; and the ftorm was increafing every moment, when the King thought fit to diffipate it, by recalling the Duke, and fubftituting in his room, with very extenfive powers, three Polifh nobles, who were greatly in favour with the people (c). The new regents made their court to the multitude by a foft and infinuating behaviour, and talked much of laws and liberty, and the neceffity of a counterbalance to the fovereign power. Lewis died without being much regretted, though he really deferved to be fo ; and his death, which gave new vigour to the republican government,

(a) Dluglofs. p. 1102.
(b) Sarnic. p. 1149.
(c) Dluglofs. p. 49.

opened

opened alfo a profpect of farther acquifitions. In the latter part of his life, when he had no hopes of begetting an heir to the throne, he pitched upon his fon-in-law Sigifmund to fucceed him, with the approbation of the Poles, which he purchafed by ceding to them frefh Privileges *(a)*.

But the Poles were not contented with having in fome meafure difpofed of the Crown, by their confent's being afked; they were refolved to ftrike a decifive blow, by abolifhing the fucceffion. If either of Lewis's two daughters had a right to the Crown, it was undoubtedly his eldeft, the Princefs Mary, wife to Sigifmund; they therefore rejected both her and her hufband, and gave the Crown to *Hedwigia*, the youngeft; upon condition that fhe would take no hufband but of their appointing.

Among the competitors that appeared on this occafion, *Jagellon* difplayed the luftre of the Crown of Lithuania, which he promifed to incorporate with that of Poland. This offer was certainly confiderable; but it would have been nothing, if he had not fubfcribed to the republican form of government. Upon this condition he married Hedwigia, and was declared King.

A republic was now eftablifhed, compofed of three eftates; the King, the Senate, and the Equeftrian order. The King's portion was majefty; power fell to the fenate, and liberty was the fhare of the Equeftrian order; an order including all the reft of the nobility, and which foon fet up tribunes, by the name of *Deputies*. Thefe deputies reprefent the whole Equeftrian order in the general affemblies of the nation, called *diets*, and put a ftop to all proceedings there, whenever they pleafe, by their right of *Veto*. The commonwealth of Rome had no King, but the *Plebeians* were reckoned as one of its

---

(a) Orichov. Annal. p. 6.

three

three orders : they had a fhare of the fovereign power in common with the fenate and the knights, and there never was a greater or more virtuous people. Their confuls at home, and their ambaf-fadors abroad, talked in a ftrain of affurance of the *majefty of the Roman people.* Poland, actuated by different principles, has placed its people upon a le-vel with the cattle that till the ground. The fe-nate, which holds the balance between the King and liberty, can look without emotion upon the flavery of five or fix millions of men, who were much happier of old when they were Sarmatians.

It was in this fame century, that four peafants, *Meletald, Stauffacher, Waltberfurft,* and *William Tell,* delivered their country from the yoke of the houfe of Auftria; but among the Swifs, every in-dividual was free, and had a fhare in making laws; and it is certainly good policy to intereft all the members of the community in the promotion of the public good.

While the commonwealth of Poland was yet in its infancy, Jagellon feemed to forget upon what conditions he reigned. An edict iffued by the King was found contrary to the oath he had taken, and the new republicans hewed it in pieces with their fabres before his face *(a).*

Before the revolution, the Kings of Poland de-termined concerning peace and war, made laws, changed eftablifhed cuftoms, repealed old conftitu-tions, and difpofed of the public treafure; but all thefe privileges were now transferred to the no-bility, and the Kings were forced to learn the art XVI. cen-tury. of bearing contradiction. But the reign of Sigif-mond Auguftus, was the æra when the republican pride difplayed itfelf in the haughtieft manner.

(a) Okolfki, tom. 1. p. 349.

This

This Prince, confulting rather his own inclinations, than the interefts of Poland, had married, without the confent of the fenate, a young widow, daughter of George Radziwil, Caftellan of Wilna. This ftep occafioned univerfal difcontent, which fhewed itfelf on feveral occafions, but more particularly in a diet held at Petrikow, where the King was prefent. The Equeftrian order, the Senators, all cried out, " That the King was the man of the " nation, and ought not to marry but for the na-" tion's intereft. What are the advantages, added " they, which we can promife ourfelves from this " union ? If we permit it, we fhall perhaps fee our " Kings, guided only by blind paffion, ally them-" felves to families unworthy of the throne, or per-" nicious to our happinefs (a)."

The whole diet was for having the King himfelf lend a hand to break the connexion which he had formed; but his inclination, and his judgment equally oppofed this meafure, and he ftood up in his turn to juftify what he had done. This brought on feveral warm replies, which the King, no longer able to contain his indignation, roughly interrupted by commanding fubmiffion and filence. A fhort filence enfued, becaufe the firft prerogative of regal dignity is to imprefs awe and reverence. While they were looking at each other, the youngeft Senator in the affembly, *Raphael Lefczinfki*, a name refpectable in Poland, Lorrain, and France, a family which has produced more than one great foul, Lefczinfki arofe, and addreffing himfelf to the King, afked him, " If he had forgot who they were that " he prefumed to give commands to : we are Poles, " added he, and you muft be told, if you know " it not already, that the Poles pride themfelves as " much upon humbling the haughtinefs of Kings

(a) Stanifl. Orichov. p. 1486.

" who

" who defpife the laws, as upon honouring thofe
" that refpect them.   Beware of fetting us free
" from our oaths, by violating your own.   The
" King, your father, liftened to our counfels ;
" and it is our bufinefs to take care that you fhall,
" for the future, be guided by the fentiments of
" a republic, of which you feem not to know that
" you are only the firft citizen (a)."

This fpeech, and the reft, which are recorded in
the fequel of this Hiftory, are not mere ornaments
invented to embellifh the narration.   If a writer
fhould give us the opinions of Minifters, as delivered in the inacceffible cabinets of abfolute Monarchs, we fhould have a right to afk him, how
he got at them ? And the more there was in them
of that nervous eloquence, which is the child of liberty alone, the greater reafon there would be to
queftion their authenticity.   But in a republican
council, every thing is fpoke in the prefence of the
whole nation, and even under its protection ; and
pieces of fpirit are generally preferved.

Y. 1573. Sigifmund Auguftus dying without children, the
Poles took this opportunity of guarding their liberty with new bulwarks.   They examined into
their old laws, limited many, extended fome, and
abolifhed others ; and after many debates, it was
agreed that the Kings elected by the nation fhould
make no attempts to get their fucceffors appointed ;
that they fhould not fo much as propofe any one
to the State for this purpofe, and confequently
fhould never affume the title of *heirs of the kingdom* ;
that they fhould always have about them fixteen
perfons by way of council, without whofe concurrence they fhould neither receive foreign minifters,
nor fend any to other Princes ; that they fhould not
levy new troops, nor order the nobility on horfe-

(a) Stanifl. Orichov. p. 1492.

back,

back without the consent of all the Orders of the Republic; that they should admit no foreigners into the Council of the Nation, nor confer upon them any office, dignity, or *starosty*; and lastly, that they should not marry, without having first obtained the permission of the Senate and equestrian order *(a)*.

The whole interregnum was spent in contriving how to guard against what was called *the encroachments of the Throne*; it is not a Master, said they, that we want; 'tis only a Chief. All the expressions which were anciently made use of to describe the regal power, such as, *the will of the King constitutes the Law, the King must be obeyed implicitely like God, King by the Grace of God*, and others of this kind, were exterminated out of the public language : there were some who went still farther, and asserted that a free People wanted no King at all.

This Republican language became henceforward the prevailing stile in all Assemblies of State. Henry of Valois was shocked at it upon his arrival in Poland, and at his coronation. The Protestant reli-Year 1574. gion had got footing in the kingdom under Sigismund I. and it's progress increased in proportion to the violence that was exercised against it. When Henry arrived at Cracow, it was known that his brother, Charles IX. had massacred one part of his subjects, in order to convert the other: and it was feared that a Prince, who had been educated in a bigotted and persecuting court, would import that spirit with him. It was resolved therefore to oblige him to swear to certain articles which he had already sworn to in France before the Ambassadors of the Republic, particularly the article of toleration which he had sworn to in very vague and equivocal terms. There were two parties formed upon

(a) And. Max. Fredro. pag. 81.

C

this occasion, the most numerous of which looked upon the second oath that was required of him as superfluous. Every thing was ready for the coronation, and the Primate was going to begin the ceremony, when the Palatine of Cracow put a stop to all proceedings by the following discourse, addressed to his own Faction. " Vain then, it seems, " is the opinion with which you and I have flatter- " ed ourselves, of our being hitherto a free people. " Our privileges are openly made a sport of; and " almost all our citizens condemn themselves to " eternal slavery, by their infamous and traiterous " silence. Let them, if they like it, stoop under " the yoke of servitude, unworthy as they are to " enjoy liberty. But let us, my brethren, who " have both our laws and religion to defend, shew " by our resolution, or by our death, in what man- " ner tyranny is to be opposed. You undoubtedly " recollect, continued he, the unanimous resolu- " tions of the whole nation, and the equitable " conditions it was thought proper to insist on. " And can you think that they ought to be forgot " by us, because the King disclaims and rejects " them ? What a disgrace and scandal will it be to " us, if we delay any longer to make him perform " his promises ? As for myself, added he, I will " suffer it to be deferred no longer. He shall im- " mediately accept the terms he has acceded to, " and swear once more to observe them ; or from " this instant, I protest against his coronation (a)." Had it not been for the eloquent *Pibrac*, it is uncertain whether his Coronation would have taken place or not; it was however performed, without his repeating the oath ; but a few months after, Offolinski, Castellan of Sendomir, was deputed, with five others, to notify to Henry his approach-

(a) History of the Diets of Poland, pag. 51.

ing

ing depofition, if he did not more punctually difcharge the duties of the Throne (a). Soon after,
his precipitate flight put an end to the complaints
of the nation and to his reign together.

To thefe fpirited attacks, made at different times,
it is owing that Poland has retained royalty without fearing its Kings. A King of Poland, at his
very Coronation, and when he fwears to the *Pacta
Conventa*, abfolves his fubjects from their oath of
allegiance, in cafe he violates the laws of the Republic.

The legiflative power belongs effentially to the
Diet, which the King is obliged to call together
every two years, and in cafe of his failure, the Republic has a right to affemble by its own authority : a regulation wifely contrived, and which might
perhaps be advantageoufly adopted by the great Republic of Chriftendom. The little Diets or Dietines of every Palatine precede the great one; and
in thefe they prepare the matters that are to be difcuffed in the General Affembly; and elect the Reprefentatives of the Equeftrian order, out of which
is compofed the Chamber of Deputies. The perfons of thefe Deputies or Tribunes is fo facred, that
in the reign of Auguftus II. a Saxon colonel having given one of them a flight wound in revenge
for an infult that he had received from him, was
condemned to death and executed, notwithftanding
all the protection the King could give him. The
only favour he could obtain was to be fhot to
death, inftead of dying by the hands of an execu-
tioner.

The old caftle of Warfaw, in which the Kings
of Poland formerly refided, is the place where the
Diet meets. In order to form an idea of the fenate, which is the foul of this body, we muft caft

(a) Reinh. Heidenft. p. 67.

our eyes upon the Bishops, Palatines, and Castellans. The two latter of these dignities are less known than the former. A Palatine is the chief of the Nobility within his own Palatinate; presides at all their assemblies, leads them to the field of election when a King is to be chose, and to the field of battle, when the *Pospolite* or *Arriere-Ban* (a) is assembled. He has also a right to fix the price of commodities, and to regulate weights and measures: in short, he is a governor of a Province. A *Castellan* enjoys the same privileges within his own district, which always makes part of a Palatinate; he represents the Palatine in his absence. The Castellans were formerly governors of the strong castles and royal cities; but these governments are now in the hands of the *Starosts*, who also administer justice either in their own Persons, or by their deputies. One admirable institution is a register lodged in the hands of the Starosts, containing an account of all the estates in the district, whether free or mortgaged; and by this means, a purchaser is sure of having a good title.

The Starost of Samogitia is the only one who has a seat in the Senate; but there are in it two Archbishops, fifteen Bishops, thirty three Palatines, and eighty five Castellans, in all a hundred and thirty six.

The ministers of state have a seat in the Senate, without being Senators: they are in number ten, two of each denomination, by reason of the union of the two States.

The Grand-marshal of the Crown.
The Grand-marshal of Lithuania.

(a) *Arriere Ban*, in the French customs, is a general proclamation, whereby the King summons to the war all that hold of him; both his Vassals, i. e. the Noblesse, and the Vassals of his Vassals. *Chambers's Diction.*
It signifies also the persons thus assembled.

The

The Grand-chancellor of the Crown.
The Grand-chancellor of Lithuania.
The Vice-chancellor of the Crown.
The Vice-chancellor of Lithuania.
The Grand-treafurer of the Crown.
The Grand-treafurer of Lithuania.
The Marfhal of the Court of Poland.
The Marfhal of the Court of Lithuania.

The Grand-marfhal is the third perfon in the Kingdom, having only the King and the Primate above him. As mafter of the Palace, he appoints ambaffadors their days of audience; and exercifes an almoft abfolute authority in the Court, and for three leagues round it. He provides for the fafety of the King's perfon, and the prefervation of the public peace: he takes cognizance of all crimes within his Diftrict, and judges without appeal, nor can his fentences be reverfed but by the whole body of the Nation. 'Tis alfo his bufinefs to affemble the Senate, and to keep in order thofe who would difturb it; for which purpofes he has always a body of troops at his command.

The Marfhal of the Court can exercife no jurifdiction but in the abfence of the Grand-marfhal.

The Grand-chancellor is keeper of the Great Seal, as the Vice-chancellor is of the Privy Seal. One of them is always a Bifhop, with a jurifdiction in ecclefiaftical matters; and all anfwers given in the King's name upon public occafions, muft be given by one of thefe two officers, either in Polifh or Latin, as the occafion requires. It is fomething fingular, that the language of the Romans, who never got footing in Poland, fhould at this time be fo commonly fpoke in that kingdom; for every one, down to the very fervants, fpeaks Latin.

The Grand-treafurer is entrufted with the revenues of the Republic: the Poles being very careful not to leave this money, which was called by the Romans

the

Treaſure of the People, *Ærarium Populi*, at the diſ-
poſal of the King.   A vote of the whole Nation,
or at leaſt a *Senatus-conſultum*, directs how it ſhal
be employed; and the Grand-treaſurer is accountable to the Nation only.

There is very little reſemblance between theſe
miniſters and thoſe of other courts.   They are appointed indeed by the King, but the Republic only
can turn them out.   Nevertheleſs, as they are connected with the Crown, which is the ſource of all
favours, and as they are men, the Republic has not
thought fit to allow them a deliberative vote in the
Senate.

The title given to the Senators is that of *Excellence*; they claim alſo that of *my Lord*; and it is
given them by their ſervants, their ſlaves, and the
poor nobility.

The firſt man in the Senate is the Arch-biſhop
of Gneſna, who is alſo called the Great Arch-biſhop, but more commonly the Primate.   This dignity was formerly accompanied with great power,
and great abuſes of power, all over Europe.   It
was a Primate of Sweden, the Arch-biſhop of Up-
ſal, who cauſed the whole Senate of Stockholm to
be maſſacred at an entertainment, upon a pretence
that they were excommunicated by the Pope; which
made the Swedes reſolve to have nothing more to do
with either Primate or Pope.   It was a Primate of
England, Arch-biſhop Cranmer, who by annulling
the marriage between Henry VIII. and Catharine
of Arragon, broke off, in concert with his maſter,
all connections between Rome and England.   One
of the greateſt obſtacles that the Czar Peter had to
encounter in the execution of his great deſigns,
was the enormous power of the Patriarch or Primate; he therefore aboliſhed the office.   In France,
this dignity is divided among ſeveral perſons, who
are always conteſting it with one another, and therefore

fore its power is diminished. In Poland it subsists to this hour in all its strength.

The Primate, by virtue of his office, is Legate of the Holy See, and censor of the Kings of Poland: he is himself in some measure a King in every vacancy of the Throne, during which he takes the name of *Interrex*: and the honours he receives are proportioned to the dignity of his station. Whenever he goes to the King, he is escorted thither with great ceremony, and the King advances to receive him. He has a Marshal and a Chancellor, like the King, a numerous guard of horse, with a kettle-drummer and trumpeters, who play while he is at table, and sound the morning and evening march in his palace. He has the titles of *Highness* and *Prince*; but among all the great privileges of his office, the most useful to the state is the Censorship, which he never exercises but with applause. If the King governs ill, the Primate has a right to make all proper remonstrances to him in private. If the King persists in his bad measures, 'tis in full senate or in the diet that the Primate arms himself with all the power of the laws to reclaim him; and the mischief is generally put a stop to. But if the King should prove more powerful than the laws (a thing which is extremely difficult in Poland) the thread of oppression is infallibly broke at his death, without passing into the hands of his successor; for an interregnum always takes care to cut it.

When the Diet is not sitting, the springs of government are kept in motion by the Senate, under the inspection of the King; but the King can neither by authority nor violence over-rule their suffrages. The liberty they possess is visible even in their outward forms; for the Senators are seated in arm-chairs, and as soon as the King is covered, they follow his example. However, the decrees of the

Senate

Senate, when the Diet is not fitting, are only pro-vifional: but when the Diet is affembled, the Se-nate, together with the King and the Chamber of Deputies, has a legiflative power.

This Chamber of Deputies would exactly refem-ble the Houfe of Commons in England, if, inftead of reprefenting the nobility, it reprefented the body of the people. At its head is placed an officer of great weight, but whofe poft is only temporary. He has commonly great influence in the refoluti-ons of the houfe; which it is his bufinefs to carry up to the Senate, and bring back thofe of the Se-nators. He is called *Marfhal of the Diet*, or *Mar-fhal of the Deputies*. His importance at Warfaw is greater than that of the fpeaker of the Houfe of Commons at London, and equal to that of a Tri-bune of the people at Rome; and as a Patrician at Rome could not be a Tribune, fo this Tribune of the Tribunes muft be chofe out of the Equeftrian order, and not out of the Senate.

When the Diet is affembled, all the doors are left open to every one, becaufe it meets to deliber-ate upon the public good. Perfons, who go there out of mere curiofity, are ftruck with the grandeur of the fpectacle. The King feated on an elevated throne, the fteps of which are decorated with the great officers of the crown: the Primate almoft vying in magnificence with the King: the Senators forming two venerable rows: the Minifters of State over againft the King: the Deputies, more numer-ous than the Senators, difpofed round about them, and all ftanding: the foreign Ambaffadors and the Pope's Nuncio have alfo a place allotted them, but the Diet may make them retire, whenever it thinks proper.

The firft thing done in a diet, is always to read the *Pacta Conventa*, containing the obligations which the King has entered into with his people; and if he
has

has failed in any particular, every member of the affembly has a right to infift upon its being better obferved for the future.

In the other fittings, which are of fix weeks continuance, the ufual duration of a diet, are fettled all the concerns of the nation; fuch as, the nomination to vacant dignities, the difpofal of the crown lands to fuch as have ferved long in the army with diftinction, the paffing the grand-treafurer's accompts, the diminution or augmentation of taxes as circumftances require, the negotiations with which the ambaffadors of the republic have been entrufted, and the manner in which they have executed their commiffions; the alliances to be formed or broke, the making of peace and war, the abrogating or paffing laws, the ftrengthening of public liberty, and, in fhort, every thing that concerns the nation.

The laft five days, called the *great days*, are fet apart for uniting all the votes. Every decree, to have the force of a law, muft be ratified by the unanimous confent of all the three orders; the oppofition of a fingle deputy undoes every thing.

This privilege of the deputies is a ftriking inftance of the revolutions of the human mind. There was no fuch privilege exifting in the year 1652, when *Sicinki*, deputy of Upita, firft made ufe of it. His claim was univerfally oppofed, fay the hiftorians of that time; he was loaded with curfes, and efcaped the fabres of his countrymen, to die, as the report goes, by a flafh of lightning that fame year. At prefent, this very privilege is confidered as the moft facred inftitution in the commonwealth; and a fure way of being torn in pieces would be to propofe it's abolition.

There is no poffibility of denying, that, if it fometimes does good, it does upon the whole much more mifchief. A fingle deputy may not only annul a good decree, but if he has a quarrel with all, he
has

has nothing to do but to make a proteſt and leave the aſſembly, and the diet is inſtantly diſſolved. It ſometimes happens, that they do not wait till a diet is formed, before they meditate it's diſſolution. The moſt frivolous pretence becomes frequently a formidable weapon. In 1752, the deputies of the Palatinate of Kiovia, were ordered by their conſtituents to require of the King, above all things, the extirpation of the *free-maſons*, a ſociety which terrifies none but credulous perſons, and had done nothing to diſtinguiſh themſelves in Poland.

The remedy againſt theſe diſſolutions of the diet is a confederacy, in which matters are decided by a majority of votes, without paying any regard to the proteſts of the deputies; and one confederacy is frequently formed againſt another. The acts of theſe confederacies muſt afterwards be ratified or annulled by a general diet. All this muſt needs occaſion great convulſions in the ſtate, eſpecially if the army comes to meddle in the diſpute.

The affairs of private perſons are decided in a much better manner. A majority of voices always determines the cauſe, but there are no fixed judges. The nobility appoints annually a certain number to form two tribunals, one at Petrikow, the other at Lublin, the former for *Great*, the latter for *Little Poland*. The great dutchy of Lithuania has alſo its own tribunal. Juſtice is adminiſtered in a ſummary manner, as it is in Aſia. No ſuch thing as attornies, or forms of law, only a few advocates, called *juriſts*; or the parties may plead their own cauſe. What is ſtill better, juſtice is adminiſtered without any expence, and conſequently the poor can obtain it. Theſe courts are ſupreme in the proper ſenſe; for the King can neither prevent their trying a cauſe by taking the cognizance of it out of their hands, nor reverſe their ſentences.

All

All crimes of treason, or of state, are judged in full diet, where the maxim, that the *church abhors blood*, does not affect the Polish bishops. By a Bull of Clement VIII. they are permitted to advise war, to give their vote for capital punishments, and to sign warrants of execution.

Another thing which is seen no where else, is, that the same men, who deliberate in the senate, make laws in the diet, and try causes upon the bench, act also as officers in the army. We may see by this, that in Poland the long robe and the sword are not considered as incompatible professions.

The nobility, having seized the reins of government, and all the honours and emoluments of the state, have thought themselves obliged to defend it too, and to leave all the rest of the nation to cultivate the lands. Poland is at present the only country in the world, whose whole cavalry is made up of gentlemen, of which the grand dutchy of Lithuania furnishes a fourth part; and in this cavalry consists the chief strength of the state, for the infantry is scarce reckoned as any thing. It is divided into *hussars* and *pancernes*, both included under the general name of *towarisz*, which signifies *comrades*, an appellation always given them by the generals, and even by the King himself. A single word often produces great effects.

The hussars are composed of the flower of the nobility, who are obliged to pass through this service in their way to employments and dignities. All Europe cannot produce a body of horse equal to this in beauty. The Poles are naturally large and well made. Let any one then form an idea of a horseman of advantageous stature, covered with an embellished cuirass, a helmet on his head, a panther's skin with the muzzle fastened upon the fore part of the left shoulder, and coming round behind to the right thigh, a gilded lance fourteen or fifteen feet
long,

long, with a streamer hanging at it's point to frighten the enemy's horse; a pair of pistols and two sabres, one at his side, and the other under his right thigh, fastened along the saddle. Armed in this manner, he is mounted upon a fine horse, the furniture of which is ornamented with plates of enamelled gold, and frequently with jewels. One of them was once presented to Lewis XIV. who admired his fine appearance.

Ever since the reign of Sobieski, the lance has been abolished to make way for the musketoon, just as the pike formerly disappeared from among the European infantry. The pike however was the weapon of the Macedonian phalanx; and Marshal Saxe, in his *Reveries*, or Dreams, laments it's not being in use for the legion which he proposed to establish. It will be objected, that this was one of his dreams: true; but the dreams of a great man are worth more than the waking thoughts of an ordinary person.

The *pancernes*, composed also of nobles, differ from the hussars only in having a coat of mail, instead of a cuirass; and their genealogy is not scrutinized with so much rigour. They are not formed into regiments, but into companies of two hundred men each, belonging to the grandees of the kingdom, not excepting even the bishops, who, as they do not serve themselves, give great pay to their lieutenants.

This army, or rather these two armies, the Polish and the Lithuanian, have each their Grand-General, independent on one another. It has been already observed, that the office of Grand-Marshal is first in dignity after the primacy; but the Grand General is superior in power, being unconfined by almost any bounds but what he prescribes to himself. At the opening of the campaign, the King holds a council with the senators and chief officers of the army, concerning

cerning the operations of the war, and from that moment the Grand-General executes as he think fit. He assembles the troops, regulates their march, gives battle, distributes rewards and punishments, promotes, diminishes, and cuts off heads, all without being accountable to any but the republic in full diet. The ancient Constables of. France, whose power has given umbrage to the throne itself, were not near so absolute; and this great authority is suspended only when the King commands in person.

The two armies have also each of them a General, whose functions are confined to the field, called the *Petty-General*, who has no authority but what the Grand-General chuses to give him,. and who supplies his absence. A third officer of note is the *Stragenik*, who commands the van.

There is also kept up in Poland a third body of troops, consisting of foot and dragoons, the institution of which is of no great antiquity. It is called the foreign army, and made up almost entirely of Germans. When the whole is complete, which seldom happens, the ordinary defence of Poland is about forty eight thousand men.

A fourth army, the most numerous and the most useless of all, is the *pospolite*. In case of necessity, more than a hundred and fifty thousand gentlemen would mount their horses, in order to submit only to such discipline as they liked; to mutiny, if they were detained more than fifteen days in the place appointed them to meet in, without marching; and to refuse to serve, if it should be necessary to pass the frontiers.

As all the wars which I shall have to describe, both under the generalship and the reign of Sobieski, were chiefly carried on against the Turks and Tartars, it will be necessary to take a short view of these two nations, considered only in their military capacity.

The

The Tartars, thofe furious conquerors, defcended from the ancient Scythians, who, under their leader, Genzis-Kan, broke out like a torrent from the north of Afia, to over-run the milder climates of China, Indoftan, and Perfia, containing more than eighteen hundred leagues from eaft to weft, and more than a thoufand from north to fouth, did not every where incorporate themfelves with the nations they fubdued. Several of their *herds* or tribes chofe to live by them-felves, and retain their ancient manners. Towards the north of the Black Sea, there is a large penin-fula, anciently known by the name of the Tauric Cherfonefe, where the Greeks extended their arms and their commerce, and abolifhed the impious facrifices of the famous temple of Diana, where it was com-mon to fee the fkulls of human victims hung up as trophies. This peninfula is now called *Crim*, and in it's neighbourhood lies *Budziac*, formerly *Beffarabia*, and *Nogay*.

The Tartars, who inhabit thefe countries, have of all the Tartars moft to do with the prefent hiftory of Europe, and particularly with that of Poland, by reafon of their vicinity. They live under a Prince, called by us *Cham*, but in the eaft *Ham*, that is, *judge*, which was the original employment of Kings. His genealogy would dazzle any one but a Tartar, who values no nobility but fuch as is per-fonal. The Cham is defcended from Genzis-Kan, the greateft conqueror that ever exifted, by his grandfon *Batoucan*.

The features and the manners of the ancient Scy-thians are to this day difcoverable in the Tartars. They are of a fquat figure, have broad fhoulders, fhort necks, large heads, flat and almoft round faces, little pig's eyes, flat nofes, olive-coloured complexions, coarfe black hair, and very little beard. They were probably ftill more hideous in the time of Alexander the great; fince Parmenio took notice to

8   the

the King of their monftrous deformity the evening before the battle of Arbela, and advifed him to attack them in the night, left the Macedonians fhould be frighted by it in the day-time (*a*). But they feem to have been familiarized with their figure, when they went in queft of the Scythians into their own country, upon the banks of the Tanais, now called the Don (*b.*) The fame arms which the Scythians had, are now ufed by the Tartars, the arrow, the javelin, and the fcymetar: they fight alfo in the fame manner, never on foot, always on horfeback. Every Tartar has at leaft three horfes; and if that which he rides is tired or wounded, he leaps upon another without ftopping his pace. He takes care to cut the cartilage which feparates the noftrils, in order to facilitate refpiration. Twenty or thirty leagues, without drawing bit, is not too much either for the rider or the horfe; and yet they both live upon very little. The Tartar's drink is pure water, or, by way of dainty, fermented milk; his food, the flour of millet, or powdered horfe-flefh; (when it is frefh, he thinks it luxury) his habit, a fheep's fkin; his bed, the earth; his covering, the fky: his phyfic, which, they fay, fucceeds better than ours, is horfe's blood, fwallowed hot, after which he gallops as far as he can hold out. As for the horfe, he is fatisfied with fuch grafs as he can find, with mofs, and the bark of trees; and in winter he fearches for pafture under the fnow. It may eafily be conceived, that there is no care taken about magazines, or convoys in

(*a*) *At interdiù primum terribiles occurfuras facies Scytharum.* Qnint. Curt. lib. 4. c. 13.

(*b*) We muft learn to be upon our guard againft names; for this river was alfo called *Amazonius*, from the Amazons, which, according to Strabo, never exifted any where. We muft even be upon our guard againft the greateft authors; for Ptolemy and Pliny make this river rife in the Riphæan mountains; whereas the Mufcovites, who live at it's fource, have never difcovered any mountains near it.

a Tar-a Tartarian army, for every foldier carries all about him. Beaten roads are not made for them: their aim is always to conceal their march, and furprife the enemy. Rivers are no obftacles in their way, for they always fwim acrofs them.

If men of this ftamp were furnifhed with the arms, the military art, and the difcipline of Europe, under an able and ambitious leader, they would ftill be formed for vaft conquefts. But they were fupplied with none of thefe, when the Turks fet out from the eaftern coaft of the Cafpian Sea to fubjugate thofe who had overwhelmed fo. many nations.

The Turkifh empire has never ceafed increafing in power, from the time of *Ottoman,* it's firft Emperor, till about the end of the laft century; an event that is chiefly owing to it's troops, which are entirely different from thofe of the Tartars; the latter having no infantry at all, whereas the Turkifh *Gengi-Cheris,* by us called Janizaries, are defervedly in high reputation. Thofe of them that refide in Conftantinople, to the number of twenty-five thoufand, are divided into a hundred and fixty-two *odas,* or chambers. Their education begins at their very infancy, and they are inured, by the Aga who commands them, not only to the ufe of arms, but to all forts of laborious employments, to carrying burdens, cutting wood, breaking ground, bearing heat and cold, and to every thing which contributes to harden the body. There are no foldiers better clad, or better paid. Every Oda of Janizaries has its purveyor, who provides them with mutton, rice, butter, vegetables and bread in great abundance; and pays them a ftipend, which is to encreafe in proportion to their merit. This prefent happinefs of condition, and the hopes of being better hereafter, produces great effects upon thefe military machines. Accordingly, far from being cheated or forced into the fervice, in a country where defpotic power would feem to authorize any

thing,

thing, a Janizary's place is much fought after, and at leaft a year's probation is required. Inftances of defertion are never known, becaufe foldiers never defert but with a view to better their condition. The behaviour of the janizaries is a furprize to ftrangers, who fee them in their ódas, or in the ftreets of Conftantinople. No fuch thing is known among them as robbery, murder, or the leaft act of violence. Mild and gentle to their fellow-fubjects, they are formidable only to the Sultan; for they have the power, by their laws, of imprifoning, depofing, and appointing him a fucceffor (a).

The Tartars, who are a body of cavalry without pay, and greedier of plunder than glory, do not ftand their ground long in action. The Turkifh horfe advance and attack in good order. They have among them a numerous and diftinguifhed body, called *Spahis*, of very ancient origin, being inftituted by *Ali*, the companion of *Mahomet*; and their exploits from the very firft have been extraordinary. They are better educated and more civilized than the reft of the army, being all taken out of the feraglio, where they have employments in their youth. If the Turks admitted of any nobility but that of offices (b), the Spahis might be taken for the nobles of the country; but the defcendants of the *Cantacuzeni* and *Palæologi* now live at Conftantinople, in greater obfcurity than Dionyfius did at Corinth. Even the family of Mahomet, who can prove their nobility for twelve centuries, are diftinguifhed only by a green turban, and get their living by trade (c). A Spahi would

---

(a) Ricaut's Hift. of the Ottoman Empire, p. 340 et feq. The Author here quoted refided five years in Conftantinople. His employment of Secretary to the Earl of Winchelfea, Ambaffador from Charles II. to Mahomet IV. gave him an opportunity of making good remarks: he is a plain and judicious writer, who makes ornament give place to inftruction.

(b) Ricaut, p. 311.   (c) Idem p. 203. et 130.

not

not exchange his condition for so splendid a pedigree. The arms of these soldiers are a scymetar, a lance, and a dart two foot long: they have also fire-arms, of which they make little account; but the ancient helmet and coat of mail still keep their credit with them. Their pay, like that of the Janizaries, is fixed to no bounds. An enemy's head raises it two aspers (a) a day. It receives another augmentation, when a Spahi brings intelligence of the death of one of his comrades; which is a contrivance of the Sultan to avoid paying dead men. But what helps most to render the state of a Spahi advantageous, are the *timars* which are bestowed upon them. These fiefs or military benefices return into the hands of the Sultan, whenever a *Timariot* dies; a custom which always furnishes the Prince with means of rewarding merit without impoverishing himself, and produces actions of extraordinary valour. In an assault made by the Turks upon a fortress in Hungary, one of these fiefs was disposed of eight times in one day, seven Spahis who contended for it being killed, and the eighth having the good fortune to keep it (b). It should be observed, that these Spahis are only private men; and that though an officer may be satisfied with glory, (a truth however which should not be examined too nicely) a common soldier must be actuated by a stronger motive.

Besides these incentives, Mahomet, their legislator, Pontiff, and King, omitted no means of banishing fear and heightening resolution. It is written in the Alcoran, *that the days of man are irrevocably determined; and that a house which has the*

(a) An asper is worth about eight French deniers. [A French livre, which is worth about eleven pence sterling, contains twenty sols, and each sol twelve deniers; so that eight deniers is very little more than an English farthing.]
(b) Ricaut, p. 325.

plague

plague in it ought not to be avoided. It is farther said, that *whoever dies in battle is admitted instantly to the joys of heaven, with the crown of martyrdom.* The same doctrine was held before this by the ancient Romans *(a)*. A Christian soldier, if he reflects ever so little upon the duties of his religion, stands in fear of hell, at the same time that he sacrifices his life. Happy would it be, if this fear made him more considerate!

The law of Mahomet forbids the use of wine; but this law is inforced with such particular severity in time of war, that drunkenness is made a capital crime. Soldiers that are kept sober are more vigilant, more obedient, and less apt to commit violence. Tumults and quarrels seldom happen among them, and duels are never heard of: indeed no such thing is known in all the east. When the army is upon a march, no peasant comes to complain that his sheep are stolen, or his daughter ravished; and when they reach the enemies territories, no ravage is committed but what the *Seraskier*, or General, commands. No General, however, were it the Grand-Vizier himself, can punish a soldier without the consent of his officer; an admirable means of securing subordinate authority.

It is a common saying among the Turks, *that their troops are innumerable as the sand of the sea.* But this does not hold good in time of peace. It seems incredible that an Empire, which extends from the Archipelago *(b)* to the banks of the Eu-

(a) Hic manus, ob patriam, pugnando vulnera passi.
ÆNEID. Lib. vi.

(b) These limits, however extensive, do not include Turkey in Europe, which certainly deserves to be considered as part of the Ottoman Empire. The translator therefore cannot help suspecting, that either the inattention of his author, or the blunder of the printer, has substituted the word *Archipelago*, instead of the *Gulph of Venice*, or perhaps the *Adriatic*, in one word,

D 2 phrates,

phrates, fhould be guarded only by a hundred and
fifty thoufand men. It is a maxim with thefe infidels, not to let a body, which preys upon the
fubftance of the people, grow to too great a fize.
And yet in time of war, an army of three hundred thoufand men is an ordinary effort for the
Grand Seignior. And what is ftill more aftonifhing, he is never put to any difficulty about their
pay. The Spahis and Janizaries are paid equally,
whether there be peace or war. The Timariots
live upon their lands ; and the other troops, which
are raifed in Afia or Europe, have all a revenue allotted them in their own country. To all extraordinary expences, however great, the treafury of the
empire is more than adequate. No new taxes are
ever impofed ; for among the Turks their fubfidies
are as immutable as their laws, cuftoms, and manners. The nation is, in every refpect, the fame, as
when it firft came into Europe.

Befides the treafure of the Empire, the Emperor has alfo his private purfe, which is inceffantly
filling, not at the expence of the fubjects, who
conftantly enjoy their patrimony without any difturbance, but by the appointment and depofition
of Bafhaws, Beglierbeys (a), and the other great
officers of ftate. As they are all taken out of
the feraglio, they come impreffed with that defpotic maxim of the Alcoran, *that they are nothing
but clay in the hands of their mafter* : who, if he
forms them into veffels of honour, gets *purfes (b)*
by it ; and if he breaks them in pieces, comes in
for the wreck ; a temptation always inviting to a
Sultan who wants to encreafe his treafures. The
valiant Amurath IV. without being avaricious, left
behind him three hundred and fixty millions of

(*a*) Beglierbeys are Governors of provinces.
(*b*) A purfe is worth five hundred crowns.

French

French money, all in gold. Hence come thofe infcriptions in the feraglio; *here is depofited the treafure of fuch a one (a)*; and it is a rule never to meddle with thefe fums, but when the Empire is threatened with ruin. · Poffeffed of fuch refources, a Sultan is never known to give himfelf up into the hands of farmers of the revenue, or to buy the money of his own fubjects.

A view of the wealth and œconomy of the Turks, of their extenfive power, prodigious number of forces, and of the enthufiaftic fury to which they may be wrought up, fhould naturally make the Chriftian world tremble, if the Turks knew any thing of naval affairs. But they are only poffeffed of about an hundred gallies, and a few light veffels, which ferve to carry provifions to the ifle of Candy: they have no fea-charts, and rarely venture out of fight of land. It is a common faying among them, that *God has given the earth to them, and the fea to the infidels (b)*; and may they always continue to fay fo!

Not contented with having fubdued more than thirty nations in Afia, Africa, and Europe, they can reckon up a crowd of tributaries, who are fure of conftant protection. To thefe tributaries relates that paffage of the Alcoran: *Their goods and their fubftance, are our goods and our fubftance; their foul is our foul, their eye our eye.* The Turks treat them, as the old Romans treated their allies: they leave them their own laws, cuftoms, and religion, but appoint them Governors, and receive from them a tribute in money. One fhould imagine that the Chriftian world would rather have been buried in its own ruins, than fuffer fuch a vaffalage to be eftablifhed in Chriftendom. But the torrent of a mighty Empire carries every

(a) Tavernier, tom, iii. p. 479.   (b) Ricaut, p. 381,

D 3   thing

thing before it.   Walachia, Moldavia, and the republic of Ragufa, receive orders from the feraglio.
The Ukraine and Tranfylvania have but lately thrown
off this dependence.   Even the Empire of Germany
has fubmitted to the Turkifh yoke.   Bufbequius
quotes a treaty of peace made between Solyman II.
and Ferdinand I. in which the Sultan expreffes himfelf thus : *Of which agreement, peace and alliance,
the firft condition is, that your dilection fhall be
bound to fend annually to our court thirty thoufand
Hungarian ducats.*   This tribute, it is true, was
only paid two years ; but it would furnifh an ever-
lafting pretence for war, if fovereigns were ever in
want of one.

Of all the tributaries of the Porte, thofe which
furnifh the greateft fuccours, more however in men
than money, are the Tartars.   It is now a long
time fince frequent plagues, a multitude of eunuchs,
and the fterility confequent upon boundlefs poly-
gamy, have been co-operating to depopulate the
Ottoman Empire, which is repeopled by the Tartars.   There may continually be feen along the
coafts of the Bofphorus, a great number of faicks,
laden with Chriftians of both fexes, the common
produce of their inroads.   In time of war, their
commerce with Conftantinople is much increafed ;
no lefs than an hundred and fifty thoufand flaves
being carried away in 1663, out of Hungary, Moravia, and Silefia, and fold in the public markets (*a*).
They do not make war of their own motion, but
by the orders of the Grand-Seignior, which is another advantage to the Empire.   When the Sultan
commands in perfon, the Cham muft take the field
himfelf with a hundred thoufand men.   If it be
only the Vizir, the Cham fends his fon, or his Prime
Minifter with fifty thoufand ; whereas, taking only

(*a*) Ricaut, p. 109.

one

one foldier out of each village, he could furnish two hundred thoufand. Thefe villages, fome of which are called cities, are nothing but a collection of huts, made of hurdles, and covered with a coarfe hair-cloth. *Bafcia-Saray*, in which the Cham refides, is fituated near the middle of the peninfula. *Precop*, called by the Tartars, *Orapy*, or the Gate of Gold, guards the entrance; and *Caffa*, formerly Theodofia, is its principal city. The Cham is perhaps the only Prince in the world who is not permitted to refide in his own capital; it being under the command of a Turkifh Governor.

The Tartars may be looked upon as the favages of Europe. They are fenfible that they might foon civilize their manners, make laws, erect tribunals, create titles, and call in luxury and magnificence; but they hear of fo many calamities which lay wafte polifhed nations, that they chufe rather to be free, and look upon cities as fo many prifons where Kings confine their flaves. They fcarce feel the dependence they are under upon a remote mafter, and are pleafed with their Prince's being more dependent than themfelves. The Cham is always narrowly watched by the Bafhaws; and if his fubjects complain, he is depofed by an order of the Divan; but if he is too much beloved by them, this is ftill a greater crime. And yet the Cham never attempts to fhake off the Turkifh yoke. He looks upon his own family, and that of the Ottoman Emperors, as one and the fame. In fact, the Sultans have acknowledged that both fprung originally from the fame flock; and they have made a law, which gives the throne of Conftantinople to the Princes of Tartary, if the Ottoman blood fhould fail (*a*). The hope of this fucceffion is indeed very remote,

(*a*) Demetrius Cantemir's Hiftory of the Ottoman Empire, Pref. p. xxxi. This princely author (a thing not very common) had

D 4

remote, when it is confidered that a Turkifh Emperor has always three or four hundred wives, the very
flower of their fex, to furnifh him with fucceffors ;
and the Cham's chance is now ftill lefs, becaufe
the Sultans have abolifhed the barbarous cuftom of
putting their brothers to death : but ftill his hopes
are not without foundation. Befides, he has reafon to be fatisfied with his lot, if he will only conform to the eafy rules of Tartarian juftice, which
requires no more of him, than not to put any force
upon the manners of the nation, and to lead them
to frequent incurfions. A ftate of war agrees beft
with his interefts ; for he is feldom attacked firft,
but generally begins the fray ; he has no army to
maintain, his troops being paid by the Grand-
Signior : he has nothing to lofe, and every thing to
gain by plunder. The Tartars are' moft to be
dreaded, not at the time of their entering a country, but at their quitting it, being like torrents
which fweep every thing off with them. In time
of action, a fenfe of honour does not reftrain them
from running away ; but then they always return
to the combat. In their marches, they fpread themfelves before, behind, and on the flanks of the enemy's troops, which they harafs ftill more by night,
than by day : fo that an army, which has not been
ufed to make war againft them, would be conquered, without an opportunity of exerting its ftrength.
In their frequent wars with the Poles, they have ravaged and depopulated Podolia, Pokrufia, Volhinia,
Moldavia, and the Ukraine; and as thefe defarts
continued to be the feat of war, even in the time of
Sobiefki, the Poles were obliged to turn Tartars in

had at different times, fpent many years as an hoftage at Conftantinople, before he came to the Crown of Moldavia. He
underftood the Turkifh language, had read their hiftories, and
was acquainted with their manner and cuftoms. Such an author muft be quoted more than once.

order

order to fubfift; that is, they were obliged to carry with them at once all the provifions that would be
wanted in a whole campaign. To this neceffity, and
to their making ufe of waggons drawn by oxen, is
owing their affembling fo late, and marching fo flowly
in the campaigns hereafter defcribed. Every Captain
knew by experience how many waggons his troop
would want; and as foon as the country was exhaufted, they lived upon their provided ftock. When
a waggon was emptied, it was fet on fire, and the
oxen killed, to furnifh a frefh fupply; and it has
often happened that the waggons alone, exclufive
of the provifions they brought, have faved the Polifh armies. In cafes of a fudden attack, they ferve
by way of entrenchments ; and this method of defence is called *Tabor*. From them probably, the
General of the Huffites, Procopius the Bald, learnt
it, and made ufe of it with great fuccefs againft the
German cavalry, which got his foldiers the name
of *Taborites*.

The Poles are born foldiers; and though they
refemble their anceftors, the Sarmatians, much lefs
than the Tartars do theirs, yet there are ftill remaining among them fome Sarmatian features.
For inftance, they are frank and haughty; which
laft quality is natural enough in a gentleman who
elects his own King, and may come to have that
honour himfelf. They are alfo extremely paffionate,
affairs being often decided fword in hand by the reprefentatives, in their national affemblies. Hofpi-
tality is a virtue much cultivated among them, and
was learnt from the Turks and Tartars. A Tartar will go fifty leagues to attack a caravan ; but
a ftranger is always well received at his houfe, and
provided with lodgings, food, and other accommo-
dations, at no expence. The Poles are brave, ro-
buft, and inured to cold and fatigue ; but they have
departed from the fimplicity and frugality of the
Sarma-

Sarmatians. To the very end of the reign of Sobiefki, a few wooden chairs, a bear's fkin, a pair
of piftols, and two boards covered with a matrefs,
was all the houfhold-furniture of a nobleman in decent circumftances; and a fuit of furs was his drefs.
Luxury began to get footing under Auguftus II.
and the French fafhions, already adopted in Germany, were added to the magnificence of the eaft,
which difplays itfelf more in pomp than elegance.
The Poles love money, but not with a view to
hoarding. Their ftatelinefs is fuch, that a woman
of quality never ftirs abroad but in a coach and fix,
though it were only to crofs a ftreet.

When a nobleman travels from one province
to another, he is attended by five or fix hundred
horfes and as many men. There are no inns upon the road, fo that every thing muft be carried
with them; but then they make no fcruple of dif-
lodging the Plebeians, who look upon their nobles
as fo many plagues and fcourges.

One excellent cuftom among the nobles, is that
of fpending the greateft part of the year upon their
own eftates. By this means, they are more independent upon the court, which fpares no pains to
corrupt them, and the country is the better for
what they fpend; but it would be much more populous and flourifhing, if it was cultivated by a
free people. The peafants in Poland are annexed
to the glebe; whereas even in Afia itfelf there are
no flaves but fuch as are purchafed, or taken in
war, and confequently foreigners; but Poland lays
the yoke upon the neck of her own children. Every Lord is obliged to lodge his vaffals, and he
does it in a wretched hut, where the children,
which lie naked among the cattle, in a frozen climate, feem to upbraid nature with not having clad
them in the fame manner. The flave, who begot
them, would with great indifference fee his cot-
tage

tage in flames, becaufe he has nothing that he can call his own. *My field, my wife, my children,* is a language he has nothing to do with. Every thing belongs to the Lord, who has an equal power to fell his labourers and his oxen. It is not common indeed to fell women, becaufe they ferve to multiply the herd, and keep up a wretched breed, great part of which is killed by the cold.

Perhaps there never was a man, to whom the human race is more indebted, than to Pope Alexander III. who, in a council held in the twelfth century, abolifhed flavery. But Poland has proved more obdurate than the reft of Chriftendom. Woe to every flave that falls under the difpleafure of a drunken Lord! One would think that nature has made a point of refufing to fome nations the very thing that they are moft paffionately fond of. Exceffes in wine and ftrong liquors have occafioned great havock in the republic of Poland. Yet their cafuifts fpeak of drunkennefs in very gentle terms, as almoft neceffary in fuch a climate; and befides, the affairs of the public are never fettled but over the bottle.

The Polifh women are fingularly agreeable in fociety. They mix with the men in competitions at public games, in hunting, and the pleafures of the table. Lefs delicate and lefs referved than the beauties of the fouth, they frequently take a journey of a hundred, or two hundred leagues in a fledge, without any apprehenfions about inconvenient lodgings, or the badnefs of the roads.

Perfons who travel in Poland find that good morals are of more value than good laws. The number of forefts, the diftance of habitations, the cuftom of travelling by night as well as by day, the negligence of the ftarofts with regard to the fafety of the roads, all contribute to favour robbery and

murder,

murder, and yet an inftance of either is fcarce known in ten years.

The Poles were noted for the practice of this branch of morality, before they embraced the Chriftian religion. They continued idolaters long after the converfion of the reft of Europe. The names of the Grecian gods, whom they adopted, were wretchedly disfigured in their language, becaufe being ignorant of letters, and knowing nothing of Homer and Hefiod, they never opened the archives of idolatry, but were directed only by the glimmering light of confufed tradition.

About the middle of the tenth century, *Mieciflaw* the Firft, Duke of Poland, was won over to the faith by the folicitations of the fair Dambrowka, his wife, who was bred a Chriftian : and the new profelyte undertook to convert his fubjects. There is nothing but may become an inftrument in the hands of God to execute his adorable defigns. One half of Europe owes its converfion to women, who, being raifed to the throne, prevailed upon their hufbands to be baptized. Thus Hungary is indebted for its Chriftianity to *Gifella* ; Ruffia, to *the fifter of a Greek Emperor* ; England, to *a daughter of Childebert* ; and France to *Clotilda*. But if Chriftianity, at its firft eftablifhment, had fhewn every where the fame violence that it did in Poland, it would have wanted two fignatures of truth to which it owed its triumphs in the three firft centuries, namely, *meeknefs* and *perfuafion*. The Bifhop of Merfebourg, who lived in the reign of Mieciflaw, informs us, that the punifhment of all who prefumed to eat flefh in Lent was to have their teeth pulled out ; that a fornicator or adulterer was hung up by the inftrument of his crime, and a razor placed within his reach, which he might either make ufe of to difengage himfelf, or die in torment

ment (a). In the fame country, it was a cuſtom for fathers to put to death their children when born with any defect, and for the unnatural off-ſpring to difpatch their decrepid parents ; a barba-rous cuſtom of the ancient Sarmatians, which was tolerated in Poland till the thirteenth century. When the Prieſt came to that part of the ſervice of the mafs where the Gofpel is read, the aſſembly was al-ways ſtruck with terror, it being a, cuſtom for all who wore ſabres, to draw them half-way, in teſti-mony of their readineſs to ſhed the blood of ido-laters (b). That horrid Chriſtian, Mieciſlaw, had divorced ſeven Pagan wives, to make way for his union with Dambrowka, and when ſhe died, he cloſed the ſcene, if we may believe Baronius and Dithmar (c), with marrying a nun, who omitted no expedient to propagate her religion. The zeal of Mieciſlaw was animated by the hopes of obtain-ing the title of King, which the Pope had lately given to the Duke of Hungary; but he would not beſtow the ſame reward upon fucceſs obtained by ſuch ſhocking means.

His ſon and fucceſſor Boleſlas I. extinguiſhed the remains of idolatry, without having recourſe to violence. Humane, acceſſible, and familiar, he treated his fubjects, as a phyſician would his pa-tients, and made uſe of no arms to conquer their prejudices, but gentleneſs and argument. The fa-ther had commanded them, the ſon perſuaded them, to be Chriſtians.

In the fourteenth century, Jagellon, being made King of Poland, planted the Chriſtian faith, by the ſame means, in Lithuania. He was before thought to be of a fierce temper, but Chriſtianity, which he had lately embraced, undoubtedly ſoftened

(a) Dithmar. lib. viii. p. 419.
(b) Cromer. lib. iii. p. 51.　　(c) Tom. i. p. 359.

him ;

him; and he compleated, by prefents and acts of kindnefs, the converfion of fuch as ftood out againft the force of argument.

This peaceable fpirit paffed from the Kings to the nation, which accordingly had very little fhare in the religious wars which defolated Europe in the fixteenth and feventeenth centuries. Poland was never the fcene of a gun-powder-plot, of a Saint-Bartholomew-maffacre, of the murder of a Senate, of the private affaffination, or the public execution of Kings; it never faw brothers in arms againft brothers, and has been more fparing than any country in burning people at a ftake, for the crime of being miftaken in matters of opinion. Notwithftanding this, Poland continued in barbarifm much longer than Spain, France, England or Germany; which fhews that grofs ignorance is much lefs turbulent than half-fcience. When the fpirit of argumentation begun to get footing in Poland, King Sigifmund I. made a law to punifh Proteftants with death. It is a ftrange paradox, that at the very time when he was taking away the lives of fuch as only queftioned the corporal prefence of Jefus Chrift upon the altar, he gave no difturbance to the Jews who denied his divine miffion. Sigifmund's zeal had already produced bloodfhed, and would have produced more; but the Republic thought fit to interpofe, and made a law, that for the future, every King, upon his afcending the throne, fhould take an oath to tolerate all religions.

Accordingly Poland abounds with Calvinifts, Lutherans, Greek Schifmatics, Mahometans, and Jews. Thefe latter have long enjoyed the privileges granted them by *Cafimir the Great*, in favour of his Jewifh concubine *Efther*. Their trade makes them much more wealthy than the natives of the country, and they increafe much fafter. In Cra-

cow

cow alone, it is computed there are more than twenty thoufand, who are ready to give their affift-ance in all emergencies of ftate; and Poland, by tolerating more than three hundred fynagogues, is called to this day *the Jews Paradife.* If the Poles are upbraided with this indulgence, they anfwer, that Rome itfelf lets them live in peace within its walls. A Spanifh inquifitor would imagine, that the whole nation Judaized on Eafter-day; a *Pafchal Lamb* being ferved up at every table, and eaten with confecrated bread; but then they have a hundred other cuftoms with which he would be highly edi-fied.

There is perhaps no country where the outward forms of religion have been, and ftill are, better obferved. The Poles, from the very firft, found fault with Chriftianity for being too mild a reli-gion; and to remedy this defect, they begun their Lent on Septuagefima-Sunday. But this fevere work of fupererogation was abolifhed by Pope In-nocent IV. to reward them for the contributions they had furnifhed, to enable him to make war upon a Chriftian Emperor, Ferdinand II. (a). Be-fides the ufual faft on Fridays and Saturdays, they keep an additional one on Wednefdays. There was once an entertainment given by Sigifmund Auguftus, the day after his father's funeral, to the nobles who affifted at that ceremony: it happened to be a Wednefday, and part of the entertainment was flefh. The whole nation was extremely fcandalized at this profanenefs; and yet at this very time, they wanted him to break through a folemn engage-ment, contracted at the altar of God, and confirm-ed by the laws of men; that is, his marriage: " If " there be any harm, faid the Archbifhop and Pri-" mate, in repudiating a lawful wife, there is none

(a) Cromer. p. 226.

" of

" of us, who, for the fake of the common good,
" will not readily take part of it upon himfelf (a):"
and the thing wanted being a fucceffor to the Crown,
the Bifhop of Przemiflia fupported his opinion with
this paffage of Euripides, *If juftice muft be violated, let it be for the fake of a Crown.*

The bloody fraternity of Flagellants are as common in this part of the north, as towards the fouth
of Europe; and hence probably it was that Henry III. imported the fafhion into France.

No hiftory, in the fame number of centuries,
pretends to fo many miracles. About five miles
from Cracow, are to be feen the falt pits of Boch-
nia, removed, according to all the Chronicles, by
St. Cunegunda, wife of Boleflas the Chaft, out
of Hungary into Poland; and much more admired
than thofe of Velika, where there is a fubterraneous
city, full three leagues deep; an aftonifhing monument of art and induftry. At the time when fo
many apocryphal miracles were confounded with
the true ones in Poland, very little progrefs was
made in the ftudy of nature; nor can this fcience
be at prefent much advanced, fince the marvellous,
which has always ferved the vulgar inftead of reafon, preferves its dominion here more than in any
other country. The Poles have always met with
a refufal from Rome, to their frequent folicitations
for predictions of future events.

Their refpect for the Papal authority has been
remarkable in all ages. When Clement II. abfolved Cafimir from his monachal vows, that he
might change the cloifter for the throne, in 1041,
his Holinefs impofed upon the Poles fome very fingular conditions, which were moft religioufly obferved. He obliged them to wear for the future,
their hair cut in the form of a Monk's crown;

(a) Stanifl. Oriehov. p. 1489.

to

to pay for ever an annual poll-tax, for keeping up in the great church of St. Peter, the moſt coſtly lamp that ever was burnt ; and he ordered, that upon great feſtivals all the nobles ſhould wear, during the time of the ſacrifice, a linnen ſtole, like that which is worn by Prieſts; the firſt of which injunctions is obſerved to this day.

This extravagant deference for the decrees of the ſee of Rome, broke out once in ſuch a torrent as overwhelmed the regal power. Boleſlas I. had received the title of King from the Emperor Otho, in the year 1001; and Rome remembered this affront, upon occaſion of the murder of Staniſlas, Biſhop of Cracow, by Boleſlas II. It was at this juncture, that *Hildebrand,* who had exchanged a wheel-wright's ſhop for the throne of St. Peter, which he filled by the name of *Gregory* VII. was grown ſo formidable to all the ſovereigns of Chriſtendom. He had lately excommunicated the Emperor Henry IV. to whom he had been preceptor ; and he now pointed againſt Boleſlas all his thunders of excommunication, depoſition, interdiction of the whole kingdom, diſpenſation from the oath of allegiance, and prohibition to the Biſhops of Poland, ever to crown any King without the expreſs conſent of the Holy See *(a).* It is hard to ſay which is moſt aſtoniſhing, the Pope's prohibition, or the blind obedience of the Poles. No Biſhop would venture to crown the ſucceeding King; and this ſuperſtitious fear laſted upon the minds both of the ſubjects, and their Princes, till the time of Przemiſlas, who having convoked a general diet at Gneſna, was crowned in that aſſembly, and reſumed the title of King, without calling in the authority of Rome *(b).* His ſubjects believed that this ſpirited behaviour, which raiſed the indignation of the court of Rome, was the cauſe of his unhappy fate. Seven months af-

(a) Cromer. p. 90.　*(b)* Sarnic. p. 1116.

E

ter,

ter, he was affaffinated by his own nephews, and *Uladiflas Loketek*, who afcended the throne yet reeking with blood, applied to Pope John XXII. for leave to be King in his own kingdom.

In the prefent age, no Pope would venture to attempt what was then carried into execution. But it is ftill true, that the Papal power is more revered in Poland than in moft Catholic countries. A nation, which has affumed a right of chufing its own Kings, has never dared to proclaim them without leave from the Pope; and a bull of Sixtus V. has given the Primate this power.

There refides conftantly at Warfaw an apoftolical Nuncio, invefted with an extent of power which is fuffered no where elfe : but yet he has not enough to enforce the indiffolubility of the marriage-contract. It is not uncommon in Poland to hear a hufband talk of a wife, who is no longer connected with him by that relation. The Bifhops, who are both witneffes and judges of thefe divorces, confole themfelves for fuch a violation of ecclefiaftical law, with the ample revenues they enjoy. The private clergy profefs the moft refpectful veneration for the facred canons ; and they are in the right ; for moft of them hold feveral benefices with cure of fouls.

Poland, in its prefent ftate, with regard both to moral and phyfical evil, prefents us with feveral ftriking contrafts : the regal dignity exifting with the name of a republic, civil laws with feudal anarchy, a rude refemblance of the Roman commonwealth with Gothic barbarifm, and abundance united with poverty.

Nature has furnifhed the country with all the materials of opulence, fuch as corn, pafture, cattle, wool, leather, falt, metals, and minerals; and yet they are the pooreft nation in Furope. The chief fource of the wealth of Poland, is the fale of the Crown.

Both

Both land, and water, concur to invite commerce; and yet it has never appeared among them. The number of fine rivers, the *Duna*, the *Bog*, the *Niefter*, the *Viftula*, the *Niemen*, the *Boryfthenes*, serve only to make a figure in geographical maps. It has been often obferved, that it would be an eafy matter to join the Northern Ocean and the Black fea by canals, and by this means take in the commerce both of the eaft and weft. But the Poles are fo far from building merchant-fhips, that they have never thought of forming a naval force to protect them from the fleets of their enemies, by which their country has often been infulted. Their dominions are larger than France, and yet do not contain more than fix millions of inhabitants. They leave a fourth part of their lands uncultivated, and yet the land is excellent, which makes the lofs fo much the more to be lamented.

A kingdom of fuch extent, being two hundred leagues in breadth, and four hundred in length, would require numerous armies to guard its vaft frontiers, and yet it can fcarce pay forty thoufand men. A King, (*a*) who governed it for fome time, and who has fhewn what he was capable of doing in a whole kingdom, by what he has actually done in a fingle province of France; a King equally qualified for writing, and for acting, informs us, *that there are cities in Europe whofe treafury is richer than that of Poland*; and that *two or three merchants of London or Amfterdam trade for much larger fums than the income of all the lands belonging to the republic.* Such a republic can never have made the reflection, that the power of Holland was originally founded upon the art of catching, and falting herrings.

(*a*) Staniflas, King of Poland, and Duke of Lorrain, in his book entitled *La Voix libre du Citoyen*, or, *The free Voice of a Citizen*, p. 247 & 285.

The

The republic of Rome, in its days of virtue, was the very reverſe of the republic of Poland. In the former, the Senators were in moderate circumſtances, and the ſtate rich. In the latter, the Palatines can raiſe and pay armies to deſtroy one another, and the republic is unable to defend itſelf. When it does take up arms, the two bodies of troops which are its ordinary defence, the Poliſh army, and the Lithuanian, being commanded by two Grand Generals, independent of each other, are without that principle of union which makes forces act in concert. It has happened more than once, that when one has marched, the other has halted: they have even been known to threaten each other.

Luxury has got footing within doors, but the naſtineſs of the cities without, is extremely diſguſtful. It is not more than ten or twelve years ſince Warſaw was firſt paved.

The extremes of liberty and ſlavery ſeem to be contending which ſhall ruin Poland. The nobility can do whatever they pleaſe ; and the body of the nation groans in ſervitude. The example of Denmark has been hitherto an uſeleſs leſſon to the Poliſh nobles. Wherever the great have tyrannically trampled upon the people, the latter have revenged themſelves by giving up their oppreſſors into the hands of an abſolute Monarch. That all men are born upon a footing of equality, is a truth which will never be eradicated from the human mind ; and if an inequality of condition is become neceſſary, it muſt be alleviated by the enjoyment of natural liberty, and equal laws. A Poliſh noble, whatever crime he has committed, cannot be taken into cuſtody, till he has been condemned in an aſſembly of all the eſtates of the realm ; which is, in effect, furniſhing him with all imaginable means to eſcape. They have a law among them,

them, which is itſelf more ſhocking than the murder it was intended to prevent. If a noble kills
one of his own ſlaves, he is to lay fifteen livres
upon the grave of the deceaſed; but if the pea-
ſant belongs to another noble, the laws of honour
only oblige him to give another. The maxim of
an ox for an ox, is the avowed principle of the
whole proceeding.

The right of the *liberum veto* makes a ſingle noble
more powerful than the whole republic. He can,
with a word, defeat the unanimous reſolution of
the whole nation; and if he leaves the place where
the diet is held, the aſſembly muſt inſtantly ſepa-
rate. The Tribunes of Rome had anciently the
ſame power, but their number was very ſmall,
and their magiſtracy inſtituted for the protection
of the people; whereas, in a Poliſh diet, there are
three or four hundred Tribunes, created, it would
ſeem, on purpoſe to oppreſs them.

The republic has taken all ſorts of precautions
to preſerve at leaſt an equality among its nobles.
There are few countries that can ſhew ſuch extenſive lordſhips; and yet there are none that have
titles annexed to them; French cooks, and the titles
of *Marquis* and *Count* were introduced into Poland
at the ſame time; and none but ſervants and flat-
terers ever give theſe Marquiſſes and Counts their
titles. The Holy Empire has filled Europe with
Princes; a title, which, at its firſt riſe, about the
time of Frederick II. was taken only by Lords of
extenſive territories; but is now beſtowed at a much
eaſier rate upon foreigners, as well as natives, and
upon ſome Poles among the reſt. The families of
*Jablonowſki, Lubomirſki, Radziwil, Doenoff, Oſſo-
linſki,* and *Sulkowſki,* need not have been ſo fond
of this German ornament. Be this as it will, the
republic ſets no ſort of value upon it. The only
Princes that are acknowledged as ſuch in the articles

ticles of union with Lithuania, are the families of
Czartoriſki, *Sanguſko*, and *Wieſnowieſki*; and yet
their title of Highneſs does not give them a higher
rank.   The loweſt Caſtellan takes place of a Prince
who has no office, that the Poles may learn to
reſpect the republic more than birth and titles.
Even they, whoſe rank is owing to the dignities
they poſſeſs, muſt confine themſelves within the limits of their condition.   The Primate, who pre-
ſided at the election of Auguſtus II. having erected
a canopy over his arm-chair, was forced to pull it
down the ſame day.   And yet, notwithſtanding all
theſe precautions, nothing can be more cringing
than the lower nobility to the higher.   It is true,
the former have their revenge, whenever the latter
aim at *popularity*, which means no more than
forming a party in the petty diets, either for the
management of the ordinary affairs of the province,
or for the election of a King.

The kingdom being elective, it might naturally
be ſuppoſed, that the People, who are the moſt numerous, and the moſt neceſſary part of the ſtate,
ſhould have ſome ſhare in the election; and yet
they have not any, but muſt take the King that
the nobles give them, and would think themſelves abundantly happy, in not being loaded with
chains of iron in the very arms of liberty.   Whoever is not nobly born, is a mere cypher in the
city, or a ſlave in the country; and it is certain,
that every ſtate is undone, where the Plebeian has
no poſſibility of riſing, but by overturning the whole
conſtitution.   In conſequence of the ſlavery of the
people, Poland has very few artificers or tradeſ-
men; and theſe few are Scotchmen, French, or
Jews.   In all their wars, they are forced to hire
foreign engineers: there is no ſuch thing among
them as a ſchool for painting: architecture is yet
in its infancy; and theatrical entertainments they
have

have none. They write history without taste, know little of the mathematics, and less of true philosophy: they have no public building of any note, and not one great city in all the kingdom: even Warsaw does not contain sixty thousand souls. Such was the state of France itself under the feudal government; for what can be expected from any country, where the weight of the nobility crushes every thing?

The honour of being ranked among the Polish nobles has been solicited by several Princes. The nephews of King Stephen Battori obtained it; and it must be confessed, that no state can shew so numerous a nobility, of the highest antiquity; the pedigrees of all the principal families beginning earlier than the tenth century (a).

Nothing can be more pompous and stately than the Polish Lords. Their wives have adopted the French fashions, without having the arts which minister to luxury; but it must not be supposed that this magnificence implies the state to be rich. On the contrary, it is not the Plebeians only that suffer. For, while about thirty Palatines, a hundred Castellans and Starosts, the bench of Bishops, and the great officers of the crown, live like Asiatic Satraps; there are a hundred thousand of the petty nobles, who get necessaries as they can; and with all their liberty, and all their pride, are not ashamed of entering into the service of the great Lords, and earning wages from them in the lowest stations. When one of these noblemen in livery commits a fault, he undergoes the discipline of the *cancbou* *; *The whip. but out of respect to his pedigree, he is furnished with a cushion to kneel on. Some of them would have applied themselves to commerce, by way of deliverance from such meanness; but it was declared by

(a) Okolski. Orbis Polonus.

E 4

a cona conftitution made in 1677, that commerce degraded nobility. With all this, the meaneft nobleman in Poland thinks himfelf fuperior to all the nobility in Europe: and yet, this nobility which he is fo proud of, is fometimes beftowed by the republic upon flight grounds enough, when a foreigner obtains an act of naturalization. A Jew, who turns Chriftian, and is baptized, is almoft fure of being ennobled, if he can procure a few friends; and then he may make as much noife in the provincial diets, as the blood of the Jagellons.

An hiftorian is obliged to dwell much upon the nobility of Poland, becaufe the people go for nothing. The privilege that is in greateft efteem with them, but of the leaft ufe, is that of electing the King. The crown is generally fold by the nobles to the beft bidder; and though, at the time of election, they call out loudly for Princes that will govern well; yet, fince the reign of Cafimir the Great, they have ranfacked Hungary, Tranfylvania, France, and Germany, in queft of foreigners, entirely unacquainted with the manners, prejudices, language, interefts, laws and cuftoms of the kingdom.

Whoever was to fee a King of Poland in all the pomp of regal dignity, would take him for the moft opulent and defpotic of monarchs; and yet he is neither one, nor the other. The republic allows him no more than fix hundred thoufand crowns for the expences of his houfhold; and in all difputes, the Poles invariably pronounce the King to be in the wrong. As he prefides in all councils, and iffues out all decrees, they call him the *mouth*, not the *foul* of the republic; and compare him to the King of the bees, which, according to the ancient naturalifts, has no fting. They keep a conftant watch over his adminiftration; and four Senators are appointed to attend him every where,

upon

upon pain of a pecuniary forfeit. His Chancellor refuses to put the seal to whatever he thinks wrong: his High-Chamberlain has a right to search his person, and therefore the King always gives that office to a favourite. His subjects forgive in each other what they would think unpardonable in him; they are always holding up against him the buckler of that liberty which they grossly abuse themselves; and it is common with them to say to other nations, *We have a King, but a King has you.*

Yet these very men, who are so haughty to their Prince, can compliment one another in the language of slaves; such as, *I prostrate myself at your feet; I put myself under the sole of your shoes;* and they submit patiently to an exclusion of a very mortifying sort. When the King dines in public, foreign Ambassadors are admitted to his table, and the grandees of the kingdom who keep his hands tied up, are employed in serving him. Poland is perhaps the only kingdom in the world, where the King has not a right of coining, being deprived of this privilege by the republic.

And yet, a King of Poland, limited as he is, may act an important part, if he will content himself with doing good, without having a power to do harm. He not only disposes, like other sovereigns, of all the great offices of state, of bishoprics and abbeys, which last are most of them held in commendam; (for the republic has taken care that Monks, who have made a vow to renounce riches, and given up their rank in civil life, should be supplied only with necessaries) but he is possessed of another treasure which is never to be exhausted. A third part of this large kingdom is royal demesne, under the names of *tenutes, advocateships,* and *starosties,* from the value of seven thousand livres a year, up to a hundred thousand. This

royal

royal Demefne, as the King cannot appropriate it to himfelf, he is obliged to give away; and it is not tranfmitted from father to fon by the recommendation of merit only. It is a common faying, that there is not an hour in the day, in which the King of Poland has not fome favour to beftow.

To complete this fketch of Poland, it is neceffary to give a fhort account of it's moft diftinguifhed Kings. The herd of princes need not be dragged out of the obfcurity that covers them; but Poland can boaft of a greater number of intelligent, active, and indefatigable Governors than any other ftate: and it is not indebted to chance for this advantage, but derives it from the nature of it's conftitution. Ever fince the fourteenth century, Poland has elected it's own Kings, and therefore has not been governed by children born with a crown upon their heads, before they have any virtues; and inheriting a privilege of flumbering upon the throne in mature age. A King of Poland is obliged to act in perfon in the fenate, in the diets, and at the head of armies.

If military virtues engrofs all our admiration, the Poles have had almoft as many great Princes as Sovereigns. But if we reckon only thofe who have aimed at promoting the profperity and happinefs of the nation, the number muft be confiderably diminifhed.

VI. century. I. clafs.
Leck, the founder of the nation, prevailed upon the Poles to leave off wandering in forefts for a fixed and civilized life. His character is not tranfmitted to us in hiftory; but we know in general, that all founders of empires have had good heads, and active vigorous fpirits: and Leck muft have ftood in need of both, to govern favages who were acquainted only with the equality of a ftate of nature.

VII. century. I. clafs.
Cracus gave them their firft ideas of juftice, by erecting tribunals to decide the differences of private perfons. By this means, order fucceeded in the
place

place of licentiousness; and the tomb of so great a benefactor was long honoured by the idolatrous inhabitants of Cracow, as the Palladium of the city (*a*).

Piast taught them virtue by practising it himself; IX. cenand inculcated, by the soft arts of persuasion and tury. example, what he could not inforce by authority. II. class. His reign was spent in peace, and his barbarians begun to be formed into members of civil society (*b*).

Ziemovit, who was of a more martial turn, taught IX. centhem military discipline. Till his time, like tor-tury. rents which quickly leave the lands they overflow, II. class. they had been accustomed only to temporary incursions: but they now learnt to stand firm in battle, to conquer by resisting their enemies, and to keep what they had once subdued (*c*).

Boleslas Chrobri laboured to reform thei rmanners, X. cento extirpate their prejudices, and regulate their cou-tury. rage, which was too apt to make a cruel use of vic-II. class. tory. Being full of humanity himself, he accustomed them to consider their sovereign as a common father; and obedience became an easy duty (*d*).

Casimir I. gave them a glimpse of science and li-XI. centerature in a savage climate, where ignorance had al-tury. ways reigned (*e*). The rude manner in which the li-II. class. beral arts were at first cultivated by the Poles, could produce no better fruits, till the arrival of more favourable seasons. Even to this day, the literary productions of Poland are somewhat harsh: but time, which ripens every thing, will finish even here what it has already brought to perfection in other climates.

Casimir II. who did not acquire the appellation of XII. cen*just* without deserving it, protected the country-people tury. against the tyranny of the nobles. That wretched II. class.

(*a*) Dlugloss. lib. 1. p. 50.   (*b*) Cromer. lib. 2. p. 40.
(*c*) Chronic. Pol. tom. i. p. 4.   (*d*) Hartknoch. lib. 1. p. 65.
(*e*) Sarnic. Annal. Pol. lib. 6. cap. 8.

race

race was obliged to furnifh every nobleman, who travelled, with lodging, provifions, horfes, and all other neceffaries for his journey. The King abolifhed this impofition (a); and if the nobility had thought as generoufly of fome of their monarchs, there would now be no fuch thing as flavery in Poland.

XIV. century.
II. clafs.

Cafimir III. or Cafimir *the Great*, called alfo *the King of the Peafants*, attempted to fet them at liberty; but not being able to fucceed in his attempt, he gave them an ufeful hint, when they came to complain to him of their grievances, by afking if they had no fticks, nor ftones at home to ufe in their own defence. The obftinate refolution of the Polifh nobility to keep the people in flavery, could neither be conquered by the authority of Pope Alexander III; who declared, in the name of a council, that all Chriftians ought to be free; nor by the example of France and England, where feudal tyranny is abolifhed; nor by the republican form of government, which is fo oppofite to every thing that has the air of flavery. But Cafimir had the greateft fuccefs in every other branch of the adminiftration. It is to him that Poland owes its firft fortreffes, but the nation has never been fenfible of that advantage, fince inftead of increafing their number, they are fuffered to go to ruin. The fame Prince exerted his utmoft efforts to extirpate barbarifm from the domain of the liberal arts. In his time, new cities were raifed, which furnifhed models to rebuild the old ones: the public monuments that were then erected were as elegant as the age would admit of. He invited into the kingdom the ableft mafters, who unfortunately had no abilities at all (b). If he had lived two centuries later, about the time of Leo X. Poland in all probability would not have been what it is at prefent.

(a) Dluglofs. p. 512.   (b) Sarnic. Annal. Pol p. 1147.
      Cromer. p. 319.

It

It was he alfo who obferved, that the original fyftem
of laws was no longer adapted to the interefts or manners of Poland, and therefore formed a new body, by
which the kingdom is governed to this time. He had
all the great qualities of Auguftus, and more valour.
His fubjects decreed him the honours of the triumph, a cuftom which begat heroes among the nations of antiquity, who confidered emulation as one
of the principal fprings of the ftate. Cafimir was
the laft of the Piafts, a family which reigned five
hundred and twenty eight years.

Jagellon, the head of the third race, kept up, and
even added to, the improvements which his predeceffors had made. He did what he pleafed with a
nation, whofe growing liberty, by being always upon
it's guard againft regal encroachments, muft have
made government a much more difficult thing than
ufual. His fubjects were furprized at the gentlenefs
of his manners; for while he was only Duke of Lithuania, he had ftartled all the north by putting his
uncle to death: but he changed all at once, and
being elected to govern a free people, he found himfelf under a happy neceffity of being a good King.
He tried his ftrength in war againft that of Sigifmund, who, after being buried alive in a dungeon
eighty feet deep, was taken out at the end of fix
months, in order to join his own crown of Hungary
to thofe of Bohemia and the Empire. *Jagellon* might
have deprived him of the former, for it was offered
to the Polifh King by the Hungarians themfelves;
but he chofe to decline the victory which he was upon
the point of gaining, for fear of difmembering the
territories of Poland, by being too eager to enlarge
them (*a*). It is furprizing, that an elective crown,
for fuch it was now become, fhould continue in his
family for near four hundred years; while in other

(*a*) Neuglbaver. hift. Pol. p. 238.

countries

countries hereditary thrones were filled by foreign families: which shews how little the event of things corresponds to the expectations of human wisdom.

XIV. century. *Uladislas* VI. son of *Jagellon*, was only ten years old when he was raised to the crown; a strange choice in a nation which might have bestowed it's crown upon a Hero of mature abilities; but they discovered an heroic soul already beaming through the infancy of the young King. The republic appointed as many regents as it had provinces; and more than one *Burrbus* undertook the task of instructing the man of the nation. At the age of eighteen, he took into his own hands the reins of government; and though he held them only two years, he shewed himself equal to the greatest Kings. He triumphed over the whole power of the house of Austria; got the crown of Hungary to be set upon his own head, and was the first King of Poland that ventured to contend with the fortune of the Ottoman Empire. Amurath II. having laid waste Transylvania and Servia, was menacing Hungary and all Europe; when the young King put a stop to his conquests, and forced him to sue for peace, which was reciprocally sworn to upon the Bible and the Alcoran: but the Pope broke the compact, and his legate, Cardinal Julian Cesarini, absolved the King from the guilt of perjury. With such auspices, Uladislas marched towards the Black Sea, entered Bulgaria, and with twenty-five thousand Poles, attacked the Sultan, whom he found near Varna, at the head of a hundred thousand Turks. At the first onset the Mussulmen gave way, when the Sultan, taking out of his bosom the violated treaty, and fixing it on the top of a lance, called upon God, the Avenger of perjury, to punish this breach of the law of nations (*a*). No sooner had he finished his prayer, than

(*a*) Sarnic. lib. 7. chap. 6. Dlugloss. p. 793.

2

having

having rallied his retiring troops, the Turkish enthusiasm was rekindled, the right wing of the Christian army gave way, the disorder increased every moment, Uladislas fell dead upon the spot; and his
head being cut off by a Janissary, and carried from
rank to rank, made the rout complete (a). He was
hardly twenty years old at his death; and Poland,
equally dreading the future, and grieved at the past,
never shed tears of deeper sorrow. The historians
agree in saying that, notwithstanding the vivacity of
his passions, his virtues were never tarnished with any
vice. If he broke his treaty with Amurath, it was
then the common opinion that faith was not to be
kept with infidels. The legate, who sanctified this
act of perjury, was drowned in crossing a river.

The tears of the nation were not wholly dried up XVI. cen-
till the reign of Sigismund I. who had the singular tury.
good fortune of being declared King by acclamation, III. class.
without any division of suffrages (b). Great men Race of
possess the art of fixing fortune; and Sigismund ob- the Jagel-
tained of her another favour, which was that of de- lons.
molishing the power of a religious order that had
laid waste Poland for three centuries. The knights
of the Teutonic order, being expelled Palestine,
where their business was to take care of the sick, had
met with an asylum in Poland in the reign of Boleslas V. and shewed the most indefatigable zeal to XIII. cen-
convert Prussia to the Christian faith, because, be- tury.
ing more dextrous in the use of the sword than of II. class.
the cross, they usurped the sovereignty of that coun- Race of
try, which belonged to Poland. Here they forged the Piasts.
the thunders which were so often let loose upon their
benefactress; every reign, after that of Boleslas, having suffered by them more or less. It was computed,
that, under Casimir IV. a war of twelve years only
had occasioned the conflagration of eighteen thou-

(a) Dingloss. p. 808 and 811.   (b) Neuglbaver. lib. 7.
                                              sand

fand villages, and the bloodfhed of three hundred thoufand men. So extenfive a fcene of defolation, and fo many victims facrificed to their ambition, made no impreffion upon the members of this religious order. They had murdered in cold blood more than ten thoufand of the inhabitants of Dantzick, without fparing women or children (a); and had beheaded, at a public feaft, a numerous body of nobles, for refufing to join in their acts of violence. Uladiflas Loketek, Jagellon, and Cafimir, had attacked this hydra, which continually acquired frefh ftrength; but at length, it was exterminated by Sigifmund, who thereby delivered Poland from the heavieft fcourge it ever felt. The uncommon ftrength of body which Sigifmund poffeffed, infomuch that he could break in pieces the ftrongeft metals, made him pafs for the Hercules of his time (b); and the ftrength of his mind was no way inferior. He lived to the age of eighty-two, victorious in almoft all his undertakings, and refpected by the fovereigns of his time, who were all cautious of offending him, not excepting even Soliman himfelf, who fhewed that regard upon no other occafion. Under him were formed the many great captains who did honour to their country, fuch as the Duke of Oftrog, Kaminiecki, Firley, Lanczoronfki, Zaremba, Sienawfki, Tarnowfki, and Pretfiz. It was a queftion that could not be decided at that time, whether Francis I. Charles V. or Sigifmund, was the greateft monarch; but the latter was perhaps fuperior to the other two, by being more folicitous for the happinefs of his fubjects than his own glory, by applying himfelf with unremitted induftry to make his fubjects better men than even their laws required, their manners more fociable, their cities more flourifhing, their public buildings more elegant, the houfes of the nobles

(a) Dlugloff. p. 949.
(b) Paftor ab Hirtenberg. p. 207. Cromer. p. 68.

more

more commodious, the country better cultivated, arts and sciences more honoured, and even their re-ligion more refined (a).

Of all his successors, none resembled him more Y. 1575. than *Stephen Battori*, Prince of Transylvania, who IV. clas. was elected to the crown of Poland, after the abdi-cation of Henry de Valois. He made it a rule with himself to dispose of all honours and employments according to merit. He reformed the manifold abuses which had crept into the *administration of jus-tice*. He enacted military laws, which have intro-duced among the Poles and Cossacks all the disci-pline that they will probably ever be capable of. He maintained peace within the kingdom, and kept in awe the Tartars, Muscovites, and Cossacks. His reign lasted ten years, a space long enough for his own glory, but too short for the good of the re-public.

Sigismund III. Prince of Sweden, succeeded him Y. 1587. in the throne, but did not supply his place, having IV. clafs. neither the same great qualities, nor the same good fortune. He lost an hereditary kingdom to gain an elective one; and missed a fair opportunity of con-quering Muscovy, and perhaps of recovering Swe-den. He suffered Gustavus Adolphus to deprive Po-land of the cities of Elbing, and Marienburg, and Li-vonia, one of it's finest provinces. He had, in short, two faults, which generally occasion great misfor-tunes; he was very silly, and very obstinate.

(a) Cromer. p. 702 and 709.

End of the F I R S T B O O K.

F   T H E

THE

HISTORY

OF

JOHN SOBIESKI

KING OF POLAND.

BOOK II.

IN the year 1629, when Sigifmund III. reigned
in Poland, Lewis XIII. in France, the unfortunate Charles I. in England, the victorious Guftavus Adolphus in Sweden, was born John Sobiefki, the fubject of the following hiftory. At the
time when Poland was drawn into thofe wars,
which lafted till the end of that century, her defender came into the world, in the caftle of Olenf-
ko, a fmall town in the Palatinate of Ruffia. Sobiefki was defcended from two families, whofe
origin the Polifh genealogifts, full as adventurous
as thofe of France, have placed high in the obfcure ages of antiquity. It is a truth of greater
certainty, that in both thefe families there has been
a fucceffion of virtues, infinitely more valuable
than the higheft pedigree.

The

The famous Zolkiewſki, grandfather to Sobieſki by the mother's ſide, defeated the Muſcovites in 1610, took priſoner the Czar Baſilius, and
brought him to Sigiſmund III. (a). The monuments of this victory were ſtill to be ſeen upon
the cielings of the caſtle of Warſaw, when the
Czar Peter was called into Poland, to defend
King Auguſtus againſt Charles XII. The Czar
thought proper to deſtroy them, but the teſtimony
of hiſtory cannot be ſuppreſſed. In the year
1620, Zolkiewſki forced his way through a hundred
thouſand Turks and Tartars, who inveſted him
in Moldavia, and was retreating before this formidable hoſt, which purſued and haraſſed him during a march of a hundred leagues. Having reached
the frontiers of Poland, upon the banks of the
Nieſter, a ſlow ſtill river, known to Ovid by the
name of Tyras (b), he little expected to be betrayed by his own men. His cavalry, tired with
looking death in the face ſo long, took the firſt
opportunity to eſcape by ſwimming acroſs the river,
and abandoned in this manner the General, and
the foot. His ſon, who was with him in the army, beſought him to provide for his own ſafety,
but he anſwered, that *the republic had entruſted to
his care the whole army.* The foot that remained
were cut to pieces before his face; his ſon expired in his ſight; he himſelf was covered with
wounds, and ſurvived only a few hours, to die with
greater horror. The Turkiſh General cut off his
head, and ſent it to the ſeraglio, to revive the
ſpirits of the Ottoman Empire (c). The head
was afterwards redeemed, and the father and ſon

(a) Lengnich, Hiſt. Pol. p. 117.
(b) —— *Nullo tardior amne Tyras.*
　　　　　　Ex Ponto, lib. iv. epiſt. 10. v. 50.
(c) Lengnich, p. 125.

buried together in the fame grave, with this Latin infcription,

Exoriare aliquis, noftris ex offibus, ultor.

May an avenger arife out of our afhes! There ftill remained one fon, who attempted to difcharge that duty; and attacked the Tartars with a courage greatly fuperior to his forces, which confifted only of a fmall troop raifed at his own expence; but he was foon overpowered by numbers; and lofing his life in the attempt, was, after the battle, buried with his friends.

The glory of avenging the Zolkiewfkis, was referved for Sobiefki, their defcendant by the female line; who never read, without emotion, the infcription that exhorted him to vengeance. The republic did not think their merit fufficiently re-compenced by this family monument; but know-ing that immortality is both a reward, and an in-centive to heroic actions, erected a pyramid, hi-therto refpected by the Turks and even the Tar-tars, upon the fpot where this noble blood was fpilt. The defign was to inculcate upon pofterity the glorious leffon of dying in defence of their country. The infcription, compofed in four lan-guages, is ftill legible.

The hiftory of the Zolkiewfkis would furnifh us with many an act of heroifm, if it came with-in our defign: and it is not only in his mother's family, that John Sobiefki found heroes to imi-tate.

His grandfather by the father's fide, Mark So-biefki, Palatine of Lublin, left his grandfon many great exploits to copy. To him was owing the happy event of the battle, in which Michael, Hof-podar of Moldavia, was defeated. The Poles were going to take a route, by which the whole army would have been expofed to utter deftruction from

the

the want of provifions, and the fire of the enemy; when Sobiefki pointed out to them another way which led to victory; and fhewed, by his behaviour in the action, that he could execute as well as advife. He defeated alfo the rebellious Dantzickers in 1577, near the town of Dirchaw (a), and threw himfelf into the Viftula in purfuit of their General, whom he came up with, and flew with his own hand in the midft of the river. This exploit was performed in the prefence of the * King, who declared more than once, that if it fhould ever be neceffary to rifk the fate of Poland upon a fingle combat, as the fortune of Rome was once entrufted to the Horatii, he fhould not hefitate a moment to chufe the Palatine of Lublin. The intrepid Palatine met his death at the attack of Sokol, a Ruffian fortrefs which the Poles took by ftorm. Such was the grandfather of John Sobiefki; and his father, James Sobiefki, was not a degenerate fon. Before he rofe to any great office, he was four times chofe Marfhal of the diet, and confidered as the buckler of liberty. When he came into the fenate, it was to fill the fecond place in it, as Caftellan of Cracow, an officer who is greatly advanced beyond his own rank, fo as to take place even of the Palatines. When the Pofpolite is affembled, he has the honour of heading the nobility, to the prejudice of the Palatine of Cracow; a diftinction acquired as the reward of a victory, in which the Palatine run away, while his Lieutenant, the Caftellan, ftood his ground, and defeated the enemy. He is alfo the firft Lay-Senator, as the Primate is the head of the ecclefiaftics, and both have the title of *Highnefs*.

James Sobiefki was qualified to ferve the republic in more capacities than one; for the Polifh Se-

* Stephen Battori.

(a) A town of Pruffia in the Palatinate of Culm.

nators

nators are in this refpect formed upon the model of thofe of ancient Rome, and equally knowing in arms and law. Poland will long remember the famous battle of *Choczin (a)*, fought in 1621, in which the young Prince Uladiflas, fon of King Sigifmund III. had the title of Commander in Chief, but the bufinefs was in fact done by James Sobiefki, in the abfence of the Grand-General. Two hundred thoufand Turks and Tartars were defeated in that action by fixty-five thoufand Poles and Coffacks; and the hero of the day, being as able a negociator as he was a General, was fent to Conftantinople to fign the peace, which the Porte was reduced to folicit. As often as the republic wanted a man of abilities in foreign courts, in Sweden, France, and Italy, Sobiefki was the perfon pitched upon, and the event always juftified the choice. By his marriage with *Theophila Zolkiewfka*, daughter of the Great Zolkiewfki, and heirefs of the vaft eftates poffeffed by that powerful family in the Palatinate of Ruffia *(b)*, he had two fons, *Mark* and *John*, whofe education he confidered as a duty indifpenfably incumbent upon himfelf, and took a large fhare of it. Though fully employed in the Senate and the army, he neglected not the ftudy of letters, well knowing that Cæfar wrote his Commentaries, while he was fubduing Gaul. There are now extant, in the libraries of Poland, feveral

(a) A town of Moldavia upon the Niefter.
(b) Thefe eftates were much more confiderable than the dominions of many fovereign Princes in Italy and Germany. The manor of Zolkiew, a fortified town with a caftle belonging to it, includes more than a hundred and fifty villages; that of Zloczow, another fortified place, contains as many; befides Olefko, which would alone make the fortune of the firft nobleman in France: the whole is near twenty leagues in extent. Such was formerly the opulence of the French nobler, till extravagance, crufading, and minifterial policy have at length brought it to nothing.

treatifes

treatifes of James Sobiefki's; and whoever writes for the public, though but indifferently, gives always a proof of fuperior activity of mind. There are alfo in the palace of Villanow, two leagues from Warfaw, feveral pieces of painting and fculpture, much admired by the Poles, done by Italian artifts, whom Sobiefki hired with a view of introducing tafte among his countrymen. At the bottom of each piece are verfes taken out of Virgil's Georgics, to explain the fubject; which, though it be a fuperfluous oftentation of learning, and favours of Gothic aukwardnefs, becaufe the figures fhould explain themfelves, yet it fhews at leaft the erudition of the perfon who could make ufe of this expedient.

A father of this character was very capable of forming his fons. Before they learnt languages, he took care they fhould be acquainted with things; and talked to them of juftice, beneficence, and refpect for the laws, as frequently as of military glory. He gradually laid open to them the interefts of Poland, and accuftomed them infenfibly to defend thofe interefts both in writing and fpeaking: talents which are ufelefs under an abfolute government, but neceffary in a republic. He laboured particularly to form in them that habit of application which he poffeffed himfelf, and without which there will never be any fuch thing as a great man.

The eldeft fon, *Mark*, was of a mild temper, a docile difpofition, cut out to be a mother's favourite; and if he had lived long, would have had the fate of Efau, who bowed down before his younger brother.

John was of a lively, ardent, impetuous temper, ftrongly bent upon whatever he fet his mind on, greedy of praife, and more eafily wrought upon by difgrace than punifhment. If the memoirs

F 4

of

of his childhood were extant, we might perhaps discover, even in that early age, the first rays of the glory with which he afterwards shone; but possibly we should find nothing but the common occurrences of childhood; for men, like fruits, shew themselves only in their proper season.

The Poles have not the vanity to think, that every thing worth seeing or knowing may be met with in their own country. When the two brothers were grown up, they set out upon their travels, and France was the country where they made the longest stay. They arrived there, at the time when the young Duke of Anguien, afterwards known by the name of the Great Condé, had already won three battles: and the two brothers declared, that they thought his victories over veteran Generals set him in a greater light, than his being born a Prince of the blood. At the same period, France was entering into the civil war of the *Fronde*, in order to displace a single Minister, instead of turning her attention to make laws to restrain the power of all Ministers. John Sobieski, who had already just ideas of government, frequently said afterwards, that he was puzzled to account for their not assembling the states of the kingdom, according to the Polish custom. The man, whom fortune had destined to be a King, was now one of the *musketeers* of France. At that time there was only one company of them, established by Lewis XIII. in 1622, and long called the *grand musketeers:* the other company was in the service of Cardinal Mazarin, before it entered into that of the state.

In the countries which the two brothers visited after their leaving France, next to the knowledge of manners and national interests, they applied themselves to the study of languages, which are always learnt best and soonest from the nations that speak them. The younger brother became so

a per-

perfect a master of six, that each might easily be
taken for his mother tongue.   The first object of
their curiosity was Paris, and the last Constantinople;   where they prolonged their stay, with a
view of being thoroughly acquainted with a power
that was so often at war with Poland.

Little did the *Porte* imagine that its armies would
one day fly before the youngest of these inquisitive
youths.   Being now furnished with what knowledge they could collect in Europe, they had formed
a scheme of penetrating into Asia, when receiving
information that a war was kindled upon the frontiers of Poland, they thought themselves obliged,
above all things, to fly to the defence of their
country.   In all republics this is the leading virtue, and the two brothers obeyed its dictates; but
they had not the satisfaction of being received in
the embraces of a father, who had instructed them,
both by precept and example.   Sobieski was lately
dead, and had left his sons an inheritance of greater
value, in the memory of his virtues, than in his
vast possessions.

The throne of Poland was at this time filled by ^{Year 1648.}
Casimir V. a Prince, who from a Jesuit became a
Cardinal, and from a Cardinal, a King.   He was
brother to Uladislas VII. who had spent the sixteen
years of his reign in acquiring the love of his subjects; and they were both sons of Sigismund III.
who would have done admirably well in a private
station, but was a very indifferent King.

Scarce was Casimir crowned, when he saw his
kingdom become a prey to the Cossacks; a people
who formerly inhabited the islands made by the river Borysthenes, where they professed the trade of
piracy, and lived wholly by plunder; but they
were taught a better, and more reputable manner of
life by Stephen Battori, King of Poland, who by
this, and the other services he did them, fixed them
in

in the interefts of his crown. They were formed by him into a military corps of forty thoufand men, and fettled in Lower Podolia, and Lower Volhinia, with a view of being employed chiefly againft the Tartars and Mufcovites, the natural enemies of Poland. He afterwards incorporated them with colonies, which he fent to people and cultivate the country, now called the Ukraine; a territory of a hundred leagues long, and nearly the fame breadth, divided by the Boryfthenes into two almoft equal parts. Of all the great things that Battori had done, this was perhaps the moft ufeful; fince by this means he fecured the frontiers of the kingdom, and doubled its military ftrength : he cultivated, for its benefit, a barren fpot, which grew to be the moft fertile of all countries : in fhort, he increafed its dominions with a new kingdom.

But the violence of powerful individuals has more than once fubverted the profperity of ftates. The Polifh nobles in the Palatinates bordering upon the Ukraine, would needs treat the Coffacks as their flaves; and accordingly violated their privileges, invaded their property, and wounded them in a ftill more fenfible part, by demolifhing the Greek churches, where they ferved God in their own way. Uladiflas VII. King of Poland, was weak enough to connive at thefe acts of injuftice ; and a faithful people was by this means drove into rebellion ; but being totally defeated, they were forced to fave what remained of the nation, by giving up their General *Pauluk*, who was beheaded, notwithftanding a promife had been given to fave his life *(a)*.

A new crime, committed by the Poles, furnifhed the Coffacks with another General, in the perfon of *Chmilienfki*, a man who lived peaceably upon the poffeffions he inherited from his father, increaf-

(a) Lengnich, p. 158.

ed

ed by the addition of some deserted lands, which he had improved by cultivation, and the erection of new mills. A Polish noble, named *Jatinski*, who had a command in the Ukraine, envied the Cossack his fortune, and attempted to make it his own; but meeting with resistance, he burnt Chmilienski's mills, ravished his wife, and massacred her upon the bleeding body of her son. The unhappy father, and injured husband, applied to the King for justice, and he was joined by a numerous multitude, who had heavy complaints to make; but no redress could be obtained.

A refusal of justice, or any similar act of oppression, only draws tears from a nation, whose spirit is subdued by having long wore the chain. But a haughty people, who can distinguish between obedience and slavery, never quench their anger but in blood.

No sooner was this fire kindled, than Uladislas died; and Chmilienski, with greater fury than prudence, advanced with his Cossacks into the heart of Poland, put all the nobles to the sword, but spared the peasants, gained a compleat victory over the Polish army at Pilawiecz, in Little Poland, marched to Leopol, the capital of Red Russia, which surrendered, to save itself from the horrors of being taken by storm, and spread the alarm to Cracow itself, from whence the crown was removed to a place of greater safety. The Cossack took care to retaliate the injuries he had suffered, by marking his progress with murder, rape, and conflagration; nor in this torrent of fury did he forget to avenge the insult offered to his religion, by forcing the Priests wherever he came to marry nuns, and conform to the Greek ritual (a).

Year 1648.

(a) Pastor. Hist. Pol. p. 138 & 192.

If

If a regifter was to be kept, of all the crimes which efcape being punifhed upon earth, both by divine and human juftice, it would encourage villains to be ftill more unruly. Many innocent perfons perifhed by the hand of *Chmilienſki*; while the chief criminal, *Jatinſki*, efcaped his vengeance.

Another matter of wonder, is the defeat of the Polifh army; the Grand-General Potozki being an officer of great experience, whereas Chmilienfki had little or none at all. But hiftory prefents us with more than one inftance of this fort; and they muft be accounted for, by fuppofing, that defpair, when it gets poffeffion of an intrepid leader, and a brave people, fupplies every other defect.

Cafimir, who had but juft taken poffeffion of the fceptre, was upon the point of feeing it wrefted out of his hands. The age in which he lived was productive of many difafters to crowned heads. Philip IV. had lately loft Portugal, and almoft all his poffeffions in Afia. In France, the mother of Lewis XIV. was forced by a faction to defert the capital with her children. At London, Charles I. expired upon a fcaffold. Were it not for thefe interruptions of regal profperity, Kings would forget that they are men.

The ignominy of the flight of the Polifh army at Pilawiecz, was yet recent, when the two Sobiefki's arrived in Poland. Their mother, a woman of an heroic fpirit, as foon as fhe faw them, cried out, *Are you come to avenge your country? I renounce you for ever as my fons, if you behave like the combatants of Pilawiecz.*

The nobility were foliciting Cafimir to put himfelf at the head of a powerful army; but the King, who aimed at reclaiming the Coffacks by negotiation, and by making fome fatisfaction for the cruel infults offered to a brave people, anfwered, that *it was wrong to burn Chmilienſki's mills, and*

ftill

still worse to ravish his wife, and murder her and her son. This anfwer gave great difcontent; and the nobles took up arms themfelves to the number of fifty thoufand men, and advanced into Lower Volhinia, where they met with a great defeat. Their courage being not yet exhaufted, they marched towards the *Hypanis.* This river, which joins the Boryfthenes, and falls with it into the Black Sea, is now called the *Bogh.* In this manner the barbarians have disfigured the very names of thofe countries which once flourifhed with colonies from Greece. The banks of the Bogh were not more favourable to the Poles than their former field of battle, and they fuffered a total defeat.

It was in this fecond action, that Mark Sobiefki, lefs fortunate than his younger brother, was flain in the flower of his age, and at his firft entrance upon the career of glory. When the two brothers were, fetting out upon their travels into France, the father gave them this advice: *Be fure, children, to inform yourfelves of every thing that is ufeful. As for dancing, you will have opportunities of learning it here from the Tartars.* In fact, the Tartars fought in conjunction with the Coffacks on this fatal day, the Cham having a perfonal injury to avenge: for Uladiflas had fuppreffed a confiderable penfion paid by Poland to him, as well as his predeceffor. After the victory, there were brought to him three hundred Polifh nobles, loaded with chains, and covered with wounds, among whom was Mark Sobiefki. The cruel Tartar, without regarding the law of nations, which protects prifoners of war, ordered them all to be beheaded, and their bodies expofed for a prey to vultures. By this means, Sobiefki's mother was deprived of the melancholy confolation of interring her fon among the remains of his anceftors. Her grief e'er long induced her to fettle in Italy, and abandon a country where fhe had loft the object of her ten-

derest

dereſt affections; for her ſurviving ſon was leſs beloved by her, on account of ſome ſallies of youth,
and his having expoſed, in two ſingle combats, that
life which was due to his country only. That barbarous cuſtom of duelling, which is unknown in all
the eaſt, from Conſtantinople to the remoteſt part of
Japan, had it's origin in the north of Europe. It is
not ſurprizing that the Poles ſhould pique themſelves
upon it, as well as we; but they have been leſs prudent than the French, in not aboliſhing thoſe public
duels, with ſeconds on both ſides, in which the ſpectators animate the emulation of the Gladiators. The
duel Sobieſki fought proved the inſtrument of his
puniſhment; for while his elder brother was tread-
ing in the path of true glory, John was detained at
Leopol by a wound he had received. As ſoon as he
recovered his ſtrength, he haſted to obey the united
calls of vengeance and of glory.

The ſame enemies ſtill remained to be oppoſed;
and it was time for Caſimir to put himſelf at the
head of the army, in order to render it's operations
more regular, and to prevent his being deſpiſed by a
nation which reſpects only warlike Kings. Accordingly, he aſſumed the command.

Y. 1649.   What had hitherto been done by young Sobieſki,
now the chief of his family, was but a prelude to his
future exploits in war. All that had been yet obſerved in him, was an impetuous ardour which made him
inſenſible of danger, and a greedineſs after military
knowledge, which carried him where duty did not
require his preſence. He ſucceeded his father in the
Staroſty of Javorow in the Palatinate of Ruſſia; and
appeared in the army at the head of a ſelect troop.
In the many ſkirmiſhes which muſt needs happen
with an enemy who fled only to return to the charge,
he ſhewed that nature had given him all the courage
of a ſoldier, and what is much more uncommon,
that happy quickneſs of diſcernment, which indicates

a ge-

a general.   A fingular event difplayed the credit he
had acquired in fo fhort a time.   The Polifh army
mutinied in the camp of Zborow, a city of Little
Poland, upon the borders of Podolia, and every
method of quieting the fedition, perfuafion, menaces,
and even the cannon of the Lithuanian troops, was
made ufe of in vain by the General Czarnefki.   The
attempt was given up as hopelefs, when Sobiefki defired to be employed.   The temerity of extraordinary
men is juftified by the fuccefs that attends it.   It is
eafy to conceive what addrefs and eloquence he needed to perfuade men who had arms in their hands.
The young orator carried his point; and that empire over the minds of men, which would have done
honour to a confummate General,   advanced to the
height of glory a youth who had yet born no public
office.

The army now advanced towards the enemy
with that unanimity of fentiment, which is a fure
prefage of victory.   Chmilienfki, notwithftanding
the juftice of his caufe, was deferted by his good
fortune.   Being fupported by the Tartars, he undertook to force the King in the camp of Zborow.
The battle lafted feveral days, during which he loft
more than twenty thoufand men, and was difcouraged from trying his fortune any more.   A negotiation
for peace was fet on foot, and before it was ratified,
the King rewarded Sobiefki by making him great
Standard-Bearer of the Crown;   an officer of the
court and of the army, who carries the banner of the
Republic in the pofpolite, and at the coronation and
funeral of the Kings of Poland.

The peace of Zborow gave great diffatisfaction to
all the nobles; for the King, who had not given up
his defign of bringing back the Coffacks to their allegiance by fair means, had granted them terms that
might be made a bad ufe of.   All paft offences were
forgot, and twenty thoufand of them were to conti-

nue

nue armed in the Palatinate of Kiovia, which was to be given for the future to a nobleman of the Greek perfuafion. They were reftored to the unmolefted exercife of their religion, and the enjoyment of all their privileges. But as fomething muft be always done to fatisfy the offended Majefty of Kings, it was ftipulated that Chmilienfki fhould afk pardon on his knees; and the Coffack fubmitted to this humiliation for the good of his country. The Tartarian Prince found his account in the plunder he gained, and in getting his penfion reftored. All thefe regulations were prudent; but the Polifh nobles were not poffeffed of that quality. They exclaimed on all fides that the King had betrayed the Republic, and they thought of nothing but breaking a treaty, the advantages of which they were refolved not to fee.

The Coffacks foon difcovered that the nobles would get the better of the King, and that the peace they had made would be but of fhort continuance. They therefore took up arms in conjunction with Year 1651. their old allies, the Tartars; and Bereftefk, a town fituated upon the borders of the Palatinate of Beltz, was the field of battle. The Tartars, having loft fix thoufand men, betook themfelves to flight. The Coffacks entrenched themfelves in their camp, where they were at length forced; but the victory was a very dear one to the Poles. It may fafely be faid, that Cafimir, whom his fubjects had forced to renew the war, was a victor againft his will. Sobiefki, in this action, was wounded in the head; but fo many others had wounds to fhew, that this was no mark of diftinction.

Chmilienfki, though beaten, was yet alive, and had ftill refources left him. The Czar Alexis now made ufe of him to attack Poland, and the Coffack took Smolenfko, a large city, fituated on the right fide of the Boryfthenes, which returned to its ancient owners; and he opened himfelf a paffage

fage into Lithuania, which he laid wafte with fire and fword.

Our memoirs fay little of Sobiefki's behaviour in this war againft the Mufcovites and Coffacks. Fame records only actions of uncommon luftre, and fuch cannot be performed but upon extraordinary occafions. It is however probable, that he continued to difplay that union of valour and prudence, which fhews a great Captain, fince in another war, which was foon after kindled out of the fire of this, and fpread its blaze over every province of Poland, Sobiefki, who was then only making his firft campaigns, was honoured with a diftinguifhed command in the horfe. So quick a rife as this, is always founded upon good reafons in a republican kingdom, where the court muft be cautious how it proceeds, and confer rewards rather than favours.

Poland, for a long time, had not feen fo many Year 1655. enemies united to confpire its ruin. Chriftina of Sweden, that too philofophic Queen, who refigned her crown, and chofe rather to live at Rome among Cardinals, arts and letters, than to employ herfelf in promoting the happinefs of a kingdom, was fucceeded by her coufin Charles Guftavus; who, by a miftake too common among Kings, thought he could not begin his reign better than with conqueft. In a fhort time, he made himfelf mafter of Mazovia, and a great part of Poland, from whence he transferred the feat of war into Pruffia.

Sobiefki, though he ferved in an army that was beat upon all occafions, was learning how to conquer. Being at the head of four hundred horfe, between Elbing and Marienburg, he defeated a body of more than fix hundred, commanded by a near relation of the King of Sweden. If Cafimir had had many Sobiefkis, he would have efcaped the fad extremities to which he was reduced. De-

ferted

serted by his army, he fought an afylum in Silefia; and faw Lithuania, which was not yet fubdued, put itfelf under the protection of the conqueror.   One would imagine that all his fubjects had been thunder-ftruck ; and that thofe whom the bolt did not kill upon the fpot, had no fenfation left them but that of terror.   At laft, the ftorm abated, by fpreading over a vaft extent of country. People begun to recover their fenfes, and to think that Charles Guftavus might poffibly not be invincible.

Cafimir took advantage of this gleam of courage.   Among the officers who moft deferved his confidence, he had taken particular notice of Czarnefki and Sobiefki.   He had the addrefs to take off the Tartars from their attachment to the interefts of Mufcovy, and to fix them in his own. Sobiefki was commiffioned to command them, while Czarnefki headed the Poles.   They begun with putting to the fword the Swedifh troops, which had taken up their winter-quarters in Lithuania : and proceeded to cut in pieces all that were difperfed in Poland.   Not a day paffed without their breaking fome link of the chains of the nation.

In the mean time Charles Guftavus was advancing out of Pruffia with his own army, and a reinforcement of the Elector of Brandenburg's troops. Sobiefki blocked him up between the Viftula and the Sanus (a fmall river which runs into the Viftula) hindered his being fupplied with provifions, haraffed him with continual fkirmifhes ; and receiving intelligence that *Douglas*, one of the Swedifh Generals, was advancing with a body of fix thoufand men to difengage the King, he left his infantry to continue the blockade, marched with his cavalry to meet Douglas, fwam acrofs the Pilcza, a river much fwelled by the melting of the fnow, and with that *celerity* which Cæfar confidered

dered as the firſt qualification of a General, ſurprized Douglas, defeated him, and purſued his army eight miles towards Warſaw.

Some other bodies of the Poliſh army, which was obliged to face the enemy on ſo many ſides, did not do their duty ſo well as that which marched under the command of Sobieſki. It was neceſſary alſo to make another diviſion, in order to oppoſe Ragotſki, Prince of Tranſylvania, who advanced, in concert with Sweden, with a view to deprive Caſimir of his crown. In the midſt of ſo many enemies, ſome blunders were committed, of which Charles Guſtavus took advantage, and having diſengaged himſelf from the dangerous ſituation he was in, advanced towards Warſaw, which brought on a general action that laſted three days. The utmoſt efforts of valour and ſkill were exerted on both ſides, and a torrent of blood was ſpilt; but at length victory declared once more for Charles Guſtavus, though purchaſed at a very dear rate. The Tartars had never fought before with ſo much order and firmneſs. Accuſtomed to continual rapine, impatient of any diſcipline, and always ready to fly when they met with reſiſtance, they found themſelves changed to other men, under the command of Sobieſki; and when the ſeries of future events turned his valour againſt them, they always remembered, with a mixture of admiration and reſpect, the great exploits they had ſeen him perform, and were convinced that glory may well be acquired even when a battle is loſt.

The republic muſt have been inevitably ruined, had Charles Guſtavus lived a few years longer; but he died in the thirty-eight year of his age; and if war is to denominate men great, he was little inferior to Guſtavus Adolphus.

On the other hand, Ragotſki, a man of greater ambition than military talents, and who ſhewed

little

little regard to the advice of his ally Charles Guſtavus, miſſed the opportunity of conquering. George
Lubomirſki, petty General of the Poliſh army,
and Sobieſki, made an irruption into his territories,
where they committed the ſame hoſtilities with which
he had afflicted Poland. He ſucceeded no better
in defending himſelf, than attacking others; and
involved in his ill fortune, the ſect of the *Unitari-
ans*, otherwiſe called *Socinians* and *Arians*, who had
abuſed the toleration they enjoyed in Poland. They
profeſs to worſhip one only God, of incommu-
nicable perfections, who never produced any being
equal to himſelf; but it was not their doctrine,
however damnable, but their connections with Ragotſki, that occaſioned their being proſcribed in Poland. This ſect, which formerly ſeduced both the
eaſt and weſt for three centuries, and now mingles
with all religions, is perhaps ſtill the moſt numerous
of any, but has no longer any diſtinct places of
worſhip. Ragotſki looked upon his own ruin to
be equally inevitable with theirs, and was glad to
accept of a ſhameful peace, which left him no inclination to diſturb the repoſe of his neighbours.

　　As for Sweden, ſhe thought herſelf too much
exhauſted to go on with the great deſigns of her
deceaſed King, and ſigned a treaty of peace at Oli-
Year 1660. va, a famous monaſtery of Royal Pruſſia, about
a mile from Dantzick.

　　The republic had ſtill two enemies, the Muſcovites and the Coſſacks, to deal with; of which the
latter were the moſt inveterate, becauſe the reſentment of a grievous injury is more ſtimulating than
the deſire of conqueſt. The republic had for its allies the Crim Tartars, a ſuccour which might prove
of the utmoſt advantage, and was principally owing
to Sobieſki, who had lived among them as an hoſ-
tage. An ordinary man, who reſides in this capacity among a barbarous people, turns his thoughts
wholly

wholly upon the happy moment of reftoration to his domeftic pleafures ; but Sobiefki was taken up with the interefts of his country. The Tartars, who had feen his behaviour in battle, already ef- teemed him, and for this reafon pitched upon him preferably to other hoftages. The Cham in par- ticular conceived for him a friendfhip which was of fingular ufe to Poland upon this occafion. In fhort, an alliance was concluded, and the combined armies attacked the Mufcovites, fometimes by fe- cret ambufcade, fometimes in the open field, and the fuccefs, upon the whole, was nearly equal. At length they were upon the point of coming to a decifive action near Cudnow, and Cafimir, who commanded in perfon, was earneft for it ; but the Mufcovites induftrioufly delayed it, to give Chmi- lienfki and his Coffacks time to join the army. It was of the utmoft importance to prevent this junction, and there wanted a man of ability to exe- cute the commiffion. Sobiefki was detached with a body much inferior to that of the Coffacks, and attacked them at the moment of their arrival at Slobodyfzee in the Ukraine. His victory was fo complete, that their General was taken prifoner, loaded with chains as a rebel, and brought to Ca- fimir. The report of this victory fo intimidated the Mufcovites, that they furrendered their arms almoft without fighting.

Nothing now remained but to retake a few places in Lithuania, one of which was Wilna the capital, a large and populous city, but built of wood, for want of quarries of ftone. The Mufcovite of- ficer, who commanded in the citadel, would have put to death any man that had only talked of furrendering. He entertained fufpicions of a Po- lifh Prieft, and put him into a mortar, and difchar- ged this frightful bomb upon the befiegers His cruelty and obftinacy, joined to the impoffibility of

G 3　　　　　　　making

making a long defence, excited fome foreign officers of the garrifon to mutiny againft their commander, whom they gave up, together with the
city, into the hands of the befiegers. The Poles
having got this barbarian in their power, condemned him to die by the hands of a common execu-
tioner; but none being to be found, his own cook
offered his fervice, and cut off his head. It is not
hard to guefs what fort of a mafter a man muft be
that had fuch a fervant.

The war with Mufcovy was now near its end,
when Cafimir fuffered himfelf to be diverted from
it, by a project which turned the arms of the republic againft itfelf. This Prince, who feemed to
be deftined for all forts of fingularities, after having been a Jefuit and a Cardinal, had married Louifa Mary Gonzaga (a), his brother's widow. This
cafe was precifely the fame with that of Henry VIII.
King of England, who married Catharine of Arragon, his brother Arthur's widow; and the difputes which arofe in England, had alfo divided
Poland. The divines of the King's party fupported their opinion with that paffage in Deuterono-
my, which not only permits, but commands a man
to marry bis brother's wife, if fhe have no children.
The Doctors of the other fide oppofed to this a
paffage in Leviticus, which forbids a man *to un-
cover the nakednefs of bis brother's wife.* The Senators, without having recourfe to the laws of the
Jewifh nation, afked the King, " how he could
" venture upon fuch an union, after all the dif-
" afters which had befallen England under Hen-
" ry VIII. and Poland under his Father Sigifmund?

(a) Daughter of the Duke of Mantua and Nevers, the fame
who was celebrated in France for her paffion for *Cinqmars,*
Mafter of the Horfe to the King.

" It

" Is it becaufe your father married two fifters *(a)*,
" that you are refolved upon this contract with
" your brother's widow ? Our fentiments are the
" fame with thofe of the Senators of that time:
" and you know that they writ to Pope Cle-
" ment VIII. that they never fuffered fuch unions
" even in their ftables *(b)*."

The fee of Rome, which had given a fanction
to the other two marriages, faw nothing to be ab-
horred in this; and it feemed that the more oppofition it had met with, the dearer was the Queen
to Cafimir. Being of a mild and complaifant temper, adopting in every thing her inclinations, employing his thoughts as fhe directed, and often not
employing them at all, he gave himfelf up to conjugal tendernefs, more perhaps than was confiftent
with his own peace, and that of Poland. Having
no children, he formed a project, in order to pleafe
his wife, of getting a young Prince who was to
marry her niece, declared his fucceffor to the crown.
The Queen having been educated in France, had
as great an affection for the blood of the houfe of
Bourbon as for her own. The young Prince, who
was to be raifed to the crown, was Henry Julius de
Bourbon, Duke of Anguien, fon of the Great
Condé; and the Princefs intended for his wife, was
Anne of Bavaria, who by her mother was of the
Gonzaga family. The Queen, who had been ufed
to govern, flattered herfelf that fhe fhould continue
to do fo, by the influence fhe would have naturally
over a young Prince, indebted to her for his Crown,
in cafe of the King's death.

The King founded the inclinations of the Sena-Year 1661.
tors and great officers; but they anfwered him

(a) Anne and Conftance, daughters of the Emperor Ferdinand II.
(b) Zalufki, tom. i. part 1. p. 158.

with

with a silence, more expressive than words, and at
length openly declared their disapprobation (a).
Lubomirski in particular, Grand Marshal of Poland, and Petty-General of the Polish army, cried
out, that to attempt the election of a King, before the throne was vacant, was to violate the most
sacred law of the republic, and to overthrow the
strongest bulwark of liberty. He desired the King
to recollect, that all his predecessors, from the time
of Jagellon, and he himself, had sworn, never to
propose a successor. " You would not be suffered,
" added he, to do for your own son, what you
" are attempting in favour of a stranger."

Casimir meeting with such resistance from the
Senate, pretended to desist from this project. It
remained buried in his cabinet for three years, and
all this time was employed in procuring votes, by
all the allurements which Kings can offer to the ambitious, and by all the terror they can impress upon the timid. No attempt was thought proper to
be made upon Lubomirski, whose character was
too well known. Not contented with delivering
his opinion in the Senate, he had taken pains to
bring over several to his sentiments, and to dispel
the apprehensions of others. He was therefore considered by the court as the head of a conspiracy,
and no art was omitted to make him appear to the
republic in the same light.

Year 1664.   The Polish army, dissatisfied with its pay, and
still more with the money's being left in arrear,
had entered into a confederacy. Of all the asso-
ciations of this sort, which are formed in Poland,
upon pretence of the public good, that of the army
is the most dangerous. The soldiers are no longer
under discipline or restraint, but live at discretion,
and commit all sorts of excesses: the authority of

(c) Lengnich. p. 208.

the

the Grand-General is fhaken off, and another commander is chofe by the name of *Marſhal of the Confederacy*, who is in fact a real *Dictator*, and unites
in his own perſon the power belonging to the three
eſtates of the kingdom. He gives audience to the
Ambaſſadors, iſſues out orders to the courts of
juſtice, levies troops, and raifes ſupplies, commands
the army, inflicts puniſhments, and exerciſes a
power of life and death. The laws indeed condemn this ſpecies of confederacy ; but notwithſtanding the laws, it is criminal only when it is ill ſupported. Lubomirſki was not the perſon that the
army placed at its head ; but the court took it for
granted, that Suiderſki, who was chofe upon this
occaſion, was only an inſtrument wholly governed
by Lubomirſki. A diet was aſſembled, before
which no accuſation was brought againſt the apparent chief, but Lubomirſki alone was ſummoned.
Being convinced that the court was reſolved to find
him guilty at all events, he did not make his appearance ; and was tried and condemned to forfeit
his eſtate, his honour, and his life, as an enemy
to the ſtate, and guilty of high-treaſon (*a*). But
the ſentence being voted and proteſted againſt by
the Deputies, was illegal.

The illuſtrious outlaw well knew that the anger of Kings is a fire that confumes every thing in
its firſt fury. He therefore quitted Poland, and
retired to Breſlaw, to give it time to cool, and perhaps to go entirely out. He had great dependence
upon an extraordinary diet, where his intereſts
would of courſe come upon the carpet. When this
aſſembly met, a large part of the nobility refuſed
to proceed upon public buſinefs, till the King could
be prevailed on to remit his refentment againſt Lubomirſki. On the other hand, the royal party in-

(*a*) Kochov. p. 147. Lengnich. p. 215.

ſifted

fifted upon it, that the ftate muft be ruined, if
the King relented, for that Lubomirfki was of a
reftlefs and turbulent fpirit, and an incendiary,
whom it was neceffary to get rid off; while the
others, who were more numerous, reprefented him
as an upright citizen, an experienced General, an
incorruptible Minifter, and a firm fupporter of the
laws of his country, whofe deftruction was aimed at
on thefe very accounts. The difpute foon ran fo
high, that nothing was heard but confufed excla-
mations and mutual threats. The affembly feparated without coming to any conclufion.

The King, however, executed in part the fentence that was paffed upon Lubomirfki, by difpof-
ing of his offices to two perfons who were highly in
the royal favour *(a)*. Czarnefki, Palatine of Kiovia, was made Petty-General; and Sobiefki, from
ftandard-bearer of the Crown, was advanced to the
dignity of Grand-Marfhal; a poft of high diftinction, but which has no military jurifdiction. The
republic has four great officers, entrufted with the
four branches of the adminiftration; the Grand-
General, who directs the affairs of the army, the
Grand Chancellor, who prefides over the adminiftration of juftice; the Grand-Treafurer, whofe
province is the public revenue; and the Grand-
Marfhal, who has the management of the police.
They are called *Brachia Regalia*, the Arms of the
King; and he fometimes makes ufe of them to
ftrike the republic. Lubomirfki had never confented to be thus employed; and this patriotic firmnefs acquired him many partizans. Sobiefki and
Czarnefki were alfo in high reputation; it was
even confeffed that they deferved the offices they
were raifed to; but it was added, that it was unjuft
to difpoffefs a man who filled them with fo much
dignity.

(a) Kochov. p. 164. Lengnich. p. 216.

Lubo-

Lubomirſki, deſpairing of having juſtice done him by a regal tribunal, reſolved to obtain it by arms. He entered Poland at the head of only eight hundred men ; but his little troop encreaſed continually as it advanced, and was found to be five thouſand ſtrong, by the time it reached Czen-ſtochow, an inconſiderable town upon the Warta, in the Palatinate of Cracow. The King aſſembled a ſuperior force in Siradia, and was encamped near the village of Warta ; from whence he detached the Lithuanians, commanded by Polubinſki, to attack the rebel army, for ſo it was called. But the rebels defeated the loyaliſts, and took a great number of priſoners, among whom were the prin-cipal officers of the army, and Polubinſki himſelf. The conqueror treated them with all the humanity they could have expected from a friend, and diſ-miſſed them without any ranſom (a). He did not behave to Sobieſki with the ſame generoſity ; but ravaged his eſtates, and carried off his ſtuds of horſes. The pleaſure of cruſhing a rival, who is raiſed upon our ruins, muſt be owned to be a temp-tation, that ſhakes the moſt ſolid virtue.

This firſt ſucceſs laid open to him Great Poland, while the royal army was exerting its utmoſt ef-forts to ſtop his paſſage. The nobility, who at firſt heſitated between the King and Lubomirſki, now came to a reſolution, and joined the army of the ſubject. The ſtorm, which threatened the de-ſtruction of the republic, was every day increaſing ; when two Senators, who had nothing in view but peace and juſtice, Andrew Trzebiſki, Biſhop of Chelm, and Thomas Leſcziníki, Biſhop of Cra-cow, prevailed upon the two armies, to continue in ſight of each other without coming to an en-gagement, till the holding of an extraordinary

(a) Kochov. p. 173. 192.

diet,

diet, which the King appointed to meet at Warfaw on the 17th of March; and the mediators
gave hopes to Lubomirſki of his reſtoration, and
to the confederated army of the pay it required.

Lubomirſki was not inflexible, but ſhewed that
he could forgive an injury, as ſoon as ſatisfaction
was made; and did not diſdain, though victorious,
to appear in the form of a ſuppliant. To prove
that he was ſincere in deſiring peace, he quitted his
army, and waited at Breſlaw for the reſult of the
deliberations of the diet. At laſt, the great day,
which kept both the arms and minds of the Poles
in ſuſpence, arrived. The Marſhal of the Deputies (a), who acted as ſpeaker, enlarged in vague
terms upon the advantages of peace; and when
Lubomirſki's partizans gave ſigns of impatience,
he went on to the demands of the confederates.
The attention of the aſſembly was now heightened,
and the moment was ſuppoſed to be come which
would produce Lubomirſki and his intereſts upon
the ſtage. But the orator, who kept his eyes fixed
upon the King, had not the courage to enter upon
the ſubject: and a *veto*, which iſſued from the
midſt of the aſſembly, put an end to the harangue
and to the diet together.

Beſides the King's reſentment, which grew daily
more and more inflamed, time had thrown a new
obſtacle in the way of Lubomirſki's reſtoration. Czar-
neſki, who had been inveſted with part of his ſpoils,
the office of *Petty-General*, was lately dead; and
the King had inſtantly conferred this important
poſt upon Sobieſki. Were it not for his diſtinguiſhed merit, which ſpoke loudly in his favour, it

---

(a) The Chamber of Repreſentatives or Deputies from the
particular diets of every Palatinate chuſes a Marſhal, who pre-
ſides at their deliberations, ſpeaks in the name of the body,
and gives the private members leave to deliver their ſentiments.

would

would give one pain to fee him rife in the midft of confufion, and upon the ruins of a hero.

The King, by this ftep, had put himfelf in a perplexing fituation; being under a neceffity of depriving Sobiefki of the two dignities, the power and honour of which he had fcarce taken poffeffion of; and in order to give fatisfaction to one man of diftinguifhed merit, he muft injure another who made already a great figure in the republic. "There is no undoing, faid the courtiers, what " is done; nor does it become the majefty of the " throne to review its paft conduct. Better far " take up arms again." Accordingly, the war was begun with greater fury than ever. The King, at the head of twenty-fix thoufand men, marched in queft of the enemy, who had only eighteen thoufand. The armies drew near each other on the 13th of July, in the Palatinate of Cujavia. On **Year 1666.** this occafion it was, that Sobiefki firft acted as General. The armies were feparated by a morafs, which the King ordered him to pafs. Sobiefki reprefented the danger of fuch a motion, it being eafy to forefee that the enemy would fuffer only fuch a number to pafs as they were fure of beating. But paffion either fees not at all, or fees badly. The King's troops entered the morafs, were embaraffed in the mud, and croffed it with great difficulty. Befides being animated by the interefts of their country, which both parties fancied they loved, at the time they were rending it in pieces, there was alfo a perfonal animofity between the two Generals, both fkilful in war, and intrepid in action. A General, newly invefted with that office, attacked another who had been difpoffeffed to make room for him. The latter, fighting in his own caufe, as well as that of the confederacy, fell impetuoufly upon Sobiefki, without giving him time to form his troops as they came out of the morafs. By this

means

means the royal army was overpowered, before it could come to action; and the King, who beheld the defeat from the other fide, had to reproach himfelf with the blood of four thoufand men, who remained upon the field of battle. The whole army muft have been ruined, had it not been for the abilities of Sobiefki, who brought it off by a retreat equally fkilful and difficult (a). And though a defeated General is always in the wrong, yet his very enemies laid the fault upon the obftinacy of the King.

The King, full of regret at not having followed his advice, went and encamped upon the river Pilcza, in the Palatinate of Rava, where he fhewed himfelf lefs averfe to an accommodation; a thing not difficult to be brought about, as Lubomirfki, without being elated with his victory, ftill made overtures of peace. He was inflexible in no point, but what regarded the interefts of his army and his country. It was agreed that his troops fhould receive the fums they had been refufed, and that no one fhould be called to account for what what was paft. Nor was the capital article which had kindled the civil war, forgot. The King, by a fpecial diploma iffued on this occafion, entered into an engagement not to concern himfelf, in any degree with the choice of a fucceffor, but to leave it to a free election, when the throne fhould become vacant. Lubomirfki having thus procured fatisfaction for the confederated army, and for his country, forgot himfelf, and was content with having the decree of his profcription revoked, without infifting upon his reftitution to the dignities he had loft.

Being thus reftored to favour, and having difmiffed his troops, he came to Jarofzin, accompa-

(a) Lengnich. p. 219.

nied

nied only by his principal officers, where he waited upon the King. The reconciliation was like all others which are brought about between a Prince and a subject who has made himself dreaded : and Lubomirski, being well acquainted with Kings, though free to remain in Poland, returned to Breslaw, where he died suddenly six months after ; and the enemies of the court did not attribute his death to nature only *(a)*.

Sobieski having learnt to conquer, while he served under him, now prepared to surpass his master. Hitherto he had lived in a continual scene of combats, in which being unmarried, he had often risked the putting an end to his life and his family together. Besides, he now drew near the thirty-sixth year of his age. Among the *Maids of Honour* that the Queen brought from France, without suspecting that she brought among them a future Queen, the Polish nobles took particular notice of one, whom the Queen herself honoured with peculiar favour. Her name was *Mary Casimira de la Grange*, daughter of Henry de la Grange, and Frances de la Châtre, who had been Governess to Queen Louisa; two ancient families of the province of Berry, distinguished by having produced several Marshals of France. Henry de la Grange was better known by the name of the Marquis d'Arquien, Captain of the guards to Philip of Orleans, only brother of Lewis XIV. His daughter *Mary*, who followed the Queen into Poland, married Radziwil, Palatine of Sendomir, and Prince of Zamoski, a town of Poland, in the Palatinate of Beltz, by whom she had four children, who all died very young, and the father did not long survive them.

(a) Kochov. p. 251. & 55.

Sobiefki, perfuaded that favour is a good fupport to merit, and knowing that the Queen ftill
continued her protection to the young widow, inftantly afked her hand, without giving her time to
dry up her tears. The Queen, to preferve the decency of mourning, got them privately married,
and then writ to the Marquis d'Arquien for his
confent. The Marquis anfwered, " That it was
" a thing unheard of to marry again in a month
" after the death of a former hufband ; that, for
" his part, he was not dazzled with the fplendor
" of Monfieur Sobiefki's name ; but that knowing
" the little fatisfaction his daughter enjoyed in her
" firft marriage, he had refolved to fettle her again
" in her native country, hoping that her Majefty's
" known equity would leave him in full poffef-
" fion of the authority which parents have over
" their children, by all the laws both of God and
" man : but that the thing being done without
" his confent, which had confequently been con-
" fidered as unneceffary, the refpect he owed to a
" great Queen, prevented him from giving his
" fentiments upon it, but that he fhould not for-
" get the fault committed by Madam Zamofka."
Men fhould learn to fubmit to their deftiny with
a better grace. The Marquis would certainly have
writ in another manner, could he have forefeen
that this match would advance his daughter to a
throne, and be the means of loading himfelf with
wealth and honours. Pope Innocent XII. never
forgot that he gave his benediction to the nuptial ceremony, while he was Apoftolic Nuncio in
Poland ; and teftified, upon all occafions, a fingular affection for this illuftrious pair.

They had but a fhort time to enjoy the favours
of the Queen, who died in 1667, employed to the
laft in fetting fecret fprings at work to infure the
crown of Poland to the Duke of Anguien, not-
. with-

withstanding the law lately passed in the diet. She was even accused of having given a commission to the Referendary *(a)*, Andrew Morstyn, lately arrived from France, to prevail upon the Great Condé to come into Poland, where she promised him an army to set the crown upon his son's head *(b)*.

She was certainly a woman of a masculine spirit, intended by nature to wear a crown, rather than admire its jewels, and much better fitted than Casimir for the management of public affairs. She always assisted at the private council where matters were prepared for the Senate, and had an equal share with the King in the direction of secret negotiations; she even appeared publicly in the diets, where she had great influence by the suffrages of her creatures, and gave occasion to frequent complaints, that her presence lessened the dignity of the republic *(c)*. Besides these talents, she had also the virtues of her own sex, and was of a devotional turn of mind; a thing pretty uncommon in a Queen who has great credit in public affairs. If it be true, as some of the Polish historians will have it, that a Queen of this character suggested to the King her husband, the design of abdicating the throne, it can be accounted for only by supposing, that she was at length weary, as she said herself, of the fatigues of royalty, the murmurs of the nation, and the dissatisfaction even of those upon whom she had conferred favours. Besides, the declining state of her health made her wish for a quiet life, which was also agreeable to the King's taste. The grief occasioned by her death was of no long continu-

---

(a) There are in Poland two Referendaries, one for ecclesiastical affairs, the other for secular. Their office is to make a report of petitions to the King or the Chancellor, and to give their advice, when the King holds his court of justice.

(b) Lengn. p. 221. Zaluski, tom. i. part i. p. 153.

(c) Lengn. p. 222.

H

ance,

ance, except with the King, the favourites, the monasteries, and the churches. She had been twice a Queen, but left no children.

Year 1667. Sobieski still possessed the favour of the King, and the esteem of the public, two things which do not always go together. His rise was also promoted by events, which fell out in his favour with uncommon rapidity. Lubomirski, by taking up arms against the King, had left vacant for him the dignity of Grand Marshal in 1665. A year after, the death of Czarneski made him Petty-General. He had now only one step left to become the most considerable person in the republic. The Grand-General Potoski died this year (1667) and Sobieski succeeded to his *staff*, resigning that of Petty-General to Demetrius Wiesnowieski, Palatine of Beltz. The two Generals do in fact receive from the King a *staff*, called *Boulaf*, which is a short mace, terminating at one end in a large head, either gilt or of massy silver, and sometimes enriched with jewels. But in the army it is not this staff of command which indicates the General, but a long lance, adorned with a horse's tail, contrived to be seen at a great distance, either upon a march, in time of action, or in the camp. The two Generals have their tents, one on the right, and the other on the left of the line, each with this ensign of office, called *Bontchouk.*

The power of a Grand-General is limited only by his own will; the greatest inconvenience of which arbitrary authority is the abuse of winter-quarters, which he may appoint where he pleases, and oppress or relieve whom he will. There had been instances of Grand-Generals who had accumulated *Starosties* (a), by forcing the gentry to sell them,

(a) A sort of governments. The lands of which they consisted, were originally part of the royal demesnes; and granted out

them at a low rate, in order to fave themfelves from total ruin. Sobiefki, as foon as he was invefted with the command, renounced this privilege of appointing winter-quarters, in order to deprive his fucceffors of the means of being tyrants. He himfelf might have tyrannized more than any man, if he had had that unfeeling nature which is too often united with power. Befides the ftaff of Grand-General, he poffeffed, as has been faid, that of Grand-Marfhal, and by this means had in his hands both the civil and military power, a circumftance which at firft occafioned great murmuring, becaufe both the fpirit and the cuftom of the republic directed, that thefe two offices fhould be always kept feparate, as their union confers too formidable a power upon one man : but Sobiefki's conduct foon put a ftop to all difcontent.

An army of fourfcore thoufand Tartars appeared upon the frontiers of the kingdom, and was already laying wafte Podolia, Volhinia, and the Palatinate of Ruffia. The Coffacks, always irritated againft their mafters, from whom they had lately received frefh grounds of difcontent, were ready to join in any attempt that aimed at their deftruction; and they marched for this purpofe under the command of Dorofcenfko, a chief of lefs ability, but greater obftinacy, than Chmilienfki. Poland was exhaufted of men, by fo many wars : its army confifted only of between ten and twelve thoufand men ; and the ftate was fo far from being able to pay frefh troops, that the Grand-Treafurer declared there was not money enough for the old ones. The King, wholly abandoned to grief, and difgufted more than ever with the crown, no longer exerted

out by the crown to the nobles, to enable them to bear the expences of military expeditions, referving only a right of nominating to them when they fhould become vacant.

him-

Y. 1667. himself to support its weight.   In the mean time, the evil grew more urgent : the Tartars, sustained by the Cossacks, advanced daily ; and there was some reason to be under apprehensions from the Turks *(a)*.

The republic expected nothing but ruin ; but Sobieski did not despair.   If ever he wanted a second, it was upon this occasion ; but every thing failed together ; for the Petty-General, Wiesnowieski, a man of experience and abilities, was dangerously ill.   The whole weight of the war fell therefore upon Sobieski, who laboured to encrease his little army.   Being to march over his own ample territories, it was there supplied with recruits.   These he joined to such as came from other quarters, formed magazines of provisions, exhausted his own private purse, borrowed large sums to supply the public treasury, and marched with twenty thousand men towards the Palatinate of Russia, there to defeat a hundred thousand.   He was no sooner arrived, than he detached Koniecpolski towards Tarnopol, Szlienifki to Leopol, Modrewski into Brzescia ; and secured the passages of the rivers by different bodies of troops, in order to stop the inroads of the Tartars *(b)*.   He gave the command of two thousand horse to an officer, named *Piwol*, who usually led a marauding party, but had all the abilities of a general, with orders to scour the country, and harass the enemy incessantly.   He himself marched towards the enemy's camp, and, as if victory had been at his command, writ to to his wife, who was gone to visit France her native country, that " on such a day he would, with " twelve thousand men, shut himself up in a for- " tified camp before Podahiecz, a place that Do-

(a) Zaluski, tom. i. part. 1. p. 9.
(b) Id. p. 2.

rofcenfko

" rofcenfko intended to befiege; that on the mor-
" row, and the following days, he would fally
" out upon the enemy; that he had placed am-
" bufcades on all fides, and would in the end ruin
" this great army."

The Prince of Condé, to whom this letter was
fhown, could fee no poffibility of fuccefs. Moft
of the Polifh officers loudly condemned the difpofitions of their leader; they faid that to divide in
this manner fo fmall an army, was to deftroy it;
and that it was neceffary they fhould all conquer or
perifh together. This difcourfe begun to fpread
among the common foldiers, and there was reafon
to fear the army would be difheartened. Upon fuch
occafions, it is as neceffary that a general fhould
fpeak, as that he fhould *act* upon others. " I am
" determined, fays he, to make no change in my
" plan; the event will fhew whether it be well laid
" or not. As to what remains, I lay no reflraint
" upon fuch as have not the courage to face a glo-
" rious death. Let them retire, and die in flight
" by the fword of a Coffack or a Tartar. For
" myfelf, I fhall ftay here, with all thofe brave
" fouls who love their country. This crowd of
" robbers makes no impreffion upon my mind.
" I know that Heaven has often given victory to
" fmall numbers, when animated with valour;
" and can you doubt but God will be for us againft
" thefe infidels?" All who were prefent looked
at each other, and blufhed; and no one thought of
leaving the camp *(a)*.

The Barbarians were free to march on and penetrate into the heart of Poland: but they chofe rather to deprive the kingdom of its only refource,
by attacking this little army with all their forces;
and they were too well acquainted with Sobiefki to

(a) Zal. tom. i. part 1. p. 10.

leave

leave him behind them. He had already taken some prisoners, whom he made use of to menace the Tartarian General, at a time when he had every thing to fear himself. *Go*, says he to the prisoners as he dismissed them, *tell the Sultan Nuradin, that I will treat him in the same manner that he treated my brother : I will have head for head.* The only answer that Nuradin gave, was to hasten the attack *(a)*.

Among the Polish officers who defended the entrenchments, there were several who had acquired great glory in former actions; and they were now employed with all the marks of confidence and distinction that they deserved. Alexander Polanowski commanded on the left ; Uladislas Wilczowski, on the right ; the center was committed to the care of Stanislas Jablonowski, Palatine of Russia, of whom it was become a proverbial saying, *Is he greater in the senate than in the field?* The Grand General undertook the inspection of the whole *(b)*.

The enemy poured in upon the camp on all sides, and were on all sides warmly received, while the artillery kept playing briskly. At length they forced their way in a weak place, and the Poles running thither, repulse, expel, pursue them, sabre in hand, beyond the entrenchments. The plain was soon covered with dead bodies, but there fell only four hundred Poles : the Tartars carried off theirs, to burn them according to the custom of the nation. Sobieski, having stood this first assault, did not make all the advantage of this success that fortune seemed to invite him to. The assailants had much to lose, but he had every thing to save. He there-

(a) Chruscinski.
(b) Zaluski. tom. i. part 1. p. 11.

fore

fore returned to his entrenchments to make the moft of any favourable opportunity that fhould offer.

A battle is generally over in a few hours; but in this cafe there was a continued action of feventeen days together, on each of which both fides fought as if the prefent had been the decifive moment. On the part of the affailants, whofe fuperior number gave them confidence, it was attack upon attack; on the part of the befieged, defence upon defence, fally upon fally. The laft day of all was the moft bloody. Sobiefki had given orders to the feveral detachments, which had occafioned fuch murmurs in the army by their feparation, to approach infenfibly towards the camp. The Barbarians, provoked and difheartened by fo obftinate a refiftance made by fo fmall a number, had refolved upon a general affault: and the moment was near which muft determine the fafety or ruin of the republic.

Sobiefki, inftead of waiting to be attacked, quitted his entrenchments and marched to meet the enemy. His troops had learnt, from the preceding actions, that this crowd of opponents was not invincible. The Barbarians, aftonifhed at fuch boldnefs, teftified their joy by loud cries, which were inftantly fucceeded by the battle. A deluge of blood was fpilt, and victory ftill continued uncertain; but before it declared for either fide, the feveral detachments arrived, and attacked the enemy in flank. The brave *Piwot* in particular, after having laid wafte the quarters of the Coffacks, carried off their convoys, and repulfed their foraging parties, redoubled his glorious efforts, attacked, fabre in hand, with his two thoufand horfe, and drove all before him. The very futtlers and peafants converted every thing they could find into arms, and refolved to bear a fhare in the victory, which was now but feebly difputed. The carnage

H 4   would

Y. 1667. would have been univerfal, if the victors had not
been wearied with flaughter. The Tartars, little
accuftomed to pitched battles, begun to look behind them, and foon after gave way, loft their
ranks, took to flight, and drew the Coffacks after
them. At this juncture, Sobiefki, whofe bravery
and fkill had animated the whole action, hoped to
keep his word with Nuradin, and ordered his life
to be fpared, if he fhould be overtaken in the rout,
that he might facrifice him to the manes of his
brother. But Nuradin and Dorofcenfko had retired fo early as to fear no purfuit, leaving twenty
thoufand of their men dead upon the field of battle.
After their retreat, the Poles faw, with horror, all
the ravages they had committed, the villages facked,
the country-feats and town-palaces of the nobles
levelled with the ground, the churches burnt, car-
caffes piled in heaps upon the ruins, and the frontiers entirely laid wafte; but the body of the ftate
was preferved (*a*); and Sobiefki's fuccefs aftonifhed
Poland, the Prince of Condé, and France.

The Barbarians, who had begun the war, now
fued for peace, which the conquerors wanted more
than the conquered. Jablonowfki was appointed
to fettle the conditions of the treaty, which was
impeded by one difficulty. The infidels demanded
and offered hoftages; whereas the chriftians alledged
that a peace confirmed by oaths made them ufelefs.
The Tartars ftill infifted upon their demand, and
anfwered that paft events had taught them what
value they ought to fet upon oaths. At laft, the
article of hoftages was agreed to, and the peace was
figned the 19th of October (*b*).

Sobiefki, preceded by victory, returned to Warfaw. He received upon the road the homage of

(*a*) Lengnich. p. 22. and 23.
(*b*) Zalufk. tom. i. part. 1. p. 13. and 15.

the

the inhabitants for all the poſſeſſions he had preſerved them; nor was the capital ſparing of its
acclamations.

Another ſubject of joy, attended with leſs luſtre,
but perhaps more ſolid ſatisfaction, was his becoming a father. His wife was brought to bed at
Paris of a ſon, whom the virtues of his father
were deſtined to raiſe in time to the rank of princes.
The child's Godfather was Lewis XIV. and he
was named James-Lewis, uniting by this means
the names of his illuſtrious grandfather, and a great
monarch.

The winter is the ſeaſon uſually allotted for diets,
that the operations of war may not be interrupted.
That of the preſent year was opened in the month
of February. The republic of Poland has many
cuſtoms which greatly reſemble thoſe of ancient
Rome. The Grand-General gave an account of
the inſtructions he had received from the ſenate, of
the operations and ſucceſs of the campaign, and
the diſtinguiſhed actions of thoſe who ſhared his labours, dwelling upon theſe much longer than upon
his own. His diſcourſe was received with applauſe
by all the orders of the aſſembly; and the Vice-
Chancellor riſing from his ſeat at the foot of the
throne, gave ſolemn thanks, in the name of the republic, to the deliverer of his country, and all who
had aſſiſted in its preſervation (a): a cuſtom admirably calculated to raiſe emulation, but impracticable in pure monarchies, where the King engroſſes all
attention.

Caſimir had no other ſhare in this victory, but
ordering prayers for the ſucceſs of the campaign,
and giving ſolemn thanks to God in the great
church of Warſaw. A deep melancholy preyed
upon his ſpirits: he was inconſolable for the loſs of

(a) Zaluſki, tom. i. p. 33.

the

the Queen; and yet, by no uncommon contradiction between the judgment and the affections, his conscience was uneasy at having married her. The authority of the Holy See had long quieted his scruples; but he now looked upon himself as accountable for all the calamities which the voice of the public attributed to his marriage and his administration. His mind, overwhelmed with grief, was sensible only of the burdens of royalty. He recalled to his memory the many disgusts that had been given him upon different occasions, the violence done to his inclinations in taking up arms against the Coffacks, the confederacy of Lubomirski, the revolt of a great part of the nobles, the perpetual declamations against the Queen, who was accused of engaging him in the projects of foreign courts, the invectives made by the deputies in full diet against the French ambaffador, Peter de Bonzi, Bishop of Beziers, a subtle and insinuating Italian, who was highly in the King's favour, and their obstinacy in insisting upon his dismission in spite of the court. He could not get out of his mind what a deputy had told him to his face, a little before the death of the Queen, *That the calamities of Poland would not end but with his reign.* The diminution of his German guard, though paid out of his own revenue (a), was another circumstance that hurt him greatly. He could see nothing in his regal dignity but a vast burden, which the Queen no longer helped him to support, and which he wanted to remove from his shoulders.

Lewis XIV. had not laid aside his project of reigning in Poland, by procuring that crown for the Duke of Anguien. He commiffioned his ambaffador to offer abbeys instead of a kingdom, and what-

(a) Zalufki, tom. i. p. 161. The King's foreign guard may be more or lefs numerous. That which the republic provides him, confifts of 1200 men.

ever

ever place of refidence Cafimir fhould fix upon in his whole dominions. The King of Poland's cha- racter muft have been thoroughly known, or fuch propofals would never have been made him. The republic as yet knew nothing of the King's having formed a defign to quit the throne. He had in- deed dropped fuch a hint a few hours after the Queen's death; but his confidents fuppofed that he would think no more of it, as foon as the grave was clofed; and they kept it a profound fecret. The fenators had no apprehenfions but of another marriage contrary to the inclinations of the repub- lic, and therefore hafted to propofe to him one that it could approve.

There were at that time in Europe, as there are now, many Princeffes to be difpofed of in mar- riage, and but few hufbands to be got. Every ftate made an offer of fuch as it could furnifh: their pictures were to be feen in the caftle of War- faw; and the King was the only perfon who never looked at them. To get rid of fuch troublefome objects, he had nothing to do but to fay, *I abdi- cate.* Thefe words he was refolved upon pronounc- ing foon, and had already fignified his intention to all foreign courts. His letter to Pope Clement IX. contains thefe words, which gave great edifi- cation at Rome, and great fcandal at Warfaw: *The diadem for which I am indebted to the benediction of the holy apoftolic fee, I lay down at your Holinefs's feet (a).* Nothing however was effected by thefe meafures, without treating with his own fubjects, who alone could refume the crown they had given him.

He therefore affembled the fenate in the month of May, without declaring the fubject of their meeting. The fenators were all in fufpence at this

(a) Zalufki, tom. i. p. 38. and 154.

uncer-

uncertainty, till the Vice-Chancellor Olſowſki put
an end to it, by taking from the King's hands a
paper which he watered with his tears, and read
with a voice interrupted by frequent ſighs : " The
" King has reſolved to interpoſe ſome ſpace of time
" between the hurry and agitation of a throne, and
" that ſtate of eternal peace, to which he reſolves
" to dedicate entirely his future thoughts. The
" hour cannot be far off, which will render him
" unable to bear the weight of a crown ; and he
" chuſes rather to anticipate this hour, than to be
" overtaken by it. He has heard the murmurings
" of the nation againſt his government ; he knows
" the unfavourable conſtructions that have more
" than once been put upon his intentions, ſo as
" even to accuſe him of contriving to get a ſuc-
" ceſſor elected by violence. He will therefore
" deliver the republic from its apprehenſions, by
" reſigning the ſceptre into the ſame hands that
" intruſted it to him. This deſign is irrevocably
" reſolved on : he therefore deſires the ſenate to
" ſpare both itſelf and him the trouble of uſeleſs
" perſuaſions to alter it."

It was viſible on this occaſion, how greatly the
affections of men are influenced by whatever has an
air of diſintereſtedneſs, and greatneſs of mind. The
King, by quitting the throne, ſeemed to have acquired the qualifications neceſſary to fill it. All the
ſenators, with their eyes bathed in tears, made ſigns
to the Primate to ſpeak. He roſe up, and repreſented to the King, " that it was cruel to repudiate
" a nation which had ſhed ſo much blood in his
" cauſe, and to deliver up a chriſtian republic to
" the attacks of Barbarians ; that they could not
" ſubmit to have their King wander over the earth,
" in ſearch of a retreat, without being ſure to find
" it ; that if he was fond of repoſe, the republic
" had excellent Generals and Miniſters ; that if his
" con-

" confcience difturbed him, there were Bifhops and
" Popes to remedy this evil." As he went on in
this harangue, he continued advancing to proftrate
himfelf before the throne, and all the Senators with
him.

This Afiatic cuftom for fubjects to kneel when
they addrefs Kings, was, hitherto unknown in Poland, and fhewed a ftrange contradiction in the
manners of a free people. The King, more careful than they of the public honour, avoided this
proftration, by reprefenting to them that it was forgetting themfelves, and debafing the dignity of the
Senate. After which, he appointed them a day to
confider the form of abdication *(a)*.

The Poles were unprovided with a precedent on
this occafion, the flight of Henry de Valois being
an abdication, not in form, but in effect, which
forced the republic to declare the throne vacant.
Thofe who continued attached to Cafimir, maintained, that the union between the King and his
fubjects was indiffoluble; but fuch as defired a
change, thought it would be fufficient for him to
make his abdication before the Senate. After many debates, it was unanimoufly refolved, that as
Cafimir had afcended the throne by the fuffrages of all the eftates of the realm, he muft alfo defcend from it by the fame fteps. The King, who
ftill continued fixed in his defign, appointed a general diet to meet on the 30th of Auguft.

During this interval, he received letters from feveral fovereigns, who exhorted him to continue on
the throne; and confidered his uneafinefs at having quitted his ecclefiaftical profeffion, and the conftant meditation of eternity for the promotion of
his temporal greatnefs, as the effect of undigefted
fcruples. Pope Clement IX. highly pleafed with

(a) Zalufki, tom. i. p. 35 & 157.

the

the docility he had always fhewn towards the holy fee, writ to him with his own hand, that *if his confcience was difturbed, he might fend his Confeffor to Rome to bring from thence the neceffary remedies.* Thefe letters getting abroad, made it doubtful whether the King would abdicate or not; and the uncertainty was augmented by his feeming to be lefs forrowful, and employing himfelf more about public than private affairs: for he affifted in the courts of juftice, added new ornaments to his palace, encreafed his guards, and gave frequent entertainments *(a)*. It was recollected, that in a diet held a little before the Queen's death, being provoked and wearied out with the oppofition made to his meafures, he had faid in a paffionate tone: "I have liftened to what you have to fay; do "you alfo liften to me. I fee that you want to "give me pain. If you are tired of having me "for your King, I am much more tired of having "you for my fubjects." Notwithftanding this pofitive declaration, he had ftill continued to reign. His fubjects therefore, looked at each other, and none would venture to declare his thoughts. There were feveral who reproached themfelves, with having been perhaps too plain in expreffing their defire of a change.

At length the day that was to unravel the whole myftery arrived. The novelty and importance of the fcene made a ftrong impreffion upon all. Senators, Equeftrians, Deputies, Marfhals of diets, Prelates, Palatines, Caftellans, Starofts, Great Officers of the Crown, not a man was abfent. Cafimir, who was now feated upon the throne for the laft time, confidering himfelf as having already quitted it, did not employ the ufual organ of Kings to fignify his will, but fpoke himfelf in the following terms:

(a) Zalufki, tom. i. p. 158.

"People

" People of Poland,

" It is now two hundred and eighty years that
" you have been governed by my family. The
" reign of my anceftors is paft, and mine is juft
" going to expire. Fatigued by the labours of
" war, the cares of the cabinet, and the weight
" of age; oppreffed with the burdens and folici-
" tudes of a reign of twenty-one years, I, your
" King and father, return into your hands what
" the world efteems above all things, a Crown;
" and chufe for my throne fix feet of earth, where
" I fhall fleep in peace with my fathers. When
" you fhew my tomb to your children, tell them,
" that I was the foremoft in battle, and the laft
" in retreat, that I renounced regal grandeur for
" the good of my country, and reftored my fceptre
" to thofe who gave it me. It was your affection
" for me that exalted me to the higheft rank, and it
" was my affection for you that makes me quit it.
" Many of my predeceffors have tranfmitted the
" fceptre to their children or brothers; and I de-
" liver it to my country, whofe child and father I
" have been; and from this moment I defcend
" from the pinnacle of greatnefs to mix with the
" inferior throng; from a ruler I become a fubject,
" from your King, your fellow-citizen; and leave
" my throne to whoever you fhall think worthy to
" fill it. The republic will make a good choice,
" and be bleffed with profperity, if heaven liftens
" to the prayers I fhall put up in the folitude to
" which I am retiring. Nothing remains but that
" I thank the republic for all the favours it has
" done me, for all the advice it has given me, for
" all the loyalty it has fhewn me; and if, contrary
" to my intention, I have had the unhappinefs of
" difpleafing any, I defire them to impute it to
                                    " the

" the misfortune of the times, or to fate; and to
" forgive me as I forgive all who may have of-
" fended me.   I bid you all adieu, and bear you
" all in my affections.   Diſtance of place may ſe-
" parate me from the republic : but my heart ſhall
" always be with that affectionate parent; and I
" ordain that my aſhes be depoſited in her bo-
" ſom (a)."

If Caſimir did not ſhew all the greatneſs of
mind that might have been expected, while he continued on the throne, he ſeemed to come near it
upon his quitting that ſtation.   The Senate renewed its ſighs; and even the Equeſtrian order,
which had ſo often expreſſed its diſcontent, and
addreſſed him ſo roughly, upon many occaſions,
conjured him not to abandon the helm of government : tears ſtreamed from every eye; but they
were like thoſe which are ſhed at a tragedy, that
leave no impreſſion upon the heart when the ſpec-
tacle is over.   If Caſimir had been prevailed on
to reſume the helm, it is probable that the former
complaints and murmurs would have been heard
again.   It became him, however, to lend an ear
to the laſt repreſentations the republic would have
an opportunity to make him.   Sarnowſki, Marſhal
of the diet, ſpoke in the name of all, and omitted nothing which decency required, to diſſuade the
King.   But he firſt repreſented the abdication of
a throne, as the moſt heroic effort of which the
human mind is capable; he blamed Auguſtus for
deliberating about it twenty years, and not having
the courage to do it at laſt, and beſtowed the higheſt praiſes upon the few great ſouls, ſuch as Sylla,
Dioclefian, and Charles V. who had the reſolution
to part with ſovereign power (b).

(a) Zaluſki, tom. i. part 1. p. 57.   (b) Id. ibid. p. 55.

Such

Such a difcourfe was not likely to alter the King's
defign.   Night being now advancing, the diet rofe,.
and the republic employed the following days in
coming to a final refolution.   Cafimir was not a ty-.
rant ; and had he been fo, a tyrant is never univerfally
hated.   The perfons whom he had much obliged,.
or who would be lofers by his refignation, were earneft for his being folicited a-new in a ftronger manner than before.   In this number was Sobiefki, more
however out of gratitude than ambition ; for being
already Grand-General, and Grand-Marfhal, what
further could he hope ? The majority was of opinion that fufficient entreaties had been ufed : and
that after fo many tender fcenes, it was time to provide for the public good.   It was allowed, that
Cafimir was a good hufband, a good mafter,
and a good friend ; that he was of a mild and af-
fable temper, a lover of juftice, when he knew on
which fide it lay, and even a good foldier, with refpect to perfonal courage ; but the thing complained
of was his want of application and talents for government.   Do you not recollect, faid the Poles to
each other, the life he led in the arms of the queen ;
how his palace was fhut up immediately after din-
ner ; with what diligence all bufinefs was kept at a
diftance ; how many hours he threw away in his
gardens, in hunting, gaming, and other amufe-
ments, which were often protracted fo late at night,
as to encroach upon the labours of the fucceeding
day ; what a relifh he always difcovered for a private life, and how much difguft for a public one ?
Have we not feen him fly into paffions upon the
bench, in the Senate, in diets, and fhew an inde-
cent averfion for the labours of a royal ftation ? Let
us no longer weary him with ufelefs remonftrances :
to take from him a burthen, which, by his own
confeffion, he can no longer bear, is to ferve him,

I

and

Y. 1668. and shew him our affection (a). The Primate, Prazmowski, who had no objection to acting the part of interrex, supported this opinion; and they thought no longer but of settling two articles; one of which, viz. the pension of the abdicated King, was fixed at three hundred thousand florins. The other, which was the instrument of abdication, gave them more trouble; for as they had no form in readiness, it was necessary to compile one. Such an act is worth preserving in history, to be useful to such Kings, as being convinced of their insufficiency, shall be willing to imitate Casimir.

We, John Casimir, King of Poland, and Grand-Duke of Lithuania, do make known to present and future generations, that finding ourselves weakened by age, and oppressed with the many labours to which our strength is no longer equal, we have taken, of our own proper motion, a resolution to abdicate our crown, in order to apply ourselves, with less interruption, to the great business of our salvation. For this purpose, we assembled the senate at Warsaw on the 12th of June, to communicate to it our intentions. But the Senators, equally surprized at the greatness and novelty of such a resolution, referred the cognizance of it to the tribunal of the whole republic. We therefore appointed an assembly of all the estates of the realm on the 21st of August; where, no sooner had we pronounced the word of abdication, than we experienced the affection and regret of our faithful subjects, who, recollecting all the benefits conferred by our ancestors upon the republic, and in particular, all that we ourselves have done for its advantage, omitted no arguments to prevail with us to continue upon

(a) Zaluski, tom. i. part 1. p. 160.

the

the throne. But our refolution continuing un- Y. 1668.
fhaken, it becomes neceffary to proceed to a folemn
abdication before all the eftates of the realm ; and
accordingly, after mature deliberation, and with
the confent of the whole kingdom, " We John
" Cafimir, being in perfect health of body and
" mind, do freely and voluntarily refign the Crown
" of Poland, and the Grand-Dutchy of Lithuania,
" and all the dominions thereunto belonging. We
" abdicate, for the prefent, and for the future, all
" the prerogatives of royalty ; and we give back
" the crown, with all its dependencies, into the
" hands of the Senate, the Deputies, and the whole
" republic ; releafing from their oath of fidelity,
" obedience, and homage, all the eftates of the
" realm, and every fubject in particular : and in
" virtue of this abdication, an interregnum being
" now commenced, the moft reverend Archbifhop
" of Gnefna, Primate of the kingdom, is autho-
" rized to proceed, in conjunction with the eftates
" of the realm, to the election of a new King, ac-
" cording to the eftablifhed laws and ufages ; and
" we promife not to concern ourfelves, in any
" manner, with the faid election. In witnefs
" whereof, and for a perpetual ratification of the
" fame, we have affixed our royal feal to this in-
" ftrument, and figned it with our hand. Given
" at Warfaw, in the general diet of the kingdom,
" on the 17th day of September, in the year of
" our Lord 1668, and of our reign the twenty-
" firft."

By this deed, the republic was difcharged from all
obligation towards the King : but the King was not
fo towards the republic, till by a reciprocal deed
his abdication was accepted, his engagements towards his fubjects diffolved, and he himfelf releafed
from the *pacta conventa,* which he had fworn to at

his

Y. 1668. his coronation. When this was over, there fucceeded harangues of mutual farewel, in which the
head had a greater fhare than the heart ; after which
the abdicated King was conducted to the fuburbs
of Warfaw, and received upon this occafion, for the
laft time, the honours that were henceforth no longer due to him (a).

He was the laft of the race of the Jagellons,
which had reigned near three hundred years. Nothing could be more diverfified than the fortune of
this Prince. Though born the fon of a King, he
could not refift the temptation of entering into a
monaftic life ; a fort of difeafe, fays the Abbé de
Saint Pierre, which often feizes youth, and which
he calls the fmall-pox of the mind. The Pope
cured him of this diforder, by making him a Cardinal. The Cardinal was then changed into a King;
and after having governed a kingdom, he came into France to govern Monks. The two abbies of
St. Germain in the Fields, and St. Martin at Nevers, which Lewis XIV. gave him, became a neceffary revenue for his fubfiftence ; for the Poles
refufed to pay him the ftipulated penfion, which
is but a bad proof of the fincerity of the tears
that were fhed at his abdication. At the fame time
there were great murmurings in France, at a ftranger's coming to eat the children's bread. There
were others who attacked his fuppofed want of the
virtues which became his new profeffion ; for he
had frequent interviews with *Mary Mignot*, the celebrated laundrefs, whom the caprice of fortune had
firft raifed to be the wife of a Counfellor of the parliament of Grenoble, and afterwards to the fame
connection with Marfhal de l'Hopital. This fingular woman, who had been twice left a widow,

(a) Zalufki, tom. i. part 1. p. 57, 58, & 59.

affured

assured Gourville, that she was privately married Y. 1668. to King Casimir. This title of King, which he commonly went by, his former subjects refused to give him, alledging that the utmost they could allow him was the title of *Ex-King* (b). If he repented of his abdication, his regret was of no long continuance, for he was soon delivered from it by death.

(a) Zaluski, tom. i. part i. p. 140.

End of the SECOND BOOK.

I 3   THE

THE

HISTORY

OF

JOHN SOBIESKI

KING OF POLAND.

BOOK III.

AS soon as any nation wants a Governor, there is no Prince who does not think himself capable of difcharging that office, not excepting even youths, who have as yet done nothing, either in the cabinet or in the field. Upon the prefent occafion, there appeared feveral candidates; the Czar of Mufcovy's fon; Ragotfki, Prince of Tranfylvania; the young Duke of Anguien; and in cafe of his being rejected, the Prince of Condé his father. There were alfo two others, who entered the lifts; Prince Charles of Lorrain, fon of Duke Francis; and the Duke of Newburg, Palatine of the Rhine.

The republic foon difmiffed the four firft for different reafons; the Czar's fon, on account of his
reli-

religion, though he offered to renounce it; but that this offer did not proceed from conviction, was evident from his thinking no more of it, after he miffed the Crown. Ragotfki was rejected, becaufe Poland was ftill fmoking with the fire of that war which his father had kindled in the kingdom. The objections to the Duke of Anguien were, his own youth, and a crime committed by another, it being in his favour that Cafimir had attempted to bring on a premature election, againft the moft facred law of the republic. Even France had withdrawn from him her protection, and given it to the Prince of Condé his father. The fon could only give hopes of future merit; the father was already an accomplifhed hero, celebrated for almoft as many victories as he had fought battles, never defeated but by Turenne, and this without any lofs of glory; a ftatefman as well as a General. It required great efforts to ruin the intereft of fuch a competitor for the crown of Poland: the affiftance of Calumny was called in, and France furnifhed the fcandal. A libel was tranfmitted to Poland, and induftrioufly handed about among the Electors.

It was there faid, " that Troy and all its glory
" were now no more; that the hero, finking under
" the exceffes of his youth, much more than the
" weight of years, oppreffed with the gout, and with
" a diforder in his nerves, which had deftroyed all
" their elafticity, was obliged to be carried about
" like a monument of his former glory; that he
" fpent his days in indolence, being incapable of
" all application; that, if the God of War had for-
" merly animated him in battle, the Goddefs of
" wifdom had never infpired him in council; that
" he had never known peace, and breathed no-
" thing but war, for which he was no longer fit;
" that fuppofing his genius fhould revive, it would

I 4

" be

" be only to ruin the Polifh difcipline, which he
" would model after the French manner." The
libel added, " that his heart was incapable of
" any fentiments of humanity or friendfhip; that
" he had abandoned the Duke of Bouillon and Tu-
" renne, who had attached themfelves to his for-
" tune ; that he was of a haughty and violent tem-
" per; had treated the French Senate with great
" indignity, in the time of the civil war ; and had
" hired incendiaries to fet fire to the Palace where it
" was affembled. Nor was his religion reprefented in
" a more favourable light than his moral character.
" The practices of the church were the conftant
" object of his ridicule ; he had never been feen
" at confeffion; and his table was covered with
" flefh on Fridays. A Polifh nobleman had been
" prefent on fuch an occafion, and made no fecret
" of what he had feen. Another was witnefs to
" his having danced upon a Saint's day." Even
the pleafantries which were laughed at, at Paris,
gave great offence at Warfaw. It was made an
objection to him, that being once at fupper with
Cardinal Mazarin, he faid to a page, *Give me fome
of the wine that the Cardinal drinks, when he is in
private with Madam * * *.* The Polifh Bifhops
confidered this pleafantry as a want of refpect for
the Cardinalfhip and the Church: nor did they
forget his own amours, as if Princes ought not to
be excufed in every foible that has no influence upon
public affairs. In fhort, the offer which France
made to Poland of the Prince of Condé, was not
fo much, it was faid, with a view of ferving that
kingdom, as of getting rid of him *(a)*.

While Poland was fetting out the hero of *Ro-
croi* in fuch odious colours, he made himfelf mafter of *Franche-Comté* (at that time as free as its

(a) Zalufki, tom. i. p. 83.

name

name imports) in lefs than three weeks. He had indeed previoufly bribed the Governor, and the Abbé *John de Vatteville*, who, after having been an officer in the army, then a Carthufian, then a Muffulman in Turkey, and laftly an ecclefiaftic, clofed the fcene with betraying his King and his country. Neverthelefs, the Prince's expedition, in which he had both intrigues and fieges to carry on, fhewed that he had ftill ability and vigour. But the Poles were at this time difpofed to believe every thing againft France and Frenchmen: " The le-
" vity and impetuofity of that nation, faid they, will
" never fuit with our phlegm and gravity. Their
" boundlefs ambition would involve us in all their
" wars, and their arrogance deprive us of all our
" glory. Have not fome of them been heard to fay,
" that the Poles were indeed brave, when headed by
" Frenchmen? They have no efteem but for their
" own nation, and their own King, who aims at
" univerfal monarchy.[1] They have compiled a
" book(*a*), which gives him a right to all the coun-
" tries that his arms can reach. Ours, among the
" reft, muft come to take its trial; and the Sor-
" bonne, the Parliament, or a Court of Juftice,
" will give fentence for our deftruction (*b*)."

Such were the efforts made to ruin the Prince of Condé's party. It received its laft blow from Lewis XIV. himfelf, who, a little before, had treated with the Swedes to force the election in the Prince's favour. A fudden revolution had changed the interefts of France, the Elector of Brandenburg having lately joined its enemies, and made himfelf formidable in the Low-countries. It

(*a*) Entitled *Recherche des Droits*, a *Difcuffion of Rights*; compofed by order of the court of France, and containing large claims upon the dominions of moft of the neighbouring Prin-ces.

(*b*) Zalufki, tom. i. p. 84.

was

Y. 1668. was of great importance to difunite him from the allies, by prefenting to his view the crown of Poland for the Duke of Newburg, from whom he expected great advantages to his family. Lewis therefore hefitated, not to declare to the Poles, that he defifted from his firft demand, and transferred all his intereft to the Duke of Newburg. *(a)*.

Year 1669. Things were in this fituation, when the diet of election was opened in the month of May. As foon as the throne is vacant, all the courts of juftice, and other ordinary fprings of the machine of government, remain in a ftate of inaction, and all the authority is transferred to the Primate, who, in quality of interrex, has in fome refpects more power than the King himfelf; and yet the republic takes no umbrage at it, becaufe he has not time to make himfelf formidable. He notifies the vacancy of the throne to foreign Princes, which is in effect proclaiming that a *crown is to be difpofed of*; he iffues the *univerfals (b)* for the election; gives orders to the Starofts to keep a ftrict guard upon the fortified places, and to the Grand-Generals to do the fame upon the frontiers, towards which the army marches. If a foreign Minifter was to prefent himfelf there, at this juncture, he would be refufed admiffion, till he received a paffport from the Primate. The fingular fituation of affairs made the Poles think once more of Cafimir, who, notwithftanding his abdication, had not yet quitted the kingdom. He was obliged to remove forty leagues from Warfaw, that he might be out of the way of forming any party.

The place of election is the field of Wola, at the gates of Warfaw. All the nobles of the king-

(a) Zalufki, tom. i. p. 83. and 154.
(b) *Litteræ univerfales.* Circular letters fent by the Kings of Poland to the provinces and grandees of the kingdom upon public affairs.

dom

dom have a right of voting. The Poles encamp on the left fide of the Viftula, and the Lithuanians on the right, each under the banners of their refpective Palatinates, which makes a fort of civil army, confifting of between a hundred and fifty, and two hundred thoufand men, affembled to exercife the higheft act of freedom. Thofe who are not able to provide a horfe and a fabre, ftand behind on foot, armed with fcythes, and do not feem at all lefs proud than the reft, as they have the fame right of voting.

The field of election is furrounded by a ditch, with three gates, in order to avoid confufion, one to the eaft, for Great Poland, another to the fouth, for Little Poland, and a third to the weft for Lithuania. In the middle of the field, which is called *Kolau*, is erected a vaft building of wood, named the *Szopa*, or Hall for the Senate, at whofe debates the Deputies are prefent, and carry the refult of them to the feveral Palatinates. The part which the Marfhal acts upon this occafion is ftill more important than in ordinary diets, for, being *the mouth* of the nobility, he has it in his power to do great fervice to the candidates; he is alfo to draw up the inftrument of election, and the King elect muft take it only from his hand. Upon the prefent occafion, one of the Potozki family filled this important poft.

It is prohibited, upon pain of being declared a public enemy, to appear at the election with regular troops, in order to avoid all violence. But the nobles, who are always armed with piftols and fabres, commit violence againft one another, at the time that they cry out *liberty*.

All who afpire openly to the crown, are exprefsly excluded from the field of election, that their prefence may not conftrain the voters. The King muft be elected *nemine contradicente*, by all the fuffrages without exception. A fingle noble oppofed the

the election of Uladiſlas VII. and being aſked what objection he could make to him, *None at all,* anſwered he, *but I will not ſuffer him to be King.* The proclamation was ſuſpended for ſome hours, which were employed in bringing him over. The attempt ſucceeded, and the King would fain know the motive of his oppoſition. *I had a mind to ſee,* ſaid the nobleman, *whether our liberty was ſtill in being or not. I am ſatisfied that it is ; and you ſhall not have a better ſubject than me.* The law is founded upon this principle, that when a vaſt family adopts a father, all the children have a right to be pleaſed. The idea is plauſible in ſpeculation ; but if it was rigorouſly kept to, Poland could have no ſuch thing as a lawful King. They therefore give up a real unanimity, and content themſelves with the appearance of it ; or rather, if the law which preſcribes it cannot be fulfilled by means of money, they call in the aſſiſtance of the ſabre.

Before they come to this extremity, no election can poſſibly be carried on with more order, decency, and appearance of freedom. The Primate, in few words, recapitulates to the nobles on horſeback, the reſpective merit of the candidates, which has already been examined in the dietines ; he exhorts them to chuſe the moſt worthy, invokes heaven, gives his bleſſing to the aſſembly, and remains alone with the Marſhal of the diet, while the Senators diſperſe themſelves into the ſeveral Palatinates, to promote an unanimity of ſentiments. If they ſucceed, the Primate goes himſelf to collect the votes, naming once more all the candidates. *Szoda,* anſwer the nobles ; *that is the man we chuſe,* and inſtantly the air reſounds with his name, with cries of *vivat,* and the noiſe of piſtols. If all the Palatinates agree in their nomination, the Primate gets on horſeback ; and then the profoundeſt ſilence

ſuc-

succeeding to the greatest noise, he asks three times, if all are satisfied; and after a general approbation, three times proclaims the King; and the Grand-Marshal of the crown repeats the proclamation three times at the three gates of the camp. How glorious a King this, if endued with royal qualities! And how incontestible his title in the suffrages of a whole people!

This sketch of a free and peaceable election is, by no means, a representation of what usually happens. The corruption of the great, the fury of the people, intrigues and factions, the gold and the arms of foreign powers, frequently fill the scene with violence and blood. The Czar Alexis, to secure the election of his son Fædor, was advancing with an army of fourscore thousand men. He was not yet the father of Peter I. whose greatness was to astonish the earth. The Grand-Chancellor of Lithuania, Casimir Paz, saved his country by amusing Alexis, who came to destroy it; and while he flattered him with the hopes of gaining his point, without drawing the sword, the Poles were discussing the claims of two other competitors, the Duke of Newburg, and Prince Charles of Lorrain.

The former, already sixty years old, was supported not only by Sweden, and the Electors of Brandenburg and Saxony, but also by the King of France and the Emperor. This cabal presented one of those singularities which always astonish those who know nothing of Princes. Lewis XIV. abandoned a Prince of the house of Bourbon, and Leopold, a Prince of Lorrain, whom he considered as the chief of the eldest branch of his family; and both to protect a stranger.

Prince Charles of Lorrain, son of Duke Francis, and nephew of the inconstant Charles IV. who spent his whole life in losing his dominions, and recovering them again, had to recommend him the

flower

Y. 1669. flower of age, a happy countenance, an heroic figure, ftrength of body, vigour of mind, the reputation of being humane, application to bufinefs,
and talents for war, of which he had given proofs
in Hungary. There were two other circumftances which prefented him in a favourable light. Being yet unmarried, he might make fuch a choice as
the republic approved; and the Prince of Lixen,
his Ambaffador, told all the nobility, that his maf-.
ter prefented himfelf unfupported by foreign powers,
that he might owe his elevation to them only, and
teftify his gratitude as became a King.   Nor were
there wanting fome zealous jefuits, who, to increafe
his intereft, gravely affured the Poles, that he had
a great devotion for the Virgin, and that there
were three hundred faints in his own family, whofe
litanies he daily repeated (a).   Having no dominions, his private agents were only his confeffor
the Jefuit Richard, and an Irifh Monk, difguifed
in the habit of a cavalier.   Such emiffaries were
not likely to procure him great regard.

   The affembly was already proceeding to vote,
and the decifive moment approached, when Debicz-
fki, ftandard-bearer of Sendomir, a man venerable
for his fanctity of manners and grey hairs. gave
the Equeftrian order to underftand, "That the
"faction of the Prince of Condé was reviving;
"that a fufpicious affembly had been held at the
"Primate Prazmowfki's; that the ufual artifices
"of France were well known; that the Ambaffa-
"dor of that crown publicly declared one thing,
"while another was contriving in private; that
"Condé would be proclaimed at a time when it
"was leaft expected, if meafures were not fpeedi-
"ly taken to prevent it."   Immediately the Equeftrian order ran to the Senate, to infift upon the

_____

(a) Zalufki, tom. i. p. 44.

                                        exclu-

exclusion of the Prince: the demand was perplex- Y. 1669.
ing; and the Primate sought his answer in the
looks of the Senators.

Sobieski, as Grand-General, ought to have been
upon the frontiers: he was prohibited by the laws
to appear in the field of election: but the high
credit he was in had raised him above the constitution; a sure sign of weakness in a republican
government, where the laws ought always to be
more respected than great men. Sobieski observing
the perplexity of the Primate, rose up to speak. It
was for his interest that an exclusion should be pronounced against the Prince; for, though he was
not in the number of the candidates, he knew
that a free nation might, in a moment, look beyond them for some other person; and in this case,
the hero of the nation might well flatter himself
with the hopes of fixing its attention. And yet
these are the terms in which he spoke: " There
" is a wide difference between refusing to vote for
" a candidate, and excluding him. A refusal is
" only an exercise of freedom; an exclusion is a
" direct affront. If the Equestrian order pretends
" to restrain, in this manner, the liberty of the
" Senate, I will neither submit to such slavery, nor
" have any share in affronting a great Prince,
" but quit the assembly. If they are contented
" with refusing him their suffrages, it is well
" known that I always yield to the voice of the
" public." Next day the demand for his exclusion became the voice of the public; and the Primate pronounced it, against his own opinion, and
that of the Senate (a).

Tranquillity was now restored for a time, the
attention of the assembly being wholly taken up
with the Duke of Newburg, and Prince Charles.

(b) Zaluski, tom. i. p. 118.

Their

Y. 1669. Their virtues and their vices, the good and the evil that the republic might expect from them, were difcuffed. 'Tis at the tribunal of liberty that Princes fhould get themfelves tried, if they would know what the world thinks of them; for they can never know it in their own courts. The partifans of Prince Charles, that is to fay, the majority of the nobles on horfeback, never ceafed repeating, " What fhall we do with Newburg? A Prince, " already fixty years of age, who will no fooner " have tried on his crown, than we muft throw our- " felves again into confufion by thinking of a new " election; and even though he fhould live longer " than there is any ground to hope, will his ad- " vanced age permit him to learn our language, to " fafhion himfelf to our manners, and to fupport " the fatigues of the diet, the bench, the fenate, " and the camp? What good can we poffibly ex- " pect from him? Too many powers intereft " themfelves in his behalf, not to make it coft us " fomething: particularly, Sweden and Branden- " burg are our very next neighbours. He is re- " commended to us for our King; but we fhould " be told what he has done either in war or peace, " for the glory and happinefs of his own fubjects. " All that we know of him is, that he is the fa- " ther of a numerous family. Two of his fons are " intended for the Priefthood: and will not our " richeft abbies, and beft bifhoprics, be for them " only? His daughters too! What a burden will " they be to the ftate? His being a candidate for " our crown, is not, depend upon it, fo much for " himfelf, as for his pofterity, whom he wants to " fix upon the throne. If he fucceeds, we fhall " for ever be forced to bend under the ftiffnefs of " a haughty nation, and fee our court and great " offices filled by Germans of both fexes, incef- " fantly boafting of their pedigrees, and infulting

" ing us and our wives; us, the defcendants of the
" Sarmatians who have fo often made Germany
" tremble (a).

" We are prefented by fortune with another
" Prince of a very different ftamp: fprung from a
" modeft nation, and endued with that virtue him-
" felf; fierce and haughty no where but at the head
" of an army. The few Lorrainers that he brings,
" with him, if he brings any at all, will be amply
" fatisfied with being on an equality with the Poles.
" Unfupported by any cabal, without moving all
" Europe to promote his greatnefs, he wifhes to
" owe the fceptre only to our fuffrages. His age,
" his ftature, his ftrength, his virtues, the exploits
" which have already diftinguifhed him, all con-
" fpire to promife a long and happy reign. His
" children, if they are to fucceed him, will be born
" Poles, and by fuch a mother as we fhall ap-
" prove (b)."

The Senate, the Deputies, and almoft all the
grandees who were for the Duke of Newburg, allowed the portrait of the Prince of Lorrain to be
faithfully drawn; but, after having foftened that of
his rival, they boafted much of his great poffeffions,
and what he promifed to the republic; a body of
troops, maintained at his own expence, a year's
pay to the national forces, a military fchool for the
young nobility, with a fund to affift them in the expence of travelling; advantages which Prince
Charles might promife, but was not in a condition to perform, as he had not the fame fortune,
or rather had no fortune at all, the French having
lately difpoffeffed his father of his dominions. If
we refufe him, added they, we have no inconvenience to apprehend on that account; but if we
reject the Duke of Newburg, let us reflect that the

(a) Zalufki, tom. i. p. 76.   (b) Id. ibid. p. 42,

K   powers

powers who propofe him to us have armies to make themfelves obeyed.

At thefe words, the nobles could contain no longer ; a fudden fury was kindled, and the fire fpread through every rank. The Senate, the great Officers, and the Deputies, were ill defended by the entrenchment that furrounds the Szopa. One part of the republic befieged the other. Several difcharges were made, as a prelude to all the horrors that might follow. The Senators and Deputies were feen throwing themfelves from their feats, and running here and there, or lying flat upon the ground, while the balls whiftled over their heads. Some got to the gates of the camp, but were received with piftols at their breafts : two were killed ; a great number wounded ; and all forced to return to their places to fave their lives (a). The tumult was every moment encreafing, when Potozki, the Marfhal of the diet, interpofed to appeafe it. It was with great difficulty that they refrained from infulting him, but the uproar ftill continued. Nothing is more difficult than to keep within bounds a nation that makes Kings.

From the firft opening of the diet, not a night paffed in which perfons were not affaffinated in the ftreets of Warfaw, or the field of election. Sobiefki had, upon two accounts, a right to command obedience to his orders. As Grand-Marfhal, he was entrufted with the civil government ; and as Grand General, he had the army at his command. As foon as he exerted his authority, he ftruck an awe into the people of Warfaw. He threatened

(a) This violence was the occafion of the Szopa's being built in a new form. This wooden edifice was formerly open on all fides, fupported only by pillars ; but was clofed up in all future elections. The nobles murmured at this innovation ; but it ftill fubfifts.

to·fend·for troops, and· fire upon whatever party
fhould attempt to difturb the freedom of election.
The fear of his executing·thefe menaces having
fufpended the rage of the· affembly, Opalinfki,
Palatine of Kalifch, completely reftored tranquil-
lity·by·the wifdom of his remonftrances.

" To what purpofe, faid he, are we murdering
" one another, for princes that we have never
" feen,·and who perhaps·will make ufe of their
" fceptre only to·fmite us ? Our anceftors were far
" more wife.   Scarce was the nation·fettled, when
" it was divided, as it·is now, among feveral fo-
" reign candidates.   The calamities which threat-
" ened· the· public, reftored the ufe of reafon :
" *Piaft*, a native of Poland, was chofen : and this
" man, who had neither birth nor fortune, go-
" verned with fuch wifdom, that to this time eve-
" ry Polifh King is called *Piaft* out of honour and
" gratitude.   Let us leave the Duke of Newburg
" to govern his large family, and his fmall domi-
" nions.   Let the Prince of Lorrain employ his
" money in recovering his hereditary territories.
" But let us imitate our anceftors, and chufe a
" *Piaft (a).*"

This is not the firft time that a wife fpeech has
calmed a tumultuous crowd.   But what *Piaft* to
chufe, was a difficulty not eafy to be got over.
The affembly turned their eyes upon Sobiefki.   If at
this juncture he flattered himfelf with the hopes of
the crown, the illufion was of fhort duration.   The
more any one reflects upon ancient and modern
hiftory, the more will he be convinced that human
affairs are the fport of fortune.   The man whom
fhe fecretly deftined for the throne, was the laft
that the public would have thought of.   He interefted himfelf fo little in the election, that he was

(a) Hiftory of the diets, p. 194.

not

Y. 1669. not found in his tent, but in a convent at Warſaw. H's name was Michael Wieſnowieſki. The two Palatines, Opalinſki and another, conduct him to the field of election without informing him of their deſign, and there preſent, propoſe, and nominate him. Oliowſki, Biſhop of Culm, and Vice-Chancellor of Poland, a prelate reſpectable for his virtue, cries out in an enthuſiaſtic ſtrain, *Long live King Michael.* The cry immediately flies from mouth to mouth; all the orders repeat it, and nothing is now wanting but the Primate's proclamation : the nobles force him to it with a piſtol at his breaſt, and Wieſnowieſki is King.

The man in the nation that was moſt ſurprized, was he himſelf. He wept as they dragged him to the throne, and proteſted that he was incapable of filling it; and the truth is, that ſince the Poles rejected all foreign candidates, and reſolved upon chuſing a *Piaſt,* it would ſeem they ſhould not have heſitated a moment between Wieſnowieſki and Sobieſki. Wieſnowieſki was ſcarce thirty years old; Sobieſki, being ten years elder, had nearly reached that maturity of age which is ſo neceſſary in the Governor of a great nation. Wieſnowieſki's youth had been totally unemployed : Sobieſki had ſpent his in travelling, in the ſtudy of public buſineſs, and in the fatigues of war: Wieſnowieſki had held no office in the ſtate; Sobieſki had obtained the higheſt by actions of diſtinguiſhed glory, and ſtill went on to acquire new triumphs. Wieſnowieſki even wanted that importance which riches beſtow; he ſubſiſted upon a penſion of ſix thouſand livres which Queen Louiſa had given him, and upon the liberality of the Biſhop of Plocſko; Sobieſki had a vaſt eſtate, and numerous vaſſals. Wieſnowieſki came to the election among the crowd of nobles to join his ſuffrage with theirs; Sobieſki, the firſt perſon of the republic, ſeemed to preſent him-

himſelf rather to receive the ſuffrages of the aſſembly than to give his own. One circumſtance only, if ſuch a circumſtance can make a nation happy, ſpoke in favour of the new King; and this waş his birth. He was deſcended from Koribut, uncle of the great Jagellon; his father was Jeremiah Wieſnowieſki, Palatine of Ruſſia, who having poſſeſſed a great eſtate in the Ukraine, was ſtripped of it before his death by the Coſſacks; ſo that the ſon, having nothing left him but an empty name, could have little reaſon to expect ſo diſtinguiſhed an honour.

There is nothing in other countries that reſembles this ceremony. Let any one figure to himſelf, more than a hundred thouſand nobles on horſeback, who would ſooner reduce themſelves to the loweſt poverty than not diſplay their pomp; the grandees in all the Aſiatic ſtatelineſs; a whole nation of curious ſpectators; the numerous troops that guard the camp; and the roar of artillery, joined to the acclamations of an aſſembled kingdom. Such is the military and civil pomp, with which the King elect is conducted, firſt to the great church of St. John, and then to the royal palace. Upon the preſent occaſion, the Poles, in the firſt moments of their enthuſiaſm, diſcovered many a happy preſage; for their prejudices in favour of the ancient Romans, diſpoſe them to put all the faith in omens that Chriſtianity will permit. During the election, a dove had flown acroſs the incloſure where the Senate was debating. An eagle had hovered over the nobles. A ſwarm of bees had buzzed about Wieſnowieſki without hurting him, a thing that had formerly happened to a ſtatue of Antoninus Pius. To all this, were added ſeveral preſages that had happened to Monks at the altar. Every thing concurred to promiſe a happy reign: but we ſhall ſoon ſee,

Y. 1669. fee, that the dove, the eagle, the bees, and the Monks, were all miftaken (a).

Cafimir, however, was not; for being told whom they had chofen, *What*, faid he, *have they fet the crown upon the head of that poor fellow?* His reign was thought fo unpromifing in foreign countries, that, foon after his election, the Elector of Brandenburg, whofe houfe was far from being fo powerful as it is now (Frederick II. was then unborn) ordered a Pruffian gentleman to be feized under the very windows of his palace; and that afylum was violated without any reparation being made.

Never was there a King who wanted more to be governed; and in this cafe, it is not always the moft able and moft upright that get the government into their hands. The Grand-Chancellor of Lithuania, Cafimir Paz, poffeffed all his confidence: a man of eminent talents, great natural eloquence, and improved abilities; but ambition being more prevalent in him than love for his country, he aimed only at promoting the greatnefs of his own family, which was already the moft flourifhing in Lithuania, though not originally of that country, but a branch of the *Pazzi* of Florence. This relationfhip with *Saint Magdalen de Pazzi* had coft the Chancellor near two millions to build a monaftery of Camaldules under the patronage of his kinfwoman: a fingular inftance of profufion in a ftatefman. His brother, Michael Paz, of a turbulent, fiery, and capricious temper, was Grand-General of Lithuania, a profeffed rival to Sobiefki, well acquainted with military affairs, but wanting that fuperiority of genius which fupports a tottering ftate.

If Sobiefki had not ftood up in its defence, Poand was on the point of being fubjected to ra-

(a) Zalufki, p. 13:, 146.

vage

vage and defolation. The Coffacks, notwithftanding the peace they had made with the republic in the
reign of Cafimir, begun to entertain great fufpicions of
the defigns of the new King Michael. They apprehended he might have a mind to recover the large
poffeffions of his own family in the Ukraine, and
thofe of all the other Polifh nobles who had been
difpoffeffed of their eftates. To difpel their fears,
the Coffacks demanded a renunciation of all thefe
claims. The Poles, on their fide, were unwilling to
begin a war, at a time when the kingdom was greatly
exhaufted. The King employed Sobiefki to ne-
gociate the affair; though he could have wifhed for
any other fit Ambaffador, for he begun to take
umbrage at a fubject who was too much efteemed
by the nation. The leader of the Coffacks, that
fame Dorofcenfko whom Sobiefki had already beat,
was inflexible. It was neceffary, therefore, to have
recourfe to that laft reafon of Kings, which has
fpilt fuch ftreams of blood fince the time that men
firft chofe to fet mafters over their heads. Sobiefki fhed as little as he could; for he confidered
the blood of the Coffacks as belonging to the republic, fince they had actually been good fubjects
before the Poles had made them bad flaves. Another caufe of Sobiefki's treating them fo mildly,
was his having but few troops; he therefore called
in the affiftance of art, and fowed divifion among
the Coffacks. He fet up a new leader againft the
old one, Hanenfko againft Dorofcenfko. He reduced to the obedience of Poland the cities of Bar,
Nimirow, Kalnick, and Braclaw, and all the country between the Bog and the Niefter. Dorofcenfko
being entirely overpowered, had no way to fave the
reft of the Ukraine but by threatening to give up
the country to the Turks, if he was drove to extremities; and this threat made Sobiefki fufpend his
victories. The congratulations he received fhew
plainly the importance of the campaign. "We

" can-

Y. 1671.   " cannot sufficiently admire your valour and pru-
" dence in this expedition. With such a handful of
" men, how could you recover so many places,
" and particularly Braclaw, which alone is worth
" a victory? You have opened to us a passage into
" the Ukraine, and will doubtless compleat its re-
" duction. Even envy itself is forced to own,
" that Poland is indebted to you for its safety (a)".
These are the terms in which the Vice-Chancellor
writ to him in the name of the King and the whole
republic ; and in this manner the Grand-General
took his revenge for having missed the crown.

But he insisted upon it, that, without abusing
their victory, the Poles should treat the Cossacks
gently, and bring them back to their allegiance by
clemency, and the alluring hopes of future prosperity.

Y. 1672.   Such was also the opinion of all the Deputies,
and the greatest part of the Senate assembled in the
diet ; but the King and his council thought diffe-
rently. The reign of the weak Michael was the
reign of favourites. His council was made up of
pensioners to the Emperor Leopold, whose sister
he had lately married. Leopold was apprehensive
of a formidable armament that was preparing in
Turkey ; and had laid a plan that was likely to
divert it upon Poland. He knew that Dorofcensko
had threatened to give up the Ukraine to the Turks,
if he was driven to extremities ; and he conjectured
that the Turks would not be indifferent to the acquisition of so fine a province, which would lay
open to them Poland and Muscovy, two kingdoms
that had produced so many enemies to the Ottoman empire. He knew besides, that Michael, if
he could recover the Ukraine by open force, flattered himself with recovering also the immense pa-

(a) Zalufki, tom. i, p, 133, 146.

trimony

trimony of his anceſtors, perhaps with ſome additions.   Acquainted with all theſe circumſtances,
Leopold had no difficulty to perſuade him, that all
negotiations with the rebels were no leſs dangerous
than they were mean ; and that to pardon Doroſcenſko was to weaken the royal authority.   Michael therefore thought himſelf great, by ſhewing
himſelf inflexible.

In the mean time the diet, by the laws of the
kingdom, might force him to make peace : to prevent which, he bribed a Deputy, who made a proteſt, left the aſſembly, and the diet was diſſolved.
A plain proof that the proteſt of the Deputy was
only an artifice of the court, is, that the King
took no ſteps to bring him over, and reſtore to the
council of the nation its power of proceeding upon buſineſs.

Doroſcenſko was ſoon acquainted with what had
paſt, and fearing to fall into the hands of a provoked ſovereign, went to look for a new one at
Conſtantinople.

Mahomet IV. in his way to the throne, had
paſſed over the body of his father, Ibrahim I.
whom the janizaries had ſtrangled.   He had beat
the Imperialiſts, made great conqueſts in Hungary,
ſubdued Tranſylvania, and taken the Iſle of Candy,
anciently called Crete.   The Turks thought they
could not do a greater honour to the Count de
Guilleragues, Ambaſſador from France, and his
attendants, than by calling the French the kinſ-
men of *Mehemmed-Tetib*, Mahomet the Victorious.
Hitherto, however, he had been victorious only as
moſt ſovereigns are, who do every thing without
doing any thing.   He had never yet appeared in
perſon at the head of his armies ; but his ſucceſs
ſeemed unalterable under the management of the
Grand-Viſir *Cuprogli*, of abilities equally exalted
with his ſtation.   A Grand-Viſir is Conſtable, Chancellor,

cellor, and Firſt Preſident, all together; and each
of theſe offices was well filled. He ſucceeded his
father in the Viſir's place, againſt the policy of the
Empire, which does not ſuffer honours to be perpetuated in the ſame family. Another ſingular circumſtance was his obtaining this ſupreme honour
at the age of thirty, whereas the cuſtom is for no
one to hold great offices under forty (a). The
Turks, who never give into hyperbole but upon
great occaſions, called him *the light of nations,*
the *guardian of the laws,* the *formidable Commander.*
The ſaying of Montecuculi, upon his retiring from
public life, when his rivals finiſhed their courſe, is
well known; *ſhould a man who has had the honour of fighting with Turenne, Condé, and Cuprogli,
hazard his glory againſt perſons that are only beginning to command armies?* The military part of
Cuprogli's character was all that Montecuculi was
acquainted with.

This able Miniſter, reflecting upon Doroſcenſko's offers, formed a deſign to conquer Poland,
deferring, till another campaign, the deſtruction of
the empire of Vienna, as a victory which would
be facilitated by this; and he was for having his
maſter come in perſon to gather the laurels he had
prepared for him. The Viſir's inſiſting upon Mahomet's preſence in the army, was a proof both of
his policy and attachment to the Sultan, who, notwithſtanding the victories of his reign, was beginning to incur the hatred and contempt of his ſubjects, becauſe he was entirely given up to his pleaſures, and ſpent more money in his ſeraglio, than he
would have done in conquering the Chriſtians.

But the Divan repreſented, that this war could
not be a juſt one, without a previous ſummons to
the Poles, and a refuſal on their part to give ſatis-

(a) Ricaut's Hiſtory of the Ottoman Empire, p. 135.

faction

faction to the Coffacks, The *Mufti* in particular, that is, the Pontiff of the Mahometan religion, re-fufed his *Fetfa*. This Mufti is a perfonage of great importance, being the only one in the empire to whom the Grand-Seignior rifes ; but were he de-tected in any double dealing, he would be pounded to jelly in a mortar *(a)*. The Fetfa which he re-fufed on this occafion, is a fort of Epifcopal man-date, that always accompanies the public orders of the Grand-Seignior ; becaufe, without this oracle, the people would not obey fo well. Cuprogli, who was himfelf too much a friend to juftice and reli-gion, not to liften to their dictates, addreffed the following manifefto to the republic of Poland.

" You affert that the Ukraine belongs to you,
" and that the Coffacks are your fubjects, as if
" we did not know that this nation was formerly
" free, and depended only upon itfelf. It is true,
" they have given themfelves to you of their own
" accord, and upon certain conditions ; but they
" little expected that you would prove tyrants, and
" commit fo many outrages. They have therefore
" taken up arms, as they are authorized to do by
" the laws of nature, to recover their former ftate
" of liberty. They have befought the Sublime
" Porte, to take them under its protection, and do
" for them what it does for all the unhappy. The
" invincible Mahomet has therefore fent to Doro-
" fcenfko, chief of the Coffacks, the fabre and
" the ftandard. Know then, that if you do not
" haften to compofe this difference with my maf-
" ter, who is already in motion towards Adria-
" nople, but fuffer him to arrive upon your fron-
" tiers with his immenfe forces, the difpute will
" no longer be decided by a treaty, but by the

(a) Ricaut's Hift. of the Ottoman Empire, p. 190.

" fword,

" fword, and the wrath of the God of venge-
" ance (a)."

At the grumbling of this thunder, the Senate affembled, and begun with expreffing great indignation, that the letter containing the declaration of war was not writ by the Sultan himfelf,
but by the Vifir; which was conftrued to be a
contemptuous piece of arrogance. The King's
partifans laid hold of this moment of indignation, to infinuate that the declaration was not made
in earneft : " Why, faid they, fhould the Porte,
" in general fo faithful to treaties, break with us,
" who have given her no offence? Can it be to
" enlarge her empire? But it is well known that
" fhe is more folicitous at prefent to preferve her
" immenfe dominions, than to extend them. Can
" it be with a real defign of fupporting Dorofcen-
" fko? But it was much more natural to favour
" him, while his ftrength was yet entire. Would
" Mahomet come with all the weight of his power
" to enter into a league with a robber? The Vi-
" fir's declaration has all the appearance of being
" a menace extorted from him, by the importunity
" and falfhoods of Dorofcenfko. But fuppofe the
" thunder fhould follow the lightning, the Czar
" offers us a powerful diverfion, in which he pro-
" mifes to engage the Perfians; and can we think
" that the empire of Germany is not equally in-
" terefted to reftrain the Tyrant of Afia? Here is
" alfo a fuccour that may foon be called for (b).

To all this the true patriots anfwered, that it
was a much eafier way to fatisfy the Coffacks, and
by this means deprive the Turks of all pretence to
difturb Poland. Sobiefki being abfent at this juncture, the Primate propofed to fufpend all debates
about war, till the arrival of the hero who under-

(a) Zalufki, tom. i. p. 360.   (b) Id. ibid. p. 352, & feq.

            ftood

Y. 1672.

ftood it fo well. This propofal was by no means agreeable to the King, who was apprehenfive of the Grand-General's becoming of ftill greater importance. Night coming on, it was propofed to carry on the debates by candle-light; but the Primate oppofed this defign, for fear that, as the difputes ran high, they might be tempted to ufe their poniards in the dark; a thing that had happened more than once in thefe affemblies. Perhaps alfo he apprehended an attempt upon his own perfon, from fome of thofe villains, who are always ready to do more than Kings even defire.

The next morning Sobiefki arrived, and moft of the Senators went out to meet him. He had the pleafure of hearing his own praifes in full Senate: he was told, that the gown and the fword became him equally, that he had twifted the laurel with his fafces, and had the abilities both of a Senator and a General. All this was true; but it was neceffary, without lofing a moment, to fix upon fome expedient, to fave the republic. Sobiefki fpoke with great warmth for appeafing the Coffacks, pointed out the articles in which Poland might make conceffions. But there is no fuch thing as perfuading weak minds, much lefs Princes who are accuftomed to make no diftinction between might and right. Michael perfifted in his obftinacy, and returned the Porte no anfwer, as if its menaces had been of no confequence.

From this period may be dated the rife of the league that was formed to dethrone him. It is a maxim with the Poles, that whatever nation has a right to make a King, has a right to unmake him alfo; fo that what would be called a confpiracy in other countries, they look upon only as an exertion of a national privilege. Among the chiefs of this league were the Primate Prazmowfki; Sienawfki

awſki, the Great Standard-Bearer; Lubomirſki, Palatine of Cracow; Ledchinſki, of Mazovia; Potozki, of Kiovia; Vielopolſki, and other nobles of equal importance. The enterprize was not ſo hazardous as it would have been in an hereditary kingdom, but yet it had its dangers.

The confederated nobles thought proper to ſhew their regard to the Emperor, by acquainting him with their deſign, on account of his ſiſter, who ſhared the throne of Poland with Michael. They therefore laid before him all the grievances of the ſtate, and particularly Michael's incapacity to govern. In proud and haughty nations, a King who is deſpiſed, generally totters upon the throne, while uſurpers, who are eſteemed, ſit firmly. The Engliſh never thought of depoſing Cromwell; for Cromwell had humbled Holland, preſcribed the conditions of a treaty to Portugal, beat the Spaniards, forced France to court his alliance, and given the empire of the ſea and of commerce to England; but Michael was fit for nothing but to ruin Poland.

The confederated nobles repreſented therefore to the Emperor, the neceſſity there was of chuſing another Governor; that the only obſtacle in their way was their reſpect for his Cæſarean Majeſty, and their Queen Eleonora, whom they were ſorry to involve in the King's fate. They therefore deſired him to ſay in what manner he wiſhed ſhe might be treated.

The emperor, after having expreſſed his pity for his brother-in-law, in having no talents for a throne, anſwered, that he pitied the republic ſtill more, but could not conſent to ſee his ſiſter without a crown. The method that he propoſed, to avoid all difficulties, was this : The moſt Serene King (ſuch was the title his Cæſarean Majeſty gave to Michael) was of a weak conftitution, of unfettled health, and hitherto without children: the validity of his marriage might, by the canons, be queftioned, on account of impotence, a way that had often fucceeded with crowned heads. The Queen confented to fupport this accufation, for the good of the republic; but then it muft be exprefsly ftipulated, that after the diffolution of her union with Michael, fhe was to marry the Prince who fhould fucceed him in the throne. A parallel inftance had happened fo late as the year 1667, when the Queen of Portugal, who had a paffion for Don Pedro, brother to her hufband King Alphonfo, accufed the latter of impotence, and obtained a bull from Rome to marry her brother-in-law, and fhare with him the throne.

Another difficulty was, to fettle upon what head they fhould place the crown. The Emperor infifted upon the exclufion of all heretics, and Frenchmen. His averfion to the former he carried fo far, as to extend it even to heretics who fhould change their religion with a view to the crown; and the French were profcribed " as a reftlefs, turbulent, and in-" flammatory nation, faid Leopold, in his difpatches on this occafion. " Their machinations, added he, " againft all Europe in general, and againft " the houfe of Auftria in particular, are well " known. It would be unreafonable, that I fhould " expofe my own family and the empire, for the " fake of your intereft. The King that I propofe " to you is Prince Charles of Lorrain, whom you " were upon the point of crowning in the laft " election. Do not confider him as a Prince with-" out fortune, and without power, who would be " burdenfome to the republic. His father is in-" deed difpoffeffed of his dominions; but this is " only a temporary evil, for which he is indebted " to France, and which that nation will, in the
" end,

Y. 1673. " end, have more reafon to repent of, than rejoice
" at (a)."

In the laft election, Leopold had preferred the
Duke of Newburg to the Prince whom he now fo
warmly recommended ; but policy will not permit
fovereigns to fpeak always the fame language, and
wear the fame afpect. After having laid open his
plan, he again expreffed his forrow, that the fceptre
fhould be forced out of the hands of the moft Serene King Michael, and lamented over fo melancholy a neceffity, concluding with a moft earneft
requeft to the republic, to provide for his fubfiftence.

Hitherto the confederated nobles, uncertain of
Sobiefki, whofe conduct feemed to indicate an un-
willingnefs to break with the court, had communicated to him nothing of their defign ; but reflecting upon the neceffity of gaining him over, they
now laid it before him. The part he fhould take
upon him to act, was likely to decide the fate of
the King, and the kingdom. With all the weight
of his dignities of Grand-Marfhal and Grand-
General, of Commander and Father of an army,
which thought itfelf invincible when headed by him,
he efpoufed the caufe of the kingdom againft the
King. But whether, when he refolved upon the
depofition of Michael, he aimed at fixing the attention of the nation upon himfelf, or had nothing
in view but the public good, it is certain that he
reprefented how dangerous it would be to take the
Emperor's nomination of a King ; that it was putting the ftate under the tuition of the council of
Vienna ; and that they had felt the melancholy effects of it ever fince Michael had been upon the
throne : " but juft as it is, added he, to take the
" crown from a man who is incapable of wear-

(a) Zalufki, tom. i. p. 342, & feq.

ing

" ing it, it would be equally unjuft to deprive him
" of his wife ; and the republic cannot, without
" difgrace, engage in fo infamous a plot. And as
" to a new King, if Poland cannot fupply that
" want, France has one to offer us, of as war-
" like a genius as Prince Charles, and who can
" involve us in no difagreeable connections. The
" perfon I mean is the Duke of Longueville *(a)*,
" defcended from the famous Count of Dunois,
" who faved Charles VII. his King, and France,
" his country. The Duke inherits the blood and
" virtues of his anceftor, and is deftined to fave
" Poland."

The Queen did not think with Sobiefki, that fhe
was infeparably connected with a hufband without
a crown. She would indeed have preferred Prince
Charles to the Duke of Longueville ; but fhe was
determined, at all events, to continue upon the
throne. She therefore infinuated to the Grandees,
that fhe would confent to marry the Duke. His
picture had been already fhewn her, and fhe did
not diflike it.

Sobiefki's propofal was conformable to the affection he always retained for France, and the in-
tercourfe he kept up with Lewis XIV. As for the
Prince whom he propofed, all his merit confifted in
valour, which alone will never make a great King.
But the confederated nobles were too eager for a
revolution to weigh things maturely, and therefore
acquiefced implicitly. They made the utmoft expedition to form their meafures with France; and
the thing was conducted with fo much fecrecy by
Sobiefki, that neither the court of Vienna, nor that
of Warfaw, had the leaft fufpicion of what was
carrying on.

(a) Known alfo by the name of Count de Saint-Paul.

L

The

The abrupt diffolution of the laft diet furnifhed a pretence for demanding another in the beginning of the fpring. Michael durft not refufe it; efpecially as it was neceffary to put the republic in arms, for intelligence came that the Turks were actually upon their march.

Never was a King treated in fo rough a manner before all his fubjects. A grievance which had, in fome meafure, been forgiven him, was revived in this diet. He had taken an oath at his coronation, not to marry without the approbation of the republick; and he had not even afked its opinion, when he married Eleonora, Arch-Duchefs of Auftria.

The Czar offered him his daughter, and the reftitution of the dutchy of Severia, with other confiderable advantages: and this propofal was highly agreeable to the republic, whereas the Arch-Duchefs brought nothing. But the King liftened only to the Chancellor *Paz*. The bringing about this alliance had coft him five hundred thoufand livres, which fum he attempted to reimburfe himfelf privately out of the national ftock; and this was interpreted as a crime againft the republic, which ought to know how her finances are difpofed of, and had nothing to do with the expences of a marriage that fhe difapproved. The fame match brought upon him another reproach; his acceptance of the order of the *Golden Fleece* being confidered as a mark of vaffalage, equally difgraceful to the King and to his fubjects, and as an engagement to efpoufe the interefts, and avenge the wrongs of the houfe of Auftria. It was even pretended that he had exprefsly fworn to do fo, when he accepted the order, the ceremony of which was performed in private. " Far different, added they, was the beha-" viour of Stephen Battori, when the Spanifh Am-" baffador made him an offer of the fame order.
" That

" That excellent King, whose loss we still de-
" plore, ordered a collar to be made, in which,
" instead of a *sheep*, there hung a *wolf*, arm-
" ed with threatening teeth (*a*). *This*, said he,
" is my order; I will accept yours, when my bro-
" ther, the King of Spain, accepts mine."

The comparison was carried on to a still greater
length. " Stephen consulted only with the Senate
" and the diets: Michael manages all public bu-
" siness with the Queen and the Austrian Ambas-
" sador, who is employed night and day in con-
" triving our ruin. Stephen always headed our
" armies in person: Michael has never yet been
" seen there. Is it reasonable that the members
" should expose themselves for a head, who always
" keeps himself out of the reach of danger (*b*)?"

The Primate, taking advantage of this ferment,
addressed him in terms which, in an absolute monarchy, would be considered as high-treason.
" The nation, said he, has made you its King,
" and you are compassing its destruction. In-
" stead of endeavouring to pacify the Ukraine,
" you have irritated its sense of pain. You have
" neglected to repair the fortifications of Kami-
" nieck, the bulwark of Poland. You still keep
" the German guard, which the republic saw with
" discontent attending upon your predecessor,
" though he paid it with his own money. You
" have persons in your court, and your cabinet,
" who sacrifice the interests of the nation to those
" of the King. The Deputies were preparing
" to address you, to remove these public pests;
" and you have discovered an expedient to re-
" move the Deputies themselves. You violate our

(*a*) The arms of Transylvania, of which Battori was Prince,
before he came to the crown of Poland.

(*b*) Zaluski, tom. i. p. 168. & seq.

L 2

" con-

" conſtitution, in diſpoſing of Staroſties and ſeats
" in the Senate, before the death of thoſe who
" hold them. You have broke off two diets, in
" order to ſcreen your authority from the animad-
" verſion of the laws. You have openly laid claim
" to the ancient prerogatives of our Kings, and
" proteſted againſt all encroachments upon them.
" Theſe ancient prerogatives, which may be ex-
" tended to ſo enormous a pitch, where do you
" propoſe to ſearch for the records that contain
" them? Probably in the Archives of Vienna or
" Madrid. 'Tis time, Senators, that we tremble
" for ourſelves, if we behave as becomes our
" rank. That ſaying which you was heard to
" make uſe of, after your coronation, that you
" ſwore to the *Pacta Conventa*, with a mental re-
" ſervation, is but too true. What faith can we
" poſſibly put in your oaths (a)? We therefore
" break ours, after your example." The firmneſs
of mind which ſuch a diſcourſe ſeems to imply,
is by no means a prodigy in a ſtate, where the liberty of the ſubject, and particularly of perſons
in public ſtations, who ſpeak boldly what they think,
and truſt to the laws for their protection, is inviolably ſacred.

..The Primate was ſtill ſpeaking, when the confederated nobles, whoſe number was greatly increaſed in the national aſſembly, ſignified to Michael, without any ceremony, to quit the throne
by a voluntary abdication, or to expect to be forced
to it. As ſoon as he ſaw Sobieſki in the league,
he deſpaired of keeping his crown, and the cataſ-
trophe daily approached. The magnificent equipages of the nobles advanced towards the ſea-coaſt
to receive the Duke of Longueville, who was deſtined for the throne. That Prince was yet upon

(a) Zaluſki, tom. i. p. 168. 263. & ſeq.

                                    the

the banks of the Rhine, which Lewis XIV. was attempting to pass; where every one knows that the Duke met with his death, by firing a pistol wantonly upon some Dutchmen, who begged their lives upon their knees. *These scoundrels* (to make use of his own expression) to whom he ordered the French to *give no quarter*, gave him none; and with him ended the branch of *Orleans-Longueville*. The death of this Prince disconcerted the league, and restored some hope to Michael.

The King, uncertain whether he was still a King or not, assembled all the nobility of the lower order, amounting to a hundred thousand, in the field of Golemba, upon the banks of the Vistula, in the Palatinate of Lublin. He had formerly made one of their body, and lived upon a level with them. To them he was principally indebted for the sceptre; he was beloved by them as an equal, and respected as a King. He chose *Stephen Czarneski* for Marshal of the Royal Confederacy, with a power of raising a new army, and restoring the ancient militia, called *Hastata*, on account of the lance it was armed with. Poland acknowledges only two Grand-Generals; but Czarneski now made a third, and indeed a great deal more; for being armed with the thunder of war, and the sword of justice, he was in fact a Dictator, who could either acquit or condemn at pleasure. The confederates took an oath to him, to maintain King Michael upon the throne at the hazard of their lives and fortunes; and the religion of an oath is as much respected in Poland, as it was in the time of their ancestors, the Sarmatians. The Senators and all persons in office were summoned to join them in a limited time, upon pain of confiscation of goods and loss of dignity. The time allowed was a very short one, and had it not been for the resolution Sobieski took, they must all have thrown themselves at the feet of a provoked King,

Y. 1672. King, and a Dictator, from whom no mercy was to be expected.

The Grand-General affembled his army at Lovicz, in the Palatinate of Rava, the citadel of which town was built by an Arch-Bifhop of Gnefna. There are few inftances in Poland of convents built by Princes of the church ; and the reafon is, becaufe they are all Senators and ftatefmen. Whoever would fee that divifion of the republic to which the majority of the Senate adhered, muft have feen it at Lovicz.

The army, which now formed a confederacy in its turn, (a fpecies of league always to be dreaded) oppofed oath to oath, and fwore by the name of God and of Sobiefki, to maintain the rights and privileges of their country, as delivered down by thofe ancient warriors who had fealed them with their blood ; to recognize as Generals thofe only who had been invefted with the command before the breaking out of the difturbances ; to difcover to the Generals whatever they fhould learn, that tended to the detriment of the prefent confederacy ; to reveal none of its fecrets ; and to confider as an enemy to his country, every foldier who fhould not inlift under its banners (a).

While the republic was thus arming againft itfelf, Cuprogli having received no anfwer, procured the war he had threatened againft the Poles to be declared a juft one, and the Mufti fanctified it with his Fetfa. The orders were already iffued out, and the horfetails flying upon the feraglio. It was not mere whim, but the gaining of a victory, that made the Turks adopt this banner. Their troops being put to flight in an action, and the Great Standard taken, the General ftruck off a horfe's tail with his fabre, and fixing it to the

(a) Zalufki, tom. i. p. 396.

top

top of a pike, rallied his men, and got the victory.

Mahomet now advanced like an angry sea, ready to overwhelm Poland. The King, instead of going to meet him with the hundred thousand nobles that supported his tottering throne, and shewing by this behaviour that he deserved to reign, was employed in prosecuting the first subjects in his kingdom with all the rigour of the law. Confiscation of goods, loss of honours and dignities, degradation from nobility, was decreed against all ; but against the ringleaders, loss of life. In the last class were included Sobieski and the Primate ; and to complete the whole, a price was set upon their heads. The sentence of death made little impression upon the criminals, who were surrounded with an army that could bring their judges to the scaffold. But twenty thousand ducats might possibly tempt an assassin, especially as the sentence took off all ignominy from such an action, and converted it, upon the present occasion, into a title of honour *(a)*.

At this news, the soldiers gave a shout of indignation against the King and the confederated nobles, and laying their sabres in the form of crosses, swore to defend and avenge their General. It was necessary that such a man should either perish, or become in the end the first man of the kingdom. *I accept your protestations,* answered he, *but let us, before all things, defend our country.* He foresaw that Mahomet would open the campaign with the siege of Kaminieck, the capital of Podolia ; a place still stronger by nature than by art ; being built upon a steep rock, surrounded with the river Smotricz, and a circle of hills, extending all round the river. It had been, in all ages, the bulwark of

(a) Zaluski. tom. i. p. 444. & seq.

Poland

Poland againſt the Turks and Tartars; and had long been looked upon by the former with eyes of indignation; nor did it give the Tartars leſs offence. Sobieſki ſent thither eight regiments of foot to reinforce the garriſon : but the Governor, who was wholly devoted to the King, was afraid that theſe troops would give Sobieſki too great an authority in the place, and therefore refuſed to admit them; a fatal effect of the civil diſſentions.

Mahomet, at the head of a hundred and fifty thouſand men, paſſed the Danube, near Siliſtria, a city of Bulgaria, croſſed Walachia and Tranſylvania, threw bridges over the Nieſter at the foot of the walls of Choczin, and appeared before Kaminieck about the end of July. A hundred thouſand Tartars arrived there, by his orders, at the ſame time; commanded, upon this great occaſion, by the Cham Selim-Gjerai in perſon. The nation had not had, for a long time, a leader of ſuch diſtinguiſhed talents, both in war and peace. The Turkiſh Generals paid great regard to his Judgment; and the Tartars were ready to undertake any thing, when they had him at their head. In another country, he would have introduced politeneſs, ſciences, and arts. Whenever he could lay aſide the ſabre, he took up the pen; and Cantemir calls him an excellent Philoſopher and hiſtorian (a). His Lieutenant-Generals were his two ſons, Sultan Galga, and Sultan Nuradin. Scarce had they paid their reſpects to the Grand Seignior, when he ordered them to make incurſions as far as the Viſtula; while the Coſſacks, ſtimulated by reſentment, carried deſolation on another ſide. Mahomet was the idol of this great multitude which exhauſted the earth; but the great Cuprogli was its ſoul.

(a) Çantemir, tom. ii. p. 139.

Sobieſki, with thirty-five thouſand Poles, could not give battle to an hundred and fifty thouſand Turks before Kaminieck : he therefore abandoned this fortreſs to its dreadful fate. It was of ſtill greater importance to ſtop that torrent of Tartars which was going to overwhelm the heart of the kingdom. The Cham was ravaging Pokruſia; Sultan Nuradin, Volhinia; and Sultan Galga took the middle way through the center of the Palatinate of Ruſſia.

We muſt not loſe ſight of the hundred thouſand nobles, under the command of the King at Golemba, and Sobieſki, with his little army at Lovicz. An imprudent ſtep of Nuradin diſcovered on which ſide lay true courage, and regard for the welfare of Poland. The young Tartar, as he coaſted the Palatinate of Lublin, took his march between the two camps. The King and the nobles took it into their heads, that this motion of the Tartar was planned in concert with Sobieſki; and the alarm was ſo great, that the King did not think himſelf ſecure in the midſt of a hundred thouſand nobles; but took refuge within the walls of Lublin (a), a town about ſix leagues diſtant from his camp, and the nobility diſperſed.

Sobieſki, having nothing farther to fear from his countrymen, diſplayed all his greatneſs. The man, who had juſt been condemned to death, exerted his utmoſt to ſave his judges. He went in ſearch of the Tartars wherever they appeared. His firſt victim was Nuradin, whom he came up with and de-

(a) This capital of the Palatinate of the ſame name, is a place of great note. The courts of juſtice for all Little Poland which are eſtabliſhed here, draw thither many of the nobility, and traders of every nation. Among its buildings, the moſt noted is the palace of Mark Sobieſki, Palatine of Lublin, grandfather to John.

feated

Y. 1672. feated at the gates of Krasnobrod (a). The victory was so complete, that the General escaped almost alone to the army of Sultan Galga, his brother; who, to avoid the like disaster, marched towards the Niester, in order to join forces with the Cham. But he was prevented by the amazing diligence of Sobieski, and his loss exceeded that of his brother. The plain of Nimirow was covered with Tartars breathing their last upon the booty they had carried off; and those that remained took to flight.

Sobieski, leaving his infantry with the baggage, followed the runaways with his horse. A new battle was fought at Grudeck, and another at Komarna, whence the two Sultans escaped in the utmost disorder. Having passed the Niester, they expected to have some respite with the shattered remains of their army, but Sobieski still pursued them. They then threw themselves across two other rivers, the Stry and the Chevitz, which Sobieski also passed; and at length the two Sultans joined their father. The Cham, who had as yet been in no engagement, was strong enough to avenge his sons; but being intimidated by their disaster, and still more solicitous about the preservation of his vast booty, which also embarassed his army, and rendered it less fit for combat, he sought only to avoid an action. This booty, being the spoils of Poland, interested Sobieski still more than than the Tartar. Besides furs, silver, and gold, the Tartars were carrying off a vast quantity of cattle, both for war and agriculture; and thirty thousand slaves of all ages, sexes, and conditions, most of whom were usually em-

---

(a) This is only a village in the Palatinate of Lublin; but heroes confer distinction upon every place that is the scene of their actions.

ployed

ployed in tillage. The leaft valuable part of the
fpoil was a number of Monks. The Cham.kept
flying; Sobiefki never loft fight fight of him; and
having more experience than the Tartar, waited
for an opportunity to attack him with advantage.
He found it at laft at Kaluffa, at the foot of the
Crapack mountains, in a narrow pafs where the enemy had not room to draw up their troops. The
action was very bloody; for the Cham left upon
the field of battle fifteen thoufand flain, and all his
booty. It was an affecting fight, when the irons
were taken off from thirty thoufand Poles, to put
them upon the Tartars that were taken after the
action (*a*). This multitude of unhappy wretches,
who never more expected to fee their wives, their
children, or their homes, fell proftrate before their
deliverer, who himfelf fell proftrate before the God
of battle.

Poland was now delivered from the Tartars, but
not from the Turks. If the hundred thoufand
nobles encamped at Golemba, that Pofpolite which
the republic fo much boafts of, and which perhaps might have done wonders under a great King;
had attacked the Turks while Sobiefki preffed upon
the Tartars, who knows but Kaminieck might have
been faved? The Turks were perfectly acquainted
with fieges before the Chriftians: at that of Candy
they made parallel lines in their trenches. Upon
the prefent occafion, Cuprogli exerted all the military art. For near a month, an enormous train
of artillery had been playing upon the place, fo that
nothing was left but ruins and the rock they flood
on. This rock, however, was acceffible only by
a bridge; and the able Vifir fhuddered at the Muffulman blood that muft be fhed in an affault. He
therefore took advantage of the fault the Governor

(*b*) Lengnich. p.239.

bad

had committed. He knew that when he refused to admit Sobieski's soldiers, he had received into the town all the nobility of Podolia, men, women, and children. The Visir had recourse to bombs, which falling within so small a compass where so many people were crowded together, heaped the dead upon the dying. The cries of the women and children enervated the soldiers, and slackened the vigour of the defence. But there was yet no talk of surrendering. Cuprogli next employed another species of terror; and gave the besieged to understand, that if they did not surrender in twenty-four hours, they should all be put to the sword, old and young, down to the very infant at the breast. This menace, accompanied by all the dispositions for a general storm, struck terror into every breast, and a parley was beat on the 29th of August.

A Major of artillery, enraged at the surrendry of a place which might have been better defended, resolved not to survive so great a loss. At the entrance of the bridge there was a large tower, that served for a magazine of powder, in which he placed a match, and mounted the platform, from whence he saw the Turks enter the place, and the Poles run out to implore the mercy of the conquerors. The magazine soon blew up, and buried the officer, and all that were within a certain distance, both Turks and Poles, in its burning ruins. The Poles that escaped had great difficulty to obtain their pardon for a crime of which they were innocent.

Mahomet adhered strictly to the articles of the capitulation; but the Poles were struck with consternation, when they saw him enter the cathedral church on horseback, as Mahomet II. had formerly done the church of Saint Sophia at Constantinople. But the Poles, who were offended at this profanation, did not recollect that the Christians had

had more than once treated the Turkiſh moſques in the ſame manner, and that the outrage was reciprocal.

It is confidently ſaid, that the news of the taking of Kaminieck, which arrived in France in the month of October, had a fatal effect upon Caſimir, the late King of Poland. In extreme misfortunes, it is natural enough to reproach ourſelves with things that we could not poſſibly foreſee. If Caſimir, inſtead of abdicating, had continued upon the throne, it is highly probable that Poland would have eſcaped the cruel deſtiny that now afflicted it; for, though he was not a great King, his incapacity was not ſuch as to commit the faults of his ſucceſſor. He died at Nevers three years after his abdication, leaving his heart to France and his body to Poland: preſents of very little value, when a King does not leave great actions behind him.

Mahomet, being now maſter of Kaminieck and Podolia, ſent garriſons into all the Places of the Ukraine that were poſſeſſed by the Coſſacks, whom the Poles repented too late that they had oppreſſed. Their misfortunes however did not end here; for the Sultan reſolved to puſh his conqueſts into the heart of the kingdom; and while he himſelf ſtaid with the main body of the army, at Boudchaz, he detached forty thouſand men towards Leopol, under the command of *Caplan* Baſhaw, Governor of Aleppo. The name of *Caplan*, which was conferred upon the Baſhaw by the voice of the public, as a title of honour, ſhews the difference of ideas that prevails in different nations. An European General might perhaps be pleaſed with the title of *Lion*, but he would certainly be offended at being called *Tyger*, which is what *Caplan* means. Whether of the two has reaſon on his ſide, will admit a doubt. Be this as it will, Leopol, which was but a weak place, made a better defence than

could

Ỹ. 1672. could be expected; and when it could hold out no longer, saved itself from being pillaged and burnt, at the price of all its gold.

Every day continued to produce some new disaster. Sobieski brought back his victorious troops from the foot of the Crapack mountains, which divide Poland from Moldavia, Transylvania and Hungary. If at this juncture he had attempted to get himself proclaimed King, he would probably have succeeded. But he was wholly taken up with the Turks, and contriving a plan to attack them in the least disadvantageous manner. He sent out a large detachment to reconnoitre the camp at at Boudchaz; and the officer who commanded it, marched with such secrecy, that he surprized the Quarters of the Sultanas. The chief of the Eunuchs, who was accountable for them with his head, had not time to stab them, to prevent the prostitution of the Grand-Seignior's mistresses. They were saved by a Christian, named *Cantemir*, the *Calaux*, or Major-General of the Moldavians, a Tartar by descent, who repulsed the Poles. This service was too great to be forgot by the Sultan; and we shall see Cantemir acting hereafter in a higher sphere. The detachment rejoined the body of the army, not without some loss; but it brought the intelligence that was wanted, and Sobieski prepared to make the best of it.

Michael was in such a situation, that he dreaded the success of his own General as much as that of the Turks. Instead of generously forgetting what had past, and uniting with him for the public preservation, instead of leading to battle the hundred thousand nobles that adhered to him, he acted a part that proved the ruin of Poland. He sent to sue for peace of Mahomet at his camp at Boudchaz, leaving him master of all the conditions, except one, which was not disagreeable to the Sultan;

2 and

and this was to maintain him upon the throne of
Poland. The Ukraine and Podolia, at that time
two flourishing provinces, were yielded to the conqueror. This was the loss sustained by Poland;
the ignominy it underwent was in engaging to pay
an annual and perpetual tribute of a hundred thousand golden ducats (a). This haughty republic,
so proud of its independence, now stooped under
the yoke; and its King, like so many other Princes, became one of the first slaves of the Porte, obliged to march, at its command, against all the
enemies of its power, Christians as well as others.
Such was the infamous treaty of Boudchaz.

If we recollect the circumstances of Michael's
election, the aversion he shewed to the throne, the
tears he shed upon ascending it; and consider him
at present, keeping his seat in spite of the grandees
of the kingdom, exposed to universal contempt,
and bound in the chains of servitude; it will be
difficult not to believe, whatever moralists may say,
that a crown brings with it more pleasure than
pain. It is not Kings that deserve our pity, unless
they have great abilities, great virtues, and great
misfortunes.

The peace which Michael had just signed upon
his knees, not only covered Poland with ignominy, but was an open violation of its laws; for a
King of Poland can neither make peace nor war
without the consent of the nation; and of all the
laws which Philosophers have invented, this perhaps is the wisest.

Cuprogli, who was a good judge of men, esteemed Sobieski as much as he despised Michael: but
he wished, for the interests of the Porte, that Michael's reign might be a long one. He removed
all the Poles out of Podolia to the other side of

(a). Lengnich. p. 238.

the

the Danube, and acrofs Mount Hœmus; where thefe unhappy wretches, torn from their religion and their country, were to cultivate and people the territories of their enemies, and two thoufand Spahis, from the neighbourhood of Bender, came to fupply their place, and occupy their poffeffions.

But Cuprogli did not think this body of troops fufficient to infure his conquefts, and therefore left fourfcore thoufand men encamped at Choczin, with orders to ftay there till the Poles had forgot their liberty; and returned himfelf to Conftantinople with victory and his mafter, who had difcovered in this campaign, that there are other pleafures befides thofe of the feraglio.

The two potentates that made the moft noife this year in Europe, were the Sultan and the moft Chriftian King, both by attacking Chriftian republics, one paffing the Niefter, the other the Rhine: Mahomet with a hundred and fifty thoufand men and Cuprogli: Lewis XIV. with an hundred and thirty thoufand, and Turenne, Condé, Luxembourg, and Vauban. But the event of the two expeditions was greatly different. Lewis abandoned his conquefts with as much rapidity as he made them, and Holland remained free. Mahomet preferved his, and Poland was enflaved.

In the whole kingdom of Poland, Michael's conduct was applauded only by himfelf. Contented with preferving his Crown, and unconcerned about the judgment of pofterity, he reigned over the nobility that he had affembled in the camp of Golemba. But though all was over with the Turks, the civil war was not yet extinguifhed. Sobiefki, whofe hands were tied up by the peace, was returned to his camp at Lovicz. Michael would needs make a fhew of generofity and dignity, without being poffeffed of either: and fent an order to the army, and to the Grand General by name, to
take

take a new oath of allegiance to him; upon which condition he promised to forget what was paſt, and to reſtore all the proſcribed to their honours and eſtates.

Sobieſki anſwered, that he himſelf and the army would take the oath required, provided that the King would take a new one to the republic, without any equivocation; and ſwear to obſerve the articles which had been omitted in the *Paſta Conventa* by a deſigned precipitation. Theſe articles were a ſecurity againſt all the violations that the Primate had reproached him with. The King, highly incenſed at being put upon a level with the nation, as if it had been an affront to that Majeſty which the nation only had conferred upon him; and provoked at their refuſal of the proffered pardon, breathed nothing but vengeance *(a)*.

To ſee, in oppoſition to each other, two names, ſo reſpeċtable in the conſtitution of Poland, as that of the King and Grand-General, two confederacies ſo highly incenſed, two armies mutually menacing one another, one would have thought that a deluge of civil blood muſt have been ſpilt, and that the republic was going to dig its own grave. Upon this ſuppoſition, the following epitaph was writ for the expiring commonwealth by a royaliſt.

Sprung from the too great indulgence of Kings, nouriſhed by the arrogance of the Senators, diſturbed by the licentiouſneſs of the Equeſtrian order, proſtituted by the avarice of all the orders, reduced to pay tribute to the infidels, here lies the republic of Poland, buried at laſt under its own ruins *(b)*.

The author of the epitaph was however in too great haſte; for it is not with Warſaw as with ancient Rome, whoſe civil fury was never extinguiſh-

_____

(a) Zaluſki, tom. i. p. 434.   *(b)* Id. ibid. p. 415.

M   ed

Y. 1672. ed but in its own blood; whereas the former, more accuſtomed to combat with the laws than with arms, often puts a ſtop to the violence of its Marius's and Sylla's without coming to blows.

There yet elapſed ſome time longer in a dreadful uncertainty of what would happen. Sobieſki was reſolved not to begin the attack, his aim being to reclaim the King to a ſtricter obſervance of the laws of the republic, and a better government; a deſign which Kings will always pardon, when they prefer juſtice to arbitrary power. Michael, who liſtened only to the dictates of his revenge, had no ſcruples about ſhedding blood; but one reflection moderated his ardor. Having nothing to execute his vengeance but an undiſciplined body of nobles, and a few new raiſed troops, he was afraid of a veteran army, inured to victory, under an experienced general. In this perplexity, he liſtened to propoſals of peace. The Queen his wife, and the Auſtrian Ambaſſador made an offer of their mediation. 'Tis only in caſe of ſuch convulſions, that the republic permits its Queens and foreigners to meddle with affairs of ſtate. Rome was at all times excepted from this excluſion, and upon the preſent occaſion gave proofs of its zeal. Sobieſki received from Clement X. a very honourable brief; in which the Pontiff, after an encomium upon his great talents and glorious actions, exhorted him to ſacrifice his reſentments to the ſafety of his country, and of Chriſtendom in general, which was greatly weakened by the calamitous ſtate of Poland.

In the preſent ſituation of things, it was of much more conſequence to appeaſe Sobieſki than the King. Sobieſki was armed, and his party preſſed him to make uſe of his advantages. The King yielding to neceſſity, erazed his name, and thoſe of all the confederated nobles, out of the act
of

of proscription; after which, he sent a deputation to the camp at Lovicz, to assure them of his affection, and to invite them to a diet of pacification, which was held at Warsaw in the beginning of February.

Whether it would be prudent for Sobieski to be present at it or not, was a question of some difficulty, now discussed in the army. The officers and soldiers represented to him, with great emotion, the dangers that might attend his going. But heroes depend for protection upon the superiority of their talents, and the majesty of their virtue. Besides, it was well known at Warsaw, that the army would be ready to avenge the wrongs of its General; and fear is frequently necessary to make Kings shew a proper respect to heroes. The greater severity the King had before shewn towards Sobieski, the more he now affected to shew respect to him. At his arrival, he sent the Great Chamberlain to compliment him at the Palace of Oviasdow. Upon his coming to court, he received him with a smiling countenance, and a rankling heart, being under great anxiety what would be the event of the diet.

If any one had a right to assume a high tone in this assembly, it was certainly the man who had triumphed over the Tartars, and would have saved Poland, if Poland would have fought with him in its own defence. But he forgot the scaffold that was intended him, and the price put upon his head: no complaint escaped him upon these subjects; but he painted, in the strongest colours, the grievances of his country. He entered again upon all those that the Primate had laid open in the last diet, and went to the bottom of such as he had only touched superficially. He traced out to the Senate and Equestrian order, a plan of the regulations they ought to make, in order to reform abuses, and restore domestic tranquillity. The King was present,

as

Y. 1673. as his ſtation obliges him to be in all the aſſemblies of the nation ; but the genius of the throne
was awed by that of Sobieſki ; and Michael felt by
experience what happens too ſeldom to thoſe who
abuſe their power ; he loſt part of that which the
laws had given him.

He had alſo another wound to bear in a very ſen-
ſible part.   Sobieſki ſhed tears over the treaty of
Boudchaz, and appealed from the King to the republic, which had not ſigned its own ſlavery and
ruin.   The concluſion they came to, was to declare it void.

Such a proceeding was eaſy enough at Warſaw ;
but the queſtion was aſked, how it would be received at Conſtantinople. " With extreme indig-
" nation, no doubt, replied Sobieſki ; but we have
" courage and ſabres ſtill left us.   We will not
" wait for the enemy's coming to us, but muſt in-
" ſtantly go to them."

This loud alarm to war put the whole aſſembly
in a conſternation.   Even they who moſt diſapproved the infamous treaty of Boudchaz, were terrified at a new war with a power that had ſo lately cruſhed them.   They repreſented that the army
was not numerous ; that new levies would neither
be capable, by their experience or number, to face
the enemy ; that the revenues of the kingdom were
exhauſted ; that the people, loaded with taxes, dür-
ing a war of ſuch long continuance, were unable to
bear new ones ; and that the Ukraine and Podolia,
being in the hands of Mahomet, and fourſcore
thouſand Turks upon the frontiers, fixed the unhappy fate of Poland.   " We are indeed, ſaid they,
" reduced to ſlavery, but yet we live. Should we like
" to ſee our cities ſacked, our wives and children
" butchered, and breath our laſt upon their pant-
" ing bodies ? If we muſt again try our fortune
" againſt the Turks, let us wait at leaſt till our

I   " ſtrength

" strength is recovered, and take time to form al-
" liances and solicit subsidies. It is the common
" concern of all Christendom, as well as ours." It
was so in effect ; for from the mouth of the Borysthenes to the territories of Venice, the arms of
Mahomet preyed upon Muscovy, Hungary, Greece,
and the islands, each in their turn ; and the Poles
were of opinion, that all the Christian world should
make it a common cause.

These arguments seemed to admit of no reply.
Sobieski had occasion for all that strength of genius which subdues multitudes. It were to be
wished that the annalists of nations had preserved
those pieces of eloquence which determine the destiny of free states. For my part, I pretend to give
no more than the substance of Sobieski's discourse,
such as I find it.

" I am acquainted, says he, as well as you, with
" the small number of our forces, and the ex-
" hausted state of our finances ; but neither of
" these evils is without a remedy. The boors
" that cultivate our lands acquire a sort of liberty
" by taking arms; and soon become soldiers, if
" they are headed by a General. I demand only
" sixty thousand men to free you from the Otto-
" man yoke. But you will ask me, where we
" can find a fund to pay them ? If I were to pro-
" pose the sale of your consecrated plate, you should
" not hesitate to give your consent ; for our coun-
" try is more sacred than the implements of reli-
" gion. But I make no such proposal.——The
" republic possesses a treasure in the Castle of Cra-
" cow. Will you wait for Mahomet's coming
" to take it, as soon as he knows that it is there ?
" Let us rather employ it to break in pieces the
" chains he has laid upon us. You chuse to wait
" for a more favourable opportunity, for alliances
" and subsidies. Negotiations are tedious, the fu-

" ture

" ture is uncertain, the prefent is in our power,
" Your anceſtors would have preferred death to a
" ſingle year of ſlavery."

Whoever has di nity and eloquence ſhould never deſpair of prevailing upon great aſſemblies. The
fire of the Poliſh Démoſthenes caught the Senate
and Equeſtrian order. The treaty of Boudchaz
was declared void, the peace broke, and war re-
kindled. They fancied already that they ſaw Mahomet humbled under the ſword of the Grand-
General. The Poles, in their commendations,
have always ſomething of the ſwelling ſtile of the
Aſiatics. Some ſaid, that the Greeks would have
taken Sobieſki for the God Apollo, whoſe oracles
diſcloſed Futurity. Others were for reviving the
doctrine of Pythagoras, and inſiſted upon it, that
the ſouls of all the ancient heroes had united in one,
and paſſed into his body. It is certain that he was
greater than the King, who heard all this from his
throne.

But it is dangerous to be too great : the murmurs
of envy, and the indignation of the court, were
excited. *Lozinſki*, one of the nobles, whoſe want
of fortune made him a Plebeian in that body, as
is frequently the caſe in Poland, a man of an audacious ſpirit, and voluble tongue. roſe up and
ſaid, that he had a crime of the deepeſt dye to lay
before the republic ; that a traitor had called in
the Turks and Tartars ; that Kaminieck had been
ſold for twelve hundred thouſand florins ; that he
had ſeen this treaſure in waggons, without knowing at firſt what it was ; but that having queſtioned
the guards about it, he was told that it was the
price of Kaminieck ; that beſides this, he had ſeen,
by accident, in the hands of an officer at *Zloczow (a)*, a note for a ſum of money that was to
come from Conſtantinople for a grandee of the re-

(a) A country-houſe belonging to Sobieſki.

Y. 1673.

public; and that it was with the utmost reluctance that he accufed the Grand-General of this crime, whofe correfpondence with the enemy might complete the ruin of the ftate. (a).

It is impoffible to defcribe the aftonifhment which appeared upon every countenance. Sobiefki, without changing colour, and unmoved at every eye's being fixed upon him, addreffed himfelf to the King and the two orders, faying, " If I am guilty " of this crime, I deferve to be punifhed, and " never more to appear in the Senate. I there-" fore leave the affembly, and will not ftir from " my own houfe, till I am convicted or acquit-" ted."

There was not the leaft probability, that the man who had beat the Tartars, had called them in ; or that he who had fent eight regiments to defend Kaminieck, had fold it. The firft motion the Senate made, was rifing to ftop Sobiefki, and conjure him to defpife this calumny which deftroyed itfelf. The King thinking himfelf obliged to do the fame, came down from his throne, but Sobiefki was inflexible, and went out accompanied by the Primate and the other nobles of the confederacy. The accufer was immediately arrefted ; and the trial, by a decree of the diet, committed to four Senators and eight provincial Deputies. This proceeding was neceffary, both for the honour of the accufed, and the fafety of the ftate.

A fcene of this fort very feldom happens in abfolute monarchies, where no one dares to accufe men in high ftations : the public murmurs, but the monarch protects the crime, and thinks to fecure his authority by defending thofe who abufe it. It is only in countries of liberty, that the law tries all fubjects, without any diftinction of rank or birth.

(a) Zalufki, tom. ii.

M 4 The

The informer did not make good his charge upon the trial ; but prevaricated, and varied in his
evidence ; and besides, it was proved that *Prufi-
nou fk:* (the pretended bearer of the note in queftion) had not fet his foot in Zloczow fince the taking of Kaminieck. His falfhood being detected,
he confeffed that a powerful party had fet him upon
this calumny, by promifing to make his fortune ;
and he named two nobles of the firft rank, one a
Senator, and the other one of the chief officers of
the crown (*a*).

Sobiefki, dreading the confequences that might
follow, not to his own perfon, but to the peace of
a great number of families, perhaps alfo to the
public tranquillity, came to the Senate and declared,
that he was fatisfied with his own acquittal, and
defired the republic to flop the progrefs of this affair ; that he gave up his refentment to the ftate,
which required that its members fhould be otherwife employed than in the punifhment of private
wrongs. But the republic thought it neceffary to
pafs fentence ; and the informer being condemned
to death, was delivered up to Sobiefki himfelf, to
order his execution as Grand-Marfhal. This was
in effect faving the life of the criminal, who owed
his prefervation to the generofity of the man whom
he attempted to ruin ; but he lived, hated by all
good men, and tormented with the remorfe of his
own mind.

The two nobles who had fuborned this informer, got off for only expreffing their forrow

---

(*a*) The manufcript that I follow fuppreffes their names,
out of regard for their families ; but the fecret is krown by
all Poland. One of them, while the trial was depending, put
feveral captive Tartars to torture by fire, in order to make
them confefs that Sobiefki had ftirred up their nation againft
Poland. But virtue had more power over thefe infidels, than
over the Chriftians, who tormented them to no purpofe.

a hone Inftance of Virtue !   to

to Sobieſki, in the preſence of the twelve commiſ-
ſioners. Sobieſki took care to make the mortification as light as poſſible. The palace where he
reſided being about a hundred paces from the city,
he gave them notice that at ſuch an hour he ſhould
get on horſeback to come to the Senate. The two
nobles met him, and every thing paſſed off light-
ly. By expreſſing their ſorrow, they certainly confeſſed their crime. Why then was their ſentence
different from that of Lozinſki? But it has been
a complaint in all ages, that the inſtruments of
crimes are puniſhed, and the authors ſpared.

The acquittal of Sobieſki gave great ſatisfaction
to all who loved their country, and particularly
to the confederated nobles, who were now no
longer united by that bond. The King himſelf
thought he was obliged to expreſs his joy. Every
thing was calmed in the diet, and the public wel-
fare was the only object of its conſultations.

The Primate Prazmowſki did not long enjoy
that reſtoration of public order to which he had
ſo much contributed. He appeared at Warſaw, even
before the arrival of Sobieſki, without any thing
to protect him but his dignity. A dangerous illneſs confined him to his bed, which he was fated
never more to riſe from. The court ſent frequently to enquire after his health, rather to know the
moment of its getting rid of him, than to lament
his death. He did not live to ſee the end of the
diet; but before he cloſed his eyes, he proteſted, in
words, and declared in his will, that whatever he
had done in the preſent reign, had been for the
ſake of the laws, of liberty, and his country, and
that he expected his reward from the Sovereign
Lord of Kings and people. He was a Prelate,
who, with great qualities, had perhaps carried the
zeal of his patriotiſm to too great an exceſs againſt
the King. But love for one's country is ſo noble
a paſſion,

a passion, that its excesses, even at the hour of death, still pass for virtues ; and the opposite party were obliged by decency to lament the man they hated (a).

The diet ended happily with recommending to the care of the Grand-General, all the preparations for a war which must end in the preservation of Poland, or its total ruin. The treasure of Cracow, which had been laid up for several centuries, was brought to the capital. It consisted of Jewels of every sort, set in gold. The Grand-Treasurer Morstyn claimed a right of being entrusted with it, in order to its distribution : and indeed it was a privilege belonging to his office. But in so pressing a juncture, the Grand-General dreaded every thing that looked like form, as being a source of delay; and therefore the treasure was put into his hands. The arts of Luxury were, at that time, so little known in Poland, that they were forced to send for workmen from Vienna, Venice, and Breslaw to value the jewels; and the money they sold for was distributed to the officers to raise recruits.

It was soon discovered that this fund would not be sufficient to pay the great number of troops which it was resolved to keep on foot. The republic therefore imposed a new subsidy, which was paid with surprising readiness, considering how much the nation was exhausted. But extraordinary imposts are not so much dreaded, in a free government, as under an absolute monarchy. The subjects of the former know that they are laid on in cases of necessity only, and will last but a short time.

While the recruits were raising, Sobieski dispatched spies into Walachia and Tartary, towards

(a) Zaluski, tom. i. p. 439, & seq.

the

the Danube, and to the camp at Choczin; who brought back intelligence, that there were some commotions in Walachia, that Tartary was quiet, that after Mahomet's departure, the bridges over the Danube were broke down, and that there was no appearance of their being erected again. But they gave a terrifying account of the camp at Choczin, which they described as looking like an immense fortress, erected to command Poland, on account of the communication it had with Podolia and Kaminieck by its bridges over the Niester.

Sobieski, without deceiving himself as to the risk he ran, but pleased with the greatness of the attempt, dispatched courier after courier to the Grand-General of Lithuania, Michael Paz, to hasten the march of his troops. The Lithuanian army did not arrive till the end of September in the plain of Glinian, a few leagues from Leopol, where the Poles waited for them with great impatience, and not without reason; for it was time to put an end to the campaign, rather than to begin it.

Sobieski dissembled the vexation he felt at this delay, but had soon a greater to bear. He was far from imagining that the King, who neither loved nor understood war, and had hitherto never quitted the court, would put himself at the head of the troops upon so critical an occasion. But dark suspicion is sometimes a more active principle than the love of glory. The King, who was credulous to excess, could never efface from his mind the reports which had been so often confuted, that Sobieski was not always inaccessible to the gold of the infidels; and besides, having been long jealous of that esteem which he could not obtain himself, he saw with pain the army acquiring a habit of obeying only its General. He therefore came to take upon him the command. Sobieski, and

4 all

all who loved their country, foresaw great inconveniencies from this step.   Never was there greater need of a commander who could act in person : all others were fit only to hinder and perplex the operations.

The King's first proceeding was to call a council in his tent, where he proposed it as a matter of debate, whether it were prudent to provoke so formidable a power as the Turk. The Grand-Chancellor, Andrew Olsowski, one of his favourites, answered, at the hazard of displeasing him, *We have already passed the Rubicon : it is now too late to look back (a).* Paz, who beheld with an eye of dissatisfaction Sobieski's laurels, though he had gathered some himself, said, in an ironical tone, *I have provided my army for a seven year's expedition, and since we are bent upon a crusade, I am sorry that the true cross is no longer at Jerusalem.* Sobieski rose to speak in his turn : " I expected, says he, " that our deliberations would have turn-" ed upon other subjects. To what purpose is " it to debate in a private council upon what a " national assembly has already decided ? Have we " forgot that we ourselves made part of that assem-" bly ? And do we also forget the obedience we " owe to the republic ? Every thing is already " settled ; we have nothing to do but to execute. " We have lost already too much time."   Paz, being hard pressed with this reasoning, had nothing to object, but that he expected to be joined by more troops ; a time of junction was therefore assigned him, and he accepted it.

The King, after this useless council, would make a review of the army. Those who are acquainted with Poland will be astonished that it could assemble fifty thousand men in so short a time. But

(a) A saying of Cæsar's, when he marched against Rome.

Sobieski

Sobiefki created every thing. The King commended the fine appearance of the troops, but they were not difpofed to return him any compliment; for they confidered him only as a weak Prince, who had fet his hand to the flavery of Poland. Such an act of meannefs could not be expiated under whole centuries of virtue; and befides, he had not that warlike air, which takes fo much with the foldiery; that exalted mien, which indicates a hero.

He was dreft in the French manner, (a fure way of giving offence, becaufe every country is attached to its own cuftoms) covered with ribbands, his hat adorned with a plume of feathers, and a cane in his hand inftead of the ftaff of command. He looked as if he were to lead up a ball, when they were marching to the field of battle. He did not go through with the review; for his colour changed on a fudden, and a cold fweat ran down his face. An illnefs feized him in the reins, and he was carried to Leopol, where he had more need of phyfic than the army had of him (a).

Sobiefki, whofe prefence was more valued than the King's, put himfelf in motion, and entered upon a march of fix weeks. When he arrived upon the banks of the Niefter, he halted fome days to wait for the Lithuanians, who there joined him. Hitherto the troops had fhewn great alacrity; but provifions begun to grow fcarcer, the roads more difficult, and winter was advancing with its frofts. There was in the army a party devoted to the court, always ready to take every opportunity of fowing difcontent. They now difguifed themfelves under the mafk of regard to the public, and demanded a council of war; which accordingly affembled, and was very numerous. The harangues that were made were dictated by fear

(a) Lengnich. p. 243.

only;

only: nothing was dwelt upon but rivers swelled by rain, immense forrests to cross, superior armies to attack, sickness and famine to encounter. Where was the prudence, it was asked, of beginning the campaign so late, and destroying, by this means, the heroes of the senate, the power of the Equestrian order, and all the strength of Poland?

Sobieski, filled with indignation to see Poland conquered before it had fought, spoke in strong terms, of the ignominy there would be in turning back after a march that must have attracted so much notice, and of the danger of leaving the republic any longer in chains. " I know, says he, that an Aga is
" set out from Constantinople to come and demand
" that infamous tribute which we submitted to in
" the last peace; and that he is bringing to our
" King that ignominious (a) vestment, which will
" rank him among the slaves of the Porte. You
" are afraid, you say, of famine. Do you suppose
" that I have not taken all proper precautions?
" You shall have supplies of provisions where you
" least expect it. You are apprehensive of the
" number of your enemies. Must we therefore
" be equal in number in order to beat them? But
" the Porte has not yet brought into the field those
" immense bodies of troops which strike Europe
" with terror. It has only fourscore thousand men
" under the walls of Choczin; and 'tis to Choczin
" that I am conducting you. If the officers de-
" sert me, I flatter myself, at least, that the sol-
" diers, with whom I have so often been victori-
" ous, will follow where I lead them. I will ei-

(a) The Caphtan, which the Sultan sometimes gives to the Ambassadors of foreign Princes, who consider it as a mark of honour; but to their masters it would be a badge of dependence.

" ther

" ther return with victory, or expire upon the car-
" cafs of fome Turk (a)."

Difcourfes of this fort are more neceffary where
men are free, than in abfolute governments, where
every thing fubmits to the dictates of blind obedience. They often raife the finking fpirits of an
army ; but on the prefent occafion, no fuch effect
was produced. Sobiefki's harangue was not followed with that agreeable murmur which betokens ap-
plaufe. On the contrary, the difobedience encreafed ; and next morning, at break of day, Sobiefki was told that the Lithuanians refufed to
march any farther. We have here an inftance of
the ill confequences that follow from an army's
confifting of two independent parts, one of which
may induftrioufly avoid the mark that the other
aims at. Paz alledged that the Polifh army fhewed
no concern whether the Lithuanians followed or
not; that by marching firft, it left nothing but famine behind it ; that the term for which the army
was paid, was expiring, and the campaign near
its end ; with many other fpecious reafons, which
are never wanting, when a man aims at diftreffing
his rival.

Sobiefki fent to him the Standard-Bearer of Pofnania, Scorazowfki, a man of eloquence, and agreeable to him whom it was neceffary to perfuade. He
did his country more fervice upon this occafion,
than if he had expofed his life in a field of battle,
for Paz liftened to his reafons, and from this moment the paffage of the Niefter was refolved on.
The river being greatly fwelled, and no ford to be
found, thofe who had fhewn moft reluctance, were
now the foremoft to fwim acrofs it, as if they aimed
to wipe off the ftain upon their characters. So-

(a) Zalufki, tom. i. p. 493.

biefki

biefki put a ftop to this rafh impetuofity, which coft the lives of feveral; a bridge was made, which he himfelf was the laft in paffing; and the army advanced into the Bucovine, a foreft of thirty leagues long, and as many broad, where a branch of the Crapack mountains forms defiles, fo extremely difficult to pafs, that even a traveller cannot do it without fhuddering.

It feems probable, that at Conftantinople they knew nothing as yet of the breach of the treaty, and the march of the Poles. The army met the Turkifh Envoy coming to demand the firft payment of the tribute. He behaved with all the haughtinefs that he thought might be fhewn with impunity to conquered tributaries. Sobiefki afked for his letters, in order to open them. *That honour*, replied he, *belongs only to thy mafter, to whom they are directed; and nothing but death fhall hinder me from obeying the orders of the invincible Mahomet*. Sobiefki was tempted to put him in irons, or at leaft to cut off his beard, which in the eaft is the greateft of all affronts. But he refpected the law of nations, and fuffered him to continue his journey, while the army advanced into the foreft, where they expected to have the paffes difputed. But the enemy did not appear till they arrived in the plain on the other fide, and then only a few fmall bodies, which retired with great expedition.

Sobiefki haftened his march along the banks of the Pruth, antiently called Hierafus, which falls into the Danube. 'Twas on the banks of this river that the Czar Peter in 1711, found on a fudden his army without provifions, or forage, and a hundred and fifty thoufand Turks in front. At this moment he was more wretched than his rival Charles XII. at Pultowa; but this moment was quickly over. A woman faved him and his army by

by negotiating the peace of the Pruth; and from
being the wife of a common dragoon, she married
the Emperor, and succeeded him in the throne.

Sobieski, leaving the Pruth, appeared on the 9th
of November before the camp of Choczin. The
town on the right side of the river was defended by
a high citadel, and a fort on the left side covered
the head of a bridge. In this very place, it was,
that fifty years before, when Sultan Ofman was defeated, Sobieski's father had performed such great
exploits: the son was now attempting greater, with
this difference only, that at that time the Poles defended the camp, and at present they came to attack it. The Serafkier Hufleim, a disciple of the
famous Cuprogli, was Commander in Chief, and
had with him fourscore thousand of those veteran
troops that had conquered the isle of Candy. There
were in the army several Bashaws with three tails;
but Mahomet had sent Hufleim a *fourth*, that he
might have the command. The title of *Serafkier*
is given to all Commanders in Chief, who represent the Vifir. Hufleim had exhausted the country
for ten or twelve leagues round, to supply his
camp with provisions, while the Poles, who had
most of them never been in any action, were in
want of many neceffaries.

A council of war was held in the night, in which
Paz, weighing the inequality of forces, protefted
that it would be a punishable piece of temerity to
expofe to certain deftruction the laft refource the
republic was poffeffed of; and that, as for himself,
he would retire at fun-rising with his Lithuanians,
to preferve them for the fervice of his country.

Sobieski, more haraffed by friends than enemies,
anfwered, that he had forefeen every thing that
now prefented itfelf, except this refolution of Paz;
that the fituation of things was far from giving
him any terror; that it was much more dangerous

N   to

to retire before an enemy of fuperior ftrength than to attack them; and that, in fhort, the only favour he defired of him was to ftay and be a fpectator of the firft blows.

Paz himfelf loved glory; and fince Sobiefki was obftinately bent upon feeking it, he would have been greatly mortified at his finding it without him.

On the 10th every thing was prepared for the attack. There was in the Polifh army a body of Coffacks, gained over by Sobiefki's liberality. Their leader, Samuel Motovildo, impatient to fignalize himfelf at their head, opened the fcene, without waiting for the General's order. He was already mounted upon the entrenchments, when he fell dead upon the body of a janizary whom he had juft killed. This brave man had been a flave nineteen years in the Turkifh galleys, and had fet himfelf at liberty by his courage, with three hundred companions of his ill fate. He made himfelf mafter of the galley in which he was chained, and landed at Venice dyed with the blood of his Tyrants. Such a man deferved to die in freedom (a). His men were all cut to pieces.

But this was not the day that Sobiefki deftined for the effufion of blood. He continued with his army in battalia, hoping that the enemy, with fuch a fuperiority, would come out of their camp. But the day was fpent in cannonading. Towards the evening an unexpected event increafed the forces of the Poles. On the right of the Turks, there was a feparate camp of between feven and eight thoufand Walachian and Moldavian horfe, which, tho' Chriftians, were under the command of the infidels. Thefe troops did not anfwer the expectations of the Serafkier, either in number or beauty; and the two Hofpodars who conducted them were there-

(a) Zalufki, tom. i. p. 498.

fore

fore treated like flaves. The Serafkier forgot him-felf fo far as to ftrike the Moldavian with his battle-ax. The Princes, ftimulated by revenge, came and offered Sobiefki themfelves and their troops. The Turks beheld this defertion with indignation, but were unable to prevent it *(a)*.

The following night was extremely fevere for the foldiers to continue under arms. They were froze by the fnow, which fell in great abundance, but they faw Sobiefki vifit the pofts, reft himfelf upon the carriage of a cannon, and refufe a tent. At break of day, he obferved that the ene-my's ranks were thinner than ufual. The fame number of colours was flying upon the parapet; but much fewer janizaries were to be feen. The Turks, accuftomed to a mildnefs of climate, which the Poles are unacquainted with, are lefs capable of fatigue. Their ftrength was exhaufted by hav-ing been four and twenty hours under arms in fuch fevere weather, and thinking that the Poles would not dare to attack them in open day-light, they were retired to take a little reft.

This is the moment that I waited for, faid Sobi-efki to the officers who were about him: *carry my orders for the attack* ; and he inftantly fet them an example, which, upon any other occafion, would be found fault with in a General. Obferving that the firft brigades were wavering between courage and fear, he made his own regiment of dragoons, a troop formed by himfelf, alight from their horfes, and putting himfelf at their head, he marched up to the Turkifh entrenchments. He was too bulky to mount with eafe; and while his men were affift-ing him, he was all the while expofed to the ene-my's fire, but at length appeared upon the para-pet with his dragoons. The foot, feeing his dan-

(a) Cantemir, tom. ii. p. 96.

ger,

Y. 1673. ger, and trembling for him, rushed on violently on the right and left to sustain him, and forcing the first posts one upon another, turned their own cannon against them.

In the mean time, Jablonowski, Palatine of Russia, made a motion of the utmost importance. The cavalry had not yet forced their way, and the infantry was afraid of being surrounded, if they advanced too far. He therefore came round by the camp which the Moldavians had quitted, and forced through with the Pancerns. Sobieski had fought on foot for near an hour: he was at length supplied with a horse, and the rest of the cavalry soon entered through the entrenchment itself.

Surprize occasions greater confusion than fire and sword. The Turks being pushed on all sides, lost many men and much ground. But the Poles, finding a greater number of empty tents than of enemies, stopped to pillage; a common fault with troops that are not under the strictest discipline. If the victory was at all uncertain, it was at this juncture. The Turks, charmed at the power of their wealth, took courage and repulsed the victors. Sobieski with the Towariiz sustained this first shock: and was seconded by Jablonowski with the Pancerns. Lesczinski, Palatine of Podalchia, brought up the plunderers to their colours; and victory, which seemed to be departing, appeared again, accompanied with order.

Sobieski, in the heat of the action, did not neglect to take care of consequences. He ordered the Baron de Boham, a French officer, to march to the bridge to cut off the enemy's retreat (a). By this time, there were none who stood their ground but the janizaries only, who durst not give

(a) He broke down the bridge, apprehending he might be forced from his post.

way

way in the prefence of the brave Soliman who commanded them. The Serafkier, on his part, did all
that could be expected from a General who was
forced in his camp. He rallied and brought back
to action his broken fquadrons.

But when fome of the runaways, being repulfed
from the bridge, brought intelligence that the retreat was cut off, the Turks, inftead of deriving
frefh courage from defpair, had no fenfation left
but that of terror. A body of between fix and
feven thoufand horfe endeavoured to efcape in a
place where the rock was lower than ufual; but
were charged by the Lithuanians, who forced their
way by that very entrance, and drove them back
upon the field of battle, where they ran full fpeed
againft a body of Polifh horfe. Sobiefki, who
was every where, happened to be in this body.
Wo be to that General, who, on fuch an occafion, cannot act the foldier. Sobiefki could; and
fortune affifted him as much as his own valour.
A Turk aimed at him a mortal blow, which was
received by a young hero, named Zelinfki, whofe
death was quickly revenged; and there fucceeded
a feries of fingle combats in the midft of a general action. At laft, the Palatine of Kalifch and the
Caftellan of Pofnania, came up with a body of horfe
and difengaged the Poles. The whole camp was
covered with expiring infidels. Soliman was juft
wounded and taken prifoner in the midft of the janizaries; and that brave corps at length gave way.
The Spahis pufhed on their horfes at random, with
no other view but to avoid the fabres of their pur-
fuers. The Serafkier covered with wounds, thought
only how to fave the wretched remains of his army;
but how to effect it, was the difficulty. The only
way of retiring that he could difcover, was either
a few paths acrofs the rocks, or the waves of the
Niefter.   N 3

From

From this moment, the ftate of the Turkifh army no longer prefented the idea of a battle, but of a complete rout, where deftruction was multiplied in all its various forms. Here the flying fquadrons throw themfelves from the top of a rock, and are dafhed in pieces againft other rocks below, where men and horfes are heaped one upon another, to the height of feveral Pikes. There the broken infantry take refuge towards the citadel, which being capable of containing no more, fends them back to the fabres of the enemy. At a greater diftance, the cavalry plunge into the river, and are delivered, by being fhot in the midft of it, from this fcene of horror. Even fuch as reached the other fide, or had croffed before the breaking of the bridge, were not fafe. They drew themfelves up in battalia, to receive and protect fuch of their companions as fhould attempt the paffage; but the impetuous Mandreofki, a Brigadier of horfe, could not bear to fee them live. He throws himfelf into the river, followed by his brigade: but receives a wound from a mufket-ball in the midft of the river, which deprives him of all fenfe. He was brought back to the place he fet out from, and loft his life ten years after in a ftill more celebrated battle. His troop ftill purfuing its point, is joined by other fquadrons; and the enemy being every where broke, retires for fafety under the walls of Kaminieck.

The river was covered with ten thoufand turbans, and the earth with twenty thoufand flain, among which were eight thoufand janizaries. The victory coft the Poles between five and fix thoufand killed and wounded; among which, the death of the Great-Huntfman of the Crown was particularly lamented. Biginfki was dragged from under a heap of carcafes the next day after the battle, and had the pleafure of knowing that his fuppofed death was regretted. If we confider the vaft fuperiority

riority of the conquered army, the whole looks like a fable. But one of these two suppositions will account for it; either it is a great disadvantage to wait for an enemy in entrenchments, or heaven fought on the side of the Poles. There is a third, which will perhaps give a still better solution. When men fight, not for the whim of a sovereign, but for the real interest of themselves and their country, they are raised above the level of humanity.

The Poles took a great number of prisoners, whose destiny stained the brightness of Sobieski's laurels. It is highly proper, that the mischiefs, which men in power do to their fellow creatures, should be related by history. If they would have nothing but good recorded of them, they should take care that all their actions be of that sort. No sooner had Sobieski returned thanks to God, by having mass said in the magnificent pavilion of the Turkish General, than he commanded the prisoners, who made no farther resistance, to be all massacred; and to this first act of barbarity he added a second, by an order to the inhabitants of the country, to put to death every infidel that had taken refuge in their houses, upon pain of being put to death themselves. He forgot that the God of battle (a title which he never assumes but when madmen disturb the earth) is still more the God of mercy. More than one Bashaw perished in this slaughter; but he had not the cruel satisfaction of involving in it the Serafkier Husseim, who had escaped in time (a).

He shewed more humanity to the wretches who waited for their fate in the citadel of Choczin, which contained vast riches, being the place where the Greeks, Armenians, and Jews kept their ma-

(a) Zaluski, tom. i. p. 498, & seq.

N 4

gazines

gazines for the camp. The artillery was brought up againft it the fame day ; and it could not poffibly hold out : a detachment which came to its relief from Kaminieck being quickly repulfed by Samuel Cofacowfki. After which, Sobiefki fent them a Polifh Deputy, accompanied by the Bafhaw Czaufio, a prifoner of diftinction, to fummon them to furrender, or to expect to be all put to the fword. Thefe unhappy people had ftill the courage to demand an honourable capitulation, and to be conducted to Kaminieck, with as much of their effects as they could carry away upon forty waggons. The honeft Turk, who read the conditions to Sobiefki, watering the paper with his tears, admonifhed him to reflect, that victory is not invariably appropriated to any nation ; that God punifhes fuch as make a bad ufe of it; and that he has more than once abafed, on the morrow, thofe whom he had exalted the day before. Sobiefki granted almoft all he afked; and the Bafhaw who commanded at Kaminieck, immediately acknowledged the favour, by difmiffing, without ranfom, fifty Polifh prifoners. The Poles, in all their writings, treat the Turks as barbarians : but thefe barbarians fometimes give leffons of virtue even to Chriftians.

The Lithuanian General, Paz, is reproached in hiftory, for his behaviour upon the march, and before the attack ; but hiftory does him alfo the juftice to own, that, during the action, his natural courage and love for his country regained the afcendant ; that he and his Lithuanians behaved like heroes, and left it doubtful whether the Poles or they deferved the palm of valour.

While this was paffing between the Pruth and the Niefter, the Turkifh Aga proceeded on his journey ; and arriving at Leopol about the beginning of November, found the King lying there at

the

the point of death. The diforder, which firft attacked him at the review, was fo increafed as to leave no hopes of recovery. An ulcer in his kidnies, blood inftead of urine, convulfions in his ftomach, and continual vomitings, left him fo fmall a remnant of life as would not permit him to give audience. And yet the Ambaffador infifted upon it, with greater haughtinefs than he had even fhewed in the army. He declared, that at all events, he would deliver to the King the Sultan's letter, and the cafket committed to his charge. The great officers of the crown and the court were in a tormenting dilemma. They apprehended the letter might be writ in an imperious manner, in the ftile of a Lord to his vaffal; they were afraid even to look at the fuperfcription, which might be changed, fince the time that Poland became tributary to the Porte. The Vice-Chancellor, before he would propofe the audience to the dying King, demanded a fight of the letter, and of the cafket, which gave ftill greater uneafinefs. Their imaginations ran upon nothing but the ftaff of command, and the veftment, which are the mortifying tokens of vaffalage that the Grand-Seignior fends to his tributaries in three quarters of the world. To put fuch a veftment upon the dying Prince, would be a fatal blow to his life, and an eternal affront to Poland. What increafed their apprehenfions was, that there was no letter for the Vice-Chancellor. This unufual circumftance left them in a ftate of uncertainty and fufpence, which made them fear the very worft, and in the mean time the Ambaffador was obftinate in his refufal to make any difcovery, except at the King's bed's-fide. It would feem, that they might have left him to vent his diffatisfaction, without endeavouring to get the better of his obftinacy; but the confequences, even in this cafe, appeared tremendous. They

knew

knew not what fuccefs the army would have; the laft intelligence from it was not promifing; and if the expedition to Choczin mifcarried, what yoke would for the future be heavy enough for the van- quifhed? Addrefs is ufually called in to the affift- ance of weaknefs; the Poles diffembled, and flat- tered the Aga; giving him to underftand that the King was recovering his ftrength, and in a few days would be able to give him an audience. In effect, the ulcer was opened, and the phyficians entertained hopes; but nature, which fo often deceives them, both on the favourable and unfavourable fide, had decided againft them. Michael died on the 10th of November, without leaving any iffue, at the age of thirty-five, after four years fpent upon the throne, or rather, fpent in uneafinefs, infamy, difturbance and horror. If the fceptre is capable of making any man happy, it muft be him only who is able to wield it. Michael, who was naturally of a hu- mane temper, would have been a good King, if he had been a great one; but his want of capacity made both himfelf and his fubjects unhappy. All that he got by being exalted to the regal dignity was, to be drenched with gall, without the leaft infufion of comfort; he felt all the evil, but none of the good; for he expired on the evening, before the victory of Choczin.

Three days after, the hope of a new triumph gave frefh pleafure to Sobiefki, who being inform- ed by the Moldavian Prince, that ten thoufand Turks had croffed the Danube, and were advan- cing through Moldavia to come and increafe the camp at Choczin, took with him part of his ca- valry, without baggage; and after a forced march of four days, arrived at Pererita, upon the banks of the Pruth. Here he had the mortification of finding that he had miffed his aim; for Kaplan Bafhaw, the Turkifh General, having learnt by the

way

way the defeat at Choczin, had marched back to-wards the Danube.

Sobieſki, upon his return to the army, formed a plan to make the greateſt advantages of his ſuc-ceſs; but every thing concurred to hinder him. Paz, who had been dragged on to victory, was in no humour to follow him; and had taken the road to Lithuania with his troops during Sobieſki's ab-ſence. The Poles were ſtill earneſt in the cauſe; but the news of the King's death either changed their inclinations, or furniſhed many of them with a fair pretence for going home. Such as were load-ed with the ſpoils of the eaſt were impatient to lay up their booty ſafe: others, who were tired with the labours of ſo ſevere a ſeaſon, eagerly wiſhed for the end of it: and all alledged, that the election of a new King was the only thing that ſhould em-ploy the attention of Poland.

Sobieſki repreſented, that the election could not come on before the ſpring; and that the winter might be uſefully employed in driving the Turks out of the Ukraine, and perhaps in making an at-tempt upon Kaminieck. He produced a letter from the Grand Chancellor, adviſing them to purſue the victory, and notifying the death of the King. It is ſurprizing that Sobieſki, who had ſo many claims to the crown, if merit be any claim at all, ſhould be ſo little in haſte to return to Warſaw, and form a party in his own favour. Inſtead of this, he was buſy in animating the Poles to new enterprizes; but was ſtopped by an order from the Primate Czartoriſki, requiring him to bring back the army, without delay, into Poland. The will of the In-terrex, is more ſacred than that of the King, and nothing was left but to obey. All that the Grand-General could do, was to leave a garriſon at Choc-zin, where the Poles raiſed a hillock which they call *Mogila*, to be a rude monument of a glorious victory.

The Victory was in my opinion great, but not glorious [*handwritten marginalia, partly illegible*]

Y. 1673. victory. It would have been unjuft, to abandon, to the vengeance of the Turks, the Moldavians and Walachians, who came and joined Sobiefki. He therefore detached a body of eight thoufand men, under the command of the Grand-Standard-Bearer Sienawfki, to defend the two Hofpodars, and their territories; but the defence was of very little fervice. The Moldavian *Petreczeïcus*, foon funk under the Ottoman power, and took refuge in Poland, where the loweft Staroft affumed a fuperiority over an ejeted Prince. He heartily repented his not having bore one affront, rather than expofe himfelf to a thoufand. At length death delivered him. The Walachian *Gregory*, after having been amufed by the Emperor, applied for protection to the Pope, who made a propofal to him of entering into the Roman communion: but he made his peace with Conftantinople, and continued a Schifmatic and a Prince (*a*). Sobiefki, however, was not wanting in gratitude; for he did every thing for them that lay in his power; after which, he took, much againft his own inclination, the road to Poland.

If we confider this celebrated expedition on the fide of conqueft, it prefents no very advantageous idea. The only acquifition was Choczin, a heap of cottages covered with ftraw. The citadel, which was a good one for the country, was retaken by the Turks in the winter. But if we view it on the fide of glory, and as being the prefervation of Poland, there are very few of equal luftre, or fo highly interefting. It prevented the treaty of Boudchaz from being ratified by the firft payment of the tribute; fufpended the flavery of Poland; weakened the Turks by the deftruction of a veteran army; and taught them, that Poland, with only mo-

(*a*) Cantemir, tom. ii. p. 139.

derate

derate forces, was capable of braving their enormous power.

Sobieſki, covered with [glory,] now came to Leopol, where he received the congratulations of all the orders of the ſtate. The moſt diſtant Palatinates ſent Deputies to the deliverer of his country. Let Kings be intoxicated, if they can, with the incenſe which is ſo profuſely, but involuntarily, offered them after victories, in which they have commonly no ſhare: that which Sobieſki received was the tribute of gratitude and joy. At the report of the triumph of Choczin, every one left off mourning for a King who was not lamented, to appear in colours, and aſſume the language of joy. If any regretted the King's death, it was the Turkiſh Envoy, becauſe he was hindered thereby from executing his commiſſion, and dreaded the ſeverity of the Porte. But the Primate gave him a certificate, atteſting that Michael was dead before the Envoy could fulfil his inſtructions.

In the mean time Warſaw was filled with intrigues that were forming for the crown; and Sobieſki ſtaid at Leopol, as if he had no pretenſions. The beſt title to it, he thought, was continuing to defend his country. He therefore fixed his reſidence at Leopol for the winter, where he was in readineſs to reſtrain the incurſions of the Tartars and the Coſſacks, or to endeavour, if an opportunity offered, to win over the latter.

End of the THIRD BOOK.

THE

THE

HISTORY

OF

JOHN SOBIESKI

KING OF POLAND.

BOOK IV.

Y. 1674. THE diet of Convocation, which precedes that of election, was summoned to meet on the 15th of January. It was to have ended in fifteen days: but the defire which every one had to fee Sobiefki prefent at it, caufed it to be prorogued to the 22d of February. He refufed however to gratify this earneft wifh, being wholly taken up with the enemy. Every thing went on quietly in the diet, under the direction of the Primate, to whom the republic was indebted for the general tranquillity it enjoyed during the whole interregnum, which is commonly a time of confufion, of which robbers and feditious perfons take advantage. The death of the King, and the time of election were notified, according to cuftom, to the powers of Eu-

4

rope :

rope : and the field of election was opened on the first of May. It muft be remembered, that there are two ways of chufing the Kings of Poland ; either in the General Affembly of the nobility, called *the diet on horfeback*, or only by the votes of the Senators and the Deputies who reprefent the nobility and the provinces. The Primate, fearing the dangers of the former method, which is generally attended with tumult and violence, managed matters with fuch dexterity, that he got the latter to be preferred ; in which cafe, the nation being reprefented by its wifeft members, may expect a better choice.

Sobiefki fhewed fo much indifference for the crown, that, notwithftanding the repeated inftances of the Electors, who had a mind to profit by his fuperior talents, he did not arrive till the 10th of May. Perhaps his delay might be partly founded in policy, in order to be more taken notice of. This was the firft time of his appearing before the affembly of the Eftates fince the victory of Choczin ; and he was received with a pomp which might well aftonifh the foreigners then prefent, who were not accuftomed, in their own countries, to fee Generals receive the honours of the triumph.

There were fix competitors bidding for the crown by their Ambaffadors.

Prince Thomas of Savoy offered two millions, which would pay the troops of the republic for fome months, together with a fupply of five thoufand foot till the conclufion of a peace with the Turk. Befides this, he promifed to fell all his poffeffions in Savoy and France, amounting in value to nine millions of florins, which fum fhould be applied to the ufes of the republic, in order to rid it of the inconvenience it fuffered by the quantity of bad coin ;

Y. 1673. coin; and for the execution of thefe promifes, the Duke of Savoy his uncle was to be guarantee.

The Duke of Modena had little of his own to give, but was profufe in offering the protection of others. The intereft of the two Cardinals Barberini, which was at his difpofal; his alliances and connections of friendfhip with all the fovereigns of Europe, and particularly with the houfe of Auftria. The great grandfon of Philip II. flattered himfelf with being powerfully affifted by the two branches of that family againft the Turks.

Prince George of Denmark, who was afterwards hufband to a Queen (a), without being a King, befides pecuniary offers, made a promife of a defenfive alliance between the two kingdoms. Another article, of greater confequence perhaps, but which made little impreffion upon the Poles, was his offering to initiate them into commerce, by laying open to them immediately that of the Eaft-Indies.

The Prince of Tranfylvania made an offer of fifteen millions, engaged to unite his principality with the crown of Poland, and to maintain a body of fifteen thoufand men, as long as the war with the Turks fhould continue. The propofal feemed fo confiderable, that it was not thought to be in his power to execute it.

Prince Charles of Lorrain, over whofe head the crown had hung fufpended in the laft election, appeared again with the hopes of fixing it there upon the prefent occafion. He was no richer than before, but had found good fecurity, no lefs than the Emperor and the King of Spain, for the performance of his promifes. He engaged to furnifh five thoufand foot for the expedition againft the Turks, to take five hundred Polifh nobles into his

(a) Anne, Queen of England.

body

body of guards, to found an academy for the education of a hundred more nobles, to erect two forts, one against the Turks, the other against the Muscovites, to advance nine months pay for the Polish army, with a promise of assigning over to Poland one half of the revenues of Lorrain and the dutchy of Bar, as soon as he should be in possession of them.

Prince William of Newburg, who was afterwards Elector Palatine, flattered himself with having better success than his father, who was rejected in the last election, and bade higher than all his rivals. Instead of six or nine months pay for the army, he stipulated for a whole year. His father was to give up to him immediately the revenues of the Dutchy of Juliers to be applied to the exigencies of the republic, till, by means of the immense possessions that were hereafter to fall to him, his liberality should be as boundless as his gratitude. A still more tempting circumstance in the present critical situation, was his offering to take into his pay twenty thousand Swedes and six thousand Brandenburghers, to be employed against the Turks (a). If the crown were to be purchased of the republic only, it would be an advantage to the nation; but it is purchased also of private persons, who put it up to the highest bidder; and what increases the misfortune is, that the magnificent offers which an ambitious candidate makes to the republic, are forgot by him when he is seated upon the throne.

Of the six competitors, there were four who had not even the transitory satisfaction of suspending the inclinations of the voters; these were, Prince Thomas of Savoy, the Duke of Modena, Prince George of Denmark, and the Prince of Transylvania. The

(a) Zaluski, p. 586.

O

other

Y. 1674. other two, Prince Charles, and the Prince of Newburg, entered the lifts.

The Emperor Leopold, who had given up Prince
Charles in the former election, had the ftrongeft reafons to fupport him upon the prefent occafion. He
was a proper hufband for Queen Eleonora, who, by
marrying him, would ftill be Queen of Poland:
it would do honour to the Emperor, to continue the
Auftrian blood upon the throne, and it would alfo
be advantageous to the Poles, who might expect
every thing from Leopold againft the Turks, by
fhewing this deference for him and his fifter. Prince
Charles was nominated by almoft all the grandées,
and the Primate-Interrex raifed his voice even higher
than the reft. " When we thought of depofing
" King Michael, faid he, our firft intention was to
" give our crown to Prince Charles, and to marry
" him with Queen Eleonora. What could not then
" be accomplifhed without violent convulfions, may
" now be done by the freedom of fuffrage, and with
" the greateft advantage to our country. Why
" then fhould we change our fentiments? We
" have nothing better to hope for from any other
" fettlement, and fhall have two Queens, inftead of
" one, to burden the republic with their mainten-
" ance." What contributed greatly to ftrengthen
this party, was the intereft of the two Paz's, the
one Grand-General, the other Grand-Chancellor of
Lithuania, who drew after them the Lithuanians.
The zeal of this faction was fo blind, that they were
for giving Prince Charles's Envoy the precedence before the French Ambaffador: but the propofal appeared fo abfurd, that it fell of itfelf. The French
Ambaffador, Touffaint de Forbin, Bifhop of Marfeilles, recommended to the attention of the republic a circumftance that made a greater impreffion;
which was, not to elect a Prince who was an enemy
to

to his master; and he supported the Prince of Newburg.

This Prince's party was not so much dazzled, as
the grandees were, with the splendor of the Austrian
name. They feared that very Queen Eleonora, who
was to continue upon the throne, if Prince Charles
were elected; and they feared still more the influence
which the council of Vienna would have in the government of Poland: whereas they had no such apprehensions from the Prince of Newburg, nor from
the Princess he should marry, since he offered to be
directed in his choice by the inclinations of the republic. The marriage of the Kings of Poland is a
circumstance always attended with great difficulties.
In other countries, they marry for themselves, without consulting their subjects: in Poland, they marry
for the republic; and as there is no such thing as an
hereditary right to the crown, the republic would be
better pleased, if they continued single. The great
offers made by the Prince of Newburg, and the interest of the same powers who supported his father
in the late election, spoke for the son in this; and if
his party was not the most considerable for the eminence of the persons that composed it, it was certainly so for their number.

Sobieski raised up a third party, by representing,
that in the present situation of the republic, when it
was on the eve of being attacked by the whole Ottoman power, it wanted an hero of tried abilities, whose
bare name might be an omen of victory; that this
hero would not be found in the Prince of Newburg,
who had never paid his addresses to military glory, nor
even in Prince Charles, who had only been honoured with her first smiles: but their want would be
amply supplied by the Prince of Condé, who had received all the favours she could bestow, and was so
celebrated in Europe, that they ought to have given
him the crown, when the throne was last vacant,

O 2   without

Y. 1674. without attending to a wretched libel, the authors of which durft not fhew themfelves ; but that it was not yet too late to chufe themfelves a King, whom all nations would be ambitious of, if they had a power to difpofe of themfelves (a).

This new candidate, who had made no propofal to the republic, and was not expected by any one, gave room to fufpect that France was not fincere in it's recommendation of the Prince of Newburg. The two oppofite parties expreffed their doubts, by the diftruftful looks they gave the French Ambaffador. They fancied that he had been fecretly diftributing money in favour of the Prince of Condé, and that Sobiefki had not been found inacceffible ; but they were miftaken in their conjectures.

Sobiefki's propofal continued a myftery, which was not long before it came to light. It was furprizing that the diet fhould never think of giving the crown to him, who was the hero of Poland. But while his talents and his virtues brought him near the throne, there were two pretences that kept him at a diftance from it. Mary d'Arquien, his wife, was looked upon by the grandees as unworthy of that ftation : " That higheft of all honours, faid they, " is fitter for the blood of the houfe of Auftria." Thus it is that men often facrifice their happinefs to a mere fantom. Another obftacle of greater weight, was the pofitive exclufion given by the Lithuanians to every Piaft. " A nation, faid they, which has " fuffered fo much from the weak government of " Michael, fhould look out for a foreign King." The Queen had fecretly brought about this exclufion, which was fuch a difgrace to Poland. The Lithuanians did not alledge the true reafon. The Queen and the Paz's could not be perfuaded that Sobiefki had no defign upon the crown. He appeared

1 (a) Id. Ibid. p. 555. and feq.

in

in the diet with all the magnificence of a King, and had all the merit requisite for that station : it was necessary therefore to exclude him under the title of a *Piaſt*.

Sobiefki being in this situation, and conscious of his own capacity for filling the throne, hit upon the expedient of embarassing the election with difficulties. He had in his way two powerful rivals; and his object was to triumph over them, by opposing to them the Prince of Condé. He knew very well, that he could not gain the Prince a majority of votes : and therefore aimed only at dividing them still farther, in order to unite them afterwards, if possible, in his own favour. His scheme of division succeeded instantly beyond his hopes. At the name of Condé, the Newburghers shuddered; and the Lorrainers declaimed against him with the utmost virulence. The most odious charges in the libel were revived, and even aggravated: and every thing indicated a division of the republic, and perhaps a civil war. It was obvious, that Sobiefki was strong enough to make himself master of the election, being already master of the Polish army, which called out loudly for the Prince of Condé, and followed in this particular the directions of it's general, without penetrating into his designs. The Paz's, with the army of Lithuania, less numerous indeed than the other, prepared to support the interests of the Queen and Prince Charles. The two brothers had all the ascendant they could wish over the Lithuanians. They knew that Prince Charles was in Silesia, with a body of troops, which, when joined to theirs, would be a match for the Polish army. These dispositions for a civil war struck with horror all who sincerely loved their country.

In this fermentation of opposite factions, Sobiefki proposed a method of reconciliation, which was fit only to embroil things still more. Queen Eleonora

should

should break off her engagements with Prince Charles, and give her hand to the Prince of Newburg, from whom the republic had more to expect on account of his great fortune; and upon this condition, the Prince of Condé should withdraw his pretensions. To bring about this scheme, a deputation from the senate waited upon the Queen *(a)*, who having engaged her heart and her jewels to Prince Charles, shewed, by her answer, that she continued inviolably attached to him; and the Ambassador of Vienna protested loudly that his court would never give up it's candidate. The grandees persisted in giving him their votes; and he would probably have had the crown, if Florian Czartorifki, the Primate and Interrex, had lived a few days longer. He died suddenly at an entertainmentt given by Sobiefki at Villanow : and as his death was of service to Sobiefki, he was suspected of contributing to hasten it. His enemies were busy in spreading reports of the Primate's being poisoned; but history, which never adopts reports without proof, informs us, that a grain of sand in the Primate's reins, which had encreafed to a considerable bulk, was the cause of his death *(a)*. He was a man of an active genius, had great power over the minds of others, was impetuous and full of fire, like the sun which draws the planets into it's vortex. His death weakened Prince Charles's party, and changed the whole face of the election.

Andrew Trzebifki, Bishop of Cracow, a man of less warmth, took his place in the diet of election, and performed the functions of Interrex, but could not unite the votes of the assembly. In one part, was heard the name of Prince Charles, in another, the Prince of Newburg; and louder still, that of

(a) Id. Ib.
(b) Lengn. p. 245. Zalufki, tom. i. p. 556.

Condé

Condé.   At laft, the palatine of Ruffia, Staniflas
Jablonowfki, a Senator, equally refpeétable for
his birth, and his fortune, his knowledge of the
law, and his behaviour in arms, who always fpoke
as he thought, and was a friend to Sobiefki, becaufe
he loved his country (a), rofe up, and endeavoured
to put an end to this ftate of uncertainty : " If in
" our choice of a King, faid he, we were to be de-
" termined-by appearances only, it would be nearly
" equal whether we chofe the Prince of Lorrain, or
" the Prince of Newburg : both of them have blof-
" foms to fhew, but it is fruit that we want; and
" upon this footing I would give my fuffrage to the
" great Condé, were it not, that fruit, which is too
" ripe, is on the point of decaying. I defpife, as
" you do, the infamous libel which was levelled at
" his reputation in the laft eleétion, and dwell only
" upon what is obvious and ftriking. Sobiefki, in
" propofing him, confiders only his heroic qualities.
" As for myfelf, I attend to his age, his infirmities,
" and the habits he has formed. He is accuftomed
" to another climate, to another way of making
" war, to other cuftoms, other manners, and other
" laws. He knows nothing, either of our language,
" or our liberty ; and has no idea but of that arbi-
" trary form of government under which he has
" lived fo long. It is too late for him, under gray
" hairs, and in that ftate of incapacity which is ad-
" vancing faft upon him, to acquire a new body
" and a new foul. His life will be worn out before
" he has made himfelf mafter of any portion of that
" knowledge which he muft neceffarily have, in or-
" der to govern us well. Once more be it obferv-
" ed, that Sobiefki confiders only that blaze of
" glory which gilds over the ruins of this hero ; but

(a) His grand-daughter, a worthy defcendant of this great
man, is married in France to the Prince of Talmont.

O 4   " is

' is his forgetting himfelf a reafon for our following
' his example? Sobiefki is in perfon before your
' eyes.   His age, his health, his vigour, his ta-
' lents, and his fortune, all fpeak loudly in his
' behalf.   He was born in the fame country, and
' educated in the fame principles and fentiments
' with yourfelves.   You have often profited by his
" fuperior abilities in the fenate and the diet; and
" have repeatedly been led to victory under his au-
" fpices.   He has fupported the crown of Poland,
" and will know how to wear it.   By looking out
" for a King among foreigners, do you mean to
" have it faid, that Poland produces no heroes of
" it's own?   By chufing out of fovereign families,
" we have more than once brought ruin upon
" our country.   You are difcharged of all obliga-
" tions towards Queen Eleonora, by her refufing
" the hufband that was offered her; but you are
" ftill bound to your country, whofe welfare de-
" pends upon your choice of Sobiefki."

Jablonowfki's harangue contained without queftion many truths; but there were in it feveral extremely rafh affertions.   The hero, whom he painted in a ftate of imbecility and exhauftednefs, fought
this very year the battle of Senef, in which he was
hurried away by his impetuofity to expofe his own
life and that of his foldiers more than upon any other
occafion; and though feverely tormented with the
gout, he would fain have renewed the battle the
next day; " but there was no one, except himfelf,
" fays an officer who was prefent, that had any fto-
" mach left for fighting."

Scarce had Jablonowfki done fpeaking, when five
Palatinates, that is to fay, their deputies, Caftellans,
Palatines, and many other nobles cried out, *Sobiefki
for ever; we will all perifh together, or have him for
our King.*   The Palatinate of Ruffia, which was Sobiefki's native country, diftinguifhed itfelf by it's

zeal above the reft; and before the end of the day the acclamation became general among the Poles; but the Lithuanians were extremely averfe to this choice. The two Paz's quitted the affembly abrupt- ly with their friends, to enter, before the regifter of the chancery, a proteft againft the election as not be- ing unanimous. The crown continued in this ftate of fufpence during the fucceeding night, which was fpent in agitation and difcord. Jablonowfki and the Interrex did all they could to unite the fuffrages. They applied in particular to a French lady, Elizabeth Clara de Mailly, wife of the Grand-Chancellor Paz; but fhe refufed to abandon the interefts of Queen Eleonora, to whom fhe was lady of the bed cham- ber, after having held the fame office under Queen Louifa, who brought her into Poland. It was faid upon this occafion, that women are fometimes cap- able of great fteadinefs. The two Paz's, after having fpent the whole night to no purpofe in contriving me- thods of making the election mifcarry, and reflecting upon the inferiority of their number, and the dan- ger that might attend their obftinacy, appeared again in the field of election on the 19th of May; and So- biefki, by unanimous confent, was proclaimed *King*. The faint and languid pleafure of a King, who reigns by right of blood, is not to be compared with that of a King, who is made fo by the election of a free people, conferring the crown upon the object of it's love and efteem.

Never did the nation difcover more joy than upon this occafion. The fenate, the equeftrian order, the army and the people, conducted the new King with civil and military pomp, with the roar of cannon and repeated acclamations, to the great church of St. John, to return thanks to God, who had often been thanked at the fame altar for Kings that he had given in his anger: but the Poles now flattered themfelves they had got a good one.

Sobiefki's

Sobieski's elevation to the throne was attributed throughout all France, except in the cabinet of Versailles, to the power of Lewis XIV. and the intrigues of his Ambassador Forbin. But this opinion is confuted by the following fact. As soon as the five first Palatinates, cried out, *Sobieski for ever*, the Baron de Boham galloped away full speed to the garden of the Casimir-Palace, where the Grand-Marshaless then was, to carry her this good news. Forbin, who was then giving her his hand, said to her, that if it ended so, he questioned much whether his master would be pleased. *Pleased or not pleased*, answered she, *who is there that would refuse a sceptre?* Forbin's instructions related only to the Prince of Newburg; and he came too late to form another cabal. He had only three days before the decisive hour; and it is impossible in Poland, more than in any other place, to gain so many persons in so short a time. The most effectual service that France did to Sobieski, without intending it, was disconcerting all Prince Charles's measures, who was so provoked at this treatment, that, though he was naturally discreet and moderate, he swore he would be revenged of Lewis XIV. and he had opportunities in process of time to keep his word. Of all Sobieski's partisans the most serviceable to him was Jablonowski; but his own merit was still more so. Whoever assumes the office of an Ambassador, must bid adieu to truth. They all testified to the new King, and even the Ambassador from Vienna amongst the rest, the satisfaction their masters would receive from this election.

While all Warsaw was filled with rejoicing, Queen Eleonora was sick out of mere convenience. The new King paid her a visit; but this King was not Prince Charles, and the throne must be resigned to Mary d'Arquien. Eleonora's creatures in the senate attempted instantly to avenge her cause, and perhaps to

to give Sobieſki a diſtaſte to the throne before he was Y. 1674.
ſeated in it. With this view, they drew up the *pac-*
ta conventa in terms which confined the expences of
the King's houſhold and the royal authority, within
narrower limits than had anciently been ſet to
them *(a)*.

Sobieſki ſaw the ſnare that was laid for him, and
avoided it by exerting a noble ſpirit of diſintereſtedneſs which always ſucceeds with great men. " You
" have choſen me, ſays he, for your King, but the
" work is not yet compleated; and I am ſtill in a
" ſtate of heſitation. The republic has not yet de-
" livered to me the inſtrument of election, nor
" have I yet accepted it in that ſolemn form which
" ratifies the whole tranſaction: and therefore, if
" you ſhew a diſtruſt of me, by laying fetters upon
" me, which my predeceſſors would have refuſed,
" I reject them and the crown together."

This generous behaviour ſtopped the mouths of
theſe diſturbers; and the fifth of June was deſtined
for tying the knot between the King and the republic, by the formal delivery of the inſtrument of election, and it's acceptation on the King's part. But
there aroſe, a few days before the time, a freſh ſtorm
which made him ſhake upon that throne, where he
was yet ſcarce ſeated. The ſame turbulent ſpirits diſputed the validity of the election; alledging that the
grand-dutchy of Lithuania had ſhewn a manifeſt diſſent; that Sobieſki, before he was elected, had promiſed to pay the army for ſix months; and that, after his election, he retracted his promiſe.

Jablonowſki and the Interrex, at the head of all
thoſe who loved peace and their country, anſwered
to the firſt article, that the diſſent of the grand-dutchy
of Lithuania confirmed the election inſtead of invali-
dating it, ſince that diſſent had been withdrawn by a

(a) Zaluſki, tom. i. p. 548.

free

V. 1674. free and deliberate acceffion; that Michael's election had been held valid, notwithftanding the violence that had been made ufe of to bring it about, and though the fenate yielded at laft with no other view than to avoid difturbing the republic.

The other objection, though of lefs weight, was not fo eafy to get rid of. It was true, that Sobiefki, before he was elected, had promifed to maintain the army at his own expence for fix months; but after the election, he had examined into the ftate of his affairs, and found it impoffible to keep his promife. " If his defign had been to deceive you, faid Jablo- " nowfki, he needed only to have let you continue " in this hope, without fulfilling his engagements: " and how could you have forced him to it, when the " fceptre fhould be firmly fettled in his hands? On " the contrary, he tells you frankly, I have deceived " myfelf; my finances are not adequate to fuch an " expence; and if this condition be abfolutely ne- " ceffary in order to wear your crown, I can only " thank you, and return it to you again. Let us " not, countrymen, be outdone by him in gene- " rofity. You had a hundred reafons, of which it " is hard to fay which was the ftrongeft, for de- " throning your late King Michael; and yet you " did not do it. Can you think then of annulling " a lawful election, for fo trivial a caufe, and de- " priving yourfelves of fo great a King? What he " now promifes, upon maturer deliberation, he will " affuredly perform. It is part of the *pacta conventa* " which he is to fwear to before you all, that he " will pay out of his houfhold revenue the penfion " you affign to King Michael's widow; that he will " redeem, out of his private income, the jewels of " the crown that have been mortgaged; will found a " a military academy for the young nobility, and " erect two forts in whatever place and manner the " republic fhall direct."

Th:

The face of the republic assumed at last an air of serenity and peace; and every thing being really quiet, or at last seeming to be so, the new King received in form the instrument of election in the same great church to which he was conducted upon quitting the field of election.

It is customary for one part of this solemnity to consist in an harangue, which always places the new King above all that have ever preceded him. The orator, according to the usage of the country, made an aukward mixture of sacred and profane learning. The following extract from his discourse may give some idea of the strain of the Polish eloquence. His harangue was delivered in a church dedicated to St. John.

"As St. John anciently prepared the way be-
"fore the Messias, so the republic, by deliver-
"ing the diploma of royalty to John Sobieski,
"prepares the way before her Lord, whose name
"is John. The virgin Mary blessed John in his
"mother's womb; and Queen Louisa Maria, wife
"of Casimir, heaped blessings upon King John,
"by marrying him to Mary d'Arquien, that ocean
"of angelical qualities. The republic was deceived
"in the former election by chusing Michael; but
"it now corrects that error by taking John. John
"is a name of *grace* which will re-establish military
"discipline and the fortune of Poland. The Molda-
"vians and Walachians have paid homage to John,
"and taught us to worship him ourselves as the Sa-
"viour of all Christendom. The sun generally ap-
"pears when the clouds are gone, but frequently
"produces others. The new sun, which rises in our
"horizon, promises us bread and not thunder. We
"have waited for the Holy Spirit on the feast of
"Pentecost, and have received him in the person of
"John. On the same day that the church celebrates
"the festival of God our Saviour concealed under
the

Y. 1674. " the form of bread, behold we chuse ourselves ano-
" ther Saviour under the figure of a man. It was
" on a Saturday, the eve of the feast of the Trini-
" ty, that we all concurred in electing *John*; who
" is also a Trinity himself, being *our son, our fa-*
" *ther, and our King.* It is not merely by chance
" that the election was delayed till the time of these
" great festivals. That of the Trinity indicates
" that the family of *John* will reign at least three
" hundred years : God grant it may be three thou-
" sand! It is the seed of Jacob which shall never be
" extinct, but be for ever a blessing to the repub-
" lic, &c. *(a)*.

It should be observed, that it was not a *Monk* who
talked in this manner, but *Gninski*, Palatine of
Culm, who had himself the happiness of bearing
the name of *John*. It must not however be imagined, that the Polish eloquence always runs in this
strain. There are illustrious instances to the contrary, where panegyric is not concerned, and particularly in defence of liberty; for upon such occasions
every free man, who is born with any talents, is animated with the same spirit that inspired Cicero and
Demosthenes. The Polish orators are often seized
with this enthusiasm, but they are too apt to swell
into bombast. Upon the present occasion, they were
not contented with bare panegyric, but produced Latin prophecies concerning all the Kings of Poland,
past and future, of equal value with those of St. Ma-
lachias concerning the Popes. The oracle which
related to Sobieski, was *Manus Congregatorum*, the
hand, or strength, of assemblies, with the letter *I*,
which seemed to be a designation of his name *John*.
Several Polish nobles, whose name was *James*, had
flattered themselves that the oracle meant them.

Sobieski, at the time of his election, was forty-five
years old; an age equally distant from the heat of

(a) Zaluski, tom. i. p. 548.

youthful

youthful paſſions, and the cold of decrepit age, when all the talents diſplay themſelves in full luſtre: and if the throne were to be given to the advantages of figure, he would have deſerved it in this view alſo. A tall and graceful perſon, a full face, regular features, an aquiline noſe, eyes full of fire, a frank and open countenance, made up his picture. He had not yet that bulkineſs of body, which in time made him leſs graceful; he had only that plumpneſs, which indicates vigorous health, and ſuits ſo well with the Poliſh habit. He derived from nature that majeſtic air, with which courtiers compliment every ſovereign. He took the appellation of John III. a name which the two Kings, who had borne it before him, had done no honour to.

John Albert, grandſon of the great *Jagellon*, is known only for ill-contrived projects, ſucceſsleſs wars, imprudent treaties, and betrayed allies; a weak, and indolent Prince, who lay open to every prejudice, and ſaw only with the eyes of others. His preceptor *Buona-Corſi*, better known by the name of Callimachus, that Greek poet whom he ſo little reſembled, corrupted and enſlaved his mind from his very infancy, and in effect reigned for him.

We have ſeen that the other *John*, *John-Caſimir*, was never more properly diſpoſed of, than when he did himſelf juſtice by reſigning a kingdom to poſſeſs an abbey.

John III. extremely different from the two former, though he was not of royal blood, had a royal ſoul. He was ſcarce ſeated upon the throne, when there was a pedigree formed for him, at which he himſelf was aſtoniſhed, but which he ſuffered thoſe to believe, who were diſpoſed to it. His origin was pointed out to him in Duke *Leſko* III. about the beginning of the ninth century, before Poland was governed by Kings. This Leſko had a ſon named *Sobieſlas*, who poſſeſſed

the

the fovereignty of Bohemia; and nothing could be more natural than to derive *Sobiefki* from *Sobieflas*.

The Queen too had the fatisfaction of feeing her genealogical tree grow very faft. It's root was fixed in *Hugh Capet*, from whence it fpread it's branches into the houfe of *La Grange d' Arquien*. But *Mary* was poffeffed of more folid advantages, an elegant fhape, a majeftic air, a fine complexion, fparkling eyes, a ftately look, a great deal of wit; only fhe was perhaps a little too artful.

The Auftrian Queen forgave her all this, and even her genealogy; but could not forgive the lofs of the throne, the luftre of which could for the future only give her pain. A few months after, fhe retired into Silefia, by the direction of the Emperor her brother. This retreat was concealed at firft under the pretence of a journey, that fhe might not lofe her fettlement; for, by the laws of Poland, whoever enjoys any advantages from the public, muft be an inhabitant of the kingdom. But, though fhe had loft the throne, fhe ftill preferved Prince Charles, whom fhe married in 1678; and if love could make amends to ambitious minds, Eleonora might have been fully fatisfied.

The new Queen, though her ambition had been fo amply gratified, was yet eagerly defirous of a further object. The King was contented with having deferved the crown, but fhe was impatient to try it on. To *hereditary* Kings, the coronation is a mere ceremony, which adds nothing to the authority they derive from their birth; but to *elective* Princes, it is a folemn and neceffary act which puts them in poffeffion of the exercife of fovereign power. The interval between the election and coronation is a continuation of the interregnum, which ftill leaves the government in the hands of the Primate. The new King dates his reign only from the day when he is crowned,

crowned, and his hands are so tied up, that he cannot sign himself *King*, without adding *elect*.

Notwithstanding so many disadvantages, which Sobiefki might have put an end to with a single word, he was more in haste to avenge his country, than to reign over it. He had gained the crown solely by his merit, and he now deferred his coronation to give up himself entirely to the war against the Turks. The republic repaid this act of generosity with another; for the law was broke thro' on this occasion, and he was authorized to date his reign from the day of his election, to decide peace and war, to publish *universals* under his privy seal for the assembling of the diets and the Pospolite in case of necessity. He was also permitted to send dispatches to foreign courts under the same seal, and to fill up vacant offices. That of Grand-Master was one, the staff being to be laid down by him, as soon as he took up the sceptre. We have seen that King Casimir, by an unexampled stretch of his private authority, had taken it from Lubomirski to give it Sobieski; who now did an act of justice and policy together, by restoring it to the son, who deserved it. By this means he recovered the alienated affections of a man, who might have instilled his discontent into others. The Primacy, the first place in the republic, was also vacant (a). Andrew Trzebiski had done the business of that office in the interregnum; and having contributed not a little to Sobieski's election, had reason to expect the King would now acknowledge his services. But this dignity was conferred upon Andrew Olsowski, Bishop of Culm, and Vice-Chancellor of the kingdom, a man whose distinguished abilities as a statesman had been tried in two reigns and two interregna. It appears that upon this occasion the new King made gratitude give way to merit, at the same time that

(a) Lengnich. p. 247.

P

he

he declined the pomp of a coronation for the good of his country.

He made alfo another facrifice which muft have coft him a great deal. He was born with a warm conftitution, was eminent for gallantry as well as valour, and had had more than one miftrefs. His prefent favourite, who had engroffed for three years the love which he ufed to fcatter with fome profufion among the whole fex, was fo much in his good graces that he had fworn to her an eternal paffion. But this oath was taken only by a private man : when he became a King, and confequently an example to his fubjects, he thought it incumbent upon him to break it, and he was rewarded for it during the whole remainder of his life; for the Queen, who had hitherto connived at his tranfitory amours, would now put up with it no longer, for fear a miftrefs fhould poffefs the influence of a Queen. To form an idea of the uneafinefs which the humours of fo haughty a Princefs, who had not yet loft all her beauty, would have conftantly given him, it fhould be obferved, that though fuperior to the herd of Kings in the cabinet and in the field, he was upon a level with the humbleft citizen in his love of domeftic peace; and that any cloud which threatened him in that quarter, difturbed him more than the enemy.

Mahomet had no defign of avenging this year the defeat of Choczin. Cuprogli was lately dead ; and fome of the laft words that he fpoke, fixing his eyes upon the Alcoran, were thefe : *Prophet, I fhall foon fee whether thy words are true ; but be they true or falfe, I am fure of being happy, if virtue be the beft of all religions.* The death of this great man left the Ottoman Empire in a ftate of languor; and John thought it a favourable opportunity to reap the fruits of his victory. His firft object was to recover the Ukraine : the Coffacks had given themfelves to the Turks in a mere fit of defpair; and they already felt

the

the weight of this new yoke; but they feared still Y. 1674.
more to return to their former masters. The governors of the world, by refusing to listen to penitent
rebels, and by inflicting punishments after having
promised forgiveness, have found out the art of making revolts perpetual. The Cossacks would not venture to make trial of the King's clemency; but being informed that he was marching against them,
and that Mahomet did not arm in their defence,
they looked out for a third master; and fled by
troops to the Russian territories, on the other side of
the Borysthenes (a). It was upon the banks of this
river that the Swedes laid down their arms, while
Charles XII. wounded and vanquished, after so many
victories, took refuge among the Turks.

Mahomet however sent an order to the Cham of
Tartary to defend the Ukraine with all his forces,
upon pain of incurring the displeasure of the sublime
Porte.

Paz, with his Lithuanians, joined the Polish army in the beginning of September. His equal and
his rival was now become his King; but the majesty
of the monarch did not humble the pride of the subject. Paz ordered a drum-major of his army to be
hanged, for daring to beat the General by the King's
order, without waiting for his. Hard at all times is
the fate of inferiors who come in the way of two contending powers! John took no notice of the affront.
Whether he did right or wrong, his conduct was
approved by the Senators, who were then in the ar-

(a) The head of this river, now called Niper or Driper,
was not known in Herodotus's time. (book 4. chap. 53.) but has
since been discovered in Muscovite Russia, between Wclock and
Olefchno. Herodotus represents it as navigable throughout, and
therefore he must have known nothing of the thirteen Falls called Porowis, which the Cossacks, and the Cossacks only, venture
to pass in Canoes; and when they have succeeded, make a feast
upon Millet. The Nieper discharges itself into the Black Sea.

my,

my, becaufe they had need of Paz. The King gave
up his own refentment to the republic; and exceeded the promife he made at his election, for he paid
the troops with his own money during this whole
campaign, and entered the Ukraine at the head of
between thirty and thirty-five thoufand men. Several places, fuch as *Bar*, *Nimirow*, and *Kalnik*, furrendered at the firing of the firft cannon. *Pavoloc*,
which was garrifoned only with Coffacks, prepared for a vigorous refiftance. But fome prifoners
being taken in a fally, the King gave them cloaths
and money, and fent them back into the town with
letters, advifing the befieged not to expofe themfelves to the laft extremities, and promifing them, *upon
the word of a King and the word of Sobiefki*, to detain
none of thofe who had a mind to go over to Dorofcenfko. The effect of this was the furrendry of the
town, and the Monarch's clemency induced them
all to continue in the Polifh fervice. By this humane conduct towards his rebellious fubjects, John
fpared a great deal of Coffack and Polifh blood;
for, notwithftanding his being a king, he fet fome
value on the lives of men. A miftaken zeal for religion (which was a common evil in Poland) did indeed fometimes make him behave cruelly to infidels,
who do not, however, upon that account, lofe either
the nature of men, or the relation of brethren. The
Cham, with a hundred thoufand Tartars, contented
himfelf with coafting and harraffing the Polifh army,
but would not venture a battle.

Human, the largeft and moft populous town in
the Ukraine was in daily expectation of it's fate. It
contained near twenty thoufand inhabitants, and a
numerous garrifon; but John befieged and took it
in the Cham's prefence, and to fhew his contempt
of the Tartar, divided his army in order to carry on
different operations at the fame time; for the froft
and fnow gave intimations that no time was to be
loft.

loft. Jablonowfki made himfelf mafter of every Y. 1674
place in his way that made any refiftance. Korefki
penetrated as far as Kafkow, a place upon the frontiers of Tartary, which he took poffeffion of. Paz
drove the Tartars before him, routed all their fmall
parties, and favoured by this means all the attempts
of the army; but his zeal cooled at laft, and he
took the road to Lithuania, contrary to the promife
which he had given the King (a). It is true, the
winter was extremely fevere, the fatigue continual,
and provifions difficult to be got; but it was not his
patience that failed upon this occafion, for Paz
was a foldier as well as a General. He had reafons
for chufing to be dependent on himfelf only; and
his antipathy had acquired new ftrength, fince his
rival's advancement to the throne. The reader
fhould not forget that in Poland the authority of the
King is binding only to a certain degree: the Grand-
General fcarce feels it at all.

Had it not been for this defection, the King
would have completed the conqueft of the Ukraine,
a country which had been a fcene of flaughter for
thirty years together. The Primate wrote to him,
" That the annals of Poland could furnifh no in-
" ftance of fuch a divifion, in the prefence of the
" King himfelf; that it was a crime of the moft hor-
" rid nature and moft fatal confequences; that if the
" Lithuanian army did not return to it's duty, the
" commander and the colonels ought to be proceed-
" ed againft, and tried, according to law; and that
" he flattered himfelf every good citizen would
" unite in avenging the injury done to the King, the
" regal dignity, and the republic (b)."

If John had been born to the throne, he would
probably have embraced the fevere meafures which
the Primate recommended; but he himfelf had for-

(a) Lnegnich. p. 247. Zalufki, p. 546.
(b) Zalufki, tom. i. p. 133, 645.

merly

merly been engaged in a feparation much like the prefent, excepting only that King Michael did not command in perfon when he was deferted. He recollected the time of his profcription, when he was upon the point of fhedding the blood of his fellow-fubjects, and perhaps of the King himfelf. He knew therefore, by his own experience, the danger of driving the commander of an army to extremities. He chofe to truft to time and mild meafures ; and if his moderation did not get the better of Paz's inflexibility, he at leaft avoided coming to blows with him, which muft have given great advantages to the enemy.

The King, being no longer able to keep the field with the remnant of his forces, diftributed them among the conquered places : as for himfelf, inftead of going to mix with his court in the pleafures of Warfaw, he fixed his winter quarters at Braclaw, a place that every one dreaded. It was a town, fitu-ated upon the Bog, that had been taken and facked by the Turks in 1672. A tradefman of Warfaw would have thought himfelf inconveniently lodged in the houfe which his Prince inhabited. The moft common provifions were very fcarce ; and the horfes were forced to feed upon the ftraw that was ftrip-ed from the neighbouring hovels. The King expe-rienced the labours of royalty, before he tafted it's pleafures. His prefence produced two good effects. It kept the Poles from deferting, for they durft not murmur or even caft a look towards Poland, when they faw the King fhare their fatigues. It alfo re-ftrained the Tartars, who were preparing to take advantage of Paz's defection and the extreme rigour of the feafon. No horfes in the world are comparable to thofe of the Tartars for bearing fatigue, and the Tartars are at leaft as hardy as their horfes.

The Cham, feeing the Polifh army diminifhed and feparated, gave his fon, Sultan Galga, a part of
his

his forces, in order to attack the Poles on the side of
Human and Raſkow, while he himſelf fell upon
Braclaw and Kalnik. He even undertook the ſiege
of the latter place, and employed the Coſſacks on
that ſervice; for the Tartars never make war but on
horſeback. But John did not give him time to carry
on his works: he preſented himſelf in ſight of the
Tartars, and the ſiege was raiſed.

At laſt the Cham reſolved to cloſe all with a deciſive blow. Sultan Gulga had met with ſuch a reception every where, that he durſt not make any attempt. The Cham therefore united all his forces,
and appeared before the gates of Braclaw, where
John had ſhut himſelf up with a ſmall force. The
Cham's deſign was either to draw him from behind
the walls, or to leave him the mortification of not
daring to come out. John ſuffered him to dance at-
tendance for ſome days; and at a time when he leaſt
expected it, made a ſally with his cavalry, attacked
him ſabre in hand, killed him two thouſand men,
and made three hundred priſoners in an hour's
time.

The Cham, being worſted upon all occaſions, and
no booty being to be got in a country which he was
ordered to defend, retired to his own dominions, and
left the Poles in peace; but this peace was ſoon ſucceeded by a greater alarm than ever.

Mahomet at length rouſed himſelf from his lethar-
gy, and turned his thoughts to revenge. The breaking of the treaty of Boudchaz, the defeat at Choczin, the inſolence of the Poles whom he conſidered
as revolted tributaries, their real weakneſs, and the
greatneſs of his own ſtrength, all ſerved to provoke
him. He called to mind the glorious campaign he
had made when aſſiſted by the genius of Cuprogli,
but was not tempted by it to try what he could do
alone. His love of glory was extinguiſhed by his
love of pleaſure. It is a general notion, that hunt-

ing

ing gives a difpofition for war: but Mahomet did not feel this effect: and yet all the time he could fpare from his feraglio, he fpent in rambling amidft mountains and forefts, while his fubjects were fhedding their blood to aggrandize the Empire. A ftill heavier charge againft him, was, that even in th ediverfions of the chace, he fet no great value upon the lives of men. If war has a right to deftroy them, the pleafures of a fovereign are not to be allowed the fame privilege.

The General, to whom he entrufted his revenge, was *Kara-Muftapha*, a mere courtier, educated in the feraglio, who, by the charms of his perfon, had gained the good graces of the Sultana *Validé (a)*. If it were not a conftant cuftom with the eaftern monarchs to advance beauty to the throne, without regarding either birth, or intereft, the fortune of this woman would be thought furpﬁzing. She was a native of Circaffia, the daughter of a Greek prieft, and deftined to live by the labour of her hands. Her memory ought to be held in veneration by the Ottoman family, for it was fhe that procured the abrogation of the cruel law made by Bajazet, enjoining the Sultan to fecure his own poffeffion of the throne, by putting his brothers and uncles to death. Nor was this Sultana more diftinguifhed for her humanity, than the ftrength of her amorous attachments. She was not contented with making her favourite, *Kaimakan*, or Governor of Conftantinople, but raifed him to the dignity of *Vizir*. He was nephew to Cuprogli, and had prefumption enough to aim at furpaffing his uncle in his firft campaign. Out of feveral armies he made up one, which would have been fufficient to overturn the greateft power in Europe. The rendezvous was appointed at Ben-

(a) Or Sultana-Mother, fhe whofe fon is in poffeffion of the throne. She has not the title of *Validé* till the coronation of her fon, and lofes it again if he dies, or is depofed.

der,

der, otherwife called Tekin, the place, where in
our time, Charles XII. though a prifoner, ftill made
himfelf feared.

The triumphs of the King hindered the diftreffes
of the republic from being felt; but they were now
aggravated beyond meafure, and every one murmured againft him as the author of the war. It was faid,
" that Mahomet ought never to have been provoked,
" nor the peace, which had been folemnly fworn to,
" violated; that the victory of Choczin had been
" productive of bitter confequences; that it was
" impoffible for Poland to contend long with Afia;
" that prudence required them to fubmit to their
" deftiny, and that it was better to pay a tribute,
" than be given up to total deftruction: that the
" name of *tributary* was a mere phantom, terrible
" only to miftaken pride; that the greateft powers
" of Europe, by paying fubfidies, do in effect make
" themfelves tributaries; that even the Empire of
" Germany itfelf had been fo to that of Conftanti-
" nople; and that, in fhort, this evil, if it were any
" evil at all, was preferable to all the horrors with
" which Poland was threatened."

Difcourfes of this fort, under an abfolute monarchy, pafs off like a tranfient cloud. The monarch, whether he hears them or not, ruins or faves
his people in his own way. But in a mixed government, the King muft fubdue his own fubjects by
reafon, before he can conquer his enemies by force.

In order to diffipate the apprehenfions of Poland,
John quitted the Ukraine after leaving garrifons behind him, and led the reft of his troops to Leopol
about the end of April. His army, if it deferved
that name, was much diminifhed by fieges, fkirmifhes, the feverity of the winter, and diforders.
He raifed recruits in the greateft hafte, but was forced to drag them out of the arms of confternation
and difcontent, His power over the minds of men
muft

Y. 1675. muſt have been equal to his reputation, or the republic would never have conſented to expoſe itſelf
with him. He ſent orders to the Lithuanians to
join him immediately, after having writ to the
Grand-General Paz in a ſtyle that was likely to
make an impreſſion on him: and then formed his
plan of defence. Judging of the Vizir's abilities
by his own, he doubted not of ſeeing him fall upon
the Palatinate of Ruſſia, which would open a way
into the heart of Poland. Upon this ſuppoſition;
he entruſted the wiſe Jablonowſki with ſix thouſand
men, and ordered him to entrench himſelf under the
cannon of Zloczow, that he might guard that paſs.
Zloczow belonged to the King in his private capacity, and he had converted it into a fortreſs for the
defence of his country. He had only twelve thouſand men left to ſuſtain the chief weight of the war.
Leopol, though a wretched fortreſs, is yet of the
utmoſt importance, as it covers Ruſſia and the neighbouring provinces. At the gates of this city, John
ſat down to wait for the enemy, and was greatly aſtoniſhed when he heard in the beginning of July that
the aukward Vizir had entered the Ukraine to throw
away his time in beſieging Human, inſtead of advancing inſtantly to cruſh a little army whoſe deſtruction would leave Poland at his mercy. *Since
be knows no better than this,* ſays the King, *I will
give a good account of his great army before the end
of the campaign.*

The defence of a city was at that time a dreadful
commiſſion. In a war among the powers of Europe,
the worſt that happens, when a place is ſurrendered,
is to continue a priſoner of war till an exchange be
ſettled; but between the Turks and the Poles, the
mildeſt fate is perpetual ſlavery, which to a brave
man is more terrible than death itſelf; and from
Kara Muſtapha there was reaſon to dread the worſt
of horrors.

                                        Human

Y. 1675.

Human held out fifteen days againſt ſo great a force. The artillery of the Turks was of an enormous weight, and their threats terrible. At length the place, having ſeveral breaches in it's walls, and being without hope of ſuccour, capitulated; but the Vizir, with a barbarity ſcarce to be pardoned when a town is taken by ſtorm, glutted himſelf with blood. Twenty thouſand ſouls periſhed in this ſlaughter; and many an infant was ſeen vomiting up milk mixed with blood upon it's mother's breaſt. The Vizir's deſign was undoubtedly to frighten Poland, and ſubdue it by means of terror.

Human had coſt him too great an expence of time and men to undertake more ſieges in the Ukraine. He therefore turned towards the left, and advanced by quick marches into Podolia. The few places which the republic yet poſſeſſed in that province, were ill provided with troops and ammunition. They belonged to private nobles, who had neglected them. A fort happened to be in the Vizir's route; which having taken by aſſault, he found in it ſome Walachian families who had entered, a century ago, into the Poliſh ſervice, where they had diſtinguiſhed themſelves from father to ſon. " This then, " ſaid he, is your treachery towards the Grand " Seignior, who honours Walachia with his protec- " tion; the whole world ſhall be taught, by your " example, to reſpect it's maſters." He inſtantly ordered them to be empaled.

The ſame barbarity was repeated at Mikuliny, after the aſſault was over. The Viſir then opened the trenches before Podahiecz. The King depended upon the ſtrength of the place, and ſtill more upon the experience of the Governor, Makowiſki. He was reputed a man of bravery, but men are not brave at all times. Both he and the principal officers were afraid of being empaled, and ſurrendered the place without ſtriking a blow; but though they

thus

Y, 1675. thus submitted to the victor's clemency, they were treated with all imaginable rigour, bating the effusion of blood.   The churches and sepulchres in the town were violated, its fortifications razed, its wealth pillaged, the inhabitants reserved for slavery, and the Governor put in irons among the crowd.

The atrocious cruelty of the Visir produced two different effects.   The pusillanimous surrendered at the first attack, in order to save their lives; but the courageous fought only to die with arms in their hands.

This last was the character of him who defended Sbaras, a large castle covered with some outworks, situated upon a hill, and making part of the large domain of Wiesnowieski, Petty-General of the Polish army, who had garrisoned it with six hundred foot, commanded by Des Auteuils, a French gentleman, originally of Picardy.   It was not easy to put the place into better hands.   He defended himself with vigour for fourteen days, while the Visir raved and threatened at his usual rate.   There were several noble families who had taken refuge in the castle, and pressed Des Auteuils to surrender : but he was deaf to the suggestions of fear, and threatened to turn them out of the place, if he heard any more of this cowardly proposal.   The wretches said no more ; but taking an opportunity when Des Auteuils could make no resistance, they gave him several mortal wounds, and threw him over the walls.   The Vizir himself was struck with horror at this act of villainy ; and covering his natural cruelty with the mask of justice, he cut off every head that he found in the place, to revenge, as he pretended, the death of the Governor.

The barbarian, by these bloody conquests, was only preparing the way for a complete victory, that he had planned in his own mind.   When he sat down before Sbaras, he detached fifty thousand men,

y. 1675.

men, under the command of Sultan Nuradin, with orders to attack the King, without giving quarter to any one, and to fpread deftruction on all fides as he marched.

The King's army, which was encamped at Leopol, had received fome additions: the whole amounted to fifteen thoufand men. Paz, though the danger was extreme, made no hafte to join the King with his Lithuanians.

The city of Leopol, confiderable for its commerce, its wealth, its great number of inhabitants of all nations, and all religions; for three Archiepifcopal fees, one for the Polifh Catholics, another for the Armenians, and a third for the fchifmatic Greeks: Leopol, with all this importance, is one of the worft of places to defend. It is fituated in a bottom, encompaffed on all fides with high grounds that command it, and which, in fome places, fhut it up fo clofe, that a man might throw ftones upon the rampart with his hand. On another fide, the eminences are at a greater diftance, and form a fpacious half-moon. In this fpot the King had pitched his camp, and the army being under the greateft concern on his account, conjured him to remove at leaft his own perfon out of danger: *You would defpife me,* faid he, *if I followed your advice (a).*

It is aftonifhing that the Vifir, inftead of employing himfelf in taking forry places, did not come in perfon to give battle to the King. This was the affair of honour, the capital point which would determine all the reft. The Tartar, whom he charged with this commiffion, had no contemptible reputation. The beft thing, however, that he did, was advancing with great rapidity. His march refembled a devouring fire: all the villages and ham-

(a) Zalufki, tom. j. p. 555.

lete

lets were burnt by his order: he appeared as quick as lightning before Jablonowſki's little camp: he even made an attempt upon the entrenchments; but that General ſoon convinced him, that it would not be an eaſy matter to gain any advantage over him; and the Tartar had a mind to preſerve all his forces for a more important purpoſe. The quick-neſs of his march, and his care to intercept all the Poliſh couriers were ſo well conducted, that had it not been for the flames which drew near to Leopol, the King, who was never before ſurprized, would have been ſo now. About ten in the morning, the Poles perceived the enemy's army, conſiſting wholly of Turkiſh and Tartarian horſe, in a vaſt plain terminated by the foot of the mountains. Though it was only the month of Auguſt, it ſnowed hard: there fell alſo a heavy ſhower of hail which happened to incommode the infidels more than the Chriſtians. All the Prieſts, Biſhops, and bad philoſophers in the Chriſtian army, cried out, *a miracle*; and the memoirs of that time aſſert that it really was one. The King made uſe of it to inſpire his little army with confidence, without ne-glecting the precautions of human prudence (*a*). He did not wait for the enemy in his camp, but aſcended the riſing grounds, where he ordered the Towariſz to plant their lances upon the higheſt ſummits, in order to appear more numerous to the enemy, who had already reached the foot of the mountains. He ordered his own regiment of dra-goons to deſcend the hill in ſmall parties, under cover of the buſhes; and theſe dragoons, by fir-ing at a very ſmall diſtance, forced the enemy's van-guard to retire. A Poliſh ſquadron filled the firſt vacancy; others preſſing on, formed in the ſame manner, and the whole army was ſoon drawn up in

(*a*) Zaluſki, tom. i. p. 555.

battalia,

battalia, while the lances of the Towarifz were Y. 1675. ftill to be feen upon the eminences.

The infidels feeing no more troops coming down, and trufting to their fuperior number, begun the charge with cries and howlings, which would probably have fatal effects upon an army that heard them for the firft time. The Poles felt no terror at the noife of their enemies, but their attack was really dreadful, and made them ftagger: the King reftored order, and fuffered the infidels to throw away their firft fire. They returned to the attack feveral times, and the Poles contented themfelves with giving them a warm reception. The King had placed a body in ambufcade to take them in flank; and a battery was advancing upon a hill to play upon them. This was the moment that the King waited for to attack them in his turn. Never was there a General more determined, nor did the Polifh troops ever difplay greater valour. The infidels, being attacked in front and in flank, gave way at the fecond charge, and from this inftant the confufion increafed among them. They were purfued to a deep morafs, where a great number perifhed. They left between fourteen and fifteen thoufand men upon the field of battle, and night faved the reft. Nuradin had boafted that he would take the King prifoner, and prefent him to the Vifir; but he narrowly efcaped being taken himfelf, and carried the news of his own defeat to the camp at Sbaras (a).

The Vifir, ftruck with confternation, refolved upon finifhing the campaign with fome important blow. It was not by marching in perfon againft the conqueror, and wrefting from him his victory, but by taking *Trembowla (b)*, at the entrance of

(a) Zalufki, tom. i. p. 555.
(b) The French Geographers write it *Tremblowa*: but they ought to confult the natives of the country.

I   Podolia,

Y. 1675. Podolia, a fortress with large and strong outworks, hanging upon a rock, the access to which is practicable only in one place, which leads to a little plain covered with thick wood. This accessible side is defended by two ravelins, with good ditches and a covered way. The Janow, a deep and muddy river, surrounds almost the whole rock, and consequently obliges an army to separate into several quarters, in order to form the siege.

Kara-Muftapha flattered himself with the hopes of carrying the place, before John could interrupt him ; and in order to succeed the sooner in his design, and spare the blood of the janizaries, he made use of art, before he had recourse to violence. He was uneasy at the reputation of the Governor, Samuel Chrasonowski, a renegado Jew, who had quitted the law of Moses for that of Jesus, and was more zealous against his brethren of the circumcision, than if he had never undergone that operation himself. The Visir employed his prisoner Makowiski, to represent to him by letter, " that " it would be rash to persist obstinately in the de- " fence of a place that must infallibly be taken ; " that he ought rather to think of deserving the " victor's mercy than provoking his indignation ; " that by submitting to his inevitable fate, he " might procure favourable treatment for himself, " the garrison, and the townsmen ; that notwith- " standing the severe orders of Mahomet, the Vi- " sir could shew favour to whom he pleased, and " would treat brave men with peculiar distinc- " tion."

Chrasonowski returned a double answer : one to Makowiski in these terms : " I am not surprized " that being in irons, thou hast the soul of a slave ; " but what astonishes me, is thy daring to talk of " the Visir's clemency, after what has happened to " Podahiecz, and thyself. Farewell : all the harm

" I

" I wifh thee is, that thou mayeſt live long in
" the infamy and fervitude thou deferveſt. Death
" would be to thee a bleſſing, but thou haſt not
" the courage to confer it upon thyfelf."

The anfwer to the Vifir was not lefs haughty:
" Thou art miſtaken, if thou expecteſt to find
" gold within thefe walls : we have nothing here
" but ſteel and foldiers : our number indeed is
" fmall, but our courage great. Do not flatter
" thyfelf that we will furrender ; for thou fhalt
" never take us till we have all breathed our laſt.
" I am preparing to give thee another anfwer
" by the mouth of my cannon (a)."

The Vifir, foaming with rage, ordered the place
to be battered with all imaginable fury. If he
wanted conduct, he was not without bravery. He
was often feen in the trenches, notwithſtanding
the fire from the ramparts, encouraging the janizaries to prefs on the fiege. The place defended itfelf beyond what could be expected. The fact
that I am going to relate will perhaps be treated as
a fable ; but I find better evidence for it than for
many things that are never called in queſtion.
The wife of the Jewifh Governor, equally beauti-
ful with Judith, and more enterprizing, having no
opportunity like her, to cut off the head of the
Vizir while he ſlept, made great havock of the
Turks in fallies conducted by herfelf, filled up
their trenches, and fought upon the breach. But
what can the brave do, when the timid are more
numerous, and want only to furrender?

Chrafonowfki had the fame inconvenience to
ſtruggle with, which had been the deſtruction of
Des Auteuils and Sbaras. The nobility who had
taken refuge in the place, feeing a breach made,
which grew wider every hour, and dreading the

(a) Zaluſki. tom. i. p. 155, & feq.

Q

impla

implacable fury of the Vifir, if they ftood a ftorm, loft all courage. Their defpair was the greater, as they expected no relief : but they were miftaken in this particular, for the Lithuanian army had at length joined the Poles in the camp before Leopol. The King was upon his march, and by calling in, upon the way, the fmall body under Jablonowfki, his ftrength amounted to thirty-three thoufand men : but as there was no news at Trembowla of this relief, it had no effect in the prefent critical con- juncture. Inftead of continuing to defend them- felves, as they had hitherto done, the nobles com- municated their apprehenfions to the officers of the garrifon ; and being accuftomed to fhare the Sove- reign power in diets, they confidered themfelves, in this extremity alfo, as the reprefentatives of their country, and claimed a right of deciding the fate of Trembowla.

The Jewifh heroine heard their confultations, in a place where fhe was not perceived. It was abfolutely determined to furrender. She inftantly flew to her hufband upon the breach, and acquainted him with it in the thickeft of the fire. The brave Governor ran to this affembly of cowards : " It is by no " means certain, faid he, that the enemy will over- " power us ; but is abfolutely fo, that I will blow " you up in this very room, if you perfift in your " bafe defign. There are foldiers at the door with " their matches lighted, on purpofe to execute my " orders." The profpect of inevitable death put arms again into their hands ; and they endeavoured to wipe off this ftain.

The Vifir was not ignorant that John was march- ing to relieve the town ; and therefore haftened his attacks. The place had already ftood four affaults ; and Chrafonowfki himfelf trembled for the fifth. His wife miftook this juft concern for a mark of weaknefs that boded no good. A woman who has
once

Y. 1675.

once got over the natural timidity of her sex, be-comes more than man. This Roman of the north, armed with two poniards, said to her husband: "One of these is destined for thee, if thou sur-renderest the town; the other I intend for my-self *(a)*."

It was in this moment of distress that the Polish army arrived. The Visir, not believing that the King was there in person, resolved upon a battle. A Polish spy, that was taken, undeceived him. The spy carried a letter, writ with the King's own hand; and the signals already gave notice of his arrival to the besieged, who got together the remnant of their forces with loud cries of joy. The Visir raised the siege, not daring to try his fortune against that of John: but he was forced to it in the event, because he took his measures too late. He repassed the Ja-now with all haste; but half his army being still on this side of the river, John attacked it, crying out to the foremost squadrons, *that he required no-thing of them, but what he would set them an example of himself*. The battle lasted a great while; and the Turks shewed, that with such a comman-der as they deserved, they might have laid claim to the victory. They lost between seven and eight thousand men, and retired under the cannon of Ka-minieck.

The garrisons of the places which the Turks had taken, did not wait for the vengeance of the Poles; but abandoned them to go and rejoin the army. Trembowla owed its deliverance to the intrepidity of Chrasonowski, and gratefully confessed it. He himself was raised to military honours: his wife contented herself with the applauses of the nation; and the soldiers were rewarded with money by an indigent republic. Such was always the practice of

(a) Zaluski, tom. i. p. 155, & seq.

the

Y. 1675. the conquerors of the world towards their victorious troops; they were sure either of money or lands.

Kara-Muftapha was now taught, that superior numbers, cruelty, and presumption are not sufficient to ensure victory. He staid some time at Kaminieck, and then directed his march towards the Danube. He had done great mischiefs to Poland by pillage, devastation, the demolition of towns and forts, and the great number of slaves which he carried off. The case is not the same with Poland, as with countries where commerce flourishes. In the year 1666, London was laid waste with plague and fire, in the midst of an unsuccessful war, and yet in three years time was rebuilt in a much handsomer and more commodious manner than before. The cities of Poland, when once destroyed, never recover again. But all these mischiefs were nothing in comparison of what the Visir might have done. He was upon the frontiers of the republic so early as the month of July. An experienced Captain, with the forces that he had, would have come and given law at Warsaw, and added Poland to the Turkish provinces: the least advantage he ought to have reaped from the campaign, was to fix himself in the Palatinate of Ruffia, and keep his ground in the Ukraine and Podolia. Being master, as he was, of the Niester, with Kaminieck and Choczin behind him, this position would have marked out the fate of Poland for the next campaign.

It was imputed to John as a crime, in some succeeding diets, that he had not immediately formed the siege of Kaminieck. The place had just received a convoy of five hundred waggons, with a reinforcement of janizaries; the season was far advanced, and all the country exhausted of provisions: when things were in such a situation, was it

Ɛ   possible

poffible to begin a fiege, whofe progrefs would be flow, and its fuccefs uncertain ? He contented himfelf with burning the villages, hamlets, and boats which ferved to furnifh the town with provifions. He hindered it alfo from being recruited with men and cattle, by carrying away both to the territories of the republic. By this conduct, he prepared the way for the recovery of Kaminieck ; having acquired glory enough by triumphing over fo many enemies with fuch an inequality of forces. This campaign may ferve to teach nations of inferior ftrength not to defpair, when they have a great King at their head.

The army now retired into winter-quarters, and John went to repofe himfelf at Zolkiew, a town in the Palatinate of Ruffia, three leagues from Leopol, which made part of the Eftate of the Zolkiewfki's, his anceftors by the mother's fide. The caftle paffed for a mafter piece of Architecture, in a country where that art is ftill in its infancy.

During his refidence in this place, which he was always particularly fond of, he learnt the death of a French hero, with which he was much affected, in confequence of that fympathy which great men feel for one another: but how great would have been his concern, if he could have forefeen that the blood of Turenne would one day be united with his own ?

In the mean time, Warfaw was impatient to enjoy again the prefence of its King. The eighteen months which had paffed fince his election, he had employed in a manner that made him ftill more worthy of the crown ; and the crown was not yet upon his head. He therefore complied with the wifhes of his capital, where, before his coronation, he received an honour which happens only to Princes whofe name aftonifhes the earth. Perfia, a diftant power, which had nothing to do with Poland,

fent

Y. 1675. fent him an Ambaffador. The Senate flattered it, felf at firft, that he came to propofe a league againft Mahomet; but the illufion was of fhort duration. The only object of his embaffy was to congratulate John upon his victories, and to afk his friendfhip.

Y. 1676. When this ceremony was over, the republic was wholly taken up with the coronation, which was fixed for the 2d of February. In chufing the fcene of this folemnity, Poland acts like France; and inftead of confecrating its Kings in the capital, conducts them, at a great expence, to Cracow, a city lefs commodious, and lefs magnificent, becaufe Ladiflas Loketek, in the fourteenth century, was crowned there. This ancient city, more extenfive than populous, and fituated upon the banks of the Viftula, ftill boafts an eftablifhment which does honour to France. Its univerfity, the moft celebrated in the kingdom, called the town of Sorbonne, actually owes its birth to doctors of the Sorbonne, fuch doctors as the fourteenth century could produce, invited thither by Cafimir III. furnamed, *the Great*. The two Dictionaries of *Moreri* and *Trevoux*, attribute this eftablifhment to Cafimir I. who reigned in the eleventh century, before the Sorbonne exifted in France.

Perfons who are fond of magnificent fpectacles, and do not confider what they coft the public, would be ftruck with the fplendor of this. All the magnificence of Afia was feen united with all the elegance of Europe. Slaves from Ethiopia and the eaft, clothed in azure habits, young Poles in purple robes, a whole army dreft to the greateft advantage; the equipages, men and horfes contending with each other in fplendor; the gold eclipfed by jewels; fuch was the proceffion, in the midft of which Sobiefki appeared upon a Perfian horfe, going

ing to take poffeffion of a crown which he had merited by his virtues.

The Polifh Kings, at their inauguration, are prefented with the throne and the grave together. The ceremony begins with the funeral of the late King, whofe body lies unburied till this time. Upon the prefent occafion, there happened, by a fingular event, to be two. The fame hearfe carried *John Cafimir*, who died lately in France, and *Michael.* The funeral pomp refembles, in moft particulars, that of other Kings. One fingularity deferves to be taken notice of. As foon as the body is laid upon the fcaffold erected in the cathedral, a Herald on horfeback, armed from head to foot, enters at the great door, and breaks a fceptre againft the fcaffold. Five others come in, in the fame manner; one of which breaks the crown, another the globe, the fourth a fcymetar, the fifth a javelin, the fixth a lance; the cannon, trumpets, and kettle-drums playing all the while.

A warm difpute between the Primate and the Bifhop of Cracow was like to have retarded the funeral and the coronation. They both claimed a right of officiating at the obfequies; but after a long conteft, which furnifhed employment for the whole court, the point was accommodated. The Primate officiated at the altar, and the Bifhop in the Pulpit, by delivering the funeral oration. To this day of forrow fucceeded the day of joy.

The Queen had employed every expedient in the preliminary diet, that fhe might be crowned the fame day with her illuftrious fpoufe; but had met with many difficulties, which the King had helped her to overcome. The Queens of Poland have a particular intereft in being crowned; fince, without this folemnity, the republic pays them no jointure

in

Y, 1676. in their widowhood *(a)*; and even ceafes to treat them as Queens. Notwithftanding this, there have been two Queens who facrificed all thefe advantages to their religion : viz. the wife of Alexander, in the fixteenth century, and of Auguftus II. in the feventeenth. The former profeffed the Greek religion ; the latter the Lutheran, which Auguftus had lately abjured ; and neither of them was crowned. The moment for gratifying Mary's wifhes was come : the Primate held in his hands the two crowns; but as fhe was afcending the throne, to fit down on the left hand of the King, a murmur was heard in the affembly, and feveral voices protefted. This ftorm being forefeen, was appeafed by the trufty fervants which the King had difperfed up and down in the Cathedral, and a crown was fet upon both their heads *(b)*.

The ceremony ended with a cuftom of fome fingularity. A Bifhop of Cracow, affaffinated by a King in the eleventh century, fummons to appear at his tribunal, that is, in the chapel where his blood was fhed, every new King, as if he were guilty of the crime. John went to the place on foot, and declared, as his predeceffors had done, " that the crime was atrocious, that he was inno-" cent of it, detefted it, and afked pardon for it, " by imploring the protection of the holy martyr " upon himfelf, and his kingdom *(c)*." It were to be wifhed that every ftate would preferve, in this manner, fome monument of the crimes of Kings ; for flattery can find nothing in them but virtues.

(a) This jointure or dowry is two thoufand ducats per annum, charged upon the falt-pits and the Starofties of Spiz and Grodeck.

(b) Zalufki, tom. i. p. 678.   *(c)* Id. ibid. p. 597.

The

The medals that were ftruck upon this occafion y. 1676. prefented a naked, fword paffing through feveral crowns of laurel, and at the point a regal crown, with this infcription, *per bas ad iftam*, through thefe to that : and John had completely fulfilled its fenfe. The acclamations increafed, when he proceeded to the public fquare, followed by the Senate, and great officers, all on horfeback, where he received, on an elevated ftage, covered with the richeft tapeftry of the eaft, the oath of allegiance from the magiftrates of Cracow, and ennobled fome of them. This is the only occafion on which a King of Poland can create nobles; for nobility muft be conferred only in a diet, after ten years fervice in the army at leaft.

Before the reign of John, the King's military eftablifhment confifted of fix hundred body-guards, fix companies of light horfe of a hundred men each, and a regiment of foot, of twelve hundred men. John made an addition of a company of a hundred Swifs, fuch as we have in France; of five hundred janizaries, which his victories had furnifhed him with; and two hundred *Heidukes*. Thefe *Heidukes* appear in the world under very different forms. In Hungary they fight among the infantry. In Germany, and other countries, as the fancy takes, they attend behind the coaches of the fuperior nobility; in Bulgaria, the neighbourhood of Mount Hœmus, and other paffes, they appear as robbers, and plunder travellers. The republic did not interpofe in the new regulations which the King made in his guards, becaufe the expence was to fall upon him only.

The folemnity of the coronation being over, the diet was opened. The republic begun with thanking the King for all the fervices he had done his country, fince his election, and defired him to be

more

more careful of his life in time of action. A great number of the Senators and Deputies made another requeſt to him, which diſgraced themſelves as much as it did honour to the King. Their admiration of his great qualities made them preſs him to unite to the crown the office of Grand-General, which he had not yet filled up, though vacant ever ſince his election to the throne. The perſons who made this requeſt broke through the conſtitution, and betrayed the intereſt of the republic. Thus it is, that Kings, by the weakneſs and adulation of their ſubjects, become deſpotic ; and when it is neceſſary to bring them back to their former ſtate, the convulſions it occaſions are tremendous. The King did not make a bad uſe of this inconſiderate zeal ; and ſhewed his real greatneſs, by refuſing to be unconſtitutionally great. He raiſed to this important poſt Demetrius Wieſnowieſki, Petty-General of Poland, of the ſame family with the late King, and diſtinguiſhed by the title of Prince of Mitra. When Sobieſki was Grand-General, there had been frequent diſſentions between them, which Sobieſki, when King, forgot ; and by doing ſo, ſhewed his love of peace. Had he been guided by his own inclinations, his gratitude, and the ſuperiority of merit, he would have preferred Jablonowſki, who was only made Petty-General. But he knew that his friend would acquieſce in this regulation, to avoid animoſity and diſſentions. In fact, the expedient ſucceeded ; and from this time no one ſhewed more fidelity and attachment to his ſovereign than Wieſnowieſki.

The zealots for the King having thus miſſed their firſt aim, were reſolved, at leaſt to diminiſh the power of the Generals, in order to increaſe that of the King. The General's office being for life, they voted to make it *triennial*, and to oblige him to take

take an oath to the King, as well as to the republic.

There are few men, whofe manners are proof againft a throne. The King, who, while he was General, would have been offended at fuch a propofal, fupported it in fecret. But the Queen was not of a temper to conform in every thing to the King's inclinations. Jablonowfki was much in her favour ; and fhe was for having him enjoy the office of Petty-General in its utmoft extent, and that of Grand-General too, when time fhould give it him. She therefore thwarted the defign by fecret intrigues, which oftener hit the mark than open blows (*a*) : and the Generalfhip is ftill perpetual.

Another difference arofe between the Grand and Petty-General of Lithuania. The latter, who was the Prince of Radziwil, reproached Paz with having deferted the King in the Ukraine; and pretended, that in order to punifh him, and promote, at the fame time, the public good, it was expedient to withdraw from his command the Petty-General, with his divifion. He flattered himfelf, that he fhould be the more attended to, as he had married a fifter of the King's, a King whom Paz had grievoufly offended. The members of the diet took part on each fide with great warmth. The King, who had now a fair opportunity of revenging himfelf upon Paz, ftood neuter; and things continued upon the former footing in the Lithuanian army (*b*). But it was not without long debates.

A great deal of precious time was fpent in thefe difputes. Mahomet was full of indignation at a little republic, which had dared to contend with him for four years together. His Vifir, Kara-Muftapha, was mortified at not being able to fubdue it. They were both employed in forging the

(*a*) Zalufki, tom. i. p. 678 & 679.   (*b*) Id. ibid.

decifive

Y. 1676. decifive thunders: and it was known at Cracow that they were fo. The Chriftian Princes, who, in the time of the Crufades, went to attack infidels who gave them no caufe of quarrel, refufed to furnifh Poland with the fuccours it wanted, and which they had promifed to fend. The Ambaffador of France, Forbin, Bifhop of Marfeilles, was bitterly reproached on this account. The Queen, who was under fome obligations to him, had got him a nomination to a Cardinal's hat. The Primate, who thought that he himfelf deferved it better, expreffed in high terms his difapprobation of the gratitude of his fovereign: " It is the height " of injuftice, faid he, that a ftranger fhould come " and deprive us of our country's right of nomi-" nation; and a ftranger, moreover, who abufes " his character of Ambaffador, and purchafes the " fcarlet by cheating us. Where are the fubfidies " he has promifed?"

The Primate's complaint of the preference given to ftrangers has had frequent occafions to be renewed. The court of Poland has been admitted to the nomination of crowned heads only fince the reign of Cafimir, who procured this equality with other fovereigns; but it is generally ftrangers who reap the advantage. The republic entered into this difpute by applauding the Primate, and the hat did not come till a long time after, in the year 1689. But the fubfidies from France never came at all; nor did the other courts of Europe keep their promifes better (a).

The republic therefore was forced to truft for defence to her own forces only. A decree of the diet fixed them at a hundred thoufand men, and gave orders for the levying of taxes in proportion. Had this been done, Poland would never have

_____

(a) Zalufki, tom. i. p. 651.

raifed,

raifed, on any occafion, fuch a number of regular troops. But as the plan was great, fo the execution was difficult, not to fay, impoffible ; and befides, the decree difpleafed the provinces. The origin of the difcontent was a report, induftrioufly propagated, that while the King was propofing one thing in the diet, he was negotiating another with the enemy ; that a peace was privately agreed on with the Turk, and that the great uneafinefs he affected was only a pretence for raifing money, which would never return again into the purfes of private perfons, when it was once got out of them.

It was true that John did employ the mediation of the Moldavian and Walachian ; but the anfwers he received contained extremely hard conditions. This, the provinces that were to furnifh the contributions, would not believe ; their miftake cooled their zeal, fo that the levies of men and money were flow, and fell far fhort of the decree of the diet (a).

On the other fide, the report of the great defigns of the diet made an impreffion at Conftantinople. Mahomet at all events, refolved to furpafs them ; and a hundred and twenty thoufand Turks, and fourfcore thoufand Tartars took arms to avenge the honour of the crefcent. But the Sultan was in great perplexity about the choice of a General. Kara-Muftapha had no mind to expofe himfelf to frefh mortifications : Huffeim, who commanded at Choczin, was dead of his wounds. The intrigues of the fera.lio would needs decide the queftion. The Sultana Validé fupported one perfon ; the favourite Sultana another ; and the Vifir a third ; and all the three Generals, one after another, made trial of the command when the troops were affembled, and were all three re-

(a) Zalufki, tom. i. p. 598. & feq.

called.

called.   A fourth prefented himfelf for the fame purpofe, but the janizaries having foon found him out, drove him away by their contemptuous behaviour and murmurs.   In whatever nation the Generals wreft the command from one another, it is a fign that there are few good ones, or none at all.   At laft, the feraglio recollected a forgotten Bafhaw, who had been deprived of the command the very day after a victory; and Mahomet now reftored it to him, with an order to put an end to the war in this laft and important campaign.   This General was *Ibrahim Shaitan*, a man of cool valour, great experience, and a fecond Ulyffes for ftratagem. The furname of *Shaitan*, which fignifies *Devil*, was intended to exprefs this laft quality.   The Ottoman army was long in filling up the chafms which the late loffes had occafioned.   It did not reach the Niefter till towards the end of Auguft, and was joined by the Tartars below Choczin.

Notwithftanding the victories of her King, Poland was ftill upon the brink of ruin.   Thirty-eight thoufand fighting men were affembled in the plain of Glinian, near Leopol; and with this fmall number John marched againft two hundred thoufand.   The Queen accompanied him as far as Javarow (*a*), but it was only to alarm his conjugal tendernefs.   Having lately been delivered at Cracow of a daughter, Therefa-Cunegonda Sobiefka, and fcarce recovered of her lying-in; her weaknefs, the fatigue of the journey, and more than any thing, the dangers to which her illuftrious hufband was going to expofe himfelf, threw her into a dangerous illnefs.   The King was paffionately fond of her, but he gave the preference to his other wife, *the republic*; and without the leaft delay, continued his march to defend her.   He foon joined

(*a*) A fine country-feat belonging to the Kings of Puland.

his

his army, and attended upon the motions of the enemy.

Ibrahim, in order to lead him into an error, threw bridges over the Niefter, imagining that the King would come and difpute the paffage with him; in which cafe he intended to go up higher, penetrate into Pokrufia, and get behind the Polifh army. John had no hopes of hindering his paffage over the river: fo numerous an army could do it when it pleafed, by dividing into feveral bodies; but in order to form his meafures, he refolved to affure himfelf firft of Ibrahim's intentions, by continuing in his camp. Ibrahim, after he had loft feveral days in waiting for him, broke down his bridges, and croffed the Bucovine to get into Pokrufia.

John beginning now to penetrate into the defigns of his enemy, formed a plan, which feemed to all his Generals impoffible to be executed: it was to remove and fix the theatre of the war upon the extremities of the republic, in order to preferve its vital parts; and he inftantly decamped to attempt it. Wiefnowiefki commanded the center; Jablonowfki the right wing; and Paz the left. The latter feemed at laft to be fenfible of all the regard the King had fhewn him; and the Lithuanians had but one will with the Poles. They ftill expected to receive recruits both from Lithuania and Poland, which Radziwil and Potofki were commiffioned to bring up. The King marched with the utmoft celerity; and paffed the Niefter, to the great aftonifhment of Ibrahim, who was ftill at fome leagues diftance from it.

Zurawno, a mean town of no note, acquired a celebrity which will laft to the end of time. This paltry place, in Pokrufia, fituated at the confluence of the Scevits and the Niefter, is defended only by a rampart of earth, without any other fortification.

tification. The castle of its Lord, (who was then, and is now, one of the Sapieha family) is defended by a second rampart like the first, with four small platforms, where they mount a few pieces of cannon against the incursions of the Tartars. On one side of the town, higher up the Niester, is a plain which leaves the distance of about half a league between itself and the river, and this space is filled with a large wood of tall trees, terminated by a very deep morass. From this morass there issues a large rivulet, which, after crossing the plain between two very high banks, runs into the ditches of the town, in its way to the Niester; which river, on its opposite bank, presents a chain of mountains, extending several leagues above 'and below Zurawno.

The Christian army extended itself in the plain between the town and the morass; it had on it's left the town and the Scevits, a torrent which after having swept away every thing to-day, is fordable in every part to-morrow: on it's right was the morass; and the wood and the Niester behind it. The question was how to fortify it in front, since they were in great want of time, and the infidels might make their appearance the next moment. In order to secure the labours of the infantry, John passed the Scevits, went in quest of the enemy, fell upon their van and drove it back upon the center. But when he was on the point of being surrounded by the multitude which covered the plain for several leagues round, he made his retreat in good order, repassed the river and there stopped the infidels for a whole day; a respite of the utmost consequence for strengthening the entrenchments which he found to be very weak. He was well acquainted with the military art in it's utmost extent; and a double defence was formed with redoubts, and detached forts, raised under his own inspection. Here it was that he shut
up

up the laft refource that was to fix the fate of Poland, refolved either to perifh with his country, or
to preferve it in it's ancient glory. The moft intrepid officers were not without fear; becaufe courage
is not fufficient where ftrength is wanting, *Did I
not deliver you*, faid the King, *at the camp of Pod-
bajecz, where we were only twenty-four thoufand,
and befieged by a hundred thoufand? Do you fuppofe
that the crown, by being put upon my head, has made
it weaker?* They began to entertain hopes againft all
reafons for hoping.

Ibrahim was aftonifhed, and at the fame time
pleafed with this exceffive boldnefs. He drew up his
army in the form of a bow, of which the Niefter
made the ftring; and within this fpace he included the
morafs, the wood, the Polifh army, the town, and
the large rivulet that feparated the two camps. But
this was not all; for Nuradin Sultan detaching an
army from the Turkifh army, paffed the river, and
feized the chain of mountains which was parallel to
it's banks. All communication was now cut off,
and the Poles could hope for no more convoys, no
more fuccours. When one confiders thefe thirty-
eight thoufand men blocked up by two hundred
thoufand, it is difficult not to look upon them as fo
many victims deftined for flaughter, and their country for fervitude. And if efteem is always in proportion to the difficulties that are furmounted, what
muft thefe men have been, and what their King?

Such was the fituation of things on the 21ft of
September. The 27th was expected to be the decifive day. Ibrahim drew up his troops in battalia,
with vaft bundles of fafcines carried before them, to
fill up the rivulets which feparated the two camps.
John, inftead of waiting for him behind his entrenchments, prefented himfelf in the intervals between the
detached forts. This bold ftep made the infidels
halt on the other fide of the rivulet. On the 29th
they fhewed greater refolution; for a body of Jani-

zaries

zaries croſſed the ſtream and attacked the redoubts on
the right, which were ſo well defended by the Poliſh
dragoons, that the general engagement was ſtill ſuſpended.

John continued to employ the moſt exalted and
refined expedients of the whole art of war ; and being ſo well prepared to receive the enemy, he thought
it would be no diſgrace to ſue for peace, ſtill reſerv-
ing a power to reject it, if the conditions were too ſevere. Bidinſki and Koricki were commiſſioned to
negotiate it, and they treated firſt with the Tartarian
prince : " We come, ſaid they, to aſk for peace,
" under your mediation. Theſe are the conditions
" on which we deſire it. Let the Turks reſtore the
" places they have taken from us, particularly Ka-
" minieck, and ceaſe to ſupport the revolt of the
" Coſſacks."

It ill becomes you, replied the Cham, *to aſſume ſo
high a ſtrain, when you are actually expoſed to the
thunder of the irritated Sultan. Your firſt ſtep muſt be
to pay the tribute which the ſublime Porte impoſed upon
you, by granting you peace at a time when it might
have cruſhed you with the weight of it's arms. When
this is done, the Porte will conſider what places it will
be proper to reſtore to it's tributaries.*

" It is to little purpoſe, anſwered Bidinſki, to
" talk of a tribute which was impoſed upon us at a
" time, when the republic was turning it's arms
" againſt itſelf under a weak King. He who now
" governs us is a Prince of conſummate bravery ;
" the conqueror of Choczin, as you well know :
" the republic and he will periſh together, before
" they will pay tribute to any power upon earth.
" What brought us hither, is the love of peace,
" which you yourſelves ſtand in need of. We bring
" neither the petitions, nor the looks of ſupplicants,
" but a courage that is proof againſt every thing ;
" and our ſwords ſhall procure us peace, if a nego-
" tiation cannot." As he ſpoke theſe laſt words, he
drew

drew his fabre half-way out of the fcabbard. The Cham was highly provoked at this gefture. Bidinfki undoubtedly fhewed his courage, but his prudence may be called in queftion.

The Turkifh General waited in his pavilion for the refult of this conference. As foon as he learnt it, he fignified to the Cham that he fhould break off the negotiation, and that the Poles ought rather to think of afking pardon for their victory at Choczin, which was a revolt that he fhould foon make them fuffer for, than to boaft of it (a).

The Poles, having now no further hopes, depended entirely upon their vigilance and love of glory to make up for the inferiority of their forces. On the 28th of October, they were in a dangerous fituation. Their right wing was again attacked, and during the action, Nuradin fwam a-crofs the Niefter below the mouth of the Scevits, which he croffed alfo, and came and fell upon the left. The center continued immoveable, obferving the motions of Ibrahim, who waited for a proper opportunity to make the action general, but this opportunity did not come. The two attacks, though very warm, were without fuccefs. Three thoufand infidels were flain: the Tartars repaffed the river, and the Turks the rivulet.

Ibrahim, perceiving all the difficulties of getting a victory, refolved to carry on his attacks with greater art. He now laid fiege to the army which he had hitherto only blockaded. The trenches were regularly opened, as if it had been before a fortified town; and feven great cavaliers were erected, with a labour, of which perhaps the Turks alone are capable. Ibrahim erected his tent in the midft of the labourers, to animate them to their work. The heavy artillery was foon ready to play; and a battery of

(a) Zalufki, tom. 1. p. 565. Lengn. p. 249.

forty-

forty-eight pounders kept plowing up the Polish camp from morning to night, and carrying off men and horses. The death of Major-General Gebroski was particularly lamented; and he had a military tomb erected for him, in the manner of the ancient Romans. A ball went through the King's tent; and the army defired him either to remove to a greater diftance, or at leaft to fuffer himfelf to be covered with a mound of earth : but he rejected up-on the prefent occafion this precaution, which at an-other time he would perhaps have liked. When the danger is extreme, a King muft fhare it with his fubjects, who facrifice more for his glory than their own. Several General officers, who had dug them-felves places of fhelter, now appeared again with great alacrity.

In the mean time, the Turkifh trenches were car-ried on with great vigour, and began to draw near the entrenchments. John ordered counter-trenches to be dug, and two armies were feen advancing to-wards each other under ground; a thing which had hitherto been without example. A battle would have been a relief to the Poles; for their fituation grew very alarming. The forage which they had collected in the camp was all confumed. The adja-cent foreft, which, as a laft refource, furnifhed leaves for the horfes, which they mixed with a little grain, no longer afforded any thing but naked wood; and this wood, that is to fay, the tendereft branches of the trees, ftill ferved for nourifhment. Nor were the men in a better condition : all that they had left was bread dealt out very fparingly, and the King was oblig-ed to take up with the fame fare as the foldiers. The artillery, by being obliged to anfwer a fuperior fire, had almoft exhaufted the ftock of ball : even the powder required good management, fince that which was brought from Dantzick could come no farther than Leopol. If the infidels had fuffered much in

their

their frequent attacks, the Chriftians had fuffered much more in proportion to the fmallnefs of their number, by repelling thofe attacks. Radziwil and Potofki, the deliverers who were impatiently expected, had marched with ten thoufand frefh troops; but no reinforcement, no convoy had been able to make it's way through the Turks. In fhort, all things failed the Poles, except their courage; and every hour might prove fatal *(a)*.

The Queen, who was recovering her health at War-faw, undertook to ward off the deftiny of the King and the kingdom. She called together the fenators in her palace, and laid before them the frightful fitua-tion of affairs. All voted for the affembling of the pofpolite, and the primate iffued out his *univerfals* for that purpofe, which is the ordinary practice in Poland, when all is given over for loft.

Authority muft needs be a thing of a very delicate nature; for, as foon as the King was informed of the *fenatus-confultum* that was made for his delive-rance, he complained of their having violated the royal prerogative, by which the King only has a power of affembling the pofpolite. In fact, he de-pended more upon his own courage and that of his troops, than upon the flow efforts of an undifciplin-ed body of nobles.

Ibrahim, thinking himfelf fure of conquering by famine, and being willing to fpare the effufion of Muffulman blood, deputed to the King two Bafhaws and twenty-four Janizaries, who had nothing in their hands but long white ftaffs, their only weapons when they are not going to battle; for the Turks are afto-nifhed at the Chriftians for going to fee their friends in time of full peace, with fwords by their fides. The deputies reprefented to John, " that the Seraf-" kier was fully acquainted with the extremities to

(a) Zalufki, tom. i. p. 611. and feq.

R 3

which

Y. 16;6. " which their camp was reduced; that all relief was
" impoffible; that a prudent Prince ought to fub-
" mit to the laws of neceffity; that defpair had
" ruined more armies than it had faved; that the
" Grand-Seignior aimed at no farther conquefts in
" Poland; that he required only the execution of
" the treaty of Boudchaz, which had been perfidi-
" oufly violated; that Poland, by becoming tribu-
" tary, would for the future live peaceably under
" his high protection, like the Tartars, Coffacks,
" and many others; and they all fwore by their
" beards and muftachios to enfure the fafety of the
" Polifh army, offering to continue as hoftages till
" it had paffed the Niefter, after the figning of a
" more folid peace than the former."

· John anfwered, " that if the leaft mention was
" made in the treaty of the tribute impofed upon his
" predeceffor, he would confent to no peace; and
" that if the Serafkier had orders to infift upon that
" article, he only defired him to allow him, on the
" other fide of the river, a fpot fufficient to draw up
" his troops in battalia; and that then they would
" decide the point fword in hand."   The deputies
departed with this anfwer, reproaching him with all
the blood that would foon be fpilt.

This haughty behaviour of the King ill agreed
with the extremities to which he was reduced; for
having ordered the rations to be counted, there were
found only enough for four days more. As foon as
the night came on, he gave his orders for beginning
the attack next morning at break of day. He afterwards confeffed, that he never felt any uneafinefs
equal to that of this night. He reflected, that it was
he who had drawn the republic into this war; that
it was he who had formed the plan of the campaign, contrary to the opinion of all the Generals;
that all his former victories were ufelefs, if he failed
of this; that he muft either perifh by hunger, or
force

force his way through more than a hundred and
fourscore thousand men, with little more than thirty
thousand; and in short, that, instead of continuing
to be the hero of his country, he was perhaps just
going to become it's destroyer. But when he reflected, that, in order to save the army, he must renew the infamous treaty of Boudchaz, his mind was
fixed in a resolution of putting every thing to the
risk.

Let every one, who knows not the power of courage and the mutability of fortune, learn to hope.
John was extremely surprized at seeing the two Bashaws, who had addressed him the evening before,
return before break of day. The scene had changed in the night by a concurrence of unexpected
events.

The Janizaries, from the very beginning of the
campaign, were dissatisfied at not having the Sultan,
or at least the Vizir, at their head. " They aban-
" don themselves to their pleasures, said they, while
" we are suffering for their sakes. They give us a
" simple Seraskier, as if we, who founded the Em-
" pire, were not worthy of fighting in the presence
" of the Emperor himself." The forced marches
they had made in order to surround the Poles, the
continual fatigues they had undergone without coming to a decisive action, all contributed to encrease
their murmurs, and the sedition was ready to burst
out in a flame (a).

The Tartars, who found they were detained upon
the frontiers, instead of going to plunder in the heart
of the kingdom, exerted themselves in a very feeble
manner. They considered Poland as their general
magazine; and did not wish to see it become a Turkish province, because in that case they should be
forced to respect it. The King was not unacquainted with their dispositions; and to make their weak

(a) Cantemir, tom. ii. p. 72.

R 4

efforts

efforts still weaker, having but little powder left, he attacked them with gold. He found means to get access this way to their leader; and to make Ibrahim uneasy, he took care to publish it. The Cham denied the fact; but the suspicion still remained.

To encrease his anxiety, Ibrahim had just received information that the powers of Christendom were sending ambassadors to treat of peace, or to enter into the war. The Marquis de Bethune from France, and lord Hide (a) from England, were already arrived at Leopol; and demanded passports of the Turkish General to go to the King's camp.

Another piece of intelligence disturbed him still more. An army of Muscovites was upon the march, to pour in upon the Ukraine and deliver Poland; an event which was brought about by a secret negotiation of the King's. In fine, the season which was pretty far advanced, (it being the 28th of October, the thirty-eight day of the blockade) the rain which had kept falling for some time, the long march before he could reach the other side of the Danube, the possibility that provisions might fall short for so great a multitude; all these considerations determined Ibrahim to lend a favourable ear to peace, and he gave notice of his intentions to John.

Ibrahim had very extensive powers, with a positive order to put an end to the war in the most advantageous manner he could. He no longer insisted upon the tribute, but dictated in a great measure the other conditions. He required first of all, that Poland should enter into an alliance with the Tartars against the Muscovites, who were marching to deliver it. This demand was rejected with horror as unjust and infamous; and they were on the point of

(a) He was brother-in-law to James II. by that Prince's first wife. He sent a trumpet with six Walachians and an interpreter; who had all their heads cut off by the Tartars, a people who know little of the law of nations.

taking

Y. 1676.

taking up arms again on both fides. Ibrahim, after
having ftormed at the delicacy of an enemy to, whom
he confidered himfelf as doing a favour, grew calm
again, and propofed more tolerable conditions, which
were at length accepted.

I.

The Ukraine had kindled the firft fpark of this
war. The Porte gave up two thirds of it to Poland;
and the other third to the Coffacks, who fhould continue under the protection of the Grand Seignior.
By this fettlement, the Turks kept a footing in the
Ukraine, and an entry into Poland, for any circumftance that might arife.

II.

Podolia, the other key of Poland, had been ceded
to the Turks by the unhappy Michael, who now
reftored part of it to the Poles, but kept the two
beft places, *Jaflowiecz* and *Kaminieck*. The latter
was of fuch importance, that, unlefs it had remained to the Turks, Ibrahim would never have
figned the peace.

III.

Some Hords of Tartars had fettled in Lithuania; and being probably weary of the Polifh government, it was ftipulated, that they fhould be
free to return under the protection of the Ottoman
empire. By this means, Lithuania was deprived
of many ufeful hands, both for the army and the
plough.

IV.

It was fettled, that the captives (for the name
of prifoners of war is never heard of between the
Turks and the Poles) fhould be reftored on each
fide.

V.

262

V.

As the Porte usually contrives to insert some pompous article in every treaty, Poland engaged to send a magnificent embassy to the Grand Seignior, and that, in the mean time, an Envoy should accompany Ibrahim himself, by way of harbinger. The person pitched upon was Andrew *Modrzewski*, Cup-bearer of Siradia. Ibrahim asked whether his figure, air, and carriage were such as made him fit to appear before the Grand Seignior. To satisfy his scruples, the Envoy was presented to him, and gained his approbation.

There is nothing in this delicacy of the Turks which ought to raise our astonishment. All the children that are educated in the seraglio, in order to fill public offices, are well made and handsome. Great care is taken that they have no natural defects; no court is composed of persons that make a better appearance. The Turks say, that it is impossible a base mind should inhabit a handsome body.

An article, that came last to be treated of, was warmly disputed. The Greek, *Payanotos*, that second Ulysses, who had contributed by a stratagem to the taking of Candy in 1669, had obtained a grant from Cuprogli, that the schismatical Greek church should have, for the future, the keeping of all the holy places in Palestine, notwithstanding the opposition of the orthodox Latin Monks. The Divan had decided, that, as Jerusalem was under the jurisdiction of the Greek church before the time of the Crusades, its pretensions were just. John required that the holy places should be restored to the Latins : *What signifies this to you*, said Ibrahim, *provided you can come there and worship your pretended God ? We are far from hindering you : and, after all, are*

5

not

not these Greeks, Christians as well as you? That the God, whose monuments they kept, held them in abhorrence, was a proposition he would not listen to. However, he did not think that this difficulty ought to retard the peace, and it was signed on the 29th of October.

Ibrahim had not done all that he might with so great a force: but John had done much more than could be expected. When he passed the Niester, to stop two such armies upon the frontiers, all Europe accused him of rashness, and gave him over for lost. But heroes judge better of one another. The great Condé admired his conduct, and congratulated him on it by letter.

And yet when we reflect on the cause of so long a war, who is there that will dare to be an advocate for severity? The Cossacks complained of oppression, were not listened to, and revolted. Common justice and mild treatment would have quieted the commotion; whereas rigour involved their Governors in a war of eight and thirty years continuance. The Turks took part in the quarrel, and every campaign seemed to open the grave of Poland. At length, the catastrophe came; and gave occasion for deploring equally the power of Princes, and the misery of subjects. In four campaigns, Mahomet lost more than two hundred thousand men, and expended sums sufficient to have relieved millions of unhappy persons. By so great a waste of men and money, what advantages did he reap? A few places in Podolia and the Ukraine, which he was not sure of possessing for any length of time.

On the other side, Poland thought itself sufficiently recompenced for all the ravages, burnings, depopulations, and horrors it had suffered, by being delivered from the ignominious tribute that Mahomet had imposed upon it.

The

Y. 1676. The King returned home crowned with glory; but he foon obfcured its luftre in the opinion of a haughty republic. The weak Michael had been reproached for his accepting *the order of the Golden Fleece*; John was invefted with that of *the Holy Ghoft* at Zolkiew, by the Marquis de Bethune, brother-in-law to the Queen. " It was ftooping " to the Pride of France, faid the Poles, to wear " its livery:" and the indecency was fo much the greater, as France had conftantly refufed to give the title of *Majefty* to the Kings of Poland, and particularly to John himfelf, when in the year 1674, he folicited it by his Ambaffador Andrew Chryfoftom Zalufki *(a)*. This title of *Majefty*, of which Trajan thought himfelf unworthy, and which Chriftians formerly gave to God only, was deferved by few Kings better than by *John Sobiefki*; and Lewis XIV. who refufed it him, gave in his letters, in 1655, the title of *Brother* to the ufurper *Cromwell*. The Queen was acquainted with all this; but being at that time more a Frenchwoman than a Pole, fne prevailed upon her hufband to fhew France this mark of confideration, without confulting the inclinations of Poland.

Y. 1677. The republic expreffed its refentment on this account, when in an affembly of the States-General, it was propofed to ratify the peace of Zurawno. They had nothing to accufe the King of with regard to the treaty itfelf; but they were refolved to mortify him; and the weaknefs of their objections fufficiently fhewed what difpofitions they were in. The Emperor, who was a great gainer, while Poland kept the Turks employed, and exhaufted itfelf, endeavoured by his emiffaries and his money, to embroil things ftill more. But John furmounted all obftacles, and fent away the great

(a) Zalufki, tom. i. p. 525.

embaffy

embassy which Ibrahim had required, with the
Palatine of Culm at its head. When he arrived at
Daud-Pacba, a country-seat belonging to the Sultans, about a mile from Constantinople; he thought
it would enhance the dignity of the republic to insist upon an honour which had never been granted,
viz. to be received by the Visir at the very gate of
the city.

The answer returned by Kara-Mustapha, the
haughtiest of all Visirs, was, that if the Ambassador liked his situation at *Daud-Pacba*, he might
stay there till a fresh order. He did stay there in
fact, and was very narrowly watched ; but when
the Visir was informed of his demanding provisions for a retinue of seven hundred Poles, he ordered him to be told, that " if he was come to
" take Constantinople, his number of men was
" too small; and if he came only to make a figure,
" it was too great; but, be that as it would, the
" Grand-Seignior could as easily furnish provisions
" for seven hundred Poles, as for seven thousand
" who were rowing in his gallies (a)."

There wanted only such an incident as this to renew the war between the two nations ; so little scru-
pulous are the Governors of the world about the
effusion of human blood! But the King of Poland being informed of the dispute, and not thinking that the honour of his crown was concerned to
vindicate the absurdity of his Ambassador, sent orders to him to make his entry, without insisting
upon such an unusual demand. The Ambassador
obeyed ; but resolving, after all, to do something
extraordinary, he shod his horses with plates of silver, which being fastened with only two nails, came
off in the procession. A French Ambassador once
did the same at Rome; and both were equally

(a) Cantemir, tom. ii. p. 73.

blameable ;

Y, 1677. blameable; for it is always the people that pays for thefe extravagancies. One of thefe fhoes being brought to the Vifir, *This infidel*, fays he, *has fhoes of filver, but a head of lead; fince, being fent hither by an indigent republic, he does not make a better ufe of his money* (a).

The Ambaffador was once more upon the point of breaking all off, when two *Capuji-Bachis*, taking him by each arm to conduct him to the Grand-Seignior's throne, fignified to him, that he muft lay by his fword. Such is the law which the Porte prefcribes to all ambaffadors, and he was forced to conform to it. The beft thing that he did, was getting the two following articles to be added to the treaty of Zurawno, when he delivered the republic's ratification of it.

We give orders, fays the Sultan, to our armies of the Tartars of Crim and Budziac, to the Coffacks and Tranfylvanians, to defift from this time and henceforward for ever, from entering Poland without our command; and we forbid them to commit there any act of pillage or hoftility whatfoever: and if it happens that any violation of this peace fhould proceed from them, all fuch as fhall have fuftained any damage thereby, fhall receive reftitution, upon producing proper proofs.

We promife, upon our Imperial word and oath, and proteft before God, the Creator of heaven and earth, and by the miracles of Mahomet the great Prophet, the fun of the two ages upon whom the glory of the Divine Majefty refts, that we will not break any of thefe articles, nor perplex them with difficulties or equivocations: but, on the contrary, the peace and union now accomplifhed and ratified, fhall be equal in duration with our glorious

(a) Cantemir, tom. ii. p. 74.

empire:

empire : provided always, that the King of Poland, his Palatines and Generals, fhall occafion no
impediment thereto, and fhall do nothing againft
the tenor of this peace and friendfhip, and fhall honour it according to its juft value. May the inhabitants of Poland enjoy it in its utmoft extent,
under the fhadow of our protection.

Thus every thing was at length concluded. Six
months had been fpent in regulating the ceremonial of an Ambaffador's entry ; whereas a peace
was fettled between the two nations in three days
upon a field of battle.

End of the FOURTH BOOK.

THE

THE

HISTORY

OF

JOHN SOBIESKI

KING OF POLAND.

BOOK V.

IT was now a long time that the republic had
supported itself by dint of arms. At length it
begun to take breath under the laurels with which
its hero had crowned it; and the seven succeeding
years were years of peace.

At the beginning of the present, there happened
an event, which occasioned great complaints in the
diet assembled at Warsaw. Poland follows the example which is set it by the other Catholic states.
A Cardinal without authority, without an army,
without having at his disposal either honours or
fortune, frequently sprung from the dunghill of a
cloister, extends his *protection* from the banks of
the Tiber over nations and Kings. Cardinal Ur-
sini, at that time Protector of Poland, had placed

6

the

the *arms* of the kingdom over the great gate of his palace, from whence he had removed them, by some unaccountable caprice, to a place less visible and less decent. The diet exclaimed loudly at this insult. The King promised to make Rome feel that a kingdom is well able to protect itself: and satisfaction was instantly made *(a)*.

The diets in Poland are generally turbulent, but the present was very peaceful. The King gave audience to an Ambassador from Tartary, who came to confirm the alliance with the republic. His retinue was far from being splendid. When he came to the door of the great-hall, the officers in waiting took off his bonnet, (as he shewed no disposition to take it off himself,) which left him nothing but a white skull-cap. Over against the King was a large cushion in the Turkish fashion, upon which, having made three bows, he sat down crosslegged, and made his harangue. The King, in return enquired after the health of the Cham, expatiated upon the mutual advantages of a good understanding between the two nations, and sent him away loaded with presents. He received also the homage of the Dutchy of Courland, but upon condition that the Duke should, for the future, pay it in person *(b)*. The diet expressed its satisfaction at the peace made at Zurawno, with the Turks, by bestowing thousands of blessings upon the deliverer of his country; and all the orders of the state had one and the same will with him *(c)*.

But if the republic enjoyed perfect tranquillity, a city which flourished under its protection was agitated with intestine convulsions. *Dantzick*, after having had the good fortune of escaping from the tyranny of the Teutonic Knights, and the power

(a) Zaluski, tom. ii. p. 673.
(b) Chvalc. Jur. Publ. p. 542.
(c) Lengnich. p. 252.

S   of

Y. 1677. of Kings, to enjoy the liberty of a Hanfe-Town, feemed to grow weary of being happy. The magiftrates accufed the people of being ungovernable; and the people complained of being opprefled by the magiftrates. Some of the feditious were dragged to prifon, and others broke their chains to aim them at the heads of the Minifters of juftice. If the poinard was not yet lifted up againft the Magiftrates, no fort of infult was fpared them; and every thing vifibly tended towards anarchy and bloodfhed.

The King, leaving his fubjects to enjoy the fweets of peace, hafted to appeafe thefe madmen; and was followed by the Queen, notwithftanding her being big with child. No woman, in fuch a fituation, could be lefs tender of herfelf: fhe travelled with as little delicacy as any citizen's wife of Warfaw, wearing a prefervative, the virtue of which ought to have been tried upon fome other perfon. It was a girdle made of the fkin of an *urus*, a fpecies of wild ox, with remarkably long hair, and a goat's beard.

Upon the King's arrival, the Dantzickers fufpended their fury. He heard the complaints both of the people and the Magiftrates; and if he feemed to incline towards either fide, it was according to the Chinefe rule, which, in public diffenfions, always fuppofes the Mandarins to be in the wrong. Not that he did not difcover faults on each fide; but as he could not, without injuftice, punifh the people, and fpare the Magiftrates, he convinced them, it was for their own intereft, that no fcaffolds fhould be erected. He was forced to hear all their complaints, examine a-new into all the laws, infpect the management of the public money, fettle the proportion of taxes, and wind up afrefh

(a) Lengnich. p. 252.

the

the whole machine of government, which was juft going to fall in pieces. He found greater difficulties in re-eftablifhing order than in conquering his enemies, and valued himfelf more upon his fuccefs, in reftoring peace among men, without deftroying them, than upon the acquifition of a victory.

He ftaid in this city fix months; but the fatisfaction he enjoyed there, was difturbed by the death of the Primate Olfowfki, whofe prefence and advice he had defired upon this occafion, and who deferved the tears of the republic. It is a fmall part of his praife, that he difcharged all the Epifcopal functions in an edifying manner. Neither the anger, nor the favour of Kings, was ever able to pervert his difinterefted patriotifm. He oppofed Cafimir in his plan for bringing on a premature election of his fucceffor. He openly expreffed his difapprobation of the profcription of the celebrated Lubomirfki. *The King after the law*, was his ftanding maxim. An embaffy, in which he had prevailed upon the Emperor, to withdraw his forces out of Poland, had done him great honour. His application to the ftudy of letters, which he loved himfelf, and attempted, by founding a publick library, to make loved by others, had perfected his natural eloquence. With this weapon he had fubdued more than one faction, and brought back the Lithuanian army to its duty. The Poles faid of him, that he furpaffed Cato in gravity, Cicero in eloquence, and Metellus in purity of manners. The hyperbolical flights of Polifh oratory were, in this inftance, founded upon truth (a).

The King regretted the lofs of his friend with as much real concern as any private perfon could

(a) Zalufki, tom. i. p. 694, & 695.

S 2

have

have fhewn: but his grief was affuaged by the birth of his fecond fon, Prince Alexander. Prince *James* was commonly ftiled the fon of the Grand-Marfhal; but this was called the fon of the King. The Queen was brought to bed of him in the town of Dantzick. Her accompanying the King in all his journeys, was as much out of a liking for bufinefs, as a conjugal regard for his perfon. This paffion of hers for governing difpleafed the kingdom, and brought an odium upon the King. The Queens of Poland are moft exprefsly forbid to meddle with the adminiftration. The Chancellors, Chamberlains, and even Deputies are charged to watch over all violations of this regulation, and to lay them before the diet. Not that the Poles are backward to own, that a Queen, who will apply herfelf to bufinefs, and does not make a bad ufe of the artifices and charms of her fex, may do great fervice both to the Prince and the people; but they have greater apprehenfions of her abufing this power, than value for the fervices it may do them.

When John had appeafed the difturbances at Dantzick, he made the Mufcovites fenfible that it was their intereft to live at peace with him. While he was engaged in his wars againft the Turk, they had taken poffeffion of three Polifh Starofties, which made up a whole province. They now thought proper to reftore them, with an indemnification of two millions of florins (a).

Not long after, he fuffered himfelf to be drawn into an act of injuftice, which ended but unfuccefsfully. The Elector of Brandenburgh was laying the foundations of a power, the prefent greatnefs of which would aftonifh him. He little imagined that a day would come, when *Berlin* would be a match for the united forces of *Stockholm, Peterf-*

(a) Lengnich. p. 253.

8   *burgh,*

burg, the *Germanic Body*, *Vienna*, and *Verfailles*; Y. 1678.
and that if he himfelf was the *Great Elector*, his
great-grand-fon would be a great King. The Elector commanded the army of the allies in Alface
againft France; and it was of great confequence to
find him employment at home. While Lewis XIV.
was contriving how to effect it, the Marquis de Bethune, his Ambaffador in Poland, undertook the
tafk. He was a man, who, with all the agreeable-
nefs of a fupple Courtier, poffeffed great abilities,
both as a General and a Statefman; being lively,
enterprifing, laborious, and had a talent of writing
and fpeaking with amazing facility. He entered
into a clofe connection with the Swedifh Ambaffador, and by this means got accefs to the cabinet
of Stockholm. The plot was foon laid, and the
Swedes made an irruption into the Elector's territories in Pruffia, againft the faith of treaties. A
paffage through Courland and Samogitia being neceffary for their purpofes, *John* granted it at the
inftigation of Bethune, who infinuated to him,
that part of the conquefts fhould be fettled upon
his family by hereditary right. Conqueft is the
chief title of the generality of fovereigns; and *John*
thought he might act the King upon this occafion.
But his hopes were foon fruftrated: for the Elector, at the head of ten thoufand men, ran to the
defence of his dominions. The Swedifh General,
Henry Horn, had under his command fixteen thoufand, of which fcarce two thoufand five hundred
got back into Livonia (*a*); and the King of Poland fat down, with the regret of having made himfelf an enemy, without getting any thing by it.

Soon after, he met with another mortification
on the fide of France, in a family-concern. His
father-in-law, the Marquis d'Arquien, lived in

(*a*) Lengnich, p. 253.
S 3   France

France upon his commiffion of Captain of the hundred Swifs-Guards belonging to the King's brother.
The Marquis's daughter, the Queen of Poland,
was paffionately defirous of feeing him honoured
with the title of Duke. The King, who had the
fame wifh, applied for this favour to Lewis XIV.
and had no doubt of fucceeding. In the whole
courfe of his fortune, he had always kept up a
clofe connection with that monarch; he had always been the leader of the French party in the
field of election; and in cafe he was obliged to
quit his country, on account of the odium he might
incur, Lewis had offered him an advantageous
fettlement in France; a *Marfhal's Staff*, if he retained a relifh for military glory; or the title of *Duke*,
if he aimed only at an eafy and honourable ftate
of vegetation. The latter dignity, as he had now
no occafion for it, he flattered himfelf he fhould
be able to obtain for his father-in-law. Lewis
anfwered, that he was willing to oblige him, provided the Marquis would put himfelf in a condition to receive fuch a favour, by acquiring an eftate
fit to bear the title of a *dutchy*.

While thefe propofals were making, the Marquis de Bethune, who afpired to the fame honour,
without knowing that he was his father-in-law's
rival, had engaged for himfelf the intereft of M.
de Seignelai his friend, and M. Colbert; giving
them to underftand, that he could get the protection of his brother in law, the King of Poland,
when it was time to produce it. The two Minifters promifed him, to take an occafion of men-
tioning it to the King, and actually did fo. Lewis
would have chofe rather to confer this dignity upon
Bethune, than upon one of his brother's domeftics.
" I will not make, faid he, two Dukes together
" in the fame family. The perfon that the King
" of Poland chufes fhall have the preference."

No

No one expected a third competitor, who now entered the lifts.

This new candidate was a perfon named *Brifa-*
cier, Secretary to *Maria Therefa*, Queen of France.
A Carmelite Friar arrived at Warfaw, charged with
letters for the King of Poland. The fubftance of
the firft was, " that the perfon, who had the ho-
" nour of writing to his Majefty, was obliged,
" at the expence of his mother's reputation, to re-
" mind him, that being in France, juft after his
" quitting the academy, he had an intrigue with
" a fine woman, who had placed to her hufband's
" account a fon, that had really the honour of
" belonging to his Majefty; and that this fon,
" with the fortune that his pretended father had
" left him, had fcarce been able to purchafe the
" poft of Secretary to the Queen of France; that
" fince fortune and merit together had raifed his
" true father to a throne, he had reafon to hope
" for fome promotion; and that, in fine, the
" Queen of Fránce warmly fupported his re-
" queft." At thefe words, the Monk prefented
to the King a letter from the Queen, preffing him,
in the ftrongeft terms, to acknowledge *Brifacier*,
and to folicit for him the title of Duke.

John was aftonifhed at all this, but could recollect none of the circumftances; till a third letter,
containing a bill of exchange for a hundred thoufand crowns (which in Poland is a fum even for a
King) payable at Dantzick, diffipated the confufion of his ideas. He reflected that the thing
might poffibly be as it was reprefented; and a
new ray of light completed his conviction. This
was the Queen's picture, richly fet with diamonds,
with which the Monk terminated his commiffion.
The King confented to folicit at Verfailles the title
of *Duke*, for this fon whom he had forgot in
France, and now thought fit to acknowledge.

Lewis

Y. 1678. *Lewis* thought it ftrange, that he fhould be applied to from the fame quarter for three favours of the fame fort; but he kept the thing fecret, and fent an order to his Ambaffador to find out, whether the King of Poland was really convinced that *Brifacier* was his fon. The Marquis de Bethune took the advantage of a hunting-party, which furnifhed him with one of thofe moments in which the mind is off its guard, and conceals nothing. *By Saint Staniflas*, faid the King to him, *I remember not the left thing either of Monfieur Brifacier or his wife. I was very young at the time of my living in France; and had feveral intrigues upon my hands, fome agreeable enough, and others the reverfe, in a country where the women are fo eafily got at. Brifacier's wife may poffibly have been of the number. Indeed how can I doubt her being fo? This bill of exchange, this picture fet with diamonds, and more than all the reft, the Queen's letter affures me, that her Secretary is my fon.* The Marquis de Bethune had the addrefs to get poffeffion of this letter, which he tranfmitted to his mafter. The Queen faw that it was figned by herfelf; but upon reading the letter, declared fhe never entertained a thought of fo impertinent a project, and that Brifacier muft needs be mad. Neverthelefs, fhe had certainly put her name to it; but as Princes fign without reading, Brifacier, inftead of having a ducal palace, was fent to take up his lodgings in the Baftile, where he confeffed his impofture.

This adventure, which would have made any man, but a King, ridiculous, cooled the zeal of John's folicitation for his father-in-law; and befides this, the eftate which was to be created into a dutchy, was not yet purchafed. As for the Marquis de Bethune, who was a man not to be difcouraged by difappointments, he kept a ftrict watch upon the fituation of Europe, refolving to deferve
the

Y. 1679.

the honours he afpired to, by doing fome new Y. 1679. fervice to France in the courfe of his embaffy. The diverfion he had effected in Sweden did not fully fucceed, but another attempt might be more fortunate.   Lewis XIV. laboured inceffantly to raife himfelf upon the ruins of the houfe of Auf- tria.   The Emperor Leopold, under the appear- ance of great moderation, nourifhed a profound ambition.   He poffeffed Hungary only by right of election, but wanted to appropriate it to his family ; and he governed it in the mean time with a rod of iron.   The blood of the Counts *Serini*, *Na- dafti*, *Frangipani*, and *Tattemback*, had been fhed upon fcaffolds ; and yet the only crime of thefe great fouls was, that of maintaining their laws, their liberty, and their religion.

The authors of thefe violent counfels were Je- fuits ; it being the cuftom of that age to bring a difgrace upon government by fuffering Monks to have a fhare in it.   The famous *Tekeli* burnt with impatience to revenge his friends and his coun- try.   The Marquis de Bethune knew this ; and formed a project to fupply him with arms and men, which fhould be furnifhed by Poland, but paid for by France.   The plan was tranfmitted to the cabinet of Verfailles, and approved of.   Lewis XIV. expelled the Proteftants from his own do- minions ; but protected them in Hungary againft Leopold.   In this manner, Princes fupport fac- tions abroad, which they would punifh capitally at home.

The King of Poland was gained over to the fcheme ; but there was ftill one difficulty in the way, as he could not levy troops without the con- fent of the republic.   But Kings have more expe- dients than one, in order to evade the laws.   He ftill kept the Starofty of *Strick*, which he poffeffed when he was Grand-Marfhal, and connived at
whatever

Y 1679. whatever might pafs there. His example was followed by thofe to whom the republic committed the infpection of this diftrict, and the Marquis de Bethune, with little noife, raifed in this Starofty an army of ten thoufand men, which he was preparing to conduct to Tekeli. A number of French, who came unobferved into Poland, were to join this body of troops. It would have been a mortal blow to the Emperor; but it was parried, without intending it, by a woman, the Marchionefs of Bethune herfelf. She was fifter to the Queen ; and before her marriage had been Maid of Honour to Henrietta of England, wife to the King's brother. The Marchionefs could not help being a little jealous when fhe caft her eyes upon her fifter's crown. Their father, the Marquis of Arquien, was ftill in France with his commiffion of Captain of the guards, and a great many debts.

The Queen, who had laid other fchemes for his promotion, than that of a dutchy, being earneftly defirous of his feeing her in all the fplendor of a throne ; he fold his commiffion to put himfelf in a condition to appear in Poland. But the Marchionefs prevailed on the King's brother to ftop the money, in order to fecure her fortune, which had not been paid. This little family quarrel now became an affair of ftate. The Queen, being informed of this proceeding of her fifter, complained of it to her, and to her hufband, who was wholly unconcerned in it. In order to appeafe her, they both wrote to the King's brother whatever fhe dictated ; and at the fame time acted a part, which (if double-dealing be any crime in courts) made them both really blameable. Before the Queen's courier could get to his journey's end, they fent an exprefs to the Prince, defiring him to pay no regard to what fhe required. Upon this, the Queen writ to him in the language of a crowned head : and

the

the Prince, who had often feen her at his feet, having reminded her of that circumftance, acquainted
her with the whole intrigue.

The Queen was of a proud and haughty temper. Her father's lofing his dutchy, the price of
his commiffion being ftopped, the anfwer fhe had
received from the Prince, all together opened an
old wound in her mind, which was but imperfect-
ly healed. Not long after her elevation to the throne,
fhe was very defirous of taking a journey into France,
from the natural defire of making a figure in her
own country. Her pretence was to drink the wa-
ters of Bourbon; but upon her afking the court
of France, whether fhe might expect to be treated
in the fame manner as the Queen-Dowager of
England, the Marquis de Louvois, whofe rough-
nefs fhewed itfelf upon every occafion, gave for
anfwer, that there was a wide difference between an
hereditary Queen and an *elective* one. She refolved
therefore to take her revenge for all thefe affronts
together, and to make her own family feel a part
of it.

She begun with informing the Senators, of the
levies that were raifing in the Starofty; and fend-
ing for the Grand and Petty-General, told them
that an armament, carried on without the knowledge of the republic, muft needs cover fome bad
defign. The two Generals failed not to reply,
that nothing had been done without a tacit order
from the King. *Go to him then*, faid the Queen,
*and give him an account of my having reproached
you with this affair.* No one could be more pe-
remptory than the King when he commanded at
the head of an army; but he loved domeftic peace.
He quickly took part in the Queen's refentment,
and ordered the Generals to go themfelves to Strick,
difband the troops, and difmifs all the French officers who came to fhare in the glory of the enterprize.

prize. Lewis was offended at this ſtep ; and John on his ſide made complaints of the French Ambaſſador and his wife, who were both recalled, and the latter baniſhed into Touraine. The Ambaſſador was permitted to come and give his reaſons at court, where he laid the whole blame of his ill fortune upon the conduct of his wife.

From this time, Verſailles and Warſaw no longer lived in the ſame harmony. The Marquis de Bethune continued a Marquis ; and the Captain of the hundred Swiſs guards, whom France did not make a *Duke,* was found at Rome to be fit to be made a *Cardinal.*

The King now turned towards the houſe of Auſtria, from which he expected great aſſiſtance in an expedition that he had laid the plan of. He knew, by his intelligence in the Seraglio, that Mahomet intended to attack the Emperor Leopold ; but as yet it was only a project, and as the Turks generally make immenſe armaments, there is time for action while they are getting ready. He knew alſo that Mahomet, depending upon the late treaty with Poland, had left Kaminieck and Podolia without any great defence. The loſs of the former was inceſſantly regretted by the republic ; and its recovery would bring great glory to the King. Mahomet indeed had reaſon to be without apprehenſions, if treaties between Chriſtians and infidels are obligatory ; but people form their ideas of morality upon the principles of the age, and the place they live in. Rome was always ready to abſolve the Poles from the oaths they had ſworn to the Turks. The King ſaw therefore, that if he could prevail upon Leopold, who was threatened by Mahomet, to be before-hand with him, he ſhould have time to ſeize Kaminieck on a ſudden, under a promiſe of uniting afterwards his arms to thoſe of Leopold. He thought further of engaging, in the league, the

republic

republic of Venice for a diverfion by fea, and Rome Y. 1680.
for a fupply of money.

To carry on fuch a negotiation, there needed
an Ambaffador of the moft diftinguifhed merit.
The Perfon that John pitched upon was paffionately
fond of chymiftry, and knew but little of the matter; but then he had married a fifter of the Queen's.
Prince Radziwil was the man employed, who having mifcarried at Vienna and Venice, went next to
Rome, where he proftituted the dignity of God and
of his mafter together. He gave Pope Innocent XI.
the title of Divine Majefty on earth, and laid the
crown of Poland at the feet of this new deity of
his own making. The Pope evaded, for the prefent, the article of money, and anfwered him only
with compliments, good wifhes, and benedictions.
The Prince confidered his embaffy rather as a journey of curiofity, than in the light of a public commiffion. He was the richeft nobleman in Poland;
and he flattered himfelf, that, in his rambles over
the world, he fhould find the *Philofopher's ftone.*
His death luckily fpared him the juft reproaches
to which he would have been expofed in Poland *(a).*

If the fubjects of an arbitrary government have
many cruel moments, there are fuch alfo for Kings,
who have only a limited power. While the Polifh
Ambaffador was throwing away his feeble eloquence
in foreign courts, the King difplayed the utmoft
ftrength of his in the diet held at Warfaw. He did
not enlarge upon the neceffity, but upon the eafi-
nefs, of retaking Kaminieck. The two Orders
liftened greedily, and fhewed a difpofition to enter into his views; when fome perfons, either of a
timid temper, and afraid of feeing the Turks
once more ravaging their country, or, out of en-

(a) Zalufki, tom. ii. p. 665.

mity

mity to the King's glory, put a stop to the debates. The singularity of one circumstance was remarkable; it being not a Deputy, as usual, that broke off the diet, but *Breza*, the Palatine of Posnania, a Senator. His right of doing so could not be contested; but by the novelty of the thing, the King was at a loss how to act, since he could not possibly foresee it. The vehement harangue that he made in the Senate, after this, served only to encrease the sorrow of the true patriots, and to furnish secret matter of triumph to the faction that tied up his hands. " Restore to us, said he, addressing " himself to the latter, restore to us the safety " you deprive us of, the glory you wrest out of " our hands. You talk of resuming the design to " retake Kaminieck at some other time. Imprudent " as you are! is time at your disposal? Can you " make the opportunity return? The Turk will " provide for his own security. He will be in- " formed of our project, and perhaps take his " revenge; when instead of shedding a little blood " for an important advantage, we shall be forced " to shed streams for our destruction *(a).*

Another mortification soon happened, which affected him both as a father and as a King. The Elector of Brandenburg, whom he had made his enemy, formed a design of getting the richest heiress in Poland, for the Margrave Lewis of Brandenburg, one of his sons. She was daughter to Prince Radziwil, whose death has lately been mentioned. This marriage would transfer to a family, already too formidable to Poland, the immense possessions which the Radziwils had been four centuries in accumulating; four dutchies extending from the heart of Lithuania to the frontiers of Muscovy and Sweden. The Elector expected to

(a) Zaluski, tom. ii. p. 133, 784.

meet with oppofition, and therefore fent his fon to
conclude with all expedition this formidable match,
without confulting the republic, or even the King,
though he was guardian to the Princefs.

The Poles were extremely offended at this ftep.
" What ! faid the Senate and the Houfe of Depu-
" ties, fhall a foreign Prince come and rob us of
" a treafure, which it is of fuch importance for us
" to keep in our own poffeffion ! When he has got
" it, we fhall be in a dilemma whether to grant
" or refufe him the right of *Indigenate (a.)* If we
" grant it, he will govern both in our general and
" provincial diets ; and make ufe of his power
" in Lithuania to dictate all our alliances, and
" perhaps to make leagues againft us. If we re-
" fufe it, he will employ the acquifitions he has got
" by this marriage, and the arms of his father, to
" compel us. Let us beware then of entering
" into an alliance with the lion, like the filly beafts
" in the fable : 'tis fufficient for us to be obliged to
" fuffer a King."

The King was more fenfibly affected by this marriage than even the republic ; as he had intended
the young Princefs for his eldeft fon, Prince James,
who would foon be of years of maturity. The
Queen indeed, and all the French in the Polifh
court, did not much regret the lofs of this match,
which they faid was not confiderable enough for
the fon of a King, who ought to marry a Princefs
by birth, and not one who derived her title from
the empire ; the daughter of a fovereign houfe, and
not the daughter of a Senator. Thefe monarchical
notions never entered into republican heads ; and
ftill lefs into that of the King, who knew that the

(a) The right of indigenate, in other countries called naturalization, is neceffary in Poland in order to poffefs eftates or
offices, or be admitted into the diets.

Roman

Y. 1680. Roman Emperors, that is to fay, the mafters of Kings, married into fenatorial families; and that very lately, James II. King of England, had married the daughter of Counfellor Hyde, advanced afterwards to the dignity of Chancellor, and ranked by the Englifh in the number of great men.

Befides this, the King confidered of what importance the great eftate of this young heirefs would be to his fon. An abfolute Monarch would undoubtedly have armed his fubjects for the intereft of his family; he would have painted the carrying off the Princefs as an affront to the crown and the nation; and perhaps another *Troy* would have been deftroyed for this new *Helen*. But being accuftomed to the manners of a free country and reftrained by the laws, he conformed to the fentiments of the republic; which, when it's firft fit of refentment was gone off, thought it better to give up an heirefs, than enter into a war; the event of which, however it turned out, would leave great fcars behind it. The republic only fought for an expedient to mitigate the King's vexation. The difputed Princefs was his niece: the Elector of Brandenburg promifed that this marriage fhould in no degree be prejudicial to the rights of the royal family; and then the knot was tied (a.) The King's family was foon after encreafed by the Queen's being delivered of her third fon, Prince *Conftantine*.

Y. 1681. The next year was diftinguifhed by a diet's being held in a town, which had never before been the fcene of fuch an affembly. The place appointed both by law and cuftom, was Warfaw, which by its fituation, fize, and wealth, is very well adapted for a national meeting. For fome time paft, the Lithuanians, particularly the Paz's, had demanded that it fhould be held alternately in Poland and Li-

---

(a) Puffendorf. Zalufki, tom. 2. p. 675.

thuania. The proposal had passed in 1673, with this restriction, that Lithuania should enjoy this advantage only once in six years. But the law had never been put in execution. In this year therefore, for the first time, the King, being no longer able to withstand the intrigues and clamours of the Paz's, transferred the diet into Lithuania. But instead of holding it at *Wilna*, the capital of that dutchy, he summoned it to meet at *Grodno*. By this means, he mortified the Paz's, particularly the Grand-General, who was Palatine of *Wilna*; and favoured the Starost of Grodno, a near relation of his own, who by so great a concourse of people, acquired a prodigious encrease of the revenue of his district. But Grodno is only a mean town, of difficult access upon the river Memel, ill built and very unwholsome, known only by the tomb of *Stephen Battori*, a monument which procured no conveniences for the diet. The King's own servants could not help saying, that when people resolve to mortify their enemies and oblige their relations, they ought at least to do it, without any detriment to the public. The contempt which the King shewed for these clamours, was beginning to act despotically in the very face of liberty.

The diet was opened with a very warm dispute, on occasion of the election of a Marshal, which, according to custom, was the first thing they proceeded on. The Paz's were for one person; and the King for another. The event of the election was such as the King wished; it being in favour of *Francis Sapieba*, descended from an illustrious family, which the King aimed at raising upon the ruins of the Paz's.

Another object excited a still greater ferment. The Polish nobles sometimes think fit to raise troops and take them into their own pay; as the great vassals of the crown formerly did in France under the feudal government. This had been lately done

T

done by one of the *Lubomirſki's*, (a) brother to the Grand-Marſhal and Great-Standard-Bearer of the crown, in order to favour *Tekeli*, who being ſeconded by the Baſhaw of Buda, had been endeavouring for three years paſt to raiſe all Hungary in arms. This ſtep of Lubomirſki's was a conſequence of the diſappointed ſchemes of the Marquis de Bethune. The Grand-General Wieſnowieſki accuſed the Great-Standard-Bearer of having violated the Laws ; and the Emperor's Ambaſſador, the Count *d'Altein* warmly ſollicited the puniſhment of the criminal: The ferment was riſing hourly to a greater height, when the Pope's Nuncio, *Martelli*, extinguiſhed it, by exhorting the aſſembly to take up arms againſt the Turk. An alarm for a Turkiſh war was at that time gladly liſtened to by the majority, and no farther mention was made of the criminal.

The Queen had an affair which concerned her perſonal intereſt to lay before the diet. She wanted to have her houſehould-revenue encreaſed ; but the *Eſtates*, diſſatisfied at their being aſſembled at Grodno, were not diſpoſed to grant her requeſt. The King, who gueſſed in what temper they would be, had deſired the Queen to defer her demand to a more favourable opportunity ; but the preſent only would ſuit the Queen. She was preſent, as uſual, at all the ſittings ; not indeed publicly, for that would have given offence to the republic, but in a place where, without being ſeen, ſhe heard all the debates. From hence, at a proper juncture, ſhe ſent her Chancellor to the King as he ſat upon the

(a) He was known by the name of the Chevalier de Lubomirſki. 'This appellation may poſſibly ſurpriſe the reader, ſince in Poland every gentleman is at leaſt a Knight, by being one of the Equeſtrian Order. But Lubomirſki was a Knight of Malta, and poſſeſſed ſome valuable commanderies of that order, which he afterwards reſigned to marry one of the Queen's maids of honour.

throne,

throne, defiring him to think of her. The King, with a fevere look and a gefture of refufal, dif-miffed the Chancellor, who returned to the Queen, and foon after came back to the King in confe-quence of a fecond order. The King, flying into a paffion, broke out in harfh expreffions againft a man, whofe fituation left him nothing but to obey. The Chancellor, who was a church-man, replied with equal firmnefs and refpect: *If your Majefty forgets that I am a Prieft, you fhould at leaft recollect that I am a gentleman.* " 'Tis enough for me, fays
" the King, that you are a man : I fee I am in
" the wrong, and you fhall have no more reafon
" to complain of me." The Queen knew what fhe did, in perfifting in her purpofe : fhe had gain-ed the votes before-hand, though the King could not conceive it, and meet with the fuccefs that fhe expected *(a)*.

Of all the virtues, that which the King moft valued himfelf upon, next to courage, was cle-mency. A wretch of that deteftable fpecies, whofe villainy and blacknefs of foul make them formid-able even to the Governours of the world, not con-tent with venting his fury in the moft outrageous language againft the King, had fired a bullet at his picture, as if with a defign of hardening himfelf in order to make the next attack upon his perfon. This monfter, who was of the body of the no-bles, was examined before the diet and condemned to expiate his crime by fuffering capital punifhment. The laws had decreed his death, but the King granted him a pardon. *I would not grant it*, faid he, *if his offence had been againft the nation.* The Parricide was only deprived of his liberty, and even of this for no long time. Every one cried out, what barbarian will dare any more to offend a

(a) Zalufki, tom. i. p. 704.

T 2

King

King fo ready to pardon offences? The criminal himfelf never ceafed bleffing him for the whole remainder of his life (a).

While this diet was fitting, there happened an event which would be unworthy of the gravity of hiftory, if it were not connected with public affairs. In the province of Volhinia, a ghoft that was faid to appear in the houfe of a Polifh nobleman made fuch a noife, as ecchoed over all the neighbouring provinces. The dead man faid many things that affected the reputation of the living, and the credit of the government: he even went fo far as to order, in the name of God, fome things to be done, which difpleafed the King. The Jefuit *Gnievofz*, chaplain to the Grand-General, attefted the reality of the apparition; but the King difpatched to the place an intelligent officer of the army, who had fome difficulty to perfuade himfelf, that the irrevocable laws of the other world were fufpended merely to frighten the inhabitants of this. The affair turned out, as it always does, to be a mere comedy, which however ended tragically when the Commiffioner came to make his report. The King was at that inftant furrounded with Courtiers, and his Confeffor *Pikarfki*, another Jefuit who had already had the direction of the confciences of two Kings, ftanding next to him. Every one liftened attentively to the hiftory and contrivance of the trick. At the unravelling of the plot, the King cafting an angry look upon the manager of his confcience, addreffed him in thefe words: *Well! what does your rafcal Gnievofz fay to that?* The director, who preached up patience and Chriftian refolution to every one elfe, was himfelf fo ftruck with this blow, that he furvived it only eight days. The lofs he fuftained, with refpect to this world, was

(a) Id. ibid. p. 706.

very

very great ; the King, whose confidence he possessed, having intended him the Bishoprick of Kiovia,
and the seals of the kingdom. The King lamented
the innocent sufferer, but did not punish the guilty
Gnievofz : one would imagine that his whole pleasure lay in rewarding (a).

The King's present dissatisfaction with the Jesuits
was preceded by another, arising from a dispute
of interest. That order has large possessions at
Jaroslaw, a city of Black-Russia, upon the river
San. The Queen had also an estate there, which
she wanted to keep to herself ; but the Jesuits, by
means of some confusion in the title-deeds, encroached daily upon her. The present is another
of those minute events which I should not think
worthy to be recorded, but that it serves to shew
the mildness of the King's proceedings. Instead of
adding his own authority to the letter of the law,
he writ to the General of the Jesuits in these terms :
" I shall not summon your brethren at Jaroslaw to
" appear before the diet, where I should have on
" my side both justice and the respect that is due
" to me. I am afraid of encreasing by this means
" the hatred that is already born you. I only,
" advise you to be upon your guard against those
" that have the management of your houses : they
" make it a point to extend their possessions by all
" sorts of means, without any regard to justice.
" I would have you order them to produce their
" deeds before two Commissioners whom I shall
" name ; that every thing may be settled amicably
" and without public scandal. Farewel. Remem-
" ber that I am a King." The deeds were at
length produced ; and the good fathers were obliged to own that they understood the value of estates,
better than the nature of titles (b).

(a) Zaluski, tom. i. p. 706.   (b) Zaluski, tom. ii. p. 775.

The

Y. 1681. The diet had now been open fix months, and the members begun to be tired of fo long an attention to bufinefs. The Chevalier Lubomirfki, who had juft been accufed as a criminal, was made Marfhal of the court, without the leaft oppofition. There were ftill feveral affairs to be fettled; and that they might be difpatched the fooner, the King. in one of the fittings, ventured to order candles to be lighted; which was a violation of a cuftom that had paffed into a law. The Deputy *Prziemfki*, a man gained over by France, where he had formerly ferved as a mufketeer, waited only for a pretence to diffolve the diet; and took this opportunity to proteft and leave the affembly. It may be a doubt perhaps, with fuch as know the inclination of Kings towards defpotifm, and the delicate nature of of liberty, whether they ought to blame the Deputy or not; but he was certainly criminal in obftinately refufing to reftore to the diet its capacity of proceeding to bufinefs, and in bringing over to his faction a part of the Senate and Equeftrian order *(a)*.

Y. 1682. Poland could already reckon five years of peace: the fixth paffed over in a lowring calm which foretold an approaching ftorm. The tempeft was gathering at Conftantinople, and they fancied at Vienna that it threatened Poland; while at Warfaw they were perfuaded that it would fall upon Vienna. At all events Leopold and John refolved to unite

(a) In order to judge of the power which this man had acquired over the multitude, it is fufficient to meation a fingle fact which happened long after the prefent time. At the election of a fucceffor in the room of King John, almoft all the Palatinates had already cried out, *Saxony for ever.* " What! my " brethren, cried Prziemfki, will you elect a Heretic ? What " is become of your zeal for religion ? 'Tis not to us that " you are engaged, but to this——" pulling out a crucifix which he had concealed in his bofom. Immediately they all cried, *Conti for ever.*

their

their forces by a treaty both defensive and offensive. The Emperor engaged to furnish an army
of sixty thousand men to act in Hungary, and the
King of Poland forty thousand to be employed
where it should be thought proper. The two
Sovereigns were to march to each other's assistance,
as occasion required ; and whoever of the two should
happen to be with the army, was to have the command in Chief. This last article gave it in effect
to John ; for Leopold was no warrior.

As for the article of subsidies, the war being expected instantly, and Poland being unable to raise
money without the consent of a diet, which it was
impossible to assemble so soon ; the Emperor was
to advance twelve hundred thousand florins to be
repaid him by the Pope ; and he further undertook
to engage the King of Spain to obtain a tenth from
his Italian dominions, to be employed for the benefit of the republic. Moreover the two combined
powers promised to exert their utmost in order to
extend the league, of which the Pope declared himself the head. The Papal Chair was filled by
Odescalchi, son of a banker in the Milanese, and
born a subject of the house of Austria : He had
even made two campaigns in the Austrian troops,
which made him retain something of a martial spirit.
He governed the church by the name of *Innocent*
XI. a wise Pontiff, an indifferent divine, a courageous, haughty, and magnificent Prince, fond of
enterprizes of lustre, and supporting them with his
own money and troops.

The Popes have in all ages founded the alarm
against the Turks : but it must not be supposed
that they have been animated by religion only.
While the Princes of Christendom are fighting and
exhausting themselves to wrest Provinces out of the
hands of the Infidels, the Pope extends his spiritual
authority, and Italy is better secured.

T 4 Innocent

Innocent XI. was not ignorant that Mahomet
II. after he had made himself master of Constantinople, which Constantine little thought of building
for the Turks, had advanced as far as Trieste at
the gates of Venice, and set up the Crescent in the
heart of Calabria, from whence he threatened Rome
and all Italy. He knew also that very lately, the
famous Vizir Cuprogli, after the conquest of Candy,
had laid it down for one of his projects to overturn
the *Holy See*. In the present juncture therefore, the
Pontiff cried out *to arms*, and called upon all the
Sovereigns of Europe. Some of them listened to his
call, but the greatest part turned a deaf ear. Lewis
XIV. was of the number of the latter; because
his pride, being irritated by that of the Pope,
wanted to mortify him. This reason alone would
have hindered him from entering into the league;
but he declined it also from reasons of state. Notwithstanding the peace which he had signed at Nimeguen in 1679, with the house of Austria, he
could not approve a treaty intended for its support:
on the contrary, he carried on intrigues in Poland
to hinder it from taking effect; and his Ambassadors at the Ottoman court pressed the Turks to carry
the war into Germany. His sentiments were widely different in 1664, when he sent six thousand
French, who shared in the glory of the battle of
St. Gothard, where Montecuculi defeated the Turks:
for Lewis at that time had not sworn that he would
lower the house of Austria.

But if Lewis was wanting to Leopold, Leopold
was still more wanting to himself. It was not long
before he found out that the storm was to fall, not
upon Poland, but his own dominions. Mahomet difpatched a courier to give him notice, that Tekeli and
the Hungarians, with a view to deliver themselves
from oppression, had submitted to the Ottoman Empire, of which they were henceforward the tributaries.

taries and subjects; and therefore he was expected to withdraw the troops he had sent against them, and to restore the places which he still possessed in the kingdom; unless he chose to be considered as the breaker of the peace, and to see his temerity punished *(a)*. Notwithstanding this fatal certainty, Leopold refused to give the title of *Majesty* to John, who alone was able to save him from destruction. Nor is this refusal a thing to be wondered at; since Leopold's predecessor, *Ferdinand* III. in the preliminaries to the treaty of Westphalia, would only give the title of *Most Serene* to the King of France, his conqueror; and the court of France, in its turn, shewed great unwillingness to give the title of *Majesty* to the great Gustavus, who thought that the first of Kings was he that beat the rest. One would have thought, in so critical a juncture, that Leopold chose rather to perish with all his pride, than to see a new *Majesty* in Europe. But John stuck to his point, and refused to treat but upon that condition.

There are some virtues which Christians may learn from Infidels. The Turkish armament was ready in the month of April; but the truce with the house of Austria was not yet expired. This honest dealing of the Mussulmen gave the two Sovereigns time to wrangle; and the dispute ended with the concession of a title that would have raised some sentiments of gratitude in John's mind, if it had been given with a good grace *(b)*.

While this difference was settling, Count *Albert Caprara*, Ambassador Extraordinary from Vienna, was endeavouring to appease the Sultan, who refused to make any alteration in the conditions he had laid down, and declared war against the Emperor about the end of autumn. Caprara saw the horse-

---

(a) Cantemir, tom. ii. p. 82.   *(b)* Zaluski, ii. p. 803.

Y. 1682. tails flying upon the feraglio, and departed immediately for fear of being arrested (a).. An Ambaffador at the Porte has a difficult part to act on account of the pride of the Turks; who are accuftomed to receive embaffies in ordinary from all
other courts, and never fend any themfelves. They
confider thefe perpetual embaffies as an homage
paid by the Chriftians to their fuperiority; and fhow
more regard to a merchant who makes himfelf ufeful to the ftate, than to an Ambaffador. Even
Lewis XIV. who infifted upon fuch fignal fatisfaction whenever his crown was affronted in the perfon of his Minifters, required none from the Turks
for their unworthy treatment of *M. de la Haye*. The
Ambaffador from Vienna would not have met with
better ufage. Nothing now remained for Leopold
to do, but to ratify with all expedition the treaty
Y. 1683. of the league. His Plenipotentiaries arrived in
Poland in the month of January; but the treaty was
not fworn to till the 31ft of March at Warfaw, and
at Rome about the fame time by the Cardinal-Pro-
tectors, before the Pope. A circumftance of great fingularity, but not thought fo at that time, was, that
the two Potentates expresfly ftipulated, by a feparate article, not to apply to the Pope for a permif-
fion to perjure themfelves with a fafe confcience (b).
This falfe cafuiftry in matters of confcience had
infefted Europe for many centuries: Philip. II.
at the time of the revolt of the low-countries,
went fo far as to declare, in a public edict, that his
violation of the oath he had taken to the Flemings
was not criminal, becaufe the Pope had given him
a difpenfation from it.

But, not to examine here into the religion of an
oath which is refpected even by Barbarians, nor into
the treaty with the Turks figned by John himfelf at

(*a*) Cantemir, tom. ii. p. 82.   (*b*) Zalufki, tom. ii. p. 808.

Zurawno,

Zurawno, his prudence in entering into this league may perhaps be juſtly queſtioned. He engaged by the treaty to march his troops wherever Leopold ſhould want them, whereas by entering into no engagement at all, and leaving Vienna to decide its own quarrel with Conſtantinople, he might, during that interval, have found it eaſy to retake Kaminieck, and all that Mahomet had wreſted from the republic. If we believe the author of the preſent ſtate of Poland, he was drawn into the league by the deſire the Queen had to be revenged of France, for refuſing to create her father, the Marquis d'Arquien, a Duke and Peer. Beſides this, ſhe had a perſonal affront to revenge, in the refuſal ſhe met with from France to treat her with the honours of a Queen in her intended journey to viſit her native country. Intereſts of leſs importance have often produced bloody wars. But Leopold ſet to work upon John ſprings of a more powerful efficacy. He tempted him with a promiſe of marrying an Archducheſs to his ſon Prince James, and of perpetuating in his family the crown of Poland, by getting it made hereditary, either voluntarily or by force, in a diet, where the authority of Innocent XI. ſhould intervene. Leopold, in the receſſes of his cabinet, contrived and brought about the moſt important revolutions. It is well known, that he made an Elector and a King; and that the Hungarians loſt, under him, the right of electing their Sovereign.

The King was prevailed on by thoſe tempting offers ; and when the league was formed, employed himſelf wholly in the execution of what he had promiſed ; but every ſpring that he attempted to put in motion reſiſted the impreſſion of his hand. The *univerſals* that he publiſhed inſtantly excited murmurs. The provincial diets ſeemed to aſſemble with a view only of raiſing obſtacles. The Palatinates

tinates protefted that they were exhaufted both of men and money.

The Generals knew not where to raife fo great a number of troops; and among the Senators, even thofe, who where moft devoted to the King's will, fhewed great backwardnefs. Lithuania, commonly lefs active in taking up arms than Poland, difcovered more averfion than ufual on the prefent occafion. The Paz's raifed difficulties, from the natural antipathy they had always born the King. His chief dependence was upon the Sapieha's, a family that he had refolved to raife in oppofition to that of Paz, which he wanted to humble. The Sapieha's were four brothers, of great wealth, clofely united with each other, of determined courage and high fpirit. John had conferred upon them offices of great importance; the eldeft was Petty-General and Caftellan of Wilna; the fecond, Grand-Treafurer; the third, Mafter of the Horfe; the youngeft, Grand-Mafter of the Artillery and Treafurer of the court. By means of thefe offices, their influence was great in Lithuania; but notwithftanding this, their motions were flow, and they feemed to forget what they owed to their benefactor.

Embarraffed by fo many difficulties, John fet himfelf at work to difcover the caufe; and it was not long before he intercepted fome letters of the French Ambaffador's, which difcovered the whole fecret. *Forbin*, at that time Bifhop of Marfeilles, had fhewn, in his firft embaffy to Poland, that his talents were at leaft equally fit for intrigues of ftate, as for the government of a diocefe. In his prefent embaffy, he followed the Marquis de Bethune's plan for croffing the defigns of Leopold.

He boafted in his letters, " that he would def-" troy the league with the Emperor; and told the " court of France, that by means of the Grand-" Treafurer *Andrew Morftyn*, he was acquainted with
" all

" all the counſels of the cabinet of Warſaw; that,
" by his aſſiſtance, he had gained the Grand-Trea-
" ſurer of Lithuania, and brought over the Sa-
" pieba's to the French intereſt; that he had ſtag-
" gered Jablonowſki, by giving him a diſtant pro-
" ſpect of obtaining, by means of Lewis XIV. the
" crown of Poland when it ſhould become vacant;
" that the provincial diets already acted openly
" againſt the King's intentions; that all this could
" not be brought about without money; that he
" had already-diſtributed penſions, to the amount
" of fifty thouſand *Imperials (a)*, according to his
" maſter's directions; and that he had alſo fur-
" niſhed money to Tekeli, to ſupport his party in
" Hungary. He added, that he had not attempt-
" ed to corrupt the republic, till after having at-
" tacked in vain the virtue of the King, who, for
" this time, had not only been inacceſſible by
" gold, but even by the temptation of getting his
" ſon Prince James elected for his ſucceſſor before
" the legal time, by the intereſt of France, pro-
" vided he would, in the preſent criſis, give up the
" houſe of Auſtria to the mercy of Lewis XIV. and
" moreover, that the King's inflexibility had pro-
" duced no other ill effect, than making it neceſſa-
" ry to diſtribute larger ſums among a people total-
" ly venal, and deſtitute of honour and good faith."
In this manner, the fate of Kingdoms is often decided by the gold and intrigues of an Ambaſſador.

When John had got poſſeſſion of this piece, he
ordered it to be read in full Senate. Some of the
members inſtantly betrayed their guilt, by their confuſed behaviour; while the innocence of others ap-

---

(a) A piece of money, coined by the Emperors of Germany, and worth about three livres, and fifteen ſous French, or
3 s. 8 d ¼. Engliſh.

peared

Y. 1683. peared by their fudden indignation. They all looked at each other, till the King fixed their attention, by addreffing them in thefe terms : " I know not " what opinion you entertain of thefe letters. It " feems credible enough, that *Morftyn* and others " like him, have fwallowed the bait of corruption. " But I cannot be perfuaded that the *Sapieha*'s have " bartered their honour.. Still lefs do I believe that " Jablonowfki would make his way to the throne, " by betraying his country and his King. An Am- " baffador, who carries on his fchemes in the dark, " and fcruples no means to acquire the favour of " his mafter, is very apt to flatter himfelf with the " fuccefs of his own plots. He interprets a doubt- " ful gefture, an ambiguous expreffion, to indi- " cate a concurrence in his defigns, and often " fwells the number of the confpirators to make " himfelf more important; having always a re- " fource ready, in cafe of neceffity, by imputing " his own miftakes to the inconftancy of others. " As to what he fays of myfelf, I acquit him of " the charge of falfhood. It is true, he has had " the affurance to tempt me with offers of im- " menfe fums, and with the ftill more feducing " bait, of enfuring the crown to my fon. His mo- " ney, I found no difficulty in defpifing : the " voice of nature was not fo eafy to be refifted; " but that of the republic has prevailed over all : " and if another Sobiefki is to reign over you, he " fhall owe his crown only to a free election. The " Ambaffador affronts us all, by defcribing us as " a venal nation, without honefty, and without " honour. Let us beware of confirming thefe " odious imputations by breaking a treaty, which " was entered into with the confent of all the or- " ders of the ftate, and which it would be necef- " fary to negotiate now, if it were not already con- " cluded. You know as well as I, that the Turk

" is

" is in arms. If *Vienna* falls, what power can
" enfure *Warfaw* ? Let us convince France, and
" all Europe, that we have fenfe enough to fee
" our own intereft, and have integrity and ho-
" nour to purfue it."

When the King had ended his harangue, feveral
of the Senators called out loudly for an examina-
tion into the whole affair, that all who were concerned in this act of treafon might be brought to
light; and treated as fuch. The perfon that infifted moft upon it was Jablonowfki : he valued himfelf upon his unfpotted integrity, and above all,
upon his gratitude. The King, who was under
great obligations to him, made it a point to difcharge the debt, by laying hold of every opportunity to advance him. After having given him
the ftaff of Petty General, he made him Caftellan
of Cracow, and laft of all, Grand General. In
this laft capacity, he could not have had a feat in
the Senate ; but being ftill Caftellan of Cracow, he
was the firft lay Senator, and his opinion had great
weight in the affembly. The King was afraid of
irritating the wounds of the republic by attempting
to heal them, and faw that the time which was fo
neceffary to be employed in action, was going to be
fpent in dangerous debates : he therefore perfuaded
the Senate, to leave in the dark all thofe who had
taken any meafures to conceal their crimes ; adding,
that they would find their punifhment in the fear of
being difcovered, and in the fuccefs of the treaty.
He excepted out of this fpecies of amnefty, only
the Grand-Treafurer *Morftyn*, who was convicted
by his own confeffion ; a letter of his being read at
the fame time, in which he profeffed an entire devotion to the interefts of France, and promifed to
lay open to that court the fecrets of the cabinet of
Warfaw, to difturb the provincial diets, to overturn the defigns of the Senate, to fow divifion among
all

y. 1683. all the orders, and bring the King to such a pass, that he should be forced either to break the treaty, or abdicate the crown. The means that he proposed to make use of, were not easy to be conjectured; but were probably explained in some dispatches writ in a cypher that no one had the key of (a). Upon the strength of this evidence, his trial was referred to the diet.

A plot that is once discovered is no longer formidable. As soon as the provincial diets were informed of what had happened, the sentiments of the nation changed, and no one would give room to suspect his being one of the venal tribe: the deputies came to the diet with favourable dispositions; and the first point that was laid before them was Morstyn's crime. He had long lain under suspicions, on account of his attachment to France, and his having purchased lands in that kingdom; which shewed a desire of fixing his fortune there.

The diet was inclined to give sentence against him in a summary way, and to treat him with all the severity due to a person convicted of high treason. The King moderated this heat; and the culprit undertook to make his defence before the republic; but it consisted only of vague strains of eloquence, and protestations of respectful submission to the King, to whom he recommended his honour, his fortune, and his life. The diet perceiving that the King leaned towards mercy, gave up the criminal into his hands. The key of the cyphers was demanded of Morstyn; he was sentenced to furnish the army with a body of men at his own expence, and expelled the Senate and the diets. His office of Grand-Treasurer was taken from him, with an order to give in his accounts when the republic should call for them, at a more convenient time.

(a) Zaluski, tom. ii. p. 281.

Morstyn

Morſtyn inſtantly took advantage of the plank that was left him after his ſhipwreck, and took refuge in France, where he ended his days in peace, though he had ill deſerved it. The republic had neither the key of his cyphers, nor the accounts of the public money ; of which a much ſmaller ſum, than was generally believed to be there, was found in the treaſury. The Poles have omitted no expedients to prevent the diſſipation of the public revenue ; but no precautions are ſufficient, when the manners of a people are corrupted. Cæſar plundered the treaſury of the Romans ; and Morſtyn was generally believed to be a ſecond Cæſar in this particular. It is certain, however, that the King took the faɛt for granted, in an inſtruɛtion ſent to a provincial diet (a).

The fugitive left nothing in his own country but a magnificent fragment of his former opulence, a palace ſituated in the ſuburbs of Warſaw. At his firſt ſetting out in life, he was lodged in a much humbler manner ; there were many, now he was cruſhed, that even queſtioned his being a gentleman. It was pretended that he had formerly been a domeſtic ſervant to the Grand-Marſhal Lubomirſki ; but by endeavouring to prove too much, they proved nothing at all ; for in Poland moſt footmen are gentlemen, and he himſelf had ſeveral of this rank attending him in his magnificent palace. King Auguſtus II. made a purchaſe of it in 1726, with the eſtate round it, to make it a place of reſidence for himſelf. By an ancient law, the Kings of Poland are forbidden to make any acquiſitions in a ſtate, which would fain veſt all power in the public ; and Auguſtus was obliged to get a diſpenſation from a diet. This indulgence, which has led the way to others, may one day prove fatal to Poland.

(a) Zaluſki, tom. ii. p. 283.

U   The

The diet, after the trial of Morftyn, applied all its care towards the means of fulfilling the treaty with Leopold. The fum furnifhed by the Pope, which had juft been received, was not fufficient for this purpofe: the public treafury was plundered, and John was forced to open his own. What had hitherto feemed impoffible, immediately became eafy: the inclinations of the public were changed, and their judgment changed of courfe.

This revolution was entirely owing to the King's conduct. If, by ufing all the feverity which the majefty of the throne, and the dignity of the re-public would have permitted, he had drove the French party to extremities, that faction, having no longer any meafures to keep, would have made ufe of every expedient, however violent, to oppofe his will. The utmoft ftretch of power can be exerted only by defpotic tyrants towards their flaves; and woe be even to them, if the flaves, after having champed the bit with difdain, fhould go fo far as to break it.

The King, having now got the afcendant in the diet, employed himfelf wholly about the affairs of the army. It could not poffibly be affembled under a confiderable time. Before the peace of Zurawno, the old troops were accuftomed to do-meftic rapine, which brought defolation upon the pea-fants. The King quartered them upon the fron-tiers, where they encamped in the defarts of Po-dolia, and in part of the Ukraine: a piece of ma-nagement of greater value than a victory. After the peace, the crown-army was reduced to twelve thoufand men, and that of Lithuania to fix. This number was far inferior to the fuccours that Vienna expected; and the Poles were affiduous in raifing recruits, and making new levies. The King, who refolved to march in perfon, was daily on horfe-back for four or five hours together. The French

Ambaf-

Ambaſſador, who ſaw this, aſſured his maſter notwithſtanding, that he was grown too heavy to be
able to make the campaign. ' Lewis XIV. was
afraid that he would make it with too much ſucceſs; and it has always been the practice to ſay
nothing to Sovereigns but what they like to hear.

End of the FIFTH BOOK.

U 2   THE

THE

HISTORY

OF

JOHN SOBIESKI

KING OF POLAND.

BOOK VI.

Y. 1683.   IN the beginning of May, intelligence was received that Mahomet had sent to the *Seven Towers* (the Baftille of Conftantinople) the Chevalier *Trofki,* the Polifh envoy. It is in fact, a cuftom with the Turks, to arreft the Minifters of the Princes againft whom they declare war, and this is the excufe they make for violating the moft facred article of the law of Nations: *we never make any but juft wars : the Ambaffador, who is only an bonourable fpy, is therefore an accomplice in his mafter's faithlefs violation of treaties.*

Intelligence was alfo received, that the Ottoman forces were arriving out of Afia and Africa in the vaft and fertile plains of Adrianople; their ufual place of rendezvous when they march againft the Chriftians. That city, called by the Arabs and

Turks

Turks Adranah, was formerly the feat of the little empire of Theodore Lafcaris; and afterwards the capital of the Turkifh dominions, before the taking of Conftantinople. Mahomet came thither with his court, in order to be nearer the fcene of war, and to give more life to the expedition. He might have attacked the empire of Germany, before the peace of Nimeguen, when Leopold was engaged with Lewis XIV. and then the empire muft have been deftroyed. The Porte has been generally unfortunate in chufing its time to attack the Chriftians, who, by tearing one another in pieces fo frequently, feem to prefent themfelves to its ftrokes. But, after all, if the danger was lefs now than before the peace of Nimeguen, it was ftill fufficiently great.

The road to Vienna was laid open to the Turks by Tekeli, whom Leopold would not overcome by clemency, and could not reduce by force. He had lately received from Mahomet a Turban enriched with jewels, a ftandard, a fabre, royal robes, and the title of King of upper Hungary. The Porte at that time difpofed of four crowns to Chriftian Princes, viz. thofe of Hungary, Tranfylvania, Walachia, and Moldavia. The infcription upon the new King's coin was, *pro Deo, pro Patriâ, pro Libertate*; for God, my Country, and Liberty. The malecontents whom he commanded were animated with the fpirit of their leader. Caprara and Schulz, two of the Emperor's Generals, had not been able to reduce them; and the former was more mortified at being beat by the rebels, than when he fled before Turenne in 1674.

The General of the Ottoman forces was the Grand-Vizir Kara-Muftapha, the fame who had already tried his fortune againft John, at Trembowla and Leopol. He ftill continued in favour with the Sultana Validé; and having alfo gained

the

Y. 1683. the affections of Mahomet, had lately married his daughter. The Sultan does not give to every Vizir his *Catifcherif*, that is to fay, a full power; but the prefent had that honour conferred upon him. Never had ambition and pride, two paffions that devoured him, a more extenfive field to act in: a hundred and forty thoufand regular troops, confifting of Janizaries, Spahis, and others; eighteen thoufand Walachians, Moldavians, and Tranfylvanians, commanded by their refpective Princes; fifteen thoufand Hungarians led by Tekeli; fifty thoufand Tartars commanded by *Selim-Gerai*, their Cham; and if we include volunteers, officers of the baggage and provifions, workmen of all forts, and fervants, the whole muft amount to more than three hundred thoufand men, thirty one Bafhaws, five Sovereign Princes, with three hundred pieces of cannon: and the object of this mighty armament was equally great, the conqueft of the weftern empire *(a)*.

But who, that cafts an eye upon this prodigious number of troops, would believe that there was at that time a Monarch in Europe who could exceed it? The Turkifh empire, fo powerful in Afia and Africa as well as Europe, has never had four hundred and fifty thoufand men in arms, like Lewis XIV. and in time of peace its ftanding army is only forty five thoufand Janizaries, and about the fame number of Spahis. The reafon of this oeconomy of the Turks muft be fought for in the maxim, that *the people's fubftance muft not be confumed wantonly.*

Mahomet reviewed his army in the plains of Adrianople; and fixing his refidence in that city, trufted his glory to the fortune of his Vizir.

The Imperial troops were commanded by Charles V. Duke of Lorrain, the fame who was Sobiefki's

(a) Journal of the fiege of Vienna, p. 159.

competitor

competitor for the crown of Poland in 1674. He was then young, but had already given proofs of his having the foul of a hero. Since that time, his name was ranked among the great captains; and, by his marriage with Eleonora of Auftria, Queen Dowager of Poland, he was brother-in-law to the Emperor. Thefe two great families, which are faid to have fprung from the fame origin, were deftined to be allied to each other, and to make only one at laft. The Duke's capacity, much more than his rank, procured him the command in chief, which would have frightened any man but himfelf; for he had only thirty-feven thoufand men to oppofe that torrent of Infidels, which came to overwhelm the empire.

The Vizir advanced on the right fide of the Danube, paffed the Save and the Drave, forced the Duke before him, made a feint of attacking Raab (a), while he detached fifty thoufand Tartars on the road towards Vienna. The Duke, perceiving the ftratagem, made a ftolen march in his turn, fuffered a check at Petronel, and had fcarce time to reach Vienna, where he threw in part of his infantry to reinforce the garrifon, and took poft in the ifland of Leopolftat, formed by the Danube on the north fide of the city; while the Tartars arrived about the fame time on the fouth.

Upon this occafion, was feen one of thofe fpectacles, which ought to be a leffon to Sovereigns, and which move the compaffion of their fubjects, even when the Sovereigns have ill deferved their tendernefs: Leopold, the moft powerful Emperor fince Charles the fifth, flying from his capital with the Emprefs his mother-in-law, the Emprefs his wife, the Archdukes, the Archducheffes, and part of the inhabitants following the court in great diforder.

(a) Otherwife called *Javarin*, one of the ftrongeft places in Hungary, at the confluence of the Raab and the Danube.

The

Y. 1683.   The whole country was filled with flying parties, equipages, and waggons laden with goods; the laſt of which fell into the hands of the Tartars, at the very gates of Lintz (a). Even this city, which the imperial family fled to in their firſt fright, did not ſeem a ſafe aſylum, and they were forced to take refuge in Paſſaw (b). They lay the firſt night in a wood, where the Empreſs, who was far advanced in her pregnancy, found that it was poſſible to ſleep upon ſtraw, ſurrounded on all ſides by terror. Among the other horrors of this night, they had a view of the flames which already conſumed Lower Hungary, and advanced towards Auſtria. The Turks were to be dreaded only as civilized warriors, who conquer by dint of valour; but the Tartars burnt, murdered, and carried into ſlavery. The deepeſt caves afforded an inſecure retreat: the trembling victims were diſcovered by dogs trained to hunt men; and Tekeli himſelf, upon this occaſion, was a very Tartar.

The Emperor, by only the firſt exceſſes that attended this irruption, paid dearly for his acts of violence in Hungary, and the blood of its nobles that he had ſpilt. He could not be perſuaded that Kara-Muſtapha would leave behind him ſuch places as Raab and Comora (c), and fall directly upon Vienna. The King of Poland, who knew better, as is always the caſe with Princes who make war in

(a) The capital of Upper Auſtria, with a bridge over the Danube. It is remarkable for the beauty of its ſtreets; but what is ſtill more ſtriking, is to ſee a city, full of nobles, carrying on a conſiderable trade.

(b) A city of Bavaria, upon the Danube.

(c) Comora, at the confluence of the Waage, and the Danube, owes its firſt fortifications to the famous Matthias Corvinus, who had the glory of counterballancing the ſucceſſes of Mahomet II. and of humbling the Emperor Frederick by the taking of Vienna.

perſon, gave him warning of it, but without effect.

Vienna was become, under ten ſucceſſive Emperors of the houſe of Auſtria, the capital of the Roman empire in the weſt; but fell far ſhort of ancient Rome in greatneſs of every kind, and particularly in the number of its citizens, which did not
exceed a hundred thouſand; and two thirds of theſe
inhabited defenceleſs ſuburbs. Soliman the Great
was the firſt Turkiſh Emperor that marched againſt
Vienna in 1529, after having been crowned King
of Perſia at Bagdad, making Europe and Aſia
tremble at the ſame time. He failed in his attempt
upon Vienna, by not daring to contend againſt the
fortune of Charles the Fifth, who marched to its
relief with an army of fourſcore thouſand men.
Kara-Muſtapha, who ſaw only a handful to oppoſe him, flattered himſelf that he ſhould be more
fortunate; and begun the ſiege on the 7th of July.
The Germans are undoubtedly a brave people;
but they have never appeared before the gates of
Conſtantinople, as the Turks have before thoſe of
Vienna.

The body of the place is waſhed by the Danube
on the north, and was fortified with twelve large
baſtions in the remaining part of its circumference.
The curtains were covered with good half-moons,
but no other out-works; the ditch, partly full of
water, and partly dry; the counterſcarp much neglected. That ſide of the city, which the river
waſhes, was defended only with ſtrong walls, flanked
with large towers, the whole with a good terraſs
behind it. A circle of mountains, which begins
on the ſouthern bank of the Danube, and retires
at ſome diſtance from it, incloſes a plain of three
leagues.

In this plain the Viſir pitched his camp, which
filled its whole extent; and he had the confidence
not

not to defend it with lines of circumvallation and contravallation : nor was this the only fault that he committed in the course of the siege, out of a brutal contempt for the Christians.   His camp abounded with every thing that was necessary for so vast a multitude; money, ammunition, and provisions of every kind.   The different quarters were commanded by Bashaws, who displayed the magnificence of Kings : but all this magnificence was eclipsed by the pomp of the Visir, who wallowed in luxury.   A Grand-Visir's retinue usually consists of two thousand officers and servants; but the present had double that number.   His park, that is to say, the space enclosed by his tents, near the palace of the *Favourite*, was as extensiv eas the city he besieged.   The lustre of the richest stuffs, of gold and jewels, seemed to contend with the glare of arms.   It was furnished with baths, gardens, fountains, and even curious animals for his amusement.   He shut himself up with his young Icoglans oftener than with his General-Officers. The Iman, or Minister of religion, who attended him in this expedition, threatened him with the divine indignation; but the Visir laughed at his menaces, and plunged himself deeper in debauchery.

In the mean time, the luxury of the General did not in the least diminish the valour of the janizaries, nor was the Turkish artillery at all less formidable.

No nation but the Turks, uses cannon that carry balls of the weight of sixty pounds.   There are writers who have represented them of two hundred on this occasion; but the quantity of powder which would have been necessary to discharge such bullets, cannot be kindled at once : the cannon would go off before a fourth part of it could take fire, and the ball would have very little effect.

Count

Count Staremberg, a man of abilities and experience, who was now Governor of Vienna, and had formerly been so to his master, had set fire to the suburbs, and, by a cruel necessity, burnt the subsistence of the citizens, whom his object was to preserve.　He had a garrison under him, which was computed at sixteen thousand men, but in fact amounted only to eleven thousand at most.　He therefore armed the townsmen and the university; the scholars mounted guard, and had a physician for their major. *(a)*.　Staremberg's second in command was the Count de Capliers, Commissary-General to the Emperor, a man whose knowledge, vigilance, and activity fitted him for the highest stations.

Several persons of quality, whose age and wounds had made them quit the service, and who might have abandoned Vienna to its fate, resolved to share its destiny.　Their names deserve a place in history; and therefore I insert them.　They were the Count de Trautmansdorff, who had commanded in the Low Countries; the Count of Funskirchen, whose personal interests required his presence, in another place ; the Baron de Kielmansegg, who having taken post in a bastion with fourscore hunters, incommoded the enemy greatly from his first appearance; the Count de Vignancourt, who had distinguished himself as a General and an Ambassador; the Count de Colato, a Venetian, who exposed his person, as if he had been in the Emperor's service : add to these an old Colonel, named Rumlingen, who was disqualified for action by the gout, but his head was still good.　They were all of approved bravery, and judges of true honour; for they made it a point of honour to command

(a) Journal of the siege.

the city-companies, after having diſtinguiſhed themſelves in the regular troops.

The palace of the Emperors was full of valuable furniture, but it afforded no money. The
Count de Kollonts, Preſident of Hungary, and
Biſhop of Newſtadt, raiſed a hundred thouſand
crowns. The Prince of Schwartzenberg, Maſter of
the Horſe to the Empreſs-Dowager, liberally added fifty thouſand florins, and three thouſand hogſ-
heads of wine for the uſe of the garriſon (a).

The approaches to the place were very eaſy.
The trenches were opened the 14th of July, in
the ſuburb of St. Ulrick, at about fifty paces
from the counterſcarp. The attack was directed
upon the *Baſtion of the Court* and that of *Lebl*. In
two days time the works were advanced quite up
to the counterſcarp where the ditch was dry.

The Duke of Lorrain, who had taken poſt in
the iſland of Leopolſtat, and did his utmoſt to
preſerve a communication from thence with the
city, thought himſelf obliged to retire from it, by
the bridges which he had laid acroſs the Danube, and now ordered to be broke down. The
country-ſeats, with which the iſland abounded, ſerved to lodge the Turks. The Duke's quitting this
poſt has been conſidered as a great fault : if it was
ſo, he made ample amends for it by his behaviour
during the whole ſiege (b). Never was there a
General in a more deſperate ſituation ; for after he
had thrown part of his infantry into Vienna, Raab,
and Comora, he had not thirty thouſand men left
to keep the field. The Chevalier Lubomirſki, the
ſame who was accuſed in the Poliſh diet, in 1681,
of furniſhing Tekeli with ſoldiers, had quitted that
leader of a faction, and entered into the Emperor's

(a) Journal of the ſiege of Vienna, pages 37, 45 and 57.
(b) Id. ibid. p. 52.

                                        ſervice

service with a body of four thousand Polish horse, Y. 1683. who could scarce be considered in any other light than as four thousand victims more for Tekeli and the Visir.

Let any one figure to himself, the Duke of Lorrain commissioned to defend, with so small a force, Moravia, Silesia, and Bohemia; marching incessantly from one to another; sometimes retreating behind rivers, and sometimes passing them; engaged in perpetual skirmishes with Tekeli and the Bashaw of Agria; in daily expectation of succours, which he did not receive till two months after: whoever reflects upon this, must tremble for him; and if he does not sink under all these disadvantages, he may safely be pronounced to be a General.

A relation of two actions only will be sufficient to give an idea of the rest. Tekeli was marching towards Presburg, a city of Hungary, upon the bank of the Danube, which, having been long weary of the Austrian government, had already received a garrison into the town from the enemy; but the castle still held out. If Tekeli succeeded, he would throw a bridge over the river at Presburg; the Visir would send him a large detachment; Silesia, Moravia, and Bohemia would lie wholly exposed; the Duke must retire to Krems (a), which would cut off his communication with the succours from Poland, and the bridge at Presburg might be brought up as high as Vienna. The Duke flew to ward off this blow; and having thrown some troops into the castle, sum-

***

(a) A village celebrated for an abbey of great antiquity, which would never have existed if the son of Tassillon, Duke of Bavaria, had not been torn in pieces in that place by a wild boar. What a herd of Monks has lived upon his death, since the time of Charlemagne!

moned

moned the city, which furrendered after having fuffered the Turkifh garrifon to efcape. The bridge, which was begun, was broken down. Tekeli and the Bafhaw of Agria were within half a league ; but the Duke's reputation, and a mifunderftanding that was between them, made them think of retreating ; which they did not however effect, without having their rear defeated by the Poles and the Emperor's dragoons. The Duke, in a letter to the King of Poland, attributes almoft the whole glory of this fuccefs to the Poles ; and exprefles his admiration at the impetuous courage of their General Lubomirfki. In fact, no one could fhine more in action ; but in the prefent cafe he only executed the plan that the Duke had laid.

Some time after, ten thoufand Turks and Tartars advanced from the Moraw (a), towards the bridges of Vienna, which were guarded by fome fquadrons of horfe ; and the Duke marched to meet them. Nothing can be more impetuous than the Turkifh cavalry. Four thoufand Spahis fell furioufly upon the Imperial army, forced the firft and fecond line, and advanced through the intervals, hewing down all they met with their fabres. Such rafhnefs muft naturally fail of fuccefs, and fo it fell out at prefent. The Imperialifts foon recovered from their aftonifhment, charged the enemy, and drove them towards the Danube ; where a great number quitted their arms and horfes ; and the Tartars, who durft not mix in the engagement, retired towards Tekeli's army.

In fhort, every expedient that required daring courage, prudent forefight, or quick execution ; marches, countermarches, ftratagems of war, and whatever the weaker party can make ufe of againft

_____

(a) A river, called by the Germans the Marck, which runs into the Danube.

the

the ſtronger, all was put in practice by the Duke, againſt an army conſiſting of thirty thouſand men at leaſt, and continually recruited with freſh ſupplies from the grand army.

In the mean time, the ſiege went on with vigour. On the ſide of the Turks, there was daily freſh ground raiſed, works advanced, new batteries, and an encreaſing fire ; on the ſide of the Auſtrians, every expedient was tried to avert their deſtruction. At the firſt approaches of the enemy, Staremberg was wounded by the ſplinter of a ſtone ſtruck off from the curtain by a ball ; and though now ſcarce recovered, he gave ſpirit to the whole garriſon by his looks, his actions, and his humane behaviour. He treated all the ſoldiers as his brethren, commended and rewarded them, whenever they did well ; and not contented with being with them by day, paſſed the night upon a matreſs, in the guardhouſe of the Emperor's palace. This palace joined to the baſtion of the court, which was included in the attack *(a)*.

So early as the 22d of July, the beſiegers were got to the paliſade which could no longer be defended with cannon, the ſoldiers being ſo near on both ſides, that they laid hold of one another through the ſtakes, and many loſt their lives by the wounds they received this way. The Count de Daun, a General officer of diſtinguiſhed merit, ordered ſcythes to be faſtened to long pikes, which deſtroyed many of the Turks *(b)*.

The beſieged had juſt received news from the Duke of Lorrain. The perſon who brought it had ſwam acroſs the four arms of the Danube, and gave aſſurances of ſpeedy ſuccour. The intelligence was falſe ; but there are times when men can be ſerved only by deceiving them. The bold

(a) Journal of the ſiege, p. 99. *(b)* Ibid. p. 86.

4

ſwimmer,

swimmer, who would have been immortalized by the Romans, but whose very name is lost to us, returned the same way to the Duke with a letter from the Governor : but he was taken, and the letter sent back into the city by the Turks, at the end of an arrow, which brought also a billet in Latin.

. The substance of the billet was, that all letters were now useless, for that God would soon deliver up Vienna to the faithful Muſſulmen, as a juſt punishment upon the Christians, for their wanton violation of treaties *(a)*. The treaties which they reproached the Emperor with breaking, was that which followed the battle of St. Gothard { the privileges of the Hungarians that he had trod under foot ; and two truces made with Tekeli, but soon broke. The Poles were reproached with taking up arms against the Porte without being attacked, and in violation of the oaths they had ſworn at Boudchaz, and at the late peace of Zurawno.

In this confidence which the Turks had in the justice of their cauſe, they frequently came forth and made ſuch bravadoes as we read in the history of ancient wars. A champion of uncommon stature advanced one day, in a menacing manner, insulting the Christians both with his words and gestures. A ſoldier of the Imperial troops, fired at this affront, runs up to him, receives a wound, returns it upon his enemy, diſarms him, cuts off his head with his own ſcymetar, and upon ſtripping him finds fifty pieces of gold ſewed up in his clothes. This eaſineſs of circumſtances, which all the Turkish ſoldiers enjoy in a greater or leſs degree, fixes them to their profeſſion, and prevents deſertion. It is natural to ſuppoſe that the Christian champion was rewarded : on the contrary, he continued a private ſoldier, and his name is not tranſmitted to poſ-

(a) Ibid. pages 71 & 82.

terity.

terity. The besieged, who saw the action from the top of the ramparts, considered it as a good omen (a); and it served to increase their courage.

The enemy did not get possession of the counterscarp till the 7th of August, after repeated engagements for three and twenty days together, with great loss of blood on both sides. The taking of this work was greatly retarded by the bravery of Count *Serini*, who had distinguished himself on a hundred occasions, and been present in every sally. The ardour which hurried him on, prevented his feeling an arrow that he received one day in the shoulder; and he kept on fighting in the very moment that they were pulling it out (b). His uncle, the famous *Serini* before-mentioned, had been beheaded by order of Leopold; and yet such is the privilege of sovereigns, that the nephew exposed his life daily in Leopold's cause.

The Turks were now got to the descent of the ditch. No troops can equal them in turning up the ground: the depth of their works was astonishing, the earth they threw out of them being nine feet high, and covered over with planks and beams in the form of a floor, under which they carried on their works in safety. Their trenches are of a different form from ours, being cut in the shape of a crescent, and covering one another, with a communication kept open between them all, much like the scales of a fish, having a labyrinth beneath, from which they fire, without incommoding those who are before, and from which it is impossible to dislodge them. When the Janizaries once enter them, they scarce ever come out again. Their fire grew brisker every day, and that of the besieged flackened. It was time to husband their powder,

(a) Journal of the siege, p. 116.
(b) Ibid. pages 79 & 84.

X   and

Y. 1683. and their granadoes begun to fail; but thefe defi-
ciencies were fupplied by the Baron de Kielman-
fegg, who invented a powder-mill and granadoes
of clay, that were of great fervice. Thus induftry
is of as much ufe as courage; but this laft refource
was moft commonly employed, efpecially by thofe
who were to fet an example to others. The Prince
of Wirtemberg, Colonel of a regiment of his own
name, and who defpifed all falfe delicacy, was
wounded in doing the duty of a Captain (a).

A hundred others, with their wounds ftill bleeding, returned to the charge; but the hopes of holding out much longer grew daily lefs. The enemy's mines, their continual attacks, the decreafe
of the garrifon, the wafte of provifions, all contributed to give the utmoft uneafinefs; and to fo
many real evils, imaginary ones were added. A
report prevailed, that traitors were at work upon
a fubterraneous paffage to let in the enemy. Every
one was ordered to keep guard in the cellar of his
own houfe; and this additional duty deprived them
of their nightly reft. Other ftories were propagated, of incendiaries hired to fecond the Turks.
A young man who was found in a church juft beginning to take fire, was tore in pieces by the people,
though perhaps he was very innocent. The Turkifh artillery was more to be dreaded than all thofe
phantoms. It was a conftant employment in the
city to extinguifh the fires kindled by the bombs
and red-hot balls, while at the fame time the out-
works were falling in pieces: the half-moon, in
particular, had already fuffered much.

The Duke of Lorrain writ letter after letter
to the King of Poland to haften his march. Notwithftanding all the diligence he had ufed, his army could not be got together till towards the end

(a) Journal of the fiege, pages 147 & 138.

of

of the month of Auguft. The place of rendezvous was at Tarnowits, the firft town of Silefia,
upon the borders of Poland. He fent away the
firft bodies that arrived, under the command of the
Petty-General Sieniawfki, Palatine of Volhinia; and
while the main body was getting ready, took up
his refidence at Cracow, where he did not throw
away his time. His fondnefs for hunting, play,
and entertainments, never fhewed itfelf but when
the republic was at peace. He examined into the
details that he received of the fiege; ftudied the
fituation of Vienna by a topographical map; confidered the pofition of the Turks in every view;
fettled his order of battle; and regulated his marches,
in order to fix the decifive day.

In one of the Duke's letters, a propofal was made
to the King, to come by the way of Prefburg, and
from thence go up the river towards Vienna. The
King made choice of another plan, which he communicated to the Duke, with the reafons that determined him. The council of war decided in favour of the King, who was at the diftance of two
hundred leagues from the fpot. The Duke gave
up his own propofal, and applauded that of the
King : a behaviour which does honour to both.

The King's fon, Prince James, about fixteen
years old, attended his auguft father to Cracow,
and folicited leave to be initiated in the fatigues
of war. The King granted his requeft, well knowing, that Princes are ruined by being kept too
anxioufly out of the reach of danger.

The Queen ftaid at Cracow, where the King
eftablifhed a council, which he invefted with all
his own authority, during his abfence. At the
head of it was the illuftrious Potofki, Caftellan of
Cracow, the city where it was held, in quality of
firft lay-Senator.

X 2 The

The French Ambaſſador ſaw, with concern, all theſe preparations for the King's departure, and wanted ſtill to doubt its truth. The King, as he got on horſeback, ſaid to him, *Your Excellency may now ſafely aſſure your maſter that I am going.* When he arrived at Tarnowits, he reviewed his army, which amounted only to twenty-five thouſand men, and conſequently far ſhort of the number ſtipulated in the treaty ; which is no more than every power that treats with Poland muſt expect. Before the review was over, he received a letter from the Emperor, which was brought by General Caraffa. A copy of it may ſerve to ſhew the power of adverſity upon haughty minds, and the return of their pride, as ſoon as the danger is paſt. " We are " convinced, (ſays the Emperor) that by reaſon " of the vaſt diſtance of your army, it is abſolute- " ly impoſſible for it to come time enough to con- " tribute to the preſervation of a place which is in " the moſt imminent danger. It is not therefore " your troops, *Sire*, that we expect, but *your Ma-* " *jeſty's* own preſence ; being fully perſuaded, that " if your royal perſon will vouchſafe to appear at " the head of our forces, though leſs numerous " than thoſe of the enemy, your name alone, which " is ſo juſtly dreaded by them, will make their " defeat certain."

It muſt certainly have coſt Leopold a great deal to make this confeſſion. As ſoon as he deſpaired of ſeeing the Poliſh army, nothing hindered him from putting himſelf at the head of his own troops, and thoſe of the empire ; but the paſt and the preſent made him feel the neceſſity of another commander, to whom he no longer ſcrupled to attribute the qualities of a hero, or to give the title of Majeſty. The Turks had long poſſeſſed a ſuperiority over the Germans, which is always a forerunner of new misfortunes to the conquered. *Montecuculli*

tecuculli, who had checked their fucceffes at St. Gothard, was no more. John was the only hero capable of oppofing them, being acquainted with their manner of fighting, and the way to beat them.

The Emperor concluded his letter with a minute account of all the troops that he was affembling, and which were to arrive forthwith at the bridge where they were to pafs the Danube, affuring the King that the bridge was already finifhed. The fequel will fhew that the Emperor foon altered his language with regard to John, and was miftaken in his facts. His letter is preferved to this day in the archives of Poland.

The critical fituation of affairs, and the confidence which Leopold repofed in him, determined the King to take a ftep which expofed his own perfon to danger.

Leaving his army to the care of the Grand-General Jablonowfki, he refolved to go forward himfelf, and even to give battle without it, if the prefervation of Vienna required it. In order to get thither, he had no route to take but acrofs Silefia, Moravia, and that part of Auftria which lies to the north of the Danube; three provinces that were infefted by Hungarians, Turks, and Tartars, whom the Duke of Lorrain, with all his capacity and courage, defpaired of keeping within bounds any longer. The King, in his march, had only two thoufand horfe. Other Kings, even in the midft of an army, have a fecond army for their guard. His equipage was no greater than that of the brave foldiers that marched with him. Nothing but a chaife attended him, which even prince James made no ufe of; they both travelled all the way on horfeback. It is true, luxury and effeminacy had not yet made their way into the army: even Lewis XIV, the moft ftately monarch in Europe, made all his military journeys on horfeback. During this whole

X 3   march

Y. 1683. màrch of a hundred leagues, reckoning from Tarnowits to the Danube, the King went into no more
than two towns, encamping all the way with his
little army, and being a daily spectator of ravages,
murders, and conflagrations; a presage of what he
might expect himself. It is not every King that
is formed to be a hero; but whoever is animated
with that glorious ambition, must endure fatiguing
marches, suffer hardships, and expose himself to
dangers like a common soldier, whenever occasion requires it. John was so far from discover-
ing any fear, that he recovered the whole country
from its consternation. The peasants, who had
sown only that they might not reap, and regretted
the fate of their murdered friends, ran together
from every hamlet to see their deliverer, and considered themselves as already delivered (*a*). His
own troops, that he conducted through so many
dangers, stood also in need of being encouraged,
and he omitted no opportunity of doing it. One
morning, when he was a few leagues from Ol-
mutz, an eagle flew by him on the right; and as
the Poles have retained some faith in omens, he
told them a story out of the Roman history, and
the flight of the eagle was considered as a token
of victory. Another day, upon the weather's
clearing up, after a thick mist, an inverted rainbow
(a phænomenon not common, but which sometimes happens) was seen upon the surface of a
meadow. The soldiers fancied it to be miraculous,
and the King confirmed them in this persuasion (*b*.)

This march of the King's, through so many enemies, without ever drawing a sword, has given
occasion to some writers of that time to say, that
by a secret convention between him and Tekeli, he
was not to be attacked. If the fact be true, it must

(*a*) Dupont.   (*b*) Zaluski, tom. ii. p. 836.

be

be accounted for by suppoſing, that Tekeli was
ſtruck with that reſpectful awe of the King, which
great men always inſpire, and that, foreſeeing the
defeat of the Turks, he had a mind to ſecure himſelf a protector.   If he really had this foreſight,
it could be founded only upon the ill conduct of
their General; for to conſider the forces of each
party, the Chriſtians ſhould naturally periſh.

   At length, the King reached the banks of the
Danube, which it was impoſſible to paſs by the
bridges of Vienna, in ſight of the enemy.   He
therefore marched to Tuln, a ſmall town on the
right ſide of the river, five leagues above Vienna,
remarkable for being the burying-place of the Count
of Habſbourg, who was advanced to the empire by
the name of *Rodolph* I. for having lent his horſe, as
the ſtory goes, to a pariſh-prieſt.   Nor was this
the only ſingularity in his fortune.   He had been in
his youth Grand-Maſter of the houſhold to *Ottocar*,
King of Bohemia; and as ſoon as he was raiſed to
the Imperial throne, he ſummoned that King to
come and pay him homage.   Ottocar anſwered,
that he owed him nothing, having paid him all his
wages.   Leopold, the deſcendant of Rodolph, was
not ſure, at this juncture, of keeping the empire
that his anceſtor had left him.   He had wrote to
John that the bridge at Tuln was finiſhed, whereas
they were now at work upon it.   The ſame letter
told him, that he would find the German troops
aſſembled in readineſs, but he ſaw only the Duke
of Lorrain's little army, and two battalions that
guarded the head of the bridge.   At this ſight,
he broke out in a paſſion: *Does the Emperor take
me for an adventurer? I have left my own army,
becauſe he aſſured me that his was ready? Is it
for myſelf or him that I come to fight?*   The Duke,

X 4   whoſe

Y. 1683. whofe prudence was equal to his valour, pacified
his indignation (a).

The Polifh army was left at a great diftance,
and yet, to the aftonifhment of every one, it arrived before the Germans. The quicknefs of its
march did great honour to the Grand-General Jablonowfki, who made his appearance on the 5th
of September. The German Generals, leaving
their troops behind, were come to attend the King,
and could not help expreffing fome difquiet at the
great day that was approaching : *Confider,* fays the
King, *the General you have to deal with, and not
the multitude that he commands. Which of you,
at the head of two hundred thoufand men, would
have fuffered this bridge to be built within five
leagues of his camp? The man has no capacity* (b).

The Polifh army was by this time paffing the
bridge. The cavalry was univerfally admired for
their horfes, their drefs, and fine appearance ; but
they feemed to be fitted out at the expence of the
foot. One battalion among the reft being remarkably ill clad, Prince Lubomirfki advifed the King,
for the honour of the nation, to let it pafs in the
night. The King was of a different opinion, and
when the battalion was croffing the bridge, *Look
at it well,* faid he to the fpectators ; *it is an invincible body that has fworn never to wear any clothes
but what it takes from the enemy. In the laft war,
they were all clad in the Turkifh manner.* If this
encomium did not furnifh them with clothes, it certainly armed them with cuiraffes.

The Poles, when they had croffed the bridge,
extended themfelves upon the right, and were expofed, for twenty-four hours together, to be cut
in pieces, if Kara Muftapha had known how to

(a) Dupont,   (b) Idem.

make

Y. 1683.

make the moft of his advantages. At length, the bodies of German troops arrived, one after another, and the whole army was affembled by the 7th.

The moft diftinguifhed perfon in it was the Duke of Lorrain, at the head of the Auftrian cavalry, which had already fhed fo much blood. This Prince had acted the part of Leonidas at Thermopylæ, only he was more fortunate, in being ftill alive to try another battle.

The Elector of Bavaria, Maximilian Emmanuel, at the age of eighteen, was entering upon the field of glory. He brought with him twelve thoufand men, fome of the fineft troops that appeared on this occafion : his cavalry in particular was admirably mounted.

The Elector of Saxony, John George III. after having diftinguifhed himfelf in feveral wars for the houfe of Auftria, came again with ten thoufand men to efpoufe its quarrel.

The Prince of Waldeck led the troops of the circles.

The whole Chriftian army amounted to about feventy-four thoufand men. There were in it four fovereigns, and twenty-fix Princes of fovereign families ; three of Anhalt, two of Hanover ; three of Saxony, three of Newburg ; two of Wirtemberg, two of Holftein ; one of Heffe-Caffel, one of Hohenzollern ; two of Baden, one of Salm ; the Chevalier de Savoy, and the Prince of Saxe-Lawemburg, of the ancient and unfortunate houfe of Afcania.

The Emperor, in whofe caufe they fought, was not prefent ; and if it be true, as we are told in the Memoirs of Marfhal Villars (a), that the Count de Sintzendorff and his other Minifters diffuaded

(a) Tom. i. p. 329.

him

Y. 1683. him from coming: they have brought a ftain upon his memory, by this timid counfel.

Before the arrival of the King of Poland, all the Princes who brought fuccours, advanced claims, which inftead of faving the Emperor, would have compleated his ruin. The Elector of Bavaria afpired to the command in chief; the Elector of Saxony difputed it with him; and every other Prince that furnifhed troops aimed at being independent. The divifion of the Greeks before Troy, was revived upon this occafion. But Agamemnon appeared, and a general union was reftored, againft the common enemy (a). From the camp at Tuln they heard the horrid roar of the Turkifh batteries. Vienna was reduced to the laft extremities, and many officers of the firft merit had loft their lives. Among thefe, were the Baron de Walteri; Kottolinfki of Silefia; Rumpler, who had defended the place with the fword and the compafs; the Count de Souches, a Frenchman of diftinguifhed abilities, who prepared the way to the victory of St. Gothard for Montecuculi; Galenfels; Count Lefly, Grand-Mafter of the artillery, of which he had made great ufe; and before he fell, had been fprinkled with the blood of his brother, a young man who gave the greateft hopes. The grave continued open without ever clofing its mouth. The dyfentery, a diforder as deftructive as the fword, carried off fixty perfons in a day. Staremberg himfelf was attacked by it, and Capliers was charged with the command. There were not more than three or four officers left to a battalion; moft of thefe were wounded; and almoft all the chief officers were gone. The foldiers, worn out with fatigue, and bad diet, could fcarce crawl to the breach; and thofe who efcaped the fire of the enemy, died

(a) Dupont.

of

of weaknefs. The citizens, who at firft partook in all the labours of the fiege, had recourfe to prayer, as their only defence, and ran in crowds to the churches, where the bombs and balls carried terror after them.

So early as the 22d of Auguft, Capliers, who had eftimated with great exactnefs the forces on both fides, judged that he could not hold out longer than three days, if the enemy made a general affault *(a)*. From that day, one misfortune followed clofe upon another. The half-moon was taken: breaches of ten and twenty fathoms were made in the two baftions and the curtain; and the foldiers fupplied the place of walls. A mine was advancing under the Emperor's palace, which was already laid flat with bombs, and joined to the baftion of the court; and others were winding about in different places. Some of them indeed were countermined, but the Auftrian pioneers, who had been collected wherever they were to be found, refufed to go under ground any more, when they heard the enemy at work. The artillery could no longer anfwer the enemy's fire, moft of the cannon being either burft or difmounted.

The Duke of Lorrain had juft received a letter from Staremberg, who, in the beginning of the fiege, had the firmnefs, and even confidence to write, *I will not furrender the place but with the laft drop of my blood.* At prefent, he had fcarce a glimpfe of hope remaining. His letter contained only thefe words: *No more time to lofe, my Lord, no more time to lofe (b).*

The ftupid inaction of Kara-Muftapha cannot be accounted for. It is certain, that, if at this time he had made a general attack, Vienna muft have fallen. But avarice extinguifhed the thunder that

(a) Dupont.　　　*(b)* Idem.

he

Y. 1683. he held in his hand. He entertained a notion that the place of refidence of the Emperors of Germany muft contain immenfe treafures; and he was afraid that he fhould lofe this imaginary wealth by the city's being pillaged, as it inevitably would be, if taken by ftorm. He chofe therefore to ftay till the place furrendered, an event which he continued to flatter himfelf would happen every minute. Nor did his prefumption contribute lefs to blind him than his avarice. He jefted at the weaknefs of the Chriftian army, which he thought ftill weaker than it was; and could not fuppofe it would have the boldnefs to come and attack him. His intelligence was fo bad, that he was ftill ignorant of King John's having marched in perfon. This ignorance, befides the Vifir's neglect, was a confequence of the miftaken pride of the Porte, which receives Ambaffadors from all the courts in Chriftendom, and does not keep a fingle Refident in any. Hence it is that the Chriftians are acquainted with the fecrets of Conftantinople, while that court is often ignorant of what paffes among them in public. The Vifir, who had only a fufpicion of the King's march, brought with him the Chevalier Trofki, the Polifh Envoy, bound hand and foot, to be anfwerable for the conduct of his mafter *(a)*. Of all the Princes in the league, the Vifir dreaded him the moft; and we fhall foon fee, that he had reafon.

The King, when he was juft going to march, gave out the order of battle writ with his own hand: the following is a copy of it, as found among his manufcripts.

" The center is to confift of the Imperial troops,
" to which we fhall add the regiment of cavalry be-
" longing to the Chevalier Lubomirfki, Marfhal

(a) Dupont, Journal of the fiege.

" of

" of the court, and four or five fquadrons of our
" horfe guards ; in the room of which we expect
" to have dragoons, or other German troops. This
" body is to be commanded by the Duke of Lor-
" rain.

" The Polifh army, commanded by the Grand-
" General Jablonowfki, and the other Generals of
" that nation, is to make the right wing.

" The troops belonging to the Electors of Ba-
" varia and Saxony are to be placed on the left
" wing; to which we fhall add alfo fome fquadrons
" of our horfe-guards, and other Polifh cavalry ;
" inftead of which they are to give us dragoons
" or foot.

" The cannon is to be divided ; and in cafe the
" Electors have not enough, the Duke of Lorrain
" is to furnifh them with fome of his. This wing
" is to confift entirely of the troops belonging to
" the Electors.

" The troops of the circles of the empire are to
" extend along the Danube with the left wing, in-
" clining a little towards the right ; and this for
" two reafons ; firft, to keep the enemy in alarm,
" for fear of being charged in flank ; and fecond-
" ly, to be in readinefs to throw fuccours into the
" city, in cafe we fhould not make an impreffion
" upon the enemy fo foon as we hope. This body
" is to be commanded by the Prince of Wal-
" deck.

" The firft line is to confift wholly of foot,
" with artillery, and to be followed clofe by
" a line of horfe. If thefe two lines were to be
" mixed, they would embarafs each other in paf-
" fing the defiles, woods, and mountains. But as
" foon as we enter the plain, the cavalry is to take
" poft in the intervals between the battalions,
" which fhall be left for that purpofe. This order

" der is to be obferved particularly by our own
" horfe-guards, which fhall charge firft.

" If we draw up all our troops in three lines
" only, we fhall take up more than a German
" league and a half, which would not be for our
" advantage; and befides, we muft, in this cafe,
" pafs the little river of Vien, which ought to be
" left on our right. We muft therefore make four
" lines; and the fourth will ferve for a body of re-
" ferve.

" For the greater fecurity of the infantry, againft
" the firft attack of the Turkifh horfe, which is
" always very warm, great ufe might be made of
" *Spancheraiftres*, or *Chevaux-de-frize*, but they muft
" be very light, in order to be carried convenient-
" ly, and as often as the battalions halt, be placed
" at their head.

" I make it my earneft requeft, to all the Ge-
" nerals, that as faft as the army comes down
" the laft mountain to enter upon the plain, they
" will each take his poft, according to the direc-
" tions given in this prefent order."

They had only a march of five leagues to get
at the Turks, who were feparated from them by
nothing but a chain of mountains. Acrofs thefe,
there lay two roads, one over the higheft part of
the ridge; the other in a place where the hills were
lower, and the paffage more eafy. The council
of war being affembled, was for taking the latter;
but the King determined upon the former, which
was much fhorter; nor did any of the Princes murmur, becaufe he convinced them, that the fate of
Vienna depended upon a fingle moment; and that
there are cafes, when expedition ought to be preferred to caution.

The 9th of September, the whole army was in
motion. The Germans, after feveral attempts to

draw

draw up their cannon, despaired of succeeding and
left them in the plain. The Poles were more indefatigable; for *Konski*, Palatine of Kiovia, Grand-
Master of the artillery, got over twenty eight pieces,
and none but these were fired on the day of battle *(a)*.

This march, which was encumbered with all sorts
of difficulties, continued for three days. Two of
them passed, without the King's being seen by his
Polish army, which begun to demand where he was
with the utmost anxiety. It appeared that he had
been among the troops of the empire, employed
in raising their courage.

The army at length drew near to the last mountain, called *Calemberg*. It was yet time for the
Vizir to repair his faults: he had nothing to do but
to take possession of this hill, and mask the defiles
in order to stop the progress of the Christian army;
but he neglected to seize the opportunity. Upon
this occasion, the Janizaries, losing all patience at
so many blunders, cried out, *Come on, Infidels, the
bare sight of your hats will make us run away.*

From the top of this hill of Calemberg, the
Christians were presented, about an hour before
night, with one of the finest and most dreadful
prospects of the greatness of human power: an immense plain and all the islands of the Danube covered with pavilions, whose magnificence seemed rather
calculated for an encampment of pleasure than the
hardships of war; an innumerable multitude of horses,
camels, and buffaloes *(b)*; two hundred thousand
men all in motion; swarms of Tartars dispersed
along the foot of the mountain in their usual confusion; the fire of the besiegers incessant and terri-

(a) Dupont.
(b) The Turks make use of buffaloes, or wild oxen, to draw
their artillery, and of horses and camels to carry their baggage;
for they have no waggons in their armies.

ble,

ble, and that of the befieged fuch as they could contrive to make; in fine, a great city, diftinguifhable
only by the tops of the fteeples, and the fire and
fmoak that covered it.

The befieged were immediately apprized by fig-
nals of the approach of the army to their relief.
To have an idea of the joy that the city felt, a perfon muft have fuffered all the extremities of a long
fiege, and be deftined with his wife and children
to the fword of a mercilefs conqueror, or to flavery
in a foreign country. But this gleam of tranfport
was foon fucceeded by fear. Kara-Muftapha, with
fuch an army, had ftill reafons to expect fuccefs,
though he did not deferve it. The King, who was
examining his difpofitions, faid to the German Generals; *This man is badly encamped; he knows nothing of war; we fhall certainly beat him:* words,
which muft not be confidered as an oracle thrown
out at random, with a view of infpiring confidence.
It is well known that Marfhal Villars, then inglori-
oufly employed in the Cevennes, foretold the defeat of Tallard from the bad difpofition of his
troops at the battle of Hochftet: and every general,
who cannot prophefy in the fame manner, ought to
give up his command.

The cannon on both fides were the prelude to the
important fcene of the following day, which was
the 12th of September; a day that was to decide
whether Vienna, under Mahomet IV. fhould have
the fate of Conftantinople under Mahomet II. and
whether the empire of the Weft fhould be reunited
to the empire of the Eaft: perhaps alfo whether
Europe fhould continue a Chriftian country.

Two hours before break of day, the King, the
Duke of Lorrain, and feveral of the Generals joined in an act of religion little practifed in our days.
They implored the protection of the fon of God,
by receiving him in the holy Euchariſt; while the

Turks,

Turks were invoking the one, folitary God of Abraham by repeated cries of Allah! Allah! *(a)*

This cry was redoubled about fun-rifing, when the Chriftian army defcended from the mountain with a flow and even pace, keeping its ranks toge-ther, preceded by its cannon, and halting every thirty or forty fteps, to fire and load again. The front grew wider and deeper, in proportion as the fpace enlarged. The plain was a vaft amphitheatre, where the Turks, in the utmoft agitation, beheld the motions of their enemies. It was at this time, that the Cham of the Tartars bad the Vizir obferve the lances adorned with ftreamers belonging to the Polifh horfe guards, and faid to him, *The King is at their head;* words which filled him with uneafi-nefs *(b)*.

The Vizir, after having ordered the Tartars to put all their prifoners to the number of thirty thou-fand to death, (a barbarity worthy of fuch a com-mander) inftantly made his troops march towards the mountain, and at the fame time ordered a ge-neral affault to be made upon the place. This laft order ought to have been given fooner; for the Chriftians had now recovered courage, and the Jani-zaries, provoked at their General, had loft it.

In the mean time, the Chriftians were coming down, and the Turks afcended to meet them; fo that the action foon begun. The firft line of the Chriftian army, confifting wholly of foot, charged with fuch impetuofity, that it made room for the line of cavalry, which took poft in the intervals between the battalions. The King, the Princes, and the generals, advancing to the front, fought fometimes with the horfe, and fometimes with the

(a) An Arabick word which anfwers to thofe of *Elohim, Adonai,* and *Jehova,* or *Tetragrammaton.* They all fignify *the Being* by way of eminence, or the Divine Effence.
(b) Journal of the fiege, p. 79.

Y   foot.

foot. The two other lines followed close upon the foremoft. Konfki, whofe fkill in the military art was equal to his intrepidity in action, had the care of the artillery, which was loaded with cartridge-fhot, and fired at a very fmall diftance.

The fcene of this firft engagement, in the ground between the plain and the mountain, was broken by vineyards, rifing grounds, and little valleys. The enemy having left their cannon at the entrance of the vineyards, fuffered much from that of the Chrift-ians. The combatants, being difperfed about on this unequal ground, difputed it with great fury till to-wards noon, when the Count de Maligni, brother to the Queen of Poland, got poffeffion of a rifing ground which took the Turks in flank, who being drove from hill to hill, retired towards the plain and drew up along the border of their camp.

The Chriftian army, the left wing in particular, tranfported at this fuccefs, and crying out victory, would needs pufh their advantages without inter-miffion. Their ardor was unqueftionably noble, but the King thought it dangerous. The German cavalry, being heavily mounted, would foon have been out of wind in the diftance between them and the enemy. A ftill ftronger reafon was, that all the different bodies having been engaged, fometimes upon rifing grounds, and fometimes in valleys, had inevitably fallen into fome confufion and difturbed the order of battle. Some time therefore was taken to repair the diforder; and the plain became the fcene of a triumph which pofterity will always have a difficulty to believe. Seventy thoufand men marched to attack two hundred thoufand. In the Turkifh army, the Bafhaw of Diarbekir command-ed the right wing, the Bafhaw of Buda the left, and the Vizir was in the centre, having with him the Aga of the Janizaries and the General of the Spahis.

The

The two armies continued motionless for some time; the Christians in silence, the Turks and Tartars redoubling their cries accompanied with the sound of clarions. In this dreadful moment, a red pavilion was erected in the midst of the Infidels, and close to it the great standard of Mahomet, a sacred object to the professors of the Mussulman faith, like the *Labarum* of the Roman Emperors, or the *Oriflamme* of the ancient Kings of France. But this imposture, which sometimes inspires them with as much courage as truth can give to Christians, did not do its office on this great occasion; for the Vizir had deprived it of all its virtue.

As soon as the King had given orders for the charge, the Polish cavalry, sabre in hand, pushed directly forwards to the Vizir, whose post was marked out by the standard. The first ranks were instantly forced, and the Poles penetrated even to the numerous squadrons that surrounded the Vizir. The Spahis disputed the victory; but all the rest, Walachians, Moldavians, Transylvanians, Tartars, and even Janizaries themselves, shewed no alacrity: a fatal effect of an army's hating and despising its General. The Vizir attempted to recover their good opinion, by shewing courage and kind behaviour; but the time was past. He addressed himself next to the Bashaw of Buda and the other Generals, who answered him only with a silence of despair: *And thou*, says he to the Tartar Prince, *dost thou too refuse to help me?* The Cham saw no safety but in flight. The Spahis were now reduced to their last efforts. The Polish horse had broke and dispersed them. The great standard soon disappeared: the Vizir turned his back, and his flight made the consternation general. It was soon communicated from the centre to the wings, which were hard pressed by all the divisions of the Christian army at the same time: the left by Jablonow-

ski,

Y 1683. ſki, the right by the Electors, while the Duke of Lorrain fell upon the centre, and the King animated the whole by his actions and his orders. That immenſe multitude, which, under a ſkilful leader, ought to have ſurrounded its enemy in ſo extenſive a plain, was deprived by terror of all ſtrength and preſence of mind. Had night been farther off, it would have been a total defeat; as things were, it was only a precipitate retreat *(a)*.

The King advanced next towards the Janizaries, who were left to continue the ſiege; but they had all diſappeared, and Vienna was completely delivered. The victorious troops would fain have entered the enemy's camp, allured by the immenſe riches that the Turks had left: but the temptation was a dangerous one at this juncture. The enemy, favoured by the darkneſs of the night, might return, and cut in pieces an army, which would be too much employed in pillage to make any defence. An order was therefore iſſued to continue all night under arms, upon pain of death. The King might probably have made a better uſe of the time, by purſuing the enemy, as the Duke of Lorrain adviſed him: but great men are ſubject to faults, becauſe they are only men; and thoſe who have undertaken to juſtify him, alledge, that the Poles, after ſo long a march, were overwhelmed with fatigue, and that their baggage could not arrive under three days. Others, who have endeavoured to blacken him, pretend that a deſire of ſecuring to himſelf the beſt part of the ſpoil, was his principal motive.

Amidſt a great number of priſoners, there was brought to the King an Arabian groom, with a horſe armed and capariſoned for a tournament, as in the days of the heroes of romance. The horſe

(a) Journal of the ſiege, p. 79.

belonged

belonged to the Vizir, and the groom gave a minute account of his genealogy. The Arabs, though they set no value upon nobility in men, pay a great regard to it in their horses, because these animals never degenerate, if they are taken care of, and the breed be kept unmixed.

There were brought also some Polish deserters, who expressed great sorrow for their fault, and returned to their colours. One of them, who had had an office in the Vizir's houshold, brought with him an enamelled stirrup which his master had lost, as he was changing horses in his flight. *Take this stirrup*, said the King to one of his officers, *carry it to the Queen, and tell her that the person to whom it belonged is defeated.* The Queen loved glory, and had no objection to presents: that which the King sent her was of no great value, but time made her amends.

About six in the morning, the enemy's camp was opened to the soldiers, whose rapaciousness was at first suspended by a most shocking spectacle, of mothers butchered in several parts of the camp, some of whom had their children still hanging at their breasts. These women were far unlike those prostitutes who follow the Christian armies, and are equally pernicious to the health and morals of the soldiers : they were virtuous wives, whom their husbands chose rather to kill than expose to the lust of the Christians. The children escaped this slaughter, and five or six hundred of them were preserved, whom the good Bishop of Newstadt, to whom Vienna was already much indebted, took care of and educated in the religion of the conquerors *(a)*.

When they entered the Vizir's tents, another object of grief and joy suspended for a moment the rage of plunder. This was the Polish envoy load-

(a) Journal of the siege, p. 187.

ed

ed with irons   The Vizir had faid to him more
than once, *If thy mafter marches, I will order thee
to be beheaded.*   Fortunately the Vizir knew nothing,
of the King's march till the moment of the battle,
and he was then too much employed to think of
keeping his word.   But the unhappy Trofki had
beheld for two months together the fabre lifted up
over him.   Upon fuch an occafion it is natural to
afk, whether Sovereigns are fufficiently fenfible of
fuch great facrifices as this?

Never did an army get poffeffion of more abun-
dant fpoil; for the Turks, who are oeconomifts in
time of peace, difplay great magnificence in the field.
Their tables are far from fplendid, and no gaming
is permitted: they have a proverb, that *be who
kills a player at dice, is bleffed of the Lord*: but the
trappings of their horfes are rich, their own clothes
and the furniture of their tents valuable, their arms
finely ornamented, their pavilions magnificent, and
the camp crowded with tradefmen, who carry to a
fort of military fair, all the finery of Afia.   The
Germans and Poles got great wealth by all this
plunder; nor did even the generals neglect their own
interefts.   The manners of different nations fhould
make fome difference in the judgments we pafs
upon warriors.   We read in Homer that the Grecian heroes, after a victory, fhared the plunder; but
without having recourfe to the cuftoms of ancient
Greece, it is well known that in the time of Charlemagne, the fpoils of the Saracens in Spain were divided between the King, the officers, the foldiers.
The hero of the day had his fhare upon the prefent
occafion.   He writ to the Queen, " that the Grand-
" Vizir had made him his heir, and that he had found
" in his tents the value of feveral millions of ducats.
" So that you will have no room, added he, to fay
" of me what the women of Tartary fay, when their
                                              hufbands

" hufbands return empty-handed; You are no men,
" becaufe you come back without plunder."

Among the many things which fell into the hands
of the foldiers, there were two, which attracted the
notice of all, but excited the covetoufnefs of none.
One was a large ftandard, which in the hurry of
joy, was taken for that of Mahomet. But this
was certainly a miftake; for the fingular precautions
tions that the Turks ufe, has always prevented this
calamity. The ftandard is inclofed in an ark of
gold, with the Alcoran and the robe of the prophet.
This ark is carried by a camel which goes before
the Sultan or the Vizir; and when the ftandard is
difplayed in battle, an officer, of the race of Mahomet,
homet, called the *Naikbul-Efchret*, is appointed to
watch the event of the combat; and when the victory
tory inclines ever fo little to the fide of the enemy,
he makes off with all expedition with the facred
depofitum. The Vizir, upon the prefent occafion,
accompanied this officer in his flight *(a)*. But the
Chriftians, who were fond of being miftaken in this
fact, have perfifted in believing that they poffefs the
famous ftandard; and the hiftorians, one after another,
ther, not excepting the celebrated author of the
Annals of the empire, have adopted this miftake.
The other facred implement that made part of the
booty, was a picture of the Virgin found in the
Vizir's tent, with this infcription in latin:

Per hanc imaginem victor eris, Johannes.
Per hanc imaginem victor ero Johannes.

The firft line, *John, by this image thou fhalt conquer*,
quer, comes from the Virgin: to which John anfwers,
fwers, *By this image, I John will conquer*. It was
evidently an imitation of the fign which Conftan-

(a) Cantemir, tom. ii. p. 154.

tine

tine faw in the air, when he was marching to give battle to Maxentius.

The image gave occafion to much fpeculation. Some thought it very remarkable that the Vizir fhould have in his tent a prefage of his approaching ruin, which ought rather to have been in John's poffeffion. Others maintained, that no miraculous facts fhould be admitted, without an application of the teft of fevere criticifm. The image, however, was placed in a magnificent chappel built by the Queen of Poland; and the pretended ftandard of Mahomet was fent to the Pope as an act of homage to the Lord of Hofts. All the cannon remained to the Emperor, and the empire alfo. The Vizir had flattered himfelf that he fhould give law to both, and had brought with him all the pageantry that he intended for his triumphal entry into Vienna. He had alfo brought magazines, artillery, and workmen of every fort, in order to victual and fortify the place, where he propofed to refide till the next campaign, which he confidered as the end of Leopold's reign. By the taking of Vienna, Italy would be inclofed within a double Crefcent, no place on that fide the Rhine could make any refiftance, and there remained nothing but the fortune of Lewis XIV. to ftop his progrefs. With fuch vaft projects and great force, he ftood in need of other manners, and another head. The only act of vigour he did, was his rapid march to Vienna, while he made a feint of attacking Raab.

After all, fo decifive an action was never attended with lefs flaughter. An Italian Secretary, named *Talenti*, whom the King of Poland difpatched to the Pope, gave out all along the road, and even told the Pontiff himfelf, that he had travelled for four leagues together upon dead bodies. This fabulous tale was well calculated to amufe the court of Rome; but if the Secretary exaggerated without

out fhame, a celebrated author, who by the univerfal extent of his knowledge, and the beauty of his writings, has acquired a privilege of making miftakes, has diminifhed without probability. He eftimates the lofs of the Chriftians at two hundred men only, and that of the Turks at lefs than a thoufand (a). The Jefuit Aurigny, in his memoirs, a work of great value in other refpects, thinks he has made a better calculation, by making the lofs of the Chriftians amount to fix hundred men (b). Thus it is that miftakes are perpetuated. On the fide of the Chriftians, a fingle fquadron of Polifh gendarmes loft two and twenty men. All the fquadrons charged, and more than a hundred officers were killed. Now it is well known that ten foldiers at leaft muft be allowed for every officer. The Germans did not continue idle ; and when blows are given, they muft alfo be received. The Poles lamented the death of Zbafki, Maczinfki, the Caftellan Urbanfki, young Potofki, chief of an illuftrious family, the intrepid Mædreofki, who had acquired fuch honour at the battle of Choczin ; Lieutenant General Affuerus, and many others, whofe bodies were found at the foot of the red pavilion which diftinguifhed the Vizir's poft. The Imperialifts beftowed tears upon the Prince of Croy, as they had lately done, in the unfortunate affair of Petronel, upon the young Prince of Aremberg, and the Chevalier de Savoy, elder brother to Prince Eugene. The death of the latter had fomething in it very deplorable : a Tartar, after having wounded him with a fabre, threw him acrofs his horfe, and fqueezed him with fuch violence that he crufhed his ftomach. The unhappy Prince was refcued out of his hands, but died the third day after, at

(a) Annals of the empire, tom. ii. p. 347.
(b) Tom. iii. p. 417.

Vienna.

Vienna. As for the Turks, they loft a great many colours, and it is well known that colours are never furrendered but with great lofs of blood; and indeed, if we take only a tranfitory view of two armies difputing at firft againft each other, foot to foot, for fix hours, a fpot of ground full of eminences and vineyards, and afterwards coming to a general action, this will be fufficient to fhew that it could not be done without confiderable lofs; but this lofs will, after all, be thought fmall, and was fo in effect for fo great a victory.

The King took a pleafure, perhaps an ill-natured one, in informing Lewis XIV. of his victory. The fubftance of the letter was, *that he thought himfelf particularly obliged to congratulate the eldeft fon of the Church, upon an event fo advantageous to all Chriftendom.* The power and the victories of the French Monarch filled all Europe. John himfelf could not help being a little jealous. He even fhewed it plainly the following year, upon one of thofe occafions, when Kings, like their fubjects, fpeak frankly what they think. The news of the taking of Luxembourg, a new triumph for the arms of Lewis, was brought to Warfaw. A French furgeon, who attended the King of Poland, and was then in his chamber, cried out, *Ay! he is a King indeed—And I,* fays the King interrupting him in a paffion, *what am I then?*—To acquaint Lewis with the deliverance of Vienna and the empire, fo great an exploit performed with fo fmall an army, was making him feel, that he was not the only King who had a right to the title of *Great.*

The morrow after a victory is alfo a day of glory. Staremberg came to pay his refpects to the deliverer of Vienna, where John thought he might triumph without offending the Emperor, and entered the town over the ruins, amidft the acclamations of the people. His horfe could fcarce get through the multitude

multitude that fell proftrate before him, came to
kifs his feet, and called him their father, their fa-
viour, the greateft of all Princes. Vienna in this
moment of joy forgot that it had a jealous mafter.
The pleafure of delivering the unhappy, and the
uncommanded gratitude they expreffed, made the
King fhed tears, and confefs, that the throne could
furnifh no pleafure equal to it. He was conducted
with fhouts of joy to the cathedral, where he went
to return thanks to the God of battle. He difcovered upon this temple the Turkifh *crefcent*, a
monument of ignominy, erected there by the great
Soliman *(a)*, which the King ordered to be taken
down and trod under foot by the people. He himfelf begun the *Te Deum*, which was fung upon the
occafion. It is remarkable that no Magiftrate was
prefent at this ceremony : even the perfons of diftinction in the city that attended it were very few,
while the people, unreftrained by political confider-
ations, fung the praifes of God and the conqueror.
The text of the fermon that was preached, was :
*There was a man fent from God, whofe name was
John.* About a century before, Pope Pius V. had
exclaimed in the fame words, when he heard of the
celebrated battle of Lepanto, which the famous
John of Auftria, baftard of Charles the Fifth, gained over the fleet of the Sultan Selim. There was
however a great difference between the victory at
Lepanto and that of John Sobiefki. The former
was of very little fervice to Chriftendom, whereas
the latter faved the empire and religion together.
Had Vienna been taken, the Chriftian churches, as
was the cafe at Conftantinople, would foon have
been converted into mofques ; and who knows

(a) The condition upon which he raifed the fiege of Vienna,
which begun to make him uneafy, while the uneafinefs of the
place was ftill greater.

where

where Mahometanifm, which has already overrun fo many countries, would have ftopt ?

Leopold, who expected to have a triumph in his capital, though he had not been prefent at the battle, advanced by the Danube, fcarce venturing to caft his eye upon the fmoking ruins of fo many hamlets, villages, gardens, and country-feats; ruins fo extenfive, that it was neceffary to make a new topographical map, for the places marked in that of *Vifcher* were no longer in being *(a)*. As he drew near the city, he heard the firing of cannon, not intended for him. He was wounded to the very heart with this thought, and turning to the Count de Sintzendorf, faid to him : *The weaknefs of the counfels that you have had a fhare in, occafions me this difgrace.* Thefe words, uttered with that imperious tone which always crufhes a courtier, affected the Minifter fo much that he died the next day *(b)*. A minifter who fhould die with grief at having advifed a meafure productive of mifery to the people, would deferve tears.

The Emperor fufpended his march, that he might not be a fpectator of John's triumph. A difficulty of ceremony contributed alfo to ftop him : the queftion was, whether an elective King had ever been prefent with an Emperor, and in what manner he had been received. The Duke of Lorrain, who liftened only to the voice of gratitude, anfwered, *with open arms, if he has preferved the empire.* The Emperor was attentive only to his Imperial dignity, and gave John to underftand that he would not give him his hand, which was the reception the King of Poland expected in quality of a Sovereign Prince. After much cavilling, it was fettled that they fhould meet in the open plain. The Emper-

(a) Journal of the fiege, p. 26.
(a) Memoirs of the Duke of Villars, tom. i. p. 329.

or, in his way, paffed before the Bavarian troops, with the Elector at their head. Leopold had given him a fword enriched with diamonds, and he had juft made a good ufe of the prefent; but this did not fecure him from feeling afterwards all the rigour of the houfe of Auftria.

When the moment of the interview arrived, the King of Poland, in a Polifh bonnet, and a plume of feathers terminated by a large pearl hanging loofe, clad in the fame armour that he wore on the day of the battle, with a Roman buckler, on which were engraved, not the actions of his anceftors, but his own, and mounted upon a ftately horfe with magnificent furniture, approached the Emperor with that heroic prefence which nature had given him, and that air which his victory gave him a right to put on. The Emperor, dreft in a plain manner, as he ufually was in his own court, and mounted accordingly, talked of nothing but the fervices done the Poles in all ages by the friendfhip and protection of the Emperors. At laft, however, he let drop the word *gratitude* for the deliverance of Vienna. At this word the King turning his horfe, faid to him : *Brother, I am glad that I have done you that fmall fervice.* He was going to put an end to the difcourfe which grew difagreeable; but he obferved his fon Prince James alight from his horfe to pay his refpects to the Emperor. *This is a Prince,* faid he, *whom I am educating for the fervice of Chriftendom.* The Emperor, without faying a word, only nodded his head; and yet this was the young Prince whom he had promifed to make his fon-in-law. After this, what a reception could the Palatines, who attended the King, expect ? One of them ftept forward to kifs his Imperial Majefty's boot; but he drew upon himfelf this reprimand from his mafter : *Palatine, no meannefs*; and then they feparated. No one was more offended at Leopold's behaviour

behaviour towards the deliverer of Vienna, than the Duke of Lorrain. In the whole courfe of the, expedition, the reader muft have, obferved that the Duke fhewed a regard, a deference, and even veneration for the King; and if we recollect that John had ftood for, and carried the crown of Poland, in oppofition to him, it muft be owned that it indicated a great mind to behave thus to a rival.

The King's diffatisfaction with the Emperor fhould naturally have induced him to return to his own dominions, after having faved the empire. This was what the republic intended, and the Queen defired. The Emperor himfelf wifhed it, for reafons which he chofe not to publifh. He knew that the malecontents in Hungary, no longer trufting in the fortune of Tekeli, had offered their crown to John for his fon Prince James. They were at this time in arms, and Leopold was uneafy at feeing fo near them a victorious King, who, by accepting that crown, might fell him at a dear rate the fervices he had done him. But this ambitious defign, which John might have juftified by the fuffrages of a people refuming their liberty in order to difpofe of it again, never entered into his mind; he thought only of the common caufe of Chriftendom, and the particular intereft of Poland, by continuing to humble the Ottoman empire. He even flattered himfelf that Leopold, notwithftanding his ftrange behaviour, would ftill perform his promifes. The double, hope of a match between an Archduchefs and his fon, and of the crown of Poland's being made hereditary in his family, fupported him againft the Imperial pride.

The council of Vienna no fooner gueffed at his thoughts, than they refolved to take advantage of the Polifh troops to force *Neubaufel* from the Turks. This place, the fiege of which the Duke of Lorrain had been obliged to raife in the beginning

of

of the campaign, is situated on the North side of the Danube. To lay siege to it would furnish an opportunity of seeing the Turks again, whom they repented of having suffered to escape with so little loss.

Kara-Mustapha, after his defeat, retired to Buda *(a)*, where he expected his fate. His being son-in-law to Mahomet was of great use to him, but the Sultana Validé of still greater. The Sultans have a particular respect for their mother, even beyond what nature prescribes. If they were to admit a Sultana to their bed without consulting her, the Alcoran and the court would murmur. They give up into her hands part of the government of the seraglio ; she is permitted to assist at councils of state, and debates upon public business, having a veil over her face, with the Vizir and the Mufti *(b)*. As Mahomet was full of this filial respect for his mother, she suborned witnesses who were glad to gain preferment by compliances that are common enough in courts. The disaster at Vienna was imputed to persons far less criminal than the Vizir. The Bashaw of Buda was strangled and lamented by the whole empire. He had performed prodigies at the siege of Candy, quieted an insurrection in Egypt, increased the tribute paid by that kingdom, without oppressing the people, and gained by his merit the confidence of the great Cuprogli. It is true, he had, on the present occasion, given up the Vizir to the arms of the Christians, but such a defection scarce ever happens but to a despised or

---

(a) The capital of the kingdom of Hungary. It is disputed, whether this be the ancient *Aquincum*, where the second Roman legion, called *Adjutrix*, was quartered. The Vatican copy of Antoninus reads *Aquineo*. It may be doubted, whether this *Aquineo* or *Aquineum* be not rather *Cepol* upon the Danube. Others will have it, that it is neither Buda, nor Cepol, but *Strigonia* : an ample subject for a learned dissertation which will end with proving nothing.

(b) Cantemir, tom. ii. p. 151.

detested

deftefted General. The fault, however, was inexcufable, and he paid for it with his head. Three other Bafhaws fell with him. The Cham of the Tartars was depofed ; a punifhment which he would not have deferved under another Vizir.

The fame courier, who was charged with thefe cruel orders, brought the real criminal diftinguifhed marks of his continuing ftill in favour ; but it was upon condition of his repairing this misfortune. Vanquifhed as he was, he had ftill an army far fuperior to that of the conquerors ; and the lifts were again opened.

The King of Poland begun his march on the 17th of September, to complete the deftruction of his enemy, for he thought that nothing was done, while any thing remained to do. He was followed by the German army, but not fo numerous as it was in the affair of Vienna. The Prince of Waldeck was preparing to lead back the troops of the circles. The Elector of Bavaria was ill, and his army waited for his recovery.

The Elector of Saxony had taken part in the juft refentment of a Prince of his family, and entirely withdrawn his troops. Whenever two perfons of diftinguifhed merit appear in the fame field of action, it is as dangerous to reward only one, as to forget both. Staremberg, befides a large fum of money, had the order of the Golden Fleece, and a Field-Marfhal's ftaff. This laft honour would have fatisfied the Prince of Saxe-Lawemburg, who had deferved it by ferving the Emperor. Upon its being refufed him, he quitted the fervice, and at the fame time the Elector withdrew his troops. The garrifon of Vienna and fome other regiments filled up a part of the chafm ; fo that the Chriftian army was ftill fifty thoufand ftrong. It paffed the Danube below Prefburg, under the cannon of Comora, directing its march towards *Neuhaufel*.

The

The German Generals had not all the same deference for the King of Poland with the Duke of Lorrain. Staremberg, commander of the foot, who poffeffed the favour and was intrufted with the intentions of Leopold, did not always affent to the difpofitions made by John ; and an event happened to encreafe this mifunderftanding. Tekeli, after the defeat of the Turks, faw himfelf upon the brink of a precipice ; and fought to accommodate matters with the Emperor, under the protection of the King of Poland. The propofals of his envoys, who were heard before a council, confifted of fix articles : the prefervation of their privileges, liberty of confcience, reftitution of their eftates, the convocation of a free diet, a fufpenfion of arms during the negotiation, and for Tekeli their leader, the fovereignty of certain Counties which had been promifed him the year before. They had fcarce time to deliver their inftructions, before Staremberg interrupted them, and talked of nothing but fcaffolds and executioners. John's anfwer was in the ftrain of a merciful, but potent Prince, who had ftill arms in his hand, and expected to meet with the refpect due to the mediation of one who had juft faved the empire. The Imperialifts replied with heat, that they had not been idle fpectators of that great day. From this moment, the King refolved to fhew them that he could conquer without their affiftance, though he conquered for their intereft.

A body of between fix and feven thoufand Turks, all cavalry, had paffed the Danube at Strigonia, in order to guard the head of the bridge belonging to that town. In this place is fituated the fort of Barcan, built of earth, with fraifes and paliffadoes, of little confequence in itfelf, but made famous by being the fcene of feveral remarkable actions.

The Turkifh cavalry was commanded by a young man, who faw the Bafhaw of Buda ftrangled, and

Z

Y. 1683. was not afraid to fill his place. The young Bafhaw, named *Kara-Mehemed*, born for war, full of fire, ambition, and courage, was refolved to deferve his fortune.

The Polifh troops always encamped before the reft of the army. The King flattered himfelf with the hopes of crufhing this handful of Turks and taking the fort of Barcan : but not chufing that the Germans fhould fhare in this victory, he concealed from them his march. In the mean time, fome of his fpies returned and brought him word that the enemy was very numerous : *Let us not enquire, faid he, how many they are, but where they are.* Unfor-. tunately he found them too foon, though their number was really fmall.

The 7th of October was a day of blood. The Turks being covered with a rideau, the Polifh vanguard did not think them fo near, and was attacked before it could draw up in order of battle. Diforder and confufion inftantly feized the Poles : the officers gave no orders at all, or gave them abfurdly, a body of dragoons being made to alight from their horfes in a plain. The Coffacks were put into diforder; the Pancerns took to flight; and the Grand-General's dragoons mounted their horfes only to fave themfelves. Thofe belonging to the King had not time to follow their example, and were cut to pieces. Nothing was to be feen but flying parties, and heads falling by the fabre.

In the midft of this diforder, the King came up with the main body of the horfe ; but his prefence did not ftop the conqueror. The young Bafhaw redoubled his activity, and the King had fcarce time to form his line. He received the Turks with firm-nefs, and even charged them in his turn. But the Turks opening their ranks to inclofe the whole Polifh line, and being animated with that rage which diftinguifhed the Mahometans under the firft

Califfs,

V. 1683.

Califfs, drove back the left wing, forced the right, and made way through the centre. The Towarifz were no longer that intrepid band, which, about a century before, had faid to their King: *What haft thou to fear, with twenty thoufand lances? If the fky fhould fall, we would keep it up with their points.*

In this univerfal diforder, when every moment added the dying to the dead, and it became equally dangerous to retreat, and to refift, the Grand-General Jablonowfki befought the King to efcape with his fon, who fought by his fide, adding, that he would endeavour to rally a few fquadrons, and ftand his ground fome little time, to protect his facred perfon. The King knew that his perfon was made facred, only that it might be facrificed for the republic, and continued the fight till he was hurried along, himfelf and his fon, by the flying multitude. Never were troops ftruck with greater terror. The huffars threw away their lances, the Cornets their ftandards, which lay fcattered about, with kettle-drums, among the furrows. Let no one be confident that he fhall be always brave, and ready to expofe his own life, to fave that of his Prince. The Polifh officers, whofe profeffion it is to be brave, abandoned their Prince to the mercy of the enemy; and when the Generals attempted to ftop them, by fhewing them the King, they anfwered, that their own life was their principal concern, and that if the King was killed, or taken, they would make another. If they pretended to ufe force, they were threatened with the fabre. The Count de Maligni, brother to the Queen, was once in as much danger from the Poles, as from the enemy. The inequality of the ground contributed alfo much to increafe the carnage. The furrows being uncommonly deep, numbers of the cavalry were difmounted, and either trod to death by their

own

Y. 1683. own men, or beheaded by the enemy. Young Lubomirſki, being thrown from his horſe, offered ten
thouſand ducats to whoever ſhould ſave his life :
a groom got the money, by giving him a led horſe.
D'Henoff, Palatine of Pomerania, had not the ſame
good fortune. Being diſmounted, and wounded
with a ball, he lay weltring in his blood, till a
Turk cut off his head.

The King, being hurried away by an ungovernable horſe, loſt ſight of his ſon. He aſked after
him with the utmoſt uneaſineſs, and thoſe who were
near pretended to ſee him, and pointed him out to
his father, deceiving him, in order to quiet his mind:
The heat of the purſuit increaſed every moment,
and the flight of the Poles grew precipitate in proportion. Every one found himſelf obliged to take
care of his own preſervation, the King as well as the
reſt. Two Turks coming up with him, he put
himſelf in a poſture of defence. One of them lifted
up his ſabre, againſt a life ſo precious to Poland,
and ſo odious to the Ottoman empire. A *Reiſter*
of the King's guards prevented the infidel, and laid
him dead with his carbine. But the ſoldier had no
time to receive the thanks of his Prince, for the
other Turk inſtantly avenged his comrade, and
puſhed on towards the King. The Maſter
of the Horſe, *Mateinſki*, interpoſing to defend
him at the hazard of his own life, preſented a piſtol to the Turk, who turned aſide to avoid him:
This dreadful ſcene was over in leſs time than it
takes to relate it, and did not at all ſuſpend the
rout.

The crowd of runaways increaſed every moment
about the King, and made his ſituation more dangerous. Bruiſed all over by the continual ſhock of
horſes and arms juſtling againſt him, encumbered
with his own bulk, out of breath, and almoſt ſuf-
focated, he ſtood in great need of aſſiſtance. Mateinſki

teinſki ſupported him on one ſide, and the firſt perſon they found on the other, while his horſe, with the bridle on its neck, redoubled its ſpeed. Having thus recovered his breath, the firſt thing he ſaw, through a cloud of duſt, was a young man held by the cloak, by a Turkiſh ſoldier.——This was no other than his ſon, who got clear by quitting his garment, and eſcaped to a wood, where he found a ſafe retreat.

The rout had now continued near an hour, and the plain was covered with dead bodies; a few minutes more, and Poland would have loſt, in one day, its King, its generals, and all its cavalry. But fortunately the infantry was advancing at a great rate. The Imperial army followed, and the artillery was getting in order. The Turks, whoſe number was too ſmall to encounter ſo great a force, returned to the field of battle, of which they kept poſſeſſion.

Theſe Turks were the very ſame troops that had fled before Vienna: they then wanted a General, and had found one in the plain of Barcan. During the whole action, the young Baſhaw had been ſeen directing their motions, defying death, and teaching his ſoldiers to deſpiſe it: a little more experience would have made him a great Captain.

The loſs of the Poles was never known exactly; for they took the firſt opportunity of burying their dead, in order to conceal their number. When this ſtorm was over, the calm that ſucceeded preſented but a melancholy ſcene. The King, overwhelmed with fatigue and vexation, had laid himſelf down upon a bundle of hay. Here they brought him his ſon, whom the King little expected to inſtruct by adverſity; and yet the leſſon was of great uſe, by teaching him how to bear it. The Poliſh nobles, who had eſcaped the ſlaughter, with downcaſt eyes, and dejected countenances, ſurrounded their maſter in mournful ſilence. The German

Z 3

Gene-

Generals put on also an air of sadness: but the King knew what was in their hearts. *Gentlemen,* said he, with that candour which is never found but in great minds, *I confess I wanted to conquer without you, for the honour of my own nation: I have suffered severely for it, being soundly beat; but I will take my revenge with you and for you. To effect this, must be the chief employment of our thoughts.* This eloquence of the heart is perhaps superior to all the speeches in Livy.

The young Bashaw, proud of the advantage he had gained over so great a King, with an inferior force, was thinking, on his side, of gathering fresh laurels. He dispatched couriers the same night to Buda, with an account of his victory. The Grand-Visir, without losing a moment, sent a body of twenty thousand horse, which arrived next day by the bridge of Strigonia, the distance being no more than six leagues He writ at the same time to *Tekeli*, who waited to see the turn of affairs at the head of thirty thousand men, " that if he had his " reasons formerly for keeping measures with the " King of Poland, they were now at an end; " that his army was entirely destroyed, and he him- " self killed or taken; that they had none to deal " with but the Germans, of whom they should " have an easy bargain; and that it was his in- " terest to march with the utmost expedition to " Barcan, where he might secure his crown, by " deserving the protection of the Ottoman empire, " and by sharing in its glory."

Such were the efforts that Kara-Mustapha made to wipe off his disgrace, without coming in person to take his share of the danger.

The King of Poland, who had recovered his strength by a night's rest, employed the whole following day; which was the 8th, in collecting his scattered army, in consoling it for the misfortune
of

of yefterday, in animating it to vengeance, in com-
bining it with the Imperial troops, and in regulating the order of battle for the morrow.

The letter he writ to the Queen, dated this day,
informing her of his difafter, was enough to freeze
her blood. He told her that *he was advancing towards the enemy, and that fhe muft expect they would
be defeated, or bid him farewell for ever.*

Tekeli was not arrived in the morning of the
9th, when the engagement begun. Any one, but
the young Bafhaw, would have avoided an action,
or at leaft would not have fought it. It will fcarce
be believed, that twenty-fix thoufand Turks, all
cavalry, and without cannon, could venture a battle
againft fifty thoufand Chriftians, provided with all
the advantages of infantry, cavalry, and artillery.
If this was an act of rafhnefs, the young Bafhaw
committed another, and a more confiderable, fault.
He drew up his troops upon a fpot that fcarce left
them any retreat, having the Danube on his left, a
ridge of mountains on his right, and the river of
Gran behind him ; fo that the bridge of Strigonia,
defended by the foot of Barcan, was the only way
to efcape, in cafe of a defeat. It was telling his
foldiers, that they muft either conquer or perifh.
Such a glorious fit of defpair has fometimes fucceeded ; but prudence is a better thing to truft to.
He formed his troops into one line only, with intervals of a moderate diftance ; but this line was
fupported by columns of fifteen fquadrons each,
one behind another. The Turks pretend that thefe
columns are hard to break, eafily rallied, and very
proper for hemming in the enemy. The Poles had
lately experienced it to their coft.

The two Bafhaws of Siliftria and Caramania
commanded the wings. The General, elated with
his late victory, and promifing himfelf another, was
in the center.

The

The Chriftian army outftretched that of the Turks by a full half of its front, which was made up of German and Polifh troops, equally divided, that the two nations might fhare in the danger and the glory, if any could be got by conquering with fuch a fuperior force. The King was on the right, Jablonowfki on the left, and the Duke of Lorrain in the center.

The Chriftians were putting themfelves in motion to begin the charge, when the Turks, who were quicker, fell upon them with an impetuofity attended with howlings, which it is impoffible to defcribe. A torrent that tumbles from the precipice of a mountain's brow, is neither more noify, nor more rapid. The Chriftians received them with fuch firmnefs, that not a man loft his poft, and with a terrible fire, that brought men and horfes to the ground. The Turks wheeled round to recover a little, and inftantly returned with greater fury. It was owing to the chevaux de frize, placed at the head of the battalions of the Chriftian army, that they were not broke. The Turks were often on the point of fucceeding, and as often repulfed. Never did fquadrons perform their evolutions with greater dexterity and quicknefs; nor was the excellence of the Turkifh horfes ever more fully difplayed.

After fo many efforts, equally bold and unfuccefsful, they changed their method of attack. Hitherto they had charged only the left wing; but now they attempted at the fame time the right and the center; and if one body was repulfed, another that had had time to recover breath, diftinguifhed itfelf by frefh efforts, fuperior to ordinary valour. It was not by their fire-arms, but by ufing their fabres well in clofe combat, that they expected to gain the victory. If Tekeli had appeared at this

juncture,

juncture, as he might have done, the Christian army would have been in great danger.

The Bashaw of Silistria having forced his way on the left, his horse was killed under him, and he was surrounded by a body of cavalry. He continued to defend himself on foot, assisted by forty of his domestics, who alighted from their horses to protect him with their sabres. Jablonowski, admiring their heroism, cried out, *spare those brave fellows*, but the Germans cut them in pieces. The unfortunate Bashaw, abandoned to the fury of the soldiers, looked round for Jablonowski, and surrendered to him. The Bashaw of Caramania was taken in the same place, covered with blood.

The General being thus deprived, if I may use the expression, of both his arms, still did every thing that could be expected from the most determined courage. He forced his way into the center, but being wounded at length in two places with a sabre, and perceiving that the strength of his troops was exhausted, he thought of making his retreat.

The King of Poland, who observed his first dispositions towards it, did not allow him time to execute his intention, but advanced at the head of his cavalry to take him in flank, and cut off his retreat. The first squadrons were already seen retiring over the bridge. The Christian army now gave a great shout in its turn, and quickening its march, extended itself in form of a crescent, and got up with the enemy.

The whole was nothing now but a scene of slaughter to the Turks, whose sole object was to fly. Some got to the bridge, but the cannon swept it from end to end; and being built of boats, it was soon overloaded, and funk under the weight. Others ran towards the fort, but the fort could hold no more, and drove them back. Many threw them-

themselves into the Danube, which was covered
with men and horses; but the shot reached them
even here, and the river swallowed them up. A
body of eighteen thousand, who would not attempt
this dangerous way, staid upon the side of the river
in much greater danger. It would seem as if men had
only a certain portion of courage, as they have of
strength. Those lions, who a few minutes before
were ready to devour every thing, now suffered
themselves to be butchered, like a defenceless flock
of sheep. Though they had still arms in their
hands, they made not the least effort to sell their
lives dearly, but seemed to be struck with thunder.
They cried out *amman*, quarter, and were all put
to death. The pen drops from one's hands, at
seeing how human creatures treat one another.

The janizaries in the fort were spectators of this
slaughter, and expected their own fate. They made
all possible signals of surrendry; hung out a white
flag, and for fear it should not be taken notice of,
tore off the sleeves of their shirts and fastened them
to the end of their weapons. But this day was
not a day of mercy. Their sentence of death was
writ upon their palisadoes, upon which the Polish
soldiers saw the bleeding heads of their brethren.
The rage that seized them at this sight cost them
fresh tears, which they might easily have prevented.
The janizaries, upon the point of being forced
when they offered to surrender, made a discharge
which did great execution. It was an act of mere
despair in the last moment they had to live. The
author of the Life of the Duke of Lorrain says,
that that Prince had granted them a capitulation.
If the fact be true, every thing concurs to blacken
the Christians on this bloody day. It is to little
purpose for commanders to impute acts of unneces-
sary cruelty to their soldiers. When soldiers are
well disciplined, they are no more than brave. Of
the

the twenty-six thousand Turks that were in this
engagement, only two thousand escaped, before the
breaking down of the bridge.· The young Bashaw,
who would have deserved a second victory, if valour was a sufficient title to it, was one of the number.

Tekeli appeared upon an eminence, when the effusion of blood ceased, for no other reason but because there was no more to spill. He might easily
have come in time ; and he now disappeared again
immediately. The truth is, he was neither enough
a Christian, nor enough a Turk : a sure means of
being, sooner or later, the victim of one of the parties.

Every circumstance of this engagement,· the
bloodiest of that age, was astonishing. A young
warrior, who had never been in any command,
venturing to contend with veteran Generals, and
defying the hero of the age : twenty-six thousand
infidels fighting a pitched battle against fifty thousand Christians, who were upon the point of being
defeated. These same infidels, more than men in
the beginning of the action, and less than women
in the end. Christians embruing their hands, after the victory, in the blood of eighteen thousand
men who begged for mercy ; a truth which I would
willingly suppress, if the fidelity of history would
permit it.

This victory, which put the Christians in possession of the fort of Barcan, made them change their
plan of operations. They designed at first to be-
siege Neuhausel, but they now fixed upon Strigonia,
which was weakened by the taking of the bridge.
This city, by the Germans called Gran, situated
on the right side of the Danube, has its citadel
upon a very high rock. Staremberg, in order to
reconnoitre the place, walked slowly round it twice,
in the midst of a shower of bullets that covered him
with

with earth. His intrepidity gained him great applause, but no notice was taken of the engineers that attended him. Strigonia was abundantly provided with all neceffaries, and a long refiftance was expected. There is no nation that fuftains a fiege with fo much obftinacy as the Turks ; becaufe the head of the Bafhaw who furrenders, is generally at ftake. If the fame practice took place in Chriftendom, we fhould not fee fuch rapid conquefts. Upon the prefent occafion, however, this fevere law did not produce its effect. The Bafhaw fet fire to the fuburbs, and the lower town; and at the end of four days, he beat a parley, making it one of the articles of his capitulation, that he fhould give up Strigonia to no one but the King of Poland, and that he and his garrifon fhould be conducted to Buda.

The King entered the place on All-Saints-Day, and gave it up to the Duke of Lorrain. He would have perfuaded the Bafhaw to accompany him into Poland, in order to fave his head : but the Muffulman anfwered, that his life was in the hands of God and the Grand Seignior, and that he would rather die by their order, than live among infidels. There was no great difficulty in being thus refigned ; for it was believed, that the Vifir, not having courage to relieve the place, had ordered him to furrender it. The great Soliman had conquered it from the Emperor Ferdinand I. brother to Charles V. a hundred and forty three years before ; and it now returned to its former mafters.

The feafon was advancing faft, and the Danube had deftroyed more Poles, than had fallen in three battles. The water of this river, which Charlemagne complained of in his time, is remarkable for giving ftrangers the dyfentery. This diforder carried off Sieniawfki, Palatine of Volhinia, the firft man that marched to the relief of Vienna.

He

He was already Grand-Standard-Bearer of the crown, and Petty-General, and died in the midft of fo promifing a career. His fon, in procefs of time, obtained the Grand-General's ftaff, which the father would have defervedly acquired; and had the additional happinefs of marrying a wife that was worthy of him. She was fo much confidered in Poland, that Lewis XIV. kept up a correfpondence with her.

The taking of Strigonia put an end to the campaign, and the armies feparated. The Poles, before they could reach their native land, had a march of an hundred leagues, through a country impeded with rivers and mountains, infefted by the malecontents of Hungary, full of towns that belonged either to them, or to the Turks, and the laft ridge of mountains which feparates Upper Hungary from Poland, prefented nothing, at this feafon of the year, but fnow, ice, and torrents, through which they were to feek their way. This ridge, anciently called the *Carpathian* Mountains, is, by the inhabitants of the country, called *Krapack*. The Poles were yet at a great diftance from them, and before their arrival there, the difficulties daily increafed.

On the third day of the march, the Count de Forgafté, an Hungarian nobleman of Tekéli's party, followed by a body of his own troops, confifting of four hundred horfe, came and furrendered himfelf to the King, defiring him to intercede with the Emperor for his pardon. John granted his requeft, and prevailed upon the Emperor to forgive him. The Hungarian refolving to deferve the favour he had obtained, followed the army as far as the Carpathian Mountains, plundering and haraffing his countrymen all the way. Thefe being more exafperated againft him than the Emperor himfelf, laid an ambufh for him, in which his whole troop was cut to pieces. The leader, who

had

had made himself so odious, by his treachery to both parties, had not the courage to die with arms in his hands, but made his escape.

If John had wanted only to march home, he might have avoided the continual molestation that his troops were exposed to. Tekeli, who was still willing to keep measures with him, might easily have been prevailed on to restrain his Hungarians; but the King resolved to march like a conqueror, and reduce to the obedience of the Emperor, all the towns that lay in his way. Eperies held out three days: Sabina something longer: Levochi threw open its gates immediately: Zetchin, a place belonging to the Turks, capitulated at the first sight of the artillery; and John left garrisons in them all. The example of Forgaste, who had made his peace, was a tempting thing to several of the Hungarian nobles. The Count d'Humanai, Tekeli's brother-in law, was one of the number. The King at last obtained some favours for them from the court of Vienna, because it would have been dangerous to refuse him every thing that he asked. And in fact the service he did the Emperor, by interposing in so gentle, and yet so effectual a manner, was much greater than if he had given up the rebels into his power: their blood, which the court of Vienna was always disposed to shed, would have perpetuated the revolt, and even made it more formidable, by driving the rebels to despair.

The Count d'Humanai, and the other deserters from the malecontents, reaped little benefit from the pardon they had obtained. They fell into the hands of Tekeli, who beheaded them all, and his brother-in-law among the rest.

The King of Poland crossed the Carpathian mountains in the month of December, in the very height of all the horrors that could make his passage dreadful,

dreadful, and arrived about Chriftmas upon the territories of the republic. He found, upon the frontiers, the Lithuanian army, which had fet out fo early as the month of July, to march to the relief of Vienna: an effect of that ftrange diffonance, which muft always follow from a ftate's having two different armies, not under the command of the fame leader. The Queen was at Cracow, expecting her illuftrious hufband, and forgot all her paft concern in the exultation of victory, and the tendernefs of conjugal embraces.

Thus ended this famous campaign, which preferved Vienna and the empire: Of the moft diftinguifhed actors in this great fcene, which drew the attention of Europe and Afia, fome, at the very time of their fervices, and others afterwards, had reafon to complain of Leopold's ingratitude.

He refufed, in a difobliging manner, to grant the Elector of Saxony a military honour, which he folicited for a Prince of his family. He gave up the fon of that Elector, Auguftus II. King of Poland, to the victorious arms of Charles XII.

Towards the end of his reign, he had thoughts of putting the Elector of Bavaria under the ban of the empire ; and his fucceffor actually did it.

He would not permit the firft Senator of Poland, *Potofki*, to erect a pyramid to the memory of his fon, upon the fpot which that young hero had watered with his blood.

We have feen with what haughtinefs he behaved to the King of Poland, who had juft reftored to him his capital. Befides this, he difputed with him fome of the Turkifh cannon, out of the great number that the Poles had taken; nor could thofe brave troops obtain winter-quarters in a country that they had preferved.

The court of Rome, always devoted to the Emperors, when its intereft requires it, took part in

8 Leo-

Leopold's ingratitude. Innocent XI. who was born his subject, instituted a solemnity, in which the Emperor and himself were represented on a banner; but every one talked of him only whose effigy was not seen. Christina, then at Rome, wrote to the Conqueror, " that he had made her feel, for the " first time, the passion of envy; for she really " grudged him the glorious title of Deliverer of " Christendom."

The scene ended tragically on the side of the Turks. The deposition of the Cham of Tartary, and the sacrifice of four Bashaws imme iately after the affair at Vienna, was not sufficient to appease the murmurs of the Ottoman empire. Tekeli was sent to Constantinople, bound hand and foot. Kara-Mustapha, charged with being the principal author of the public calamities, and even accused of a design to form for himself, in Austria and Hungary, an empire independent of the Sultan, received his doom at Belgrade. The resignation of Mussulmen astonishes all religions but that of Japan. It is written in the Alcoran, *that no martyrdom is more glorious than that of dying, by the hand, or by the order, of the Prince of Believers.* Kara-Mustapha fell prostrate before the warrant for his death, kissed it, embraced the Kiahia that brought it, took out of his bosom the seal of the empire, which he delivered to the Aga of the janizaries, held out his neck to the four executioners, who strangled him, and his head was carried to Constantinople. Let all, who owe their rise to court-favour, contemplate the fate of this Visir, and tremble at their own prosperity.

All the advantages of the expedition fell to Leopold's share. Poland got nothing but glory and a title. The Letters from crowned heads, in the time of an interregnum, were before addressed, *Inclytæ reipublicæ,* to the celebrated Republic. The Im-

Imperial court in particular, was extremely fcrupulous in this refpeƈt.   Ever fince the viƈtory
of Vienna, the republic is become *Moft Serene* ;
a title void of meaning, and certainly inferior to
Celebrity ; but in the ceremonial of courts, words
take place of things.

End of the S I X T H B O O K.

A 2   T H E

THE

HISTORY

OF

JOHN SOBIESKI

KING OF POLAND.

BOOK VII.

THE King paſſed the winter at Cracow, where he received the congratulations of Europe. But, in the opinion of the republic, he had done nothing, if he did not retake Kaminieck. This was the general wiſh in all the diets; and the preſent juncture ſeemed favourable for effecting it. The Turks were employed in Hungary by the Imperialiſts, who had juſt laid ſiege to Buda; and new enemies were riſing up againſt the Ottoman empire. The Muſcovites and the Venetians were earneſt to be admitted into the league. Muſcovy had ſuffered, at different times, conſiderable loſſes in its conteſts with the Ottoman power. Venice alſo had complaints of the ſame ſort. That republic, which, in the beginning of the fifth century, was nothing but

6   the

the retreat of a few fishermen and fugitives, owed its greatness, by sea and land, to its commerce; and, in the time of the Crusades, instead of wasting its strength in that epidemical malady, had increased its power by the conquest of the isle of Candy, of Peloponnesus, and the best parts of Greece. The country which gave birth to *Pericles, Sophocles,* and *Plato,* might have recovered some part of its ancient lustre; but the Turks, by expelling the Venetians, had reduced it again to a state of barbarism. Another grievance of very late date, was, that during the siege of Vienna, the ships belonging to the republic had been insulted in the port of Constantinople. The Venetians therefore hoped, as did also the Muscovites, to repair their losses, by entering into an alliance with John, whose valour and good conduct seemed to ensure success. Their Ambassadors arrived at Warsaw, and treated with him, and at the same time with the Emperor, who seemed destined to reap the chief advantages of the league.

The Polish army was greatly weakened by its victories. The Grand-General, Jablonowski, omitted no expedient to repair its losses; but notwithstanding all his care, it continued much less numerous than in the campaign of Vienna. The soldiers still regretted the death of the Petty-General *Sieniawski*; but Andrew Potoski, Castellan of Cracow, who succeeded him, dispelled their grief. He already filled the first post in the Senate, and was now in the way of obtaining the same rank in the army. About the end of July, the Poles were joined by the Lithuanians, who were no longer headed by the Grand-General Paz. Death had put an end to his command, and he was lamented by Poland, but not by the King. There were others of the name of *Paz,* who might have been chosen to succeed him; but the King had resolved to

humble

humble that family.   The eldeſt of the Sapieha's
was inveſted with the ſupreme command, and at
the ſame time made Palatine of Wilna.

The King had a variety of plauſible reaſons to
excuſe himſelf from making this campaign.   The
ſhining exploits of the laſt, and of ſo many others,
ſeemed to give him a right to repoſe himſelf with
honour.   The ſucceſs of a ſiege, undertaken with
no great force, was very uncertain.   The maſters
of the world generally chuſe their own time to
tread the paths of glory; but the preſent occaſion
preſented nothing very tempting.   It was not
againſt Mahomet in perſon, as in 1672, that the
King was going to make war : it was not even
againſt a Grand-Viſir, inveſted with all the power
of the Sultan ; but againſt a ſimple Seraſkier, who
had more Tartars than Turks under his command.
Such an opponent was too mean to gratify the pride
of the throne; and beſides all this, the King might
commit the care of the expedition to the Grand-
General Jablonowſki, whoſe abilities he was well
acquainted with, and who would have been glad
to do ſomething without the King.

All theſe motives could not prevail upon him to
ſtay behind, and enjoy the pleaſures of Warſaw.
He put himſelf at the head of the army, and advanced towards Jaſlowiecz, a town which was the
ſecond in Podolia, before the Turks had made
themſelves maſters of that fine province.   They
had ſet fire to the town, and left nothing ſtanding but the caſtle, a fortification of immenſe bulk,
compoſed of eight large towers, and ſituated upon
a rock, which is made a peninſula by the river
Janowf.   The foot of the rock was encompaſſed by
a wall of no great height, with ſeveral ſquare towers
of the ſame elevation.   It was principally by means
of their bombs that the Poles carried this fort,
which had a garriſon of five hundred and thirty

2   jani-

janizaries, and thirteen pieces of cannon. When objects are out of fight, the imagination magnifies them as it pleafes. The noife of this exploit refounded throughout all Europe; whereas it would fcarce have been fpoke of, had it not been for the great parade that accompanied it : all the forces of the republic were in motion ; the King, and all his court, were prefent; the Queen herfelf, by being witnefs of this firft fuccefs, fancied that fhe had a fhare in the glory of it. Her foul had caught a portion of the warlike fire of her hufband : and yet fhe here ended her campaign.

The object next in view was Kaminieck ; an amufement by no means proper for a Queen. The King continued his march along the Niefter, with a defign of throwing a bridge over that river, and entering Moldavia, in order to hinder the Turks from having any communication with Kaminieck ; and even wintering in that province, if the place fhould make all the defence it was capable of. This project, which deprived the place of all poffibility of receiving fupplies, muft have reduced it, by means of a blockade of fix months, to furrender without effufion of blood : a fcheme too humane to be attended with glory.

The whole plan was difconcerted by the great diligence of the enemy. The Poles had fcarce begun to work upon their bridge, before twenty thoufand Turks, and a greater number of Tartars, appeared on the other fide of the river. In the campaign of Vienna, Mahomet had loft feventeen Bafhaws of merit, and had only three left of any reputation. Of this number *Soliman* was one ; born in Bofnia, a province noted for producing men of abilities, and eager for an opportunity of diftinguifhing himfelf, in order to obtain the dignity of Vifir, to which the courfe of events raifed him. At the firft report of the King's march,

he

he advanced into Moldavia and Walachia, where the two Cantacuzeni, *Demetrius* and *Serban* then reigned. They had been jewellers at Conſtantinople, where one of their anceſtors wore the Imperial crown. Serban had abilities, but he held a ſuſpicious corrcſpondence with Vienna and Moſcow: *I know all,* ſaid Soliman to him, *thou ſhalt be narrowly watched.* The other, unworthy of the name he bore, was a weak Prince, without talents, and unfit to command in a critical junĉture. Soliman depoſed him, and gave the crown of Moldavia to Cantemir, who had ſaved the Sultanas before Kaminieck, and whom he thought well affeĉted to the intereſts of the Porte. After this regulation, he appeared on the banks of the Nieſter, at a time when he was thought to be at a great diſtance from it; and his reſolute behaviour, after he arrived, was of a piece with the quicknefs of his march.

It was not poſſible to throw a bridge over the river in his preſence; but the Tartars did not want one to get at the Poles. That nation, which no obſtacles can ſtop, which lives upon little, and is capable of all ſorts of hardſhips, would ſtill be -the moſt formidable upon earth, if it had the European diſcipline. In its preſent ſtate, its ravages are more dreaded than its arms. The kingdom of Hungary thought itſelf happy in being delivered, upon this occaſion, from ſuch a gang of plunderers. They ſurrounded the Poliſh army, and haraſſed it on all ſides, without ever coming to aĉtion, being equally quick in running away, and in coming on, and always ready to repaſs the river, if they found themſelves forced to it.

There was one Horde among them, which diſtinguiſhed itſelf above the reſt by a more daring and obſtinate fury. Theſe were the *Lipka* Tartars, who had lived under the Poliſh government in Lithuania, and returned to their mother country by the

peace

peace of Zurawno.   This article of the treaty
proved more prejudicial to Poland, than was at
firſt imagined.   The Kingdom loſt a number of uſe-
ful ſubjects, both in agriculture and arms, by diſ-
turbing them on account of their profeſſion of the
Mahometan faith ; for though an univerſal toleration is eſtabliſhed by law, there are ſometimes
powerful zealots who make a bad uſe of their authority.   Theſe perſecuted ſubjects of the republic, became now its moſt dangerous enemies.   The
race of them having inhabited Lithuania for three
centuries, they were not diſtinguiſhable from the
Poles.   They wore the ſame habit, uſed the ſame
arms, and ſpoke the ſame language.   They had
loſt nothing but what might have ſerved to make
them known; viz. that deformity which is natural to the Tartars, the ſmall eyes, flat noſe, and
tawny complexion, which they derived from the
climate they came from ; and were Poles in every
thing but in heart.   They had ſome time before
ſurprized the fort of *Mienzibow*, and from thence
made incurſions into Black Ruſſia.   They inſinuat-
ed themſelves with eaſe into the villages, the caſtles
of the nobility, and the religious houſes, com-
mitting every where great ravages, and carrying
off many ſlaves.   Upon the preſent occaſion their
rage was greatly increaſed,   They entered the Poliſh
camp by night, and ſometimes by day, carried off
the baggage, mixed with the foraging parties, and
put them to the ſword.   Orders were iſſued, that
no quarter ſhould be given them ; but it ſeldom
happened that there was an opportunity of exer-
ciſing this ſeverity.

During this petty war, which, however, greatly haraſſed the Poles ; the Turks, on the oppoſite
ſide of the river, contented themſelves with ob-
ſtructing the paſſage.   While the two armies continued in ſight of each other, without coming to a

decifive

decisive action; a Tartar of distinction, who had formerly been at the court of Poland, to treat about the ransom of his brother, cried out, that he begged to see the great King once more. John ordered him to be told, that he would send him, not only an escort, but hostages for his security. The Tartar answered, that the King's bare word was worth more than all his hostages, and that he would come the next day. The interview did not take place, nor is it known what broke it off.

In the mean time, Kaminieck, the object of this campaign, was secured from all attempts, and the Polish army suffered much in a country that was entirely deserted. When Cuprogli, in 1672, made a conquest of Podolia, at that time a fine and fertile province, he gave leave to the Poles to retire, with all that they could carry off with them. This was not a direct order; but he chose to leave no discontented subjects in the territories of the Porte. The nobility, the clergy, and the religious houses led the way in quitting the province, and the people followed their example : a conduct not very prudent in persons that might one day hope to return again under the Polish government. The conquerors set fire to the towns and villages, which were henceforward of no use, and the whole province of Podolia existed only in the single town of Kaminieck. All the land that was cultivated extended about three leagues, from the glacis of the place to the ruins of Zwanieck, formerly a considerable town. The Polish army consumed all it could; and the rest was destroyed by fire, to the very gates of Kaminieck. This was doing mischief to the enemy, but it was not making them submit.

To lay siege in form to a place of that strength, where there was a garrison of ten thousand men,

and

and in prefence of a fuperior army, was a thing Y. 1684. impoffible.

The King refolved, if nothing more could be done, to erect a citadel againft Kaminieck, in order to pave the way for its fall at a more favourable time. He chofe for this purpofe, at the diftance of about a league, a rock that ftood by itfelf upon the bank of the fame river that runs by Kaminieck, and not far from the Niefter. He employed his infantry and dragoons to fortify this poft. The Turks beheld their labours with a jealous eye; and paffed the Niefter to interrupt them. This was what the King wifhed for, in hopes of bringing on a battle; but the Serafkier had different views, and contented himfelf with fkirmifhing inceffantly with the Polifh cavalry. The King advanced often to-wards him; but the Serafkier retired immediately under the cannon of the place. The fort *of the Trinity* (which was the name of the work now raifed) was completed in fix weeks; a garrifon was put into it, and incommoded the town greatly, during the whole time that it continued in poffeffion of the enemy; for no fupplies could be received, but at the hazard of a battle.

The feafon advancing faft, John came to a refolution to draw towards Leopol, where the Queen waited his arrival; but as he retired, being perpetually befieged by the Tartars, he endeavoured to draw them into fome fnare, where he might have an opportunity to beat them. He got them once in a narrow pafs; but the Generals objected the fatigues of the march, and the approach of night; and propofed calling a council of war, in the precious moment when it was neceffary to charge. The Power of a King of Poland is very extenfive in the army, but never abfolute. The Tartars efcaped the danger, and fhuddering at the rifque they had run, flackened the ardour of their purfuit.

The

The exploits of the Christian armies in this campaign were extremely unlike those of the last, which had been crowned with victory. The Muscovites and the Venetians had hitherto attempted nothing; and while the Poles miscarried before Kaminieck, the Imperialists raised the siege of Buda, after having lost twenty eight thousand men, and five hundred of their best officers. The besieged, in the midst of their joy, lamented the death of their Governor, the young Bashaw, who had the singular honour of beating the King of Poland in the plain of Barcan, and was killed upon the breach. The siege had already been raised a month, when Valstein, the Imperial Ambassador, assured the court of Poland, that his master's army had only sent off their sick and wounded: a false piece of policy, which is soon found out, and serves only to destroy all confidence among allies for the remaining part of a war. The Duke of Lorrain and the King of Poland were taught by experience, that great talents cannot always ensure success : all the glory of this campaign was gained by the Visir *Ibrahim* and *Soliman*, Seraskier of the army at Kaminieck : the latter of whom, preferring prudent counsels to the splendor of battles, contented himself with frustrating all the King's designs.

If we recollect that Kaminieck, besides the right of conquest, a right so sacred in the code of sovereigns, had also been solemnly ceded to the Turks by the peace of Zurawno, it is obvious that they had justice on their side. Upon the present occasion, they had success also; but such an instance must not always be depended on.

The King, not pleased with his expedition, formed a plan for letting Poland enjoy at least the sweets of peace, in the midst of a war, the end of which could not be foreseen. Instead of going to enjoy the amusements of the capital, he took up up his residence upon the frontiers, and while he restrained the Tartars, who are always ready for incursions, the nobles enjoyed their fortunes, the merchants carried on their trade, the lands were cultivated, and the peasants got bread. The court, though perhaps inwardly sighing after the pleasures of Warsaw, endeavoured to conform to the Prince, in this military life. He was always found in boots by the Ambassadors from foreign courts. Among the rest, there came one in the habit of a Friar: a character below the dignity of history, but which may be admitted to a place in it, upon having an influence in affairs of state. The person I mean was the Jesuit *Vota*, a Savoyard by birth, but an Austrian by inclination, who, without being invested with the character, he brought with him the spirit of an Ambassador. His real intentions were hid under the specious title of a missionary, sent by the Emperor into Muscovy, to bring about the reunion of that schismatical church with the see of Rome. He soon returned from thence, alledging that the Czar had refused to listen to the first overtures; but he flattered himself, that God would open the eyes of that Prince in another journey. It seemed as if he only passed through the court of Poland: and no one was more likely to be desired to stay there.

Kings, who reign in person, want amusement much more than their subjects. John could find no diversion in the little tales of a court, nor in that elegant jargon which sports itself with trifles, and leaves the mind always empty. The King wanted more substantial food. In the midst of the labours of war, he loved the arts of peace, music, painting, poetry, and eloquence. Poland would have had perhaps it *Lully's*, *Le Brun's*, *Corneille's*, *and Bossuet's*, if his reign had been less disturbed with wars and factions. He often forgot

Y. 1684. got his cares in the arms of hiftory and the fciences. When he read, he had always a pencil in his hand ; and all his marginal notes either fhewed his fine tafte, or contained fome ufeful obfervation. Quote me a great man who has not loved and protected letters ; and he will infallibly be found in the annals of the Goths or Tartars. The King of Poland fpoke five or fix languages from his youth, and befides thefe, learnt Spanifh at fifty. Of the many fpeeches that he made in the fenate [and the diets, the greateft part were in Latin ; and the method made ufe of to prevail upon Charles XII. when he was a child, to learn that language, was telling him, that the hero of Poland underftood it.

The Jefuit Vota, like the King, befides the learned languages, expreffed himfelf with eafe in French, German, and Italian. Ancient and modern philofophy, an acquaintance with the hiftory of different ages, places, and empires, an extenfive knowledge of religious opinions, and the genealogy of families ; all thefe accomplifhments, though little attended to in moft courts, made him very agreeable to a Prince of improved underftanding. Leopold intended once to make him preceptor to his fon, the Archduke Jofeph ; but thought that he might be more fuccefsfully employed in negotiation. The King was diffatisfied with the court of Vienna, and grew cold in the league. To hinder him from deferting it, was the true object of the Jefuit's miffion ; a point much more eafily gained than the converfion of the Ruffians. A perfon who negotiates without a public character, is under much fewer reftraints. The Jefuit laid claim to no perfonal refpect, was ready to join in any thing, and even encouraged the raillery of the courtiers at his own expence. He was fond of the converfation and careffes of the great, but never feemed difturb-

ed

ed when he could not obtain them. Being particularly eager to gain the confidence of the King, who grew fubject to want of fleep, he often lay upon the floor of an antichamber, to be always in readiness to amufe his weary hours. Befides the advantages of having flexible manners and an improved underftanding, of being educated in Italian politics, and acquainted with all the artifices of negotiation, he was alfo a man of confiderable abilities. He begun with making himfelf agreeable, and ended with becoming neceffary to fuch a degree, that the foreign Ambaffadors and Polifh minifters could not get admittance to the King's cabinet, but when Vota opened the door to them. Even the Grand-Chamberlain, who, though he is not reckoned in Poland as one of the fix great officers, enjoys the valuable privilege of coming to the King at all hours, no longer found the fame eafe in being admitted. Nothing gives greater offence to the grandees, or brings more contempt upon the government, than to fee the cloifter in high credit at court. One of the Palatines, Martin Matczinfki, got a picture drawn reprefenting a long proceffion, clofed by a Jefuit beating time : the Jefuit was followed by a King, and two other Jefuits held before him a book of mufic, on which he feemed to look with great attention.

Vota not only offended the Poles, but gave umbrage at Verfailles ; for if Leopold's view was to keep John firm in the league, Lewis XIV. aimed to detach him from it. The Marquis de Bethune arrived in Poland, not with the title of Ambaffador, as in his former journey, but upon a pretence of coming to pay his court to the Queen his fifter-in-law. His real errand was to pull down what the Jefuit built.

It was a long time fince Poland had feen any of its Kings with fo brilliant a court : foreign noble-

men

Y. 1634. men travelling to visit it, Ambassadors extraordinary
coming to form alliances, young Princes desirous
of learning the art of war under an accomplished
hero, and even men of letters, who always search
for Princes acquainted with the arts they profess.
John was worthy to enjoy their conversation, as he
generally did at table. He loved the pleasures of
society, when seasoned with sound philosophy, without which society has no lasting charms. The
knowledge he had acquired in every branch cost
him much application, intense reflection, and many
sleepless nights. He now reaped the fruits of his
labour, but their sweetness was often mixed with
gall. Such is the condition of all human affairs,
whether the part we act be high or low.

Y. 1685.   The diet, of which I come now to give an account, exasperated him extremely. The law ordered it to meet at Grodno in Lithuania; but the
King appointed it at Warsaw in the month of
February. In the universals issued for this purpose,
he explained the reason of his having thus violated
the law, namely, that by reason of the great distance of Grodno from the frontiers, it would be
impossible to come time enough to begin the campaign. The Lithuanians paid little regard to this
reason, and assembled among themselves at Grodno,
where they created a senate and a chamber of deputies, while the Poles met at Warsaw. Such a
separation might occasion civil commotions in the
republic. A month was spent in negotiations to
accommodate the difference. The King made a
proposal to the assembly at Grodno to elect a Lithuanian for Marshal of the diet, and to give the
name of diet of Grodno to the council of the nation held at Warsaw. The Lithuanians consented
to the expedient: nor is this the only instance, in
which policy has reconciled contending factions, by
substituting words in the room of things.

The

The diet of Grodno was therefore opened at Warfaw; but harmony did not reign in the affembly. Paz, the Grand-Chancellor of Lithuania, was lately dead: and another of that name *(a)*, who had already feen the Grand-General's ftaff transferred from his own family to that of *Sapieba*, flattered himfelf at leaft with the hopes of obtaining this other office. The King, who begun to be apprehenfive of raifing the Sapieha's too high, had indeed paft them by on this occafion, but it was not in favour of Paz. He had nominated to this important poft *Oginfki*, Palatine of Troki, in a privy council held at Javorow, a country-feat of his own in Red Ruffia. This nomination was illegal; for, by the law, it ought to be made in full diet: a regulation wifely contrived; becaufe a King may be fuppofed to be more fcrupulous of making a bad choice in the prefence of the whole nation, than before his favourites and minifters.

The Lithuanians difcuffed this point with great warmth. Some were for rejecting Oginfki, and demanding another Chancellor. All infifted at leaft upon a new nomination of the fame perfon, and upon his taking an oath to the diet, in order to preferve the refpect due to the law. Paz, who was moft interefted, was alfo moft vehement in the affair. His eloquence was fo audacious, that the King, forgetting himfelf ftill more than his fubject had done, laid his hand upon the hilt of his fabre, and drawing it half-way, faid to him; *Do not oblige me to make you feel the weight of my arm.* Paz, who was the moft impatient and haughty of men, replied with the like gefture, accompanied with thefe words: *Remember, that when we were equals, you knew by experience, bow capable I am of dealing with you in that way:* alluding to a duel

(a) Paul Michael Paz, Staroft of Samogitia, the only Staroft who has a feat in the fenate.

they

Y. 1685. they had fought in their youth, or poffibly to fome provincial diet, in which they had backed their arguments with their fabres.

Whoever reflects upon a fcene of this fort paffing in public between a King and his fubject, will be apt to fhudder at the audacioufnefs of the latter ; and to denounce a woe upon every free nation that does not diftinguifh between liberty and licentioufnefs.

The diet continued to fit, but fhewed ftill the fame obftinate averfion to comply with the King's will. The King, on his fide, wifhed that he had not advanced fo far. His fubjects held up againft him the buckler of the law, with which he had formerly forced his predeceffor Michael to retire ; but he was too much exalted with his regal dignity, to think with patience of retiring himfelf. Not but that he knew the law, and generally refpected it ; but the Queen, by abufing his conjugal tendernefs, had drawn him into this difficulty. She now formed a plan to extricate him from it ; and ordered the queftion to be put to the Lithuanian deputies, by what authority the provincial diets, that preceded the national one, had been affembled. As they could not difown that it was by the authority of that very Grand-Chancellor, the legality of whofe nomination they difputed ; it was intimated to them, that their own election was invalid, if that magiftrate was not lawfully appointed. The deputies had no mind to lofe their pofts. A fure way of fucceeding in any thing is to lay hold of men by their intereft. The difpute was going to end as the King wifhed : but Oginfki, laying hold of this moment when both parties were on the point of uniting, propofed, in order to make his nomination more fecure, to take a new oath to the republic, and by this means difpleafed the court.

The

The Queen gave another proof, in this diet, of the power of artifice when force fails. The poſt of Vice-Chancellor of the kingdom being vacant, ſhe had a mind to beſtow it upon *Radziowſki*, Biſhop of Warmia *(a)*, a relation of the King's. But the two places being incompatible by law, ſhe got the Biſhoprick to be declared vacant ; and Radziowſki, a few days after, was again Biſhop of Warmia, and Vice-Chancellor. The law indeed was evaded ; but this artifice ſerved only to diſguſt a nation which has a greater affection for its laws than its Kings. After all, the poſt in queſtion would be deſpiſed by a man of quality, in any other country in Europe : Radziowſki, however, was nearly related to the King : but the caſe is, that, in Poland, whatever has any connection with the adminiſtration of the great affairs of the public, is below no one's acceptance.

A negotiation of ſome difficulty had been carrying on with France, which it was neceſſary to conclude at laſt. The French Ambaſſador in Poland, the Marquis de Vitry, had been inſulted by ſome ſervants, who fired ſeveral piſtols into his Houſe. The Poles would have apologized for their conduct by making them paſs for drunk, and perhaps they really were ſo. Be this as it will, the King of Poland was in no haſte to make reparation for the affront. Lewis XIV. who, for inſults of this kind, had obliged Spain, Rome, and the republic of Genoa to give him ſatisfaction, by ſending ſolemn embaſſies, demanded the ſame from Poland. The Marquis de Bethune, who was privately commiſſioned to ſollicit it, had a troubleſome buſineſs upon his hands. He had republican ſpirits to deal with,

(a) Warmia is a province included within the bounds of Pruſſia. The epiſcopal city is, Hienſberg. The Biſhop takes his title from the province, of which he is Sovereign Prince, as head of the chapter to whom the ſovereignty belongs.

and none of the grandees would submit to make
the apology.   At last, *Wielopolski*, Grand-Chancellor of the crown, who had married one of the
Queen's sisters, was persuaded to undertake it.   He
was received at Fontainebleau with great pomp,
loaded with marks of esteem, and carried home
with him a picture of the French Monarch richly
set with diamonds.   All these circumstances reconciled a few individuals to the office of excuse-mak-
ing ; but the republic thought herself debased.

The campaign was opened soon after, and suspended the dissatisfaction of the public.   The King
proposed in council to resume the project of the preceding year ; which was to enter Moldavia, in
order to force the Hospodar to declare in favour of
Poland, and make use of his assistance to take Kaminieck.   The recovery of this bulwark would
have made the nation forget all the miseries of so
long a war.   The army was already assembling,
but a disorder detained the King.   The court of
Vienna discovered a mystery in this event : they
fancied that the Marquis de Bethune had got the
better of their Jesuit, and that John had a mind to
make his diversion less formidable to the Turks, by
not commanding his army in person.   But the
court of Vienna was mistaken, for the disorder was
real.

The Grand-General Jablonowski readily undertook the charge of all that might happen ; for as
often as a King, like John, commanded, it was
natural for Europe to attend to him only ; and the
Generals had complained more than once that he
engrossed all the honour of every expedition.

While the army was upon its march, John received a piece of intelligence that struck him with
amazement.   The Archduchess whom Leopold had
promised to Prince James, was married to the Elector of Bavaria ; and the King guessed from hence
                                        what

what he was to expect from the other promise, which related to the securing of the crown of Poland in his family, by the intrigues, the money, and the power of the court of Vienna. Being naturally warm and impetuous, he had great difficulty to restrain his resentment till the end of the campaign, and then take his measures as events should happen. In the army of the Grand-General there were several Frenchmen, and among others the Marquis de Souvré, second son to M. de Louvois, who came to learn the art of war. Their apprenticeship was very severe. The Grand-General, instead of attempting the passage of the Niester over-against Choczin, as the King had done in the last campaign, without success, pass'd it at Halicz (a) higher up the stream, and advanced through Pokrusia into the Bucovine, a forest thirty leagues long and as many broad, extending from the Crapack mountains to the Niester. Before the wars between the Poles and the Turks, it was peopled and cultivated in the vacant spaces, which are still to be seen. At present, taking in Pokrusia and Podolia, provinces that border upon each other, there are near a hundred leagues of ruins ; a deplorable monument of the fury of the human race, in extirpating each other from a world where their stay is otherwise so short. A detached branch of the Crapack mountains advancing into the Bucovine, supplies it plentifully with water : and the rivers, morasses, and mountains, form defiles in it extremely difficult to pass.

The army had already got through two thirds of the forest, and was encamped upon open ground, when the couriers brought intelligence that the enemy appeared. The Poles soon heard the great

(a) This city, formerly considerable, and the capital of the kingdom of Halicz, is at present very small, but has a strong castle upon the river.

drums

drums of the Janizaries, which are double to ours
in every respect.   The drummers beat them at both
ends, with a common drum-stick in their right
hands, and a switch in their left.   They are attended by lads who carry two plates of very sonorous
metal, which they strike in cadence one against the
other : and this mixture of sounds composes a loud,
and not unwarlike, noise.

The two armies drew up in order of battle, with
a defile between them.   The match was by no
means equal ; for forty thousand Turks and as
many Tartars must needs overpower thirty thousand
Poles.   The latter durst not pass the defile before
so great a multitude, but wished that the others
would pass it, to begin the engagement.   But the
Serafkier Soliman had conceived a different project.
He raised redoubts upon the side of the defile with
lines to join the works ; and detached thirty thousand Tartars to seize the passes behind the Polish
army, and cut off their retreat   These passes were
sufficiently difficult of themselves, but were now
made more so by felled trees.   The Tartars stole
off imperceptibly under the cover of the wood and
the night ; so that the Poles did not perceive their
situation, till the moment of its growing desperate.
One army in front ; another in their rear ; a river
(the Pruth) bordered with rocks, on the right ; a
morass and a hill possessed by the enemy, on the
left ; all together made up a situation like that of
the famous *Caudine Forks*, and Soliman thought
himself sure of making them pass under the yoke.
Every day consumed their provisions and augmented the terror of the army.   Some of the soldiers,
more frighted than the rest, passed the Pruth, and
ran with all speed to the frontier, where they spread
the alarm by giving out that all was lost.   The
consternation became general : the Tartars were already seen in places that they never before approached ;

ed : the inhabitants of the country took refuge in the towns, and the towns expected to be forced. The alarm increafed like a torrent, till it reached Zolkiew, a place not far from the Frontiers, where the King refided for the recovery of his health. Though he was ftill in a weak condition, he put himfelf at the head of the nobility of the neighbouring provinces, and fome Lithuanian troops, which, coming from a great diftance, could not join the army in time. But the cataftrophe was over, before the King came.

Jablonowfki, after he had been fifteen days in this fituation, perceiving more diftinctly all its horror, and reflecting that fo many brave men had no choice but death or flavery, that his country would lofe its army, and himfelf all his glory, made a motion which put a large wood between the enemy and him. This, however, was of no ufe. But in this new pofition, he formed a plan for a retreat which feemed impracticable. Behind him there was a wood of Alders, which grew in a morafs deep enough to fwallow up men and horfes. He ordered his men to take hatchets, and cut down the trees clofe by each other with the branches uppermoft : by this means he formed two bridges wide enough for five waggons to pafs in front.

The baggage begun to file off, in the beginning of the night, between the eighth and ninth of October. The cavalry followed next, and by break of day there remained behind only fifteen fquadrons. The infantry and dragoons, with part of the cannon, came in the rear, and were commanded by Konfki, General of the artillery, a man whom it was impoffible to furprize, and who had diftinguifhed himfelf in fo illuftrious a manner at the battle of Vienna. To be ready for all that might happen, he kept his infantry and dragoons in order of battle the whole night.

The

The Turks at length poured out of the great wood, that was in the front of the Polish army. The cavalry begun the attack, and charged with its usual impetuosity; but was so roughly handled, that it retired into the wood again, to make room for fresh squadrons. The charge was repeated in this manner ten or twelve times; and the different bodies succeeded each other so fast, that the Poles had scarce time to load again. Men and horses fell thick on each side, and yet the carnage was only beginning. The combatants stood in need of perhaps greater intrepidity, than if the action had been in an open plain. The distance from an inhabited country, the forest which intercepted the light of the sun, the cries of the Turks and Tartars mixed with the roar of cannon, which the nature of the place redoubled and made more dreadful, all these circumstances encreased the horror of this vast desert, where the wild beasts were less cruel than the human species.

There now succeeded a few minutes of inaction. The Janizaries who had not yet been engaged, flattered themselves they should close the scene by bathing themselves in blood. The cavalry, which supported them, trembled with rage at meeting with such resistance from so small a body. In this juncture, the Poles invoked the assistance of despair, a principle frequently more active than glory itself. The fire-arms on both sides were no longer depended upon: the Turkish sabre, and the Polish battle-ax were to decide the point. The Polish cavalry, like that of all other nations, is armed with sabres: the infantry and dragoons fight with battle-axes: a weapon anciently used by the Romans, and admirably formed not only for cutting but pushing, with a handle five feet long. The soldiers held them with both hands, and lopped off all the heads and arms that came within their reach. Even the

head

head of a horfe was often cloven in two at one blow. It is faid, that in the famous victory which *Procopius the Bald*, fucceffor to Zifca, gained over the Emperor Sigifmund, his foldiers were armed with thefe axes; and that this novelty was the caufe of their winning the battle. It was with the fame weapon that the Poles were now triumphant. On both fides there was an equal degree of fury and true courage, but the Poles fought with better conduct. The Janizaries, having loft a greater number than they, were at length obliged to regain the wood, and the battle ended. A body of between eleven and twelve thoufand men had been engaged for ten hours againft forty thoufand.

There were three circumftances, exclufive of courage, to which this little army owed its prefervation. In the firft place, the ground would not permit the Turks to prefent a more extenfive front than that of the Poles. A fecond advantage was the unfkilfulnefs of the General of the Turkifh artillery, who inftead of bringing his cannon to the edge of the wood, from whence he might have annoyed the enemy greatly, had the imprudence to place it on a high hill: by which means, the cannon being pointed downwards, the ball was buried as foon as it touched the ground, and made no rebound. But all thefe advantages would have been ufelefs, had it not been for the great abilities of Konfki. At the head of his battalions, he had placed chevaux de frife, formed a rampart of waggons, and pointed his cannon in fuch a manner as to have the greateft effect. All the different bodies fupported each other, like the baftions of a moveable fortrefs. The whole rear-guard feemed to be but one battalion performing its evolutions at a review. The fmall body of cavalry that was prefent, though not under Konfki's command, obeyed him with as much alacrity as the foot and dragoons. Never was

B b 4   any

any man poſſeſſed of cooler valour. The officers and ſoldiers cried out to him, to take care of himſelf for the common good : *I have not yet received a ſingle wound*, anſwered he, *and I ſee ſome of you fighting with ſeveral.* His behaviour in this action gave the nation ſo high an opinion of him, that, at the death of King John, he was named among the candidates for the throne, to which his civil virtues gave him alſo a fair claim. He was contented with living and dying firſt Senator ; and the laurels, which he acquired on this occaſion, will continue freſh to the end of time.

As the night drew on, the retreat was completed, the enemy appearing no more. The rear joined the cavalry which, during the whole action, was drawn up in battalia in a little plain beyond the wood of alders, expecting all the while to be attacked by the Tartars who were within view. After all, if Konſki had the honour of executing this celebrated retreat, Jablonowſki had the glory of having planned it, when it ſeemed impracticable.

The army, as it retreated, ſoon came to the famous Foſs, which the Emperor Trajan ordered to be dug, when he ſubdued the Dacians (*a*). It extends from the Crapack mountains to the Nieſter, acroſs the Bucovine ; and was the boundary which ſeparated the Roman empire from the Sarmatians. Trajan, who fixed upon this limit, ſeemed to adviſe his ſucceſſors not to paſs it.

They were ſcarce got on the other ſide, when the enemy appeared again, as if with a deſign of coming to a deciſive action. The Poles, encouraged by their late ſucceſs, returned to the Foſs, and drew up in order of battle. The enemy proceeded no farther than a cannonade, which the Poles returned. Moſt of the days, that they ſpent in get-

(*a*) Now the Hungarians, Walachians and Moldavians.

ting

ting through the Bucovine, were of the fame fort.
They marched from one defile to another, purfued
and harraffed inceffantly, without being ever defeated. At length, the foreft and the purfuit ended
together.

Notwithftanding this, Jablonowfki kept the field
for three weeks longer, to hinder the incurfions of
the Tartars, who had reafon to be greatly diffatisfied with the expedition. The only pay they receive
from the Grand-Seignior is their booty: they now
returned empty-handed, to be treated by their wives
as cowards, and effeminate wretches, unworthy to
bear arms: and this domeftic contempt is more
dreaded by a Tartar than the dangers of war. The
Polifh arms acquired great glory, but no real advantage. The Moldavians were not fubdued: Kaminieck continued in the hands of the Turks: and
the whole defign of the armament mifcarried.

The cafe was not the fame with the other powers
of the Chiftian league. While Poland kept employed a part of the Ottoman forces, the celebrated
Francefco Morofini attacked the common enemy in
Greece. He was accufed before the fenate of having betrayed the interefts of Venice, by furrendering the town of Candia. Accufations of this fort,
though often unjuft, contributed to keep up the
virtue of the ancient Greeks and Romans. The
accufed was defended with great fpirit; and he
juftified himfelf ftill better by conquering the Morea, a country formerly fo famous by the name of
Peloponnefus, when Corinth, Argos, and Sparta
really produced men. The republic of Venice, in
imitation of ancient Rome, gave its hero the name
of *Peloponnefiacus.*

Vienna gained ftill more than Venice. The
Duke of Lorrain had defeated before Strigonia the
Vifir Ibrahim, a General, who, with greater merit
than his predeceffor, Kara-Muftapha, had not better

ter fuccefs. Neuhaufel, one of the bulwarks of
the Turkifh empire in Germany, was taken by
ftorm, and made the fcene of exceffive cruelties,
which the Turks will for ever record, as a reproach to the Chriftian name. Of all the inhabitants of this wretched city, there efcaped only thirty Janizaries, who hid themfelves when they faw
that all was loft. The Kiahia, who commanded
them, was carried to Vienna, where, having attempted in vain to force his guard, he killed
himfelf with a piftol-fhot. Towards the end of
the attack, when the town made no refiftance, the
befiegers gave no quarter, even to the Chriftian
flaves, whom the befieged had forced to take arms.
The perfons who firft thought of fwallowing their
gold have been the occafion of many cruelties in
fucceeding ages. The women of the German army
were feen ripping up the bellies of the Turks,
while their bodies were yet panting, to fearch for
treafure in their bowels. The French Princes
(a) who eloped from the court of Lewis XIV. to
make this campaign, returned home with as much
horror as glory. The Abbot of Savoy, who renounced France, did not return with them. He
then begun that glorious career, which has immortalized him by the name of Prince Eugene.

The King returned to Zolkiew, where he endeavoured to confirm his health, not by that delicate and cautious way of living, which ferves only
to prolong a ftate of weaknefs, but by following
the diverfion of the chace. It has always been
faid, that hunting is the image of war. In moft
parts of Europe, this image reprefents its object of
a very fmall fize : but Poland encreafes its magni-
tude, in imitation of the Afiatic fovereigns, who

(a) The Princes of Conti, Roche-fur-Yon, and Turenne;
the latter of whom was killed at the battle of Steinkerque.

hunt

hunt with a complete army. The King kept in pay five hundred Janizaries, all real Turks, taken in battle, armed and dreſſed in their former man- ner. A circular ſpace was marked out for them in a foreſt, which they encompaſſed with nets, leav- ing an opening that anſwered to the plain. At a conſiderable diſtance, a line of dogs held in leaſhes formed a creſcent ; behind which, the King, the huntſmen, and the ſpectators were drawn up in an- other line. The ſignal being given, other dogs were let looſe into the foreſt, and drove before them whatever they found. In a ſhort time, there came out ſtags, elks, *auroxes*, (a ſort of wild bulls of ſingular beauty, ſtrength, and fierceneſs) lynxes, boars, and bears ; and every ſpecies of dogs at- tacked the beaſt that was its proper prey. The beaſt could neither get back to the foreſt, nor ſtay by the nets ; becauſe the Janizaries were poſted there to prevent it. The huntſmen did not en- gage in the combat, but when the dogs were likely to be overpower d. This mixed multitude of men, horſes, and wild beaſts, the noiſe of horns, the variety of combats, and all this apparatus of war ſet out with proper magnificence ſtruck the natives of the ſouth, who were preſent at it, with ſurprize ; nor did the republic murmur at the ex- pence, becauſe it was not defrayed out of the pub- lic coffers. –

Hunting however. was not the King's ſole amuſe- ment. s the nation was not to be aſſembled this year, and it was uncertain whether the war would be renewed or not ; he had much leiſure upon his hands. The very recreations of a laborious King are a public benefit The pleaſure of building happening to ſtrike his fancy, he pitched upon a delightful ſituation on the banks of the Viſtula, about two leagues from Warſaw. Villanow roſe out of the ground, and the north was ornamented with

with the architecture of Italy. But the satisfaction the King enjoyed in raising this edifice, did not make him forget his resentment against Leopold; and he shewed it, by declaring a resolution to quit the league. Leopold saw that it was necessary to present him with some other bait to keep him steady; and proposed to him the conquest of Moldavia and Walachia, to be possessed as a sovereignty by his family; promising him a body of German troops, which should advance from the banks of the Danube to assist him in the reduction of those provinces. They are both inhabited by Christians, and were formerly dependent upon the kingdom of Hungary, but are now properly fiefs of the Turkish empire, ever since the days of the victorious Soliman; whose successors sell the principality of them to the highest bidder. The Hospodar Duca, who died a prisoner in Poland, was servant to a merchant of Yassi, before he grew rich enough to be made a Prince; and Walachia has had Hospodars, whose birth was not more illustrious.

This double crown was a strong temptation to the King. On the other side, Mahomet, who daily sustained fresh losses, made him an offer, if he would quit the league, to restore Kaminieck, with a considerable sum of money, to indemnify Poland for the expences of so long a war.

In this competition between the republic and his own family, the King had not the greatness of mind to make a right choice. He was prevailed upon, by the insinuations of the Jesuit Vota, the solicitations of the Queen, and the voice of paternal affection, to decide in favour of his family, and leave to fortune the interests of Poland. However, he disguised his real design in this expedition, under the specious pretence of conquering only for the republic, and of recovering Kaminieck in a more glorious manner, by cutting off all its succours,

since

since it received none from any other quarter but
Moldavia.

It was a long time since Poland had seen so fine
and so numerous an army. It amounted to near
forty thousand fighting-men, the Generals having
served the King well, which is a thing that does
not always happen. Prince James, who had already his eye upon a throne that could be acquired
by merit only, endeavoured to get himself a name,
by sharing in the fatigues of war ; and besides, the
intended conquests were to fall to his lot. This
project however, was known to very few ; for the
multitude, as well officers as soldiers, are always
ignorant why they fight, and yet do not fight the
worse upon that account.

The terrifying difficulties the army had gone
through in the last campaign, of which the present
was a repetition, did not prevent its taking the same
route. The only difference was, that, upon the
present occasion, the King, as he proceeded on his
march, established fortified posts, at proper distan-
ces, from the frontiers of Poland to the very capital of Moldavia. The design of these forts was to
secure the couriers and the convoys which were to
come from so great a distance.

When the army crossed the Bucovine, a place
where it was on the point of perishing in the preceding campaign, they threw bridges over all the
passages which could either retard their march, or
hinder their return. When they came to that scene
of blood where Konski had deserved so highly of
the republic, he again received the thanks of the
King and the whole army. There were still to
be seen piles of bones, which recalled to some the
memory of a friend ; to others, that of a brother
or a father, and made them wish for an opportunity of avenging their fate. The King secured
this defile by a redoubt, strengthened with palisadoes,

fadoes, and defended by a good garrifon; and from thence, continuing his march along the Pruth, he entered the vaft plains of Moldavia, where the army fuffered extremely by the heat. The climate is naturally hot, and was made much more fo by having been three years without rain. The ponds and lakes were almoft dry: the courfe of the *Babilouf*, a river as large as the Marne, was ftopped; and the marfhy grounds were full of cracks, which, for their depth, might be taken for gulphs. In the midft of fo parched a fcene, the Poles were aftonifhed to fee the earth covered with grafs two feet high, growing thick, and excellently good. No cattle were to be found in all the country, which formerly abounded with them, and with men alfo; but the glorious profeffion of war had made it all a defart. Nothing was to be found but cities, whofe ruins being overgrown with thiftles and nettles, ferved for nothing but a retreat for ferpents. In this condition were *Pererita, Chocava, Sorock, Stefanouf, Felki, Gallacz*, and feveral others. Moft of them were converted into places of arms to favour the expedition. The difficulty of fubfifting in a country, uninhabited and uncultivated, is eafy to conceive. The armies of the middle of Europe may well afk thofe of the north, how they contrive to fubfift wherever they go. Their doing it fuppofes their convoys to be very regular, their officers and foldiers very fober, and their equipages no greater than is neceffary; fince otherwife, this laft article alone would not only embarrafs, but famifh an army. Of two nations, at war with each other, great odds may be laid on that which is moft frugal.

If all Moldavia had been like the eaftern part of the country which the Poles croffed, they would have marched to the conqueft of a wildernefs. But, in the weft, it was well peopled, and well culti-

Y. 1686.

cultivated; and the foil fo good, that it produces the richeft crops, by being only once turned up without any manure.

The reigning Prince of Moldavia was *Conftantine Cantemir*, the fame whom Soliman, in 1684, had fubftituted in the room of the weak *Cantacuzenus*. He was grandfather to that Prince Cantemir, who was not long ago the Ruffian Ambaffador in France, having before had the fame character in England. He did not ftay to furrender, till the army was at the gates of his capital: it was fcarce got out of the Bucovine, when a nobleman arrived from his court, who told the King, that his mafter thought himfelf happy in the profpect of being foon delivered from the Ottoman yoke to enter into the obedience of Poland; that he regretted his not being able to come in perfon to wait upon fo great a King; and that his view in ftaying for him in his capital, was to hinder the people from leaving it.

The King, charmed with a conqueft which would occafion the fhedding of no tears, haftened his march to the plain of Cetzora, where the army halted. This plain recalled to his mind the flaughter and the glory of his grandfather, by prefenting him with a view of the entrenchments, where the famous Zolkiewfki, with thirty thoufand Poles, repulfed an army of a hundred thoufand Turks and Tartars; and of the pyramid, which was ftill ftanding, where the manes of that hero addreffed the paffenger in thefe animating words; *Learn of me, how fweet and how honourable it is to die for one's country:* a maxim that was engraved upon the King's heart from his earlieft youth. From this plain, it is no more than fix leagues to the capital, which a detachment of eight thoufand men went and took poffeffion of, without the leaft refiftance. The corn was all ftanding; and to keep
the

the main body of the army at a diſtance, in ſuch a juncture, was taking care of the intereſts of the capital.

Yaſſi, a place of great riches, by means of its commerce with Aſia, is a large open town, without gates or walls; but it has twelve vaſt caſtles of great thickneſs, and flanked with terraſſed towers. They are all mounted with cannon, and have magazines of arms for their defence; but are in fact only ſo many monaſteries, inhabited by Greek Monks, who work out their ſalvation under the protection of the Turks. The Chriſtian world has no Monks that can vie with them for antiquity; St. Baſil having been their patriarch ſo early as the fourth century; but the Perſians and Indians had Monks long before this, in the midſt of their idolatry. It was not till later times, that the weſt grew addicted to the indolence of a contemplative life. It muſt be owned, that theſe fortreſſes of St. Baſil's ſerve alſo for an aſylum to the inhabitants of the country, when the Tartars make their inroads. It is impoſſible perhaps to find a place where ſo many Monks are aſſembled together; for another hive of them may be ſeen upon a hill over againſt the city. So great a number of men, who occaſion a great conſumption, but produce nothing of their own, muſt needs diminiſh the riches of the city, and the revenues of the Hoſpodar. Their extreme ignorance is not ſo much owing to their idleneſs or want of capacity, as to the ſlavery in which they live; and there are good reaſons to believe in general that the Moldavians would diſtinguiſh themſelves both in arms, and arts, if they were once ſet at liberty. As the Prince who governs them buys his ſovereignty, the people muſt repay the purchaſer: *Yaſſi* therefore was ſure to gain by becoming ſubject to another power.

When

When the King approached the town, he was met by the Bishop, the clergy, the principal inhabitants, and the people; but he was surprized at not seeing the Hospodar. Cantemir's situation was extremely critical. One of his sons was an hostage at Constantinople, with four nobles of the country, as pledges for his fidelity; and on the other hand, a Christian army was ready to fall upon him, without his having any hope from the Turkish forces, which were, at this juncture, at too great a distance to defend him. He had recourse therefore to a pretended submission, in order to engage the conqueror to spare his dominions; and to exculpate himself with the Porte, he took refuge with his family and his treasures in the Turkish army, which was encamped near the mouth of the Danube. His flight was not disagreeable to the King, who, as he resolved to keep his conquests, would have been puzzled how to dispose of the Hospodar; but he was displeased at his having carried over his troops to the enemy. He learned from the Moldavians themselves, that he was the worst Prince that had for a long time governed that country; that having bought his crown at a very dear rate, he was a professed usurer, and behaved in the most oppressive manner; and that the very moment of his flight had been distinguished by acts of extortion, which exceeded the ordinary measure of his rapaciousness. The King found in his palace some fine apartments, inlaid with Mosaic work: he treated the city with great tenderness, considering it as his own: the shops continued open, the markets free, and every thing was paid for by the conquerors, as punctually as by the citizens. The soldiers, who were quartered up and down the monasteries, did not disturb their regularity; and the Moldavian women, whose dress made them

C c

no

no lefs tempting than their natural charms, were treated with great refpect.

While things were in this fituation in Moldavia, the Walachians were far from being in a ftate of tranquillity. Fear, and ftill more, the humanity of the victor, which was loudly celebrated by fame, induced them to fubmit; and they obliged their Hofpodar to fend him a deputation, declaring that their gates were open. Doubtlefs *Serban Cantacuzenus*, whom Soliman had continued in the principality, notwithftanding the fufpicions he entertained of his conduct, had not removed all caufe of complaint. His poft was filled by another Prince, *Conftantine Brancovan*, who fubmitted to this apparent furrendry purely to efcape the prefent danger.

The King, being now mafter of Moldavia and Walachia, extended his views ftill farther. Before him lay the antient Beffarabia, now called *Budziac (a)*, and all that vaft country which lies between the Danube and the Niefter, up to the coaft of the Black Sea. The Crim itfelf tempted his ambition: he was pleafed with the idea of chaftifing the Tartars upon their own ground, and feemed to intend opening himfelf a paffage even to Conftantinople, by ways which were deemed impracticable. He therefore refumed his march, without quitting the *Pruth*, the water of which was neceffary for the fubfiftence of the army in fo dry a feafon; and befides this, was very wholfome, and mitigated a diforder that raged among the troops. The fol-

(*a*) The Budziac Tartars are a branch of thofe of the Crim. They obey to a certain degree their *Murfes*, that is to fay, the heads of their different Hords. The Porte calls them its flaves, but there is not a freer people upon the face of the earth. They are in a ftate of almoft perpetual war; and while other nations confider them as robbers, they call themfelves warriors.

diers,

dlers, who were fcorched with the heat, by eating
greedily of cucumbers, melons, and other fruits,
brought upon themfelves dyfenteries; for which
the water of the Pruth was an affured remedy. The
neceffity of following the river in all its windings,
augmented the fatigue of the march.

The army was already far advanced; and no
enemy, either Turk or Tartar, appeared: for Mahomet, who was acquainted with the King's march
into a country fo remote from Poland, had given
orders to his General not to quit the iflands of the
Danube, and to the Tartars not to appear on the
hither fide of the Niefter, till the Polifh army was
got a great way into the country. His defign was
to effect its deftruction in the fame plains, where
Darius I. King of Perfia, repented his having carried the war againft the Scythians, the anceftors
of thofe Tartars whom John was come in queft of
upon their own territories.

The danger increafed continually as the march
was prolonged. When the Poles came to Gallacz,
a town not far from the place where the Pruth falls
into the Danube, the plain was covered with a confufed multitude of Tartars; and foon after, the
Turks made their appearance in good order. The
King looked towards the Danube, from whence he
expected the fuccour which the Emperor had promifed him; but Leopold, attentive only to his own
interefts, was pufhing his fucceffes in Hungary.
The King, finding himfelf deceived, felt all the
danger to which he had expofed himfelf. He had
been upon the march full three months; and muft
now force his way through frefh troops, fuperior to
his own by more than half their number. The
only refource left him was to retreat; and this could
be done only by weathering a ftorm for two months
together, before he reached the port. Upon fuch
occafions as thefe, a King, who had not the abi-

lities

lities of a General, would have no prospect but of being buried in the same abyss with the companions of his labours : but the Poles looked towards their King, and conceived hopes. He threw a bridge over the Pruth, which, by this means, he placed between the enemy and himself. It happened fortunately, that forage was equally plenty on the other side ; and there was no want of wood. The two armies contended for the water of the Pruth for twenty days together ; and neither of them procured it, but at the price of blood. There was, on each side, a daily revolution of encampments and decampments on the opposite banks of the river, and the cannon was not idle all the time.

In the mean while, the Tartars swam across the Pruth, with a design of getting before the Polish army ; and attempted to effect its destruction, without coming near it. Having observed that the grass, which covered the plain, being dried by the heat of the sun, was easily inflammable, they set it on fire ; and instantly the Poles saw nothing but flames through which they were to pass. This army of incendiaries molested them in a variety of ways at the same time ; by consuming their forage ; by obliging part of the Polish cavalry to be on horseback, by night as well as by day, in order to keep the incendiaries at a distance ; and by retarding the march of the army, because they were forced to allow time for the flames to die away. But when they came to pass over this burnt land, the air they breathed was on fire also. The ashes that rose under the feet of the men and horses, enveloped the whole army in a black cloud. The sweat that covered their faces made the ashes stick ; and instead of Poles, they all looked like Ethiopians. The deserts, through which they passed, afforded nothing but fruit, and the convoys were brought up with great difficulty. The King, Prince James,

2   and

and the Generals, taught the foldiers, by their example, to bear thefe hardfhips. The French officers that ferved in that campaign, were aftonifhed
at the patience and fobriety of the Poles. As they
drew near to Yaffi, they found upon the road a
great number of hillocks, thrown up by men's
hands, which were intended as burying-places for
the warriors that have fallen in the many battles,
of which Moldavia, comprehended under ancient
Dacia, has been the fcene. One among the reft,
which was a hundred and twenty feet high, gave
occafion to critical fpeculations. The Moldavians
call it *Rebea*; and hence it was concluded to be the
Maufoleum of a Prince of that name. The King
of Poland, who piqued himfelf upon his learning, gave it as his opinion, that it was the tomb
of *Decebalus*, King of the Dacians. A King, with
no other quality but learning, would ill difcharge
the duties of the throne; but if he were, at the
fame time, the defender, the oeconomift, and the
philofopher of the nation, he would be the prodigy of the eighteenth century.

Yaffi received its conqueror again with great joy;
but if we may believe the hiftorian Cantemir, the
Hofpodar's fon, it foon had caufe to fhed tears.
He afferts (a), " that the King being abandoned
" by Leopold, and therefore too weak to preferve
" his conqueft, gave up the city to be pillaged,
" and carried away even the confecrated plate, and
" the fhrines of the faints, which were fet with
" precious ftones; that he was feen in perfon,
" with a torch in his hand, fetting fire to two mo-
" nafteries which refufed to give up their treafures;
" and that the murders and rapes which were com-
" mitted, drove away the inhabitants, both of the
" town and country; by which means his army

(a) Tom. ii. p. 118.

C c 3

" was

Y. 1686. " was reduced to great want." The Poles deny
these horrid facts; and the veracity of the historian may be doubted, as it was his father's dominions that were invaded. All nations that are at
war accuse one another of cruelty; and at the very
time of the charge, it is difficult for those who
are not upon the spot to find out the truth. Who
then will venture to decide, at so great a distance
of time and place?

Be this as it will, the King resumed his march
towards Poland; and the Tartars perceiving that
he took his route by Cornar, poisoned the lake
which supplies the town with water. " I doubt
" not, says Cantemir (a), but what I am going
" to relate will seem incredible to those who have
" not seen it; and even after having been en eye-
" witness of it myself, I cannot conceal the sur-
" prize it gives me. The Tartars are possessed of
" a secret, which is known only by three or four
" of the nation: I mean, the knowledge of a
" plant, of so poisonous a nature, that being
" thrown into water, whether standing or running,
" it destroys both man and beast without remedy."
If Cantemir saw well, these three or four poison-
ers are masters of the lives of the whole nation,
and of all that can do them any hurt.

The King, either from suspicion, or good fortune, changing his design, quitted the flat country,
to go and encamp along the *Seret*; from whence,
quite to the frontiers of his own dominions, he supplied with provisions all the ruined towns where
he had left troops, and compleated the forts he had
raised. Though all these precautions did not secure to him his conquests, there resulted from them,
however, one advantage to the country itself,
which was visible the very next year. The towns,

(a) Tom. ii. p. 166.

which

which had so long been deserted, begun to be filled again with inhabitants, under the protection of the Polish arms: the neighbouring villages were repaired: the Greek and Armenian merchants, who are inceſſantly paſſing between Europe and Aſia, were glad to find places of ſafety to lodge their goods: the Jews alſo came hither to ſeek an aſylum; and even the Poles themſelves, I mean the peaſants, in order to avoid the ſlavery in which the nobles keep them, came to enjoy the common rights of humanity in the newly-conquered country. Pokruſia, which the army croſſed before it finiſhed its retreat, a Poliſh province, in a ſtate of deſolation, equal to that of the eaſtern part of Moldavia, partook of the ſame benefits.

The King, in this expedition, enjoyed the unuſual glory of being a benefactor to the people he had conquered. Leopold, on the other hand, while he expoſed his ally, kept all his troops to be employed for his own advantage. He felt the crown of Hungary totter upon his head, while Buda continued in the hands of the Turks. The Duke of Lorrain, who had raiſed the ſiege of that town in 1684, reſumed his deſign of taking it, with more eagerneſs than before. The place was very ſtrong in itſelf, and defended by the Baſhaw *Apté*. The Viſir Soliman kept the field, with a great army. But the Duke ſurmounted all obſtacles, took Buda by aſſault, and drove the Viſir beyond the Drave. The Viſir, who was a man of reflection, now found by experience the truth of what he had often ſaid himſelf, that ſucceſs in enterprizes of the ſecond order, is no ſecurity of ſucceſs in thoſe of the firſt. The Baſhaw *Apté* was ſpared the mortification of being a witneſs of this diſgrace, by being killed upon the breach. Upon this occaſion too, Prince Eugene gave ſpecimens of his future merit.

At

At the fame time, the Turkifh arms fuffered another check in the Morea. The Venetians, who had got footing in that country the preceding year, now fortified themfelves there, by the taking of Calamata, Navarrin, Modon, and Napoli di Romania *(a)*, after having beat the Turks in feveral encounters.

If the King of Poland did not gain any great advantage over them this campaign, he at leaft kept them at bay with inferior forces. In the month of November he arrived at Leopol, where the Ambaffadors from Mufcovy expected him. The two Czars, *Iwan* and *Peter*, who reigned together upon the fame throne, which only one of them deferved to fill, had hitherto done nothing for the league. They wanted previoufly to fecure to themfelves the Polifh towns and lordfhips, which they held only in truft ; *Smolenfko (b)*, *Kiovia (c)*, *the Palatinate of Czernicow, and the Duchy of Severia.* To fupport fo long a war, Poland ftood in need of men and money. The Ambaffadors made an offer of troops, paid down one million immediately, promifed to pay another, and the ceffion was made in form.

In concluding this treaty, the King confulted rather the authority he had acquired by his virtues, than the laws. The lands of the republic cannot be alienated but by the republic itfelf, affembled

---

(a) This town, called by Ptolomy *Nauplia navale.* becaufe it was built by Nauplius, fon of Neptune and Amymone, is a feaport fituated in a gulph of ancient Argia, called *Sinus Argolicus.* In the room of the ancient Grecian temples have fucceeded mofques, fynagogues, and Chriftian churches, without any hoftile intentions towards each other ; and the traders of all nations have an entire liberty of ferving God in their own way.

(b) A town fituated upon the Boryfthenes.

(c) Kiovia or Kiow, upon the weftern bank of the fame river.

in a diet; and the prefent ceffion was authorized
only by a decree of the Senate. The Poles murmured greatly at this circumftance; and befides,
they thought it was purchafing, at too high a price,
the affiftance of a nation, whom they then looked
upon with contempt. But things are now much
changed; and the prefent age has feen Mufcovy decide the fate of Poland, by giving it its Kings.

In the fame affembly of the Senate, the King ventured upon another breach of the laws, which made
the republic exclaim loudly againft him. To underftand the foundation of the complaint, it muft
be obferved, that Poland indulges the children of
its Kings with no privileges which may induce them
to confider the throne as an hereditary poffeffion;
and in order to imprefs upon them more ftrongly
the idea of republican equality, they are fubject
to the jurifdiction of the Senate, at the time when
their father holds the fceptre. There have been inftances, particularly thofe of Albert and Ferdinand,
fons of Sigifmund III. of their foliciting to be admitted into the Senate; but thofe Princes were received only upon the exprefs condition of taking an
oath of fidelity to the republic. John, upon the
prefent occafion, attempted much more in favour
of Prince James, by feating him on the throne by
his fide, when he gave audience to the Mufcovite
Ambaffadors. This was, in fome meafure, declaring him King elect, and confequently infringing
the liberty of the nation.

The Queen alfo upon the fame occafion, arro-
gated to herfelf one of the prerogatives of royalty.
By the conftitution of Poland, the Queen is kept
at a diftance from all public affairs, and of courfe
not permitted to give audience to Ambaffadors.
The Mufcovites, feduced by the careffes of her who
now fat upon the throne, folicited of her a public
audience, and eafily obtained it. This ftep gave
occafion

occasion to general discontent; so that no one received any real satisfaction, except the Ambassadors, who were treated with extraordinary marks of distinction. They met with a different reception at Vienna, where they went next to ratify the treaty of the league. Being at that time a savage race, who felt the brutal passions, but knew not how to curb them, they seized young girls by force; and even fathers came to demand their sons, whom they had corrupted; a conduct which gave great scandal in a decent, and even austere court. The Emperor concluded the alliance in all haste, and sent away these lawless envoys to their own country, and their own manners.

The King of Poland, after their departure, united the apostolic with the regal character. The prevailing religion in Poland is the Roman Catholic; but in the southern provinces of Black Russia, Pokrusia, Podolia, Volhinia, and the Ukraine, there are ten Greeks to one Catholic. The Bishops, like the Basilian monasteries from whence they were taken, were subject to the Patriarch of Muscovy; and their most sacred Dogma is an everlasting hatred for Rome. The King thought it would be serving both God and the state, to reconcile them with that church; and as the Bishops were then at court, on account of their temporal concerns, he gratified them beyond their hopes, and then prevailed upon them to hear the point of the schism discussed. Accordingly, conferences were appointed, and the King assisted at them in person, to moderate the acrimony of the Theologians. The Bishops were but little affected by the arguments that were produced against them; but the lenity and beneficence of the King gave force to the reasons of his party; and several of these wandering pastors sent Deputies to Rome to be admitted, together with their flocks, into the fold of St. Peter.

But

But while the King was thus labouring for Rome, he was upon the point of coming to a rupture with that court. The thing in difpute was, whether there fhould be any Capuchins in Poland ; or at leaft, whether France or Italy fhould have the privilege of furnifhing the kingdom with, that precious commodity. Innocent XI. was refolved to allow none but Italians : both parties were obftinate, and grew angry, which might have been attended with bad confequences ; for even the whims of Princes become matters of ftate. At laft, fince one Capuchin was probably as good as another, the King chofe rather to receive the prefent from Italy, than to continue empty-handed.

It is difficult to reconcile the zeal which the Pope had for the league, with the little regard he fhewed for the hero of that alliance. It was now eight years fince the King had nominated to a Cardinal's hat, *Forbin*, Bifhop of Beauvais, who had been twice Ambaffador at his court. Innocent XI. after having feen the extinction of almoft the whole facred college, raifed it up again by a promotion of four and forty Cardinals ; and in all this great number there appeared not the name of the Bifhop of Beauvais ; but there were two Poles in the lift, whom the King never dreamed of : *Radziowfki*, Bifhop of Warmia, his relation ; and the Abbot of *Henoff*, his Envoy Extraordinary at Rome. It is probable, that the Pope, who had had more than one quarrel with France, had a mind to mortify Lewis XIV. in the perfon of the Bifhop of Beauvais, without regarding the refentment of the King of Poland ; who, being equally chagrined at what was granted, and at what was refufed him, would not honour the ceremony of invefting the new Cardinals with the hat, with his royal prefence. The Abbot of Henoff quitted Poland for ever, and went to receive the hat at the fountain head : an

event

7

Y. 1686. event which occafioned a law, to exclude all ecclefiaftics from being fent as Minifters to the court
of Rome. The Bifhop of Warmia was invefted
with the hat, in a private manner, by the perfon
that brought it from the Pope; and was no fooner
clothed in the purple, than he claimed a right of
precedence before his mafter's fons. Such was the
will of the court of Rome, which it fignified by
the Nuncio *Palavicini*.

It was in the age of the Emperor Charles the
fifth, that the Cardinals firft affumed fo exalted a
rank. At that time, moft of the kingdoms in Europe had a Cardinal for firft Minifter : *Ximenes* governed in Spain, always clad in the habit of a
Francifcan Fryar, but haughtier than even the
haughtieft Spaniard; *Duprat* in France; *Wolfey* in
England; *Martinufius* in Hungary; and even
Charles the fifth himfelf, after having difmiffed
Ximenés, chofe for his prime Minifter, his preceptor, Cardinal Adrian, whom afterwards he made
Pope. It is no difficult matter for fubordinate
Kings to ufurp honours; but Poland was hitherto
unaccuftomed to the claims of the Roman purple.

The King, who was nettled to the quick, forbad the new Cardinal and the Nuncio to appear in
his prefence, till the Pope had given him fatisfaction with regard to the Bifhop of Beauvais; and he
complained heavily of the affront to the court of
Rome. The King of France joined in the remon-
ftrance; but Innocent heard them with pleafure,
and continued inflexible; nor was it till after the
Pope's death, that the two Kings faw the Bifhop
Forbin converted into a Cardinal de *Janfon*.

Y. 1687.   Thefe mortifications increafed the diforders which
already preyed upon the health of the King of Poland. A wound that he formerly received at the
battle of Bereftefk, in the reign of Cafimir, had
left impreffions behind it, which became more
trouble-

troublesome as he advanced in age : and the gravel, a still more dangerous complaint, gave him frequent intimations that he was mortal. His physicians advised him to give up the command of the army, and to relax his attention to affairs of state : but his answer was, *Why was I made a King? If I am to be cured, it shall not be by sitting still.*

While the physicians were consulting in what manner to treat his case, he was informed of the death of the *Great Condé*, whom the gout had at length worn out. They had both discovered, from their earliest youth, great talents for war : they had saved their country more than once : they had both stood for, and both deserved, the same crown ; and they had congratulated each other by letter upon their victories : all which formed a sort of connection that made the King more sensibly affected with his death. In one respect however they were different, that Condé had quitted the field at fifty five ; but the King, who was farther advanced in life, and felt equally the symptoms of illness and decay, was still intent upon war ; and for this purpose quitted Leopol to come to Zolkiew.

This change of situation placed him upon the frontiers of the kingdom, in the midst of the winter-quarters of the army, and at a season of the year when other Generals are of opinion, that the smallest degree of success gives them a right to unbend themselves in the pleasures of the capital. The Queen pressed her husband to make use of this privilege ; and her intreaties were seconded by deputations from the nobility of all the provinces, who represented to him of what consequence his health was to the state, and how great a loss the kingdom would sustain by losing him. Harangues of this sort are mere empty compliments to the generality of Kings ; but upon the present occasion they expressed the real sentiments of the nation. But as

John

Y. 1687. John was not born upon the throne, he had none of that delicate attention to his own eafe, which is always the effect of effeminacy, and frequently the caufe of inconveniences to the public. He refufed to comply with their follicitations, and he had his reafons for fo doing. He was apprehenfive of incurfions from the Tartars, who are never flopped by winter : it was neceffary to reinforce and fuftain the pofts which he had eftablifhed from the Niefter to the very heart of Moldavia ; and he knew that things are always beft done, under the infpection of the mafter's eye : a maxim which is ftill more to be depended on, if the mafter be himfelf a judge of the bufinefs ; and the King was certainly a good one.

There were many Polifh prifoners, or rather flaves, confined at Kaminieck, whofe fate gave the King great concern : the republic alfo had Turkifh prifoners in its hands : the King therefore fent the officer (a), from whofe memoirs thefe particulars are taken, to treat about an exchange. By the conftitution of Poland, the power of the King is confined within fuch narrow limits, that even his fubjects are not fuffered to be exchanged by his authority, but by that of the Grand-General. Upon this occafion however, the affair was tranfacted in the King's name. The captives whom he claimed belonged to the *Gendarmes* and *Pancerns*, two bodies of cavalry entirely made up of gentlemen : the Turks he had in his power were officers of the Spahis, or Janizaries, and the two Bafhaws of Siliftria and Caramania, who were taken in 1683, at the battle of Barcan. The King made a prefent of them to the Grand General, who had not yet received their ranfom (b). There were alfo in irons

---

(a) Dupont.

(b) The ranfom of the two Bafhaws was fixed at 200 purfes, each worth about five hundred piaftres ; in the whole 700,000 French livres, or about 32,000 pounds.

on

on both sides many common soldiers, whose exchange was attended with no difficulty. At the first conference that was held upon the subject, the Bashaw Hussein, Governor of Kaminieck, declared to the Polish envoy the intentions of the Grand Seignior, in these terms : " If thy master will be contented " with exchanging the common soldiers, thou " mayest take them away with thee immediately, " and send me the captive Spahis and Janizaries. " I will even return him his gentlemen at a fixed " price : but as for the Grand-Seignior's officers, " who have suffered themselves to be taken pri- " soners, and particularly the two Bashaws, tell " them that they must never hope to see the Sub- " lime Porte again. A true Mussulman, who " bears arms, should die a thousand times, rather " than be reduced to slavery ; and if those who " command had this greatness of soul, their exam- " ple would be followed by those who obey."

The negotiation was protracted to a great length : because Hussein had no money to give, and that which he was to receive from the Poles was not ready. It is natural to pity the fate of the two Bashaws, whose chains were riveted on them afresh, if we recollect their gallant behaviour in the bloody battle of Barcan ; where they were taken in the very thickest of the action, covered with wounds, and faint with loss of blood. The Porte continued its severity towards them for eight years longer ; but the Grand-General alleviated the weight of this long captivity, by treating them like brethren.

By the laws of Poland, a diet was to be assembled this year : but the senate put it off, to save expences at a time when the continuation of the war was so heavy a burden. The nation, however, though not assembled in form, murmured greatly at the projects of its chief. His plan for the ensuing campaign, was to secure his conquest of Moldavia,

davia, by carrying his victorious arms quite to the black sea, where he depended upon making himself master of the fortresses of Kilia and Bialogrod. To execute this design, it was necessary that he should continue stedfast in the league, notwithstanding ·his dissatisfaction with the Emperor, to the end that the Turks, being attacked on all quarters, might be more easily dispossessed of their territories on the side of Poland. But Poland begun to suspect that these great projects were calculated for the benefit of his own family more than for that of the nation ; and those who had no doubt that this was his intention, observed in an angry strain, that it would be still more difficult to keep than to conquer ; that it was maintaining a war of which there would be no end ; and aiming at distant objects, while the enemy was suffered to continue undisturbed at the gates of the kingdom, in a fortress which it was a disgrace not to retake. The King could not help feeling that the complaints were just ; and the bombardment of Kaminieck was resolved on. The Polish soldiery, the chief strength of which lay in the cavalry, was by no means proper for sieges of any sort, and much less for the present service, when a place was to be attacked, that was well able to defend itself. The Turks, since they had been in possession of Kaminieck, had considerably encreased its fortifications ; and a garrison of ten thousand men, made up both of Janizaries and Spahis were resolved to sell their lives at a dear rate. It was therefore judged prudent to attack it by bombardment ; and as it expected a convoy which was supposed to be absolutely necessary for its subsistence, the Poles flattered themselves with the hopes of intercepting it, and taking the place by famine, if the fire of the bombs was found to be insufficient.

The

The army begun its march about the end of June. Y. 1687.
The King attended the expedition in a languid and
exhaufted ftate : his mind had loft nothing of its
former vigour ; but his bodily ftrength failed him
entirely at Jaflowiecz, where he was obliged to give
up the command, and Prince James took poffeffion
of it with all the enfigns of power. When a King
of Poland is at the head of his army, a lance adorned with a horfe's tail, called *Bontchouk*, is carried
before him, as a fignal of the royal prefence. The
four Generals, of Poland and Lithuania, have alfo
their Bontchouks ; but they are lowered in the
King's prefence. The fame refpect was now paid
to Prince James ; and the Generals, who are fubject to the King only, received orders from his fon.
The thing was hitherto without example, and of
great confequence to a young Prince who aimed at
regal dignity. The moft fingular circumftance of
all was, that the Generals confented to it without
reluctance; for they were afraid of difobliging a
King, who, by his virtues, difarmed even pride itfelf.

The Prince therefore, taking the thunderbolt out
of his father's hands, advanced towards Kaminieck,
where he arrived on the 10th of July. The Turks
have a degree of confidence that is unknown among
us ; for, after the place was invefted, they fent
back feveral Polifh prifoners, whofe ranfom had
been paid. In fuch a cafe as this, we fhould be a-
fraid of difcovering the defects of the place ; but
it is a maxim with the Turks, that furprize can
never fucceed againft perfons who are upon their
guard ; and yet this does not prevent their having
an eye upon fuch as are fufpected of giving intelligence. They had allowed the public exercife of the
Chriftian religion to be continued in a church, which
they called the mofque of *Iffevi* (the Turkifh word
for Jefus) where two Jefuits officiated. The Turks

D d   confider

Y. 1687. confider the Chriftians as idolaters, and yet protect them in their dominions. The two Jefuits made a bad ufe of this protection, by giving intelligence to the Poles of the difpofitions they obferved in the place. Their letters were intercepted, and they expected nothing but death. The Bafhaw only ordered them to be conducted to Prince James, and gave them leave to carry with them as much as they could of their effects. The remainder was depofited in the church, and the doors fealed, till the Grand-Seignior's pleafure was known: a lenity of behaviour, which aftonifhed the criminals and the whole Chriftian army.

The bombardment lafted fix days with a moft terrifying noife. The befiegers played upon the town with fifty pieces of cannon, and fixteen mortars; and the befieged returned their fire from three hundred. The Bafhaw *Huffein* had taken all proper precautions to leffen the effect of the bombs; and befides, the place was not now in the fame cafe, as when Mahomet took it. At that time, it was filled with all the nobility of Podolia, who dreading the laft extremities, (the women efpecially and the children, who made the air refound with their cries) ftruck the garrifon with terror and confufion, and talked of nothing but furrendering: whereas, in the prefent crifis, it contained nothing but foldiers.

The Poles foon difcovered that their powder was confuming to little purpofe; and thought proper to flacken their fire, when they faw the Tartars pafs the Niefter, and advance towards them; and a few days after, the Serafkier appeared at the head of twenty five thoufand Turks, preparing to pafs it alfo. Prince James was eager to come to blows: it was the firft time of his commanding in chief, and he was impatient to fhew that he deferved that honour. But the Serafkier whofe reputation was

4   already

already eftablifhed, refolved to fight only in cafe of neceffity, and feeing the enemy retire to a league's diftance from the place, he contented himfelf with obferving their motions, without paffing the river.

While they were thus watching each other, the King, who ftaid at Jaftowiecz, was more follicitous about the operations of the army, than his own health. He continued in this poft; in order to be ready for whatever might happen, and to be able to act with his head, though his arm was ufelefs. The fituation, however, was not without danger; being diftant only ten leagues from the Tartars, who are a wandering and rapid body, and the King was guarded by a little camp of no more than two thoufand men. The circumftance that gave him moft uneafinefs, was his being attended by the court, which was put into an alarm as foon as the Tartars had paffed the Niefter. The Queen, the Princefs of Poland, the Marchionefs of Bethune, and the maids of honour might eafily fall into the hands of thefe barbarians: it could not be expected that they fhould be all heroines; and fome were fo far from it, as to fall fick out of fear. The Queen, however, was not one of this number: her curiofity was fo great, that fhe ventured to advance to the bank of the river, though fome boatmen had been taken prifoners the fame day in that very place. A Tartarian envoy, who came to the court next day, thought proper to remind the King, that his companions did not wear bells to give notice of their approach.

In the mean time, nothing decifive happened between the two armies, who only cannonaded each other acrofs the river with little lofs. The campaign ended with no other exploit than the ruin of a few houfes in Kaminieck, and the death of three or four hundred Tartars, who fell into an ambuf-

cade;

Y. 1687. cade: inconfiderable effects to be produced by fo great a caufe.

The efforts of the league were attended with fuccefs in other places; but it was not where the greateft armies were employed, as might naturally have been expected. Prince *Galliczin*, Favourite of the Regent of Mufcovy, firft Minifter of ftate and Generaliffimo of the army, advanced through the Ukraine towards the Black Sea, with an army of three hundred thoufand foot and a hundred thoufand horfe. *Peter the Great*, who was deftined to difcipline thefe troops, was yet a child. Galliczin propofed to make himfelf mafter of the Crim, a peninfula from whence had iffued fo many fwarms of Tartars that carried terror to the very gates of Mofcow. By exterminating this hive, he would have greatly weakened the Turkifh power; but when his army, which eat up all the countries through which it paffed, had croffed the Samara, a little river which is the boundary of the Ukraine, it was prefented with a fmoking defart, fifty leagues in extent. The Tartars had burnt the whole country as far as Precop, a fortrefs which guards the Ifthmus of the Crim. Galliczin was ftopped by famine and difeafe, and a great part of his foldiers perifhed, without having feen the enemy.

Morofini, who was more fortunate and more difcreet, though his forces were but fmall, after having made himfelf mafter of the Dardanels, Lepanto, Caftelnuovo, Portoleone and ancient Attica, completed the conqueft of Peloponnefus, which was of greater value than Candia. The Venetian bombs deftroyed, in this expedition, many monuments of antiquity which the Turks had fpared; and among the reft, the famous temple of Athens dedicated *To the unknown God (a)*. That celebrated city, whofe very

(a) Some learned men affure us that the whole infcription, which St. Paul faw upon the altar at Athens, was as follows:
T•

Y. 1687.

very ruins still command respect; together with Epidaurus and Corinth, seemed to rejoice at being under the dominion of masters who were judges of arts and genius.

But the General, who gave the greatest blow to the Ottoman empire in this campaign, was the Duke of Lorrain. This defender of the house of Austria, after having defeated the Visir Soliman upon the banks of the Drave, taken his camp with the tents standing, and passed the bridge of Essek with the runaways, extended himself along that river towards Sclavonia, without losing sight of what remained to be subdued in upper Hungary. *Agria*, surnamed by the Turks *the impregnable*, was capable of making great resistance; but when the Visir intended to reinforce it with twelve thousand Spahis, they refused to obey his Commands. The spirit of mutiny, being communicated from one troop to another, almost instantaneously, made the Visir tremble for his own safety, and take refuge in Belgrade. The army, deserted by its General, chose one of its own; and instead of opposing the progress of the Duke of Lorrain, marched directly to Constantinople to change its master. Mahomet IV. who had taken Candia, and other islands, from the Venetians; the Ukraine, Podolia and Volhinia from the Poles; and Hungary from the house of Austria, was upon the point of being stripped himself of all his power by the hands of his own slaves. His reign, ever since the fatal expedition of Vienna,

---

To the Gods of *Asia*, *Europe*, and *Africa*; to the *unknown ana foreign Gods*. St. Jerom in particular is clearly of this opinion: *Comm. in Epist. ad Titum. C.* 1. And yet St. Paul, in his sermon before the Areopagites, comprehends the whole inscription in these two words *Ignoto Deo*, *To the unknown God*. St Jerom will have it that he did so, in order to give more force to his preaching: but it is difficult to imagine, that the belief of one God stood in need of this inconsiderable advantage, in order to be preached with success.

where

where the King of Poland put a stop to his victories, had been nothing but a series of disgraces.

When the mutinous troops were arrived at the gates of Constantinople, Mahomet sent to demand what they wanted of their Emperor. But, during their march, he had already made a reformation in certain points, which had long excited the murmurs of the public. He had taken off some extraordinary taxes, which the dissipation of his revenues had forced him to lay on ; he had sold his jewels, reduced his stables and hunting-equipages, diminished the expence of his gardens, dismissed from his seraglio a great number of Sultanas, who carried away with them a still greater number of slaves, and broke off his commerce with *Kulogli*, a passion equally condemned by the Alcoran and by nature. This Catamite, who was one of the pages of his music, was dressed in'the same manner with himself, never absent from his side, richer than any Bacha, and had all his wishes anticipated. But the sacrifice which must have cost the Sultan most, was to depose four of his favourites, two of whom had helped to ruin the empire : the only crime of the other two was being unfortunate. The army demanded their heads, and he was forced to send them : they were those of the *Testerdar*, or Treasurer of the empire ; of the *Giurumchi-Bachi*, or Receiver of the revenue of the Demesne-lands ; of the Visir Ibrahim, who had been disgraced two years before ; and of Soliman, his successor. The latter was a formidable instance of the revolutions of human fortune. He had distinguished himself in twenty different engagements ; and was esteemed and beloved, till the time of his being invested with all the authority of his master. His head was brought to the army last of all ; and the mutineers, at the very time when they rejoiced at its being taken off, seemed still to shew it some respect.

Hitherto

Hitherto the army had not ventured within the
limits of Conftantinople; but the Janizaries foon
led the way, crying out in the ftreets that the indolent and unfuccefsful Mahomet ought to be depofed. The *Ulema*, that is to fay, the affembly of
Lawyers and Divines, met in the mofque of St. Sophia, where the Emperor's trial was finifhed in a
few hours. He had had too long a feries of misfortunes not to be charged with all the calamities of
the ftate. On this occafion, he repented that he
had not executed, upon his brothers, the cruel law
of Bajazet ; for news was brought to the feraglio,
that it was intended to fet the crown upon the head
of his brother Soliman. It was then too late to
make away with him ; for the Boftangi-Bachi guarded the apartment of the Princes with an armed
force. The reins of government were taken from
Mahomet, and delivered into the hands of Soliman, who had languifhed in prifon for forty years.
When the Caimacan, the Cherif of the mofque of
St. Sophia, and the Nakib, or keeper of the ftandard of Mahomet, fignified to the Emperor that
he muft quit the throne, and that fuch was the pleafure of the nation, he anfwered ; *The will of God
be done, fince his indignation is deftined to fall upon
my head. Go tell my brother, that the Almighty declares his pleafure by the mouth of the people.* We
fee, by this anfwer, that thefe Sultans, with all their
defpotifm, acknowledge a power in the nation fuperior to their own ; and it is a maxim with the
Lawyers of the Ottoman empire, that this power is
inherent in all the nations of the world.

Mahomet had feveral fons, but they were too
young to reign. The Turks always chufe their
Emperors out of the Ottoman family ; but they do
not think that an infant, a weak, or a wicked Prince,
has a right to reign, becaufe he is defcended in a direct line, or happens to be the firft-born : Sons, bro-

thers,

Y. 1687. thers, or uncles, they chuſe indifferently out of all; and have often made a happy choice. As for what farther relates to Mahomet, having ſpared the lives of his brothers, he died a natural death; and was not taken off by poiſon, as was reported in Conſtantinople (a). The ground of ſuch ſurmiſes is, that the people, in all countries, ſuppoſe the great to commit all the villainies they can: a ſuppoſition not at all to the honour of their own morals.

While the Turks were employing their ſtrength in civil broils, the Duke of Lorrain completed the reduction of Hungary. There was yet remaining a woman of undaunted courage, who defended herſelf to the laſt. Being daughter of the unhappy Serini, widow of Ragotſki, and wife of Tekeli, ſhe had vowed an eternal hatred to the houſe of Auſtria. She held out for two years in Mongatz, a fortreſs where Tekeli had ſhut up his treaſures, his archives, and his children, with a ſtrong garriſon. He himſelf was wandering about in remote provinces, and could give no aſſiſtance to his wife; who being beſieged by famine, partook at laſt in the fate of Hungary; and being carried to Vienna, was reduced to repeat her Roſary in a convent, while her children were taken from her, and put under the tuition of the Jeſuits of Prague. What compleated her grief, was to ſee the Archduke crowned King of Hungary, without an election. The victorious Leopold refuſed to grant the Hungarians any terms but a ſcaffold, which he erected in the town of *Eperies*. The blood of the natives of that kingdom continued to flow from March to December; and the crown of Hungary was declared hereditary by the nobility, in the preſence of the executioners. It is but a melancholy conſideration for the people, that ſo dreadful a method ſhould ſucceed.

(a) Cantemir, tom. ii. p. 134.

One

One fatisfaction was ftill wanting to Leopold; namely, to get Tekeli into his power. The Turks, who had reftored him to liberty, did not give him up; but affigned to him the towns of *Widin*, *Ca-ranfibes*, and *Lugos*, with their territory, which he exchanged for the kingdom of Hungary.

The King of Poland, when he was informed of the horrid tragedy that had been acted in Hungary, repented that he had not fet that crown upon the head of his fon, when the Hungarians, won by his virtues, folicited him to do it, after the battle of Vienna. Being now decaying in his health, he hoped at leaft to tranfmit to him that which he wore himfelf, and refolved to take advantage of the approaching diet, to make the Poles concur in his defign.

End of the SEVENTH BOOK.

THE

THE

HISTORY

OF

JOHN SOBIESKI

KING OF POLAND.

BOOK VIII.

THE diet, which ought to have been affembled at Gródno the preceding year, was now
appointed to meet at that place. The King would
have chofe it rather at Warfaw, where he hoped to
make it turn out more to his advantage ; but the Lithuanians adhered ftrictly to the law ; and Grodno
was fixed upon for the 25th of January. The King
and all his court came there, without delay : Prince
James, who flattered himfelf with the expectation
of acting a diftinguifhed part upon this occafion,
was there before the day appointed. He had lately commanded the army, and taken his feat upon
the throne by his father's fide in 1686. Thefe
were fo many fteps towards royalty ; but there yet
remained one, which was more delicate and more
decifive

decisive than all. He had as yet been seated upon the throne, only in an assembly of the Senate, without the consent of the nation assembled by its representatives: the point now in question was, to ascend it in the most public manner; and the King, who earnestly desired it, lent his hand to help him up. In absolute governments, where the King acts contrary to the law, the grandees are silent, because they have every thing, even their liberty itself, to lose: but in Poland, they speak out, because the Prince can take nothing from them.

The King, however, had no reason to expect the opposition on that quarter from whence it proceeded. He had loaded the Sapieha's with riches, honours, and power; and it was they who thought themselves obliged to prefer the constitution of their country to private gratitude. They called to their assistance the Ministers of the Emperor and the Czar, without forgetting the Nuncio from Rome: a person, whose authority in Poland is a surprize to other nations; being allowed a jurisdiction and a tribunal in a republic, whose haughty spirit is always opposing its Kings.

The union that was formed against the projects of the court gained daily new partisans. The cry was, that the laws were no longer respected; that an attempt was made to impose a King upon the nation, without its consent; whereas it could not, even itself, dispose of the throne, till it should become vacant: and menaces were thrown out of dissolving the diet, and taking vigorous measures to secure the rights of the nation, if Prince James did not immediately leave Lithuania. A hard necessity this for the son of a King, to whom Poland was so much indebted! When the Great are thus obliged to submit to the will of the people, they endeavour, at least, to find out some specious pretext to palliate their weakness. Prince James found himself

strongly

ſtrongly inclined to pay his devotions at a celebrated monaſtery, called the Mount of Pazzi, and to hunt in the neighbourhood of Wilna; and it happened fortunately that his purſuit of the game carried him out of Lithuania.

This act of complaiſance reſtored tranquillity to the diet, and its deliberations were beginning to grow favourable to the court; but the Queen, who was highly piqued at the affront put upon her ſon, was carrying on an intrigue to diſſolve the aſſembly. The agent ſhe made uſe of was *Dombroſki*, a man of a bold front, ſtrong lungs, and turbulent eloquence, who by his clamours, and his *veto*, incapacitated the tribunal of the nation to proceed upon public buſineſs. The Queen's venturing ſo far, was owing to the aſcendant which the King had ſuffered her to aſſume.

The King, who was not in the ſecret, and who intended to take the opinion of the nation upon matters of great importance relating to the approaching campaign, attempted to remedy the evil, by ſummoning all the members of the firſt order of the ſtate, to a Senatorial aſſembly; but the ſpirit of diſcord was gone forth, and diſturbed all his meaſures. The new Cardinal Radziowſki was the firſt rock of offence. He was a Senator by virtue of his Epiſcopal character, and as ſuch, no one diſputed his right to a ſeat in the Senate; but he was alſo a Cardinal, and upon this footing claimed the firſt place. By the laws of Poland, no rank or precedence is allowed to the Roman purple; and for this reaſon, there had hitherto been only three Cardinals in that kingdom; *Oſius*, *Radziwil*, and Prince *Caſimir*, before he came to the crown. The Poles had avoided a rupture with them as well as they could; but the generality of the nation entertained the ſame ſentiments with the Greeks, in the time of the laſt Emperor of Conſtantinople :

We

Y. 1688.

We had rather, said they, *see the turban here, than the Cardinal's hat.* Radziowſki was embarraſſed with his dignity from the very day that he received it, and ſtudiouſly avoided both the court and the Senate; the former, becauſe, according to the maxims of Rome, he muſt have claimed precedence before the royal family; and the latter, becauſe the Biſhops, his brethren, would make him no conceſſions. There was only one event, which could put an end to all difficulties, by uniting the primacy with the purple; and the death of the Archbiſhop of Gneſna fell out in a lucky ſeaſon. By the favour of the King, Radziowſki was advanced to that exalted poſt, and became a ſtriking example of the power of fortune. His mother indeed was a Sobieſki; but when he ſtudied at Paris, he was obliged to live in a manner that ill became his birth. He was now, next to the King, the firſt perſon in the republic; and little imagined, that his right of precedence in the Senate would be diſputed; but the Biſhops made it an objection, that he had not yet received his bulls of inveſtiture from Rome. This new difficulty was the more puzzling, as it was unforeſeen; but after much heat and many debates, the Biſhop of Cracow convinced his brethren, that the Pope's bulls related entirely to ſpiritual functions; and Radziowſki took his ſeat, much to the ſatisfaction of the King, who expected great aſſiſtance from him in the preſent juncture. But the Primate, whoſe conduct was always dark and artful, ſecretly thwarted his deſigns; and beſides, the minds of the members were ſo exaſperated, that he could not have been of much uſe.

Inſtead of deliberating upon the means of continuing the war with greater vigour, or making an advantageous peace; the firſt perſons that ſpoke, dwelt entirely upon the preſumption of Prince James,

Y. 1683. James, the influence of the Queen in public affairs, the suspicious residence of the Marquis de Bethune in Poland, the intrigues of France, the inutility of so many expeditions against the Turks, and the disgrace of leaving Kaminieck any longer in their power. Their complaints, however, were expressed at least in respectful terms: but the Palatine of Siradia, a creature, and even a petitioner of the King's, declaimed against his benefactor in the most outrageous manner, and called him, to his face, an infringer of the laws, an oppressor of the people, and an enemy to his country (a). Examples of this sort are enough to deter men from beneficence; but great minds find a pleasure in furnishing men with opportunities of being ungrateful.

The King had learnt, from his dispute with Paz, in the diet of 1685, that though a subject forgets his duty, a King, who is the image of God, ought to command his temper; and therefore he replied to all these accusations, as if they had not concerned himself. He made a distinction between the language of passion, and what had some appearance of reason. He did not pretend to have been exempt from all faults; and defended himself with that dignity and moderation which confounds the efforts of calumny, and diminishes real faults. The only revenge he took of the violent Palatine, was not doing him the honour to address his discourse to him, but to the nation in general. He had made no preparation for this apology; but having formed an habit of speaking in public, and being thoroughly acquainted with affairs of state, he could at any time dispense with the ceremony of delivering his sentiments by his Chancellor, and speak, as the Poles call it, *ex Throno*.

(a) Zaluski, tom. ii. pages 1059, and 1090.

While

While this paſſed in the Senate, there was handed about, in Grodno, a ſatire againſt the King and the Queen, of ſo ſcandalous a nature, that the memoirs of that time have not tranſmitted it to poſterity. A clergyman alſo, who was preaching upon the ſubject of confeſſion, had the audaciouſneſs to ſay, in the Queen's preſence, that *Kings confeſſed only ſmall ſins, and ſaid nothing of great ; that it was well known, there was a Prince in the world, who thought it no crime to ſell offices of ſtate, and to ſacrifice his country to his blind complaiſance for a wife.* The preacher, whoſe enthuſiaſtic zeal offended even thoſe who agreed with him in opinion, got off for only making a recantation, in the ſame pulpit where the offence was given ; and the libel was condemned to the flames, without any enquiry after the author (a).

In the midſt of this ſcene of diſtraction, the King could not help ſeeing that the Queen alienated from him the affections of many of his ſubjects, and therefore ſent her away ; but without any diminution of his tenderneſs. She ſet out for Warſaw with great reluctance, and full of reſentment againſt thoſe whom ſhe ſuſpected of giving the King this advice.

He himſelf, when he had calmed the minds of the Senators as much as poſſible, propoſed to their conſideration the maintenance of the war, and got a ſubſidy to be aſſigned for that purpoſe, but far ſhort of what was neceſſary. He put an end to the aſſembly of the Senate, by proteſting, that, notwithſtanding the mortifications they had given him, he would not deſert the republic; that the weakneſs of his health ſhould not hinder him from commanding the army ; and that death would be welcome to him, if he left Poland victorious and

(a) Zaluſki, tom. ii., pages 1059 and 1060.

happy.

happy. He muſt needs have been highly offended with the Sapieha's; and yet he honoured with his preſence the funeral of one of the brothers, who was Maſter of the Horſe of Lithuania. The Poles diſplay as much magnificence in their funerals as in their diets. The expence the Sapieha's were at in mere pageantry, and in purchaſing prayers for the ſoul of the deceaſed, would have ſupplied the numerous retinue of gentlemen in their brother's ſervice, with bread. The ceremony and the ſorrow ended together with a great entertainment, where all the company got drunk, according to eſtabliſhed cuſtom.

At the ſame time, a ſcene of a more joyful ſort was preparing for the King at Wilna, the capital of Lithuania; a city, which, having never ſeen its ſovereign, was impatient to pay him its homage. The people took no part in theſe quarrels of ſtate; they were attentive only to the glory, and the benevolent diſpoſition of their ſovereign; and left it to the grandees to criticize his faults. He was received upon the road, and in that great city, with thoſe acclamations, and ſigns of joy which are never extorted from a free people againſt their will.

From Wilna he repaired to Warſaw, where the Queen was impatient to ſee him, as much for the pleaſure of ſharing with him in the government, as for the love ſhe bore him. She prevailed upon him to ſubmit to a courſe of phyſic, before he took up arms; and to concert meaſures for marrying Prince James to a widow, whoſe immenſe poſſeſſions were coveted all over Europe. This widow was the heireſs of the houſe of Radziwil, the ſame that Prince James would have married once before, in the year 1680, and whom he loſt by means of the Elector of Brandenburg, who procured her for his ſon, Prince Lewis. The young huſband

did

did not long enjoy his acquisition; and the court of Poland negotiated at Berlin to get possession of the widow, with greater hopes of success than ever. The treaty was already far advanced, and the Polish Envoy sent word, that Prince James's presence was necessary to ensure success. The Prince flew to Berlin, entered the town incognito, and had a conference with the French Minister, who was ordered by his master to promote the match, with a view to take off King John from the interests of the house of Austria. He had a private interview with the young widow, and got from her a formal promise to marry him in eight months, (by which time her mourning would be out,) upon pain of forfeiting all her fortune. The marriage-presents were given and received on each side, and the Prince set out for Warsaw, perfectly satisfied with his success. In consequence of this match, he would be in possession of four duchies in the heart of Poland, acquire great personal weight, and be a considerable step nearer to the throne.

The news of the Prince's success was received with great joy by the court of Warsaw, and particularly by the King, who loved his son tenderly, and stood in great need of laying his heart open to the impressions of joy. But it was only a transitory gleam, which was soon followed by grief. While Prince James was returning home with his promise, a more fortunate rival actually married the Lady at Berlin. The Husband was Prince Charles of Newburg, third son to the Elector Palatine, and brother to the Empress. The Elector of Brandenburg, to whom Leopold held out the alluring object of a regal crown, favoured this act of treachery, if the ill offices which the maxims of politics have sanctified in the morality of sovereigns, can be called by that name. It was still the Emperor

E e   Leopold

Leopold who thwarted all the views of his ally, the King of Poland.

This mortifying blow was received by the court of Poland with all the transports of grief and revenge.. While the surprize was yet recent, the Marquis of Arquien, who had quitted France without losing the vivacity of a Frenchman, proposed sending the insulted Prince to Hamburg, with his uncle the Count de Maligny, and a third champion, to challenge the successful rival. The Prince relished this expedient : but the King considering, that, if his son should fall, it would be a greater loss than he had already sustained, and that in case of his being victorious, it was very uncertain whether the Princess would marry the murderer of her husband, prevented its being put in execution. If John had been master of a force equal to that of Leopold or Lewis XIV. he would not have been affronted with impunity in the person of his son. As things were, he submitted to the only expedient he had left, and acted as his weakness, and indeed reason itself, required.. He consulted the Polish Lawyers concerning the promise given by the faithless Princess, and the penalty to which she had subjected herself. They were of opinion that the King had a right to confiscate all her estates ; but such a sentence could be pronounced only by the tribunal of the nation assembled in a general diet ; and the nation was, at this juncture, wholly intent upon war. The negotiation of Berlin, and the weak state of the King's health, put off, till the month of August, the opening of the campaign, which was attended with no success.

The King could not quit his designs upon the two crowns of Moldavia and Walachia, which he hoped to leave to his family, if that of Poland should pass into other hands. He was so much taken up with this great object as to forget Kaminieck ;

minieck ; and therefore the Poles continued their murmurs. They marched, however, under, his ſtandards, induced more by the reſpect which is due to heroic qualities, than by a conviction that it was for the intereſt of their country. He led the army, as in 1686, through Pokruſia and the Bucovine. When he came to Pererita, where he had left troops and workmen, he ſaw the ruins of that deſerted town, changed into houſes, the neighbouring villages repeopled, and the lands cultivated: and this was the only ſatisfaction he enjoyed in the whole expedition. He haſted to croſs the Pruth, in order to make ſure of Walachia, from which he had hitherto received nothing but vague expreſſions of ſubmiſſion, extorted by fear only. Though he had as yet neither eſtabliſhed poſts, nor quartered troops in that country, as he had done in part of Moldavia, he looked upon it as an eaſy conqueſt.

But an event, quite contrary to the long drought which had ſo much incommoded his army in 1686, threw him into ſtill greater difficulties. There fell ſo violent and continual a rain, that in a few days the brooks were changed into torrents, the ſtreams into rivers, and the whole country into a vaſt ſlough. The army, however, crawled on as as far as the river *Chocava*, which they paſſed with incredible difficulty. But when they came to the *Seret*, it was impoſſible to attempt to paſs it. They wandered about upon its banks, changing the ſituation of the camp every day, in order to avoid ſinking in the mire, and to divert the ſoldiers from attending too much to the hardſhips they ſuffered. Six weeks were thus loſt by means of the inundation ; and there appeared no hopes of its ceaſing. The Turks and the Tartars ſaid, that heaven undertook their defence, and they never made their appearance. The army, being defeated by the elements,

ments,

Y. 1688. ments, marched back towards Poland, having loft a greater number of horfes, and more baggage, than if it had met the enemy. The heavy artillery was buried in the Bucovine, in order to be dug up again at a convenient feafon.

But it was not in Poland only that the Chriftian arms were unfortunate : the fame want of fuccefs attended them in other parts. The Mufcovites had refumed their defign upon the Crim ; and *Galliczin*, who had failed in his former attempt, again commanded the expedition. Precop was befieged by an army of two hundred thoufand men, who attacked it with fourteen hundred pieces of cannon. The Tartars gave all up for loft, but the Cham did not defpair. The brave *Selim-Gerai*, whom the Turks had depofed after the battle of Vienna, was reftored to his throne, out of refpect to his fuperior abilities. He amufed the Ruffian General, by propofing an accommodation, as a means to prevent the effufion of blood ; and difputed the terms like one refolved to furrender, and aiming only to alleviate the weight of his ill fortune. While the conferences were carrying on, (an interval often fatal to the ftrongeft party) the Cham was daily growing ftronger from behind, and Galliczin weaker by confuming his provifions ; nor did he perceive the fnare that was laid for him, till it was neceffary to decamp in fearch of food ; and as he retreated, the Cham cut in pieces his rear-guard. Thus the Tartars were faved by the addrefs and courage of their chief, without humbling the fpirit of the Mufcovites : for Galliczin had no fooner regained the banks of the Samara, after a march of three weeks, than he difpatched couriers to Mofcow and Warfaw, with advices that he had beat the Tartars, and purfued them beyond Precop. The two capitals made public rejoicings, when they ought to have put on mourning ; and the General,

neral, before he returned home, received compliments from the Regent, and ample rewards for his army; a practice common enough in the Ruffian empire, except in the reign of Peter the Great.

The Venetians laid fiege to Negropont, anciently called Chalcis, in Euboea. This Ifland, the fineft in all the Archipelago, was taken from them by the irrefiftible Mahomet II. Morofini was animated by the recollection of the calamities that his countrymen fuffered at the time of this lofs : his imagination was full of the ideas of the brave Erizzo fawed in two, his daughter ftabbed in defending her virtue, and all the inhabitants, of both fexes, above the age of twenty, devoted to death. He hoped to avenge fo much barbarity and murder, and to reftore to his country a part of its ancient dominions. His efforts were amazingly great; but the refiftance of the Turks was ftill greater; and his attempt mifcarried.

Of all the powers engaged in this war, none had any fuccefs but the Emperor Leopold, who, without ftirring from his cabinet, purfued the Turks from one lofs to another. The new Sultan, Soliman III. was no formidable enemy. He had been forty years in prifon, ftudying the Alcoran, and was unrivalled in the practice of religious exercifes. The zealots efteemed him much; the Divan little; and the foldiery not at all. He had the merit, however, of knowing his own weaknefs; and therefore made Leopold the moft advantageous offers by his Ambaffador *Mauro Cordato*, a phyfician of Padua, whofe firft maxim in negotiation, was that faying of the Poet *Saadi*; that *a lie which gains the point, is better than truth which miffes it.* But his maxim, if he made ufe of it upon this occafion, did not fucceed; for Leopold rejected all the offers he made with his ufual haughtinefs, which was ftill encreafed by profperity.

rity. He was no greater a warrior than Soliman; but with a profound skill in politics, and great firmness of mind, he found Generals in all the Princes of Europe. He now transferred his favour from the Duke of Lorrain to the young Elector of Bavaria, whom he had lately made his son-in-law, and entrusted him with the command of the army, and the siege of the important town of Belgrade, which was taken by storm before the Visir's face.

Leopold was just upon the point of driving the Turks out of Europe; but he undertook too much at once, by entering into the famous league of Augsburg against Lewis XIV. which divided his attention and his forces. This new league placed Innocent XI. in a very singular situation: for he gave his benediction equally to the attack that was made upon the Turks, and that which was preparing to be made upon the Most Christian King. His fortune was such as must needs have astonished himself: he was the son of a banker of Milan, and came to be able to assist the empire of Poland against the Turks with his money, and the Venetians with his gallies. He was insulted indeed in Rome itself by Lewis XIV. but it was not till after he had first had the courage to affront him.

The King of France, on his side, laboured more than ever, to break the connection between the Emperor and the King of Poland, while the latter imagined he had a reason for adhering to it with more firmness than before. The taking of Belgrade had given the alarm to Walachia, and induced it to put itself under the protection of the Emperor; and John hoped that the Emperor would give it up to him, according to a secret treaty between them. By this event, the object of his late unsuccessful campaign would be happily obtained:

tained : but the Emperor only held out Wala- Y. 1688.
chia to his view, without any defign of giving it.

The King of Poland, in his prefent fituation, cannot but excite compaffion, as a Prince, who, with great qualities and little power, is made the fport of a fuperior potentate. He was deftined to be fo in more ways than one, as he experienced in the diet, of which I come now to give an account.

The kingdom grew weary of a ruinous league, Y. 1689. of which Vienna reaped all the profit ; and was inclined to make a feparate peace with the Turks. An Envoy from the Cham of Tartary came to offer that Prince's mediation, with very advantageous conditions. The Emperor was highly averfe to this feparate treaty; and the King did not much relifh it, for the reafons above mentioned. But Leopold apprehended that the republic would get the better of its Sovereign.

Another point which was to be difcuffed in the diet, gave him alfo fome concern, and this was the propofed confifcation of the Princefs of Newburg's vaft eftate to Prince James's ufe. He was difpleafed to think that his brother in-law, the Prince of Newburg, fhould marry the heirefs of the houfe of Radziwil, and be deprived of all her fortune.

To avoid thefe inconveniences, there was only one method to be taken, which was to get the diet diffolved, as foon as it thwarted his views ; and this method he took. He prevailed upon the Elector of Brandenburg, whofe bufinefs it was to court him in order to be made a King, and whofe money made him powerful at Warfaw, to enter into his fcheme. He gained over to his intereft the Sapieha's, who had great influence in the Senate, and the Equeftrian order ; and when things were thus fet in order, the diet was opened.

E e 4

The

Y. 1689.   The debates turned at firſt upon Prince James's
claim.   The lawyers had given it as their opinion,
that the Princeſs's fortune was forfeited to him,
by her having broke her promiſe; and that the penalty was juſtly incurred, becauſe ſhe had ſubjected
herſelf to it by a voluntary act.   In reply to theſe
arguments, the contrary party offered reaſons, which
at leaſt made the point doubtful.   There were others,
who, affecting to ſtand neuter, (though this was
far from their intention) cried out, that it was not
a time to mind the intereſts of the royal family,
when the republic had ſuch important buſineſs of
her own to attend to.   The proper queſtion to
be debated, was, *Whether they ſhou'd accept the ſe-
parate peace that was offered them by the Turks, or
continue the war with redoubled vigour?* Some were
eager for peace, and others as earneſt for war.
The King himſelf agreed in opinion with theſe laſt:
but the attention of the aſſembly was taken off from
this ſubject by the diſcuſſion of another point that
was ſtarted.   He was reproached with the treaty
made in 1686, with Muſcovy, by which he ceded
to that crown two cities, a Palatinate and a duchy.
This exchange of certain poſſeſſions in lieu of uncertain advantages, had been made with the conſent of the Senate only: and it being neceſſary that
the diet ſhould ratify it, it was now debated, whether it ought do ſo, againſt the public intereſt *(a)*.

This objection to the King's conduct was ſoon
ſucceeded by another.   The Queen was always ſuppoſed to have put him upon every meaſure that
was diſagreeable to the republic: and Raphael Leſc-
zinſki, Palatine of Poſnania, a man reſpectable for
his own merit *(b)*, and ſtill more ſo for being
the

(a) Zaluſki, tom. ii. p. 1135.
(b) His perſonal abilities, ſupported by the ſplendor of his
birth, raiſed him to the higheſt offices of the republic. He
was

the father of a Prince who has been long regretted by Poland, and is now adored by Lorrain, was not afraid to difpleafe the court in order to ferve his country. He knew that the Queen was caballing bufily, in order to bring on again, before the diet, the confifcation of the Princefs of Newburg's fortune, which was a queftion productive of nothing but confufion. He therefore aimed his difcourfe againft her, and faid nothing of the King. " She was exalted, he faid, above the reft " of her fex in fpirit and abilities; but a mere " woman in intrigue and artifice. Of what ufe " added he, is fuperior fenfe, if it be employed " only to foment difcord among all the orders of " the ftate? She complains frequently of the bad- " nefs of her health; we commiferate her cafe; but " fhe is indebted for it to her too great applica- " tion to affairs of ftate, which the public will " readily excufe her, for not meddling with at all." The Queen had lately loft a female confident, whofe death gave great joy to the city, and even to the court. The Palatine was very fevere upon her memory, and took occafion to make it a frefh matter of objection to the Queen (a). It would have been much lefs dangerous to offend the King than the Queen, who declared openly that fhe dif- liked all fpeakers of truth; but in Poland the laws protect the fubjects from the indignation of their fovereign.

In this manner, the feffions of the diet paffed away in quick tranfitions from one fubject to an- other, without coming to any decifion. Thefe

was Marfhal of the diet that made the league againft the Turks, in 1683, Ambaffador at Conftantinople, Grand-Trea- furer, and General of Great Poland. He married a daughter of the Grand-General Jablonowfki, by whom he was the fa- ther of King Staniflas.

(a) Zalufki, tom. ii. p. 1104, and 1147.

Y. 1689. public diffentions were the occafion alfo of private quarrels. Count Vielpolfki challenged the Standard-Bearer of Cracow, who refufed to fight, not for want of courage, or out of refpect for the laws of God or man ; but becaufe it happened to be Saturday, a day which is held peculiarly facred in the fyftem of Polifh devotion.

In the mean time, the diet continued fitting, but without any regular difpatch of bufinefs. They had refufed to hear the King upon the fubject of his family-concerns : and he and all the orders of the ftate were now obliged to lend an ear to a private quarrel between two Bifhops. Cafimir Opalinfki, Bifhop of Culm, who was one of them, made a long and abfurd harangue; and pretending that the King was prejudiced againft his caufe, addreffed him in thefe words ; *either ceafe to reign at all, or reign with juftice.* All his brethren, and particularly the Cardinal Primate, expreffed immediately their difapprobation of his behaviour. Maczinfki, Palatine of Beltz, confounding the innocent with the guilty, cried out, that all the Bifhops ought to be expelled the Senate, and fent to Rome. One of them anfwered, " We were Polifh noblemen " before we were Bifhops : in the former capacity, " we are as effentially connected with Poland as you : " in the latter, we are your paftors, which gives us " a new title to refpect." The quarrel quickly grew warm, and would have proceeded to great extremities, if the King, forgetting for a moment the affront put upon himfelf, had not interpofed and ftopped it. But the faying of the Bifhop of Culm was ftill a load upon his mind. He required that the Prelate fhould publickly retract it, and afk pardon, declaring that it was owing to a fudden ftart of paffion, and thrown out without reflection. Some of the Senators had prevailed upon the Bifhop to give the King this fatisfaction, but many more diffuaded him.

him. The ingratitude of many had a greater effect upon John than the insolence of one, and he talked of abdicating the throne, as there was little pleasure in governing a people by whom he was not beloved (a), But this thought, which derived its origin from his present chagrin, soon vanished; and the Bishop of Posnania, to suspend these frequent skirmishes, laid before the assembly a treaty of commerce proposed by the Dutch; which much for the interest of Poland, as it would have occasioned a great exportation of grain, which is one of the most considerable advantages that can happen to a corn-country. It has lately been made appear, before the Parliament of England, that in four years time, this article alone brought into the kingdom a hundred and seventy millions, three hundred and thirty thousand French livres. It is true that Poland has no marine; but the Dutch made an offer of theirs. The Bishop of Posnania laid before them all these circumstances; but their minds were in such a ferment, that they instantly hurried away to other matters.

The only thing that seemed to fix their attention, was the trial of Lysinski, a nobleman of Lithuania. He had been educated among the Jesuits, and led a studious retired life, distinguished only by acts of beneficence and humanity. His love of religious truth had tempted him to ridicule some of the Polish superstitions. He might perhaps have been forgiven this fault, if he had not been possessed of a considerable fortune, which, by the laws of Poland, was to be divided between the informer and the exchequer. He was accused of atheism by one Brzoska, a man in public office. The strongest proof that could be produced was a note writ by Lysinski in a book upon the existence of

_(a)_ Zaluski, tom. ii. p. 1105.

God.

V. 1689. God.   The author of the book was a German,
who, with the beſt intention in the world, of proving a truth which never wanted to be proved, did
in fact ſubvert it.   Lyſinſki, obſerving that the
reaſoning was falſe, writ in the margin, *ergo non
eſt Deus*, therefore there is no God.   The Poliſh
Biſhops, ſince the Primate's promotion to a Car-
dinalſhip, had acquired a reliſh for that dignity.
The Biſhop of Poſnania had long been ſeeking an
opportunity to gain the good graces of the court
of Rome ; and fancying that he had now found it,
undertook to ſupport the accuſation, and contrived
to make the whole aſſembly, and particularly the
bench of Biſhops, enter warmly into the cauſe.
The conſequence was, that Lyſinſki, after under-
going the diſcipline of the whip from the hands of
a Biſhop, and being protected, by abſolution, from
puniſhment in the other world, was burnt in this.
The ſentence of condemnation was expreſſed in
very ſingular terms; that the blaſphemer had not
only denied the exiſtence of God, but the doctrine
of the Trinity, and the divine maternity of the
Virgin Mary *(a)*.   There were few centuries that
had not produced inſtances of noblemen's being
guilty of riots, rapes, aſſaſſinations, and burning
of houſes ; but as the laws of Poland do not ſuffer a nobleman to be arreſted before he is condemned, the criminals had always had time to eſcape the puniſhment.   Upon the preſent occaſion,
the law was violated, and Lyſinſki arreſted as ſoon
as accuſed.   When the form of the proceeding was
known at Rome, that court diſapproved ſo inhu-
man a ſentence ; and the King reproached himſelf
more than once, for not having checked this furious
eruption of zeal.

(b) Zaluſki, tom. ii. p. 1120.

The

The diet had now been assembled three months, without dispatching any business but this; and no sooner were the affairs of the republic, or the royal family, brought again upon the carpet, than the Imperial faction spirited up the Deputy Sulkowski to protest and leave the assembly. The diet met again the next day, and sent repeated deputations to Sulkowski, to persuade him to return. The King himself sent after him to the house of Sapieha, Grand-General of Lithuania, where it was known that he had passed the night; but Sapieha coldly replied, that he was not Sulkowski's keeper. When this answer was brought to the diet, it gave the King, and all who loved their country, great concern: even the Grand-Treasurer of Lithuania, brother to the Grand-General, seemed affected, and made as if he would remedy the evil. He rose from his chair, and went out, saying that he would not return without bringing Sulkowski with him, and re-instating the diet in its privileges. The assembly began to entertain some hopes, but they were soon totally extinguished, by the Grand-Treasurer's not appearing any more. The Castellan of Samogitia made a last effort, by conjuring, in the name of their country, Dambrowski, a Deputy of great interest, to restore the powers of the diet, by prevailing upon his collegue and friend, Sulkowski, to return. *In the name of your country!* answered the Tribune: *say rather in the name of the King: you mind nothing but him.* These words, which were made more offensive by the manner in which they were spoke, were an affront to the whole Senatorian Order in the person of the Castellan; and the Bishop of Wilna thought himself obliged to avenge the insult, by reprimanding the Deputy in very haughty and severe terms. But Dambrowski treated the Bishop with greater roughness than he had done the Castellan; he even lifted up his hand

to

to ftrike him, and by this facrilegious gefture deprived Warfaw of the benefit of hearing mafs for three days; for the Primate laid all the churches under an interdict; and the calamity would have continued longer, if the fiery deputy had not made his fubmiffion to the offended Bifhop. Upon this, the churches were opened again, but the diet was clofed; and the members carried with them to their refpective Provinces the animofity of the contending factions. The next day, the King received a billet which the Elector of Brandenburg's Minifter had dropped. The fubftance of it was, that the Sapieha's had acted their part well, and deferved the promifed reward (a).

If we reflect upon the fpirit of difcord that agitated the nation in this diet, the condition of mankind will feem much to be pitied. Place them under the abfolute government of a fingle perfon, and they are perpetually complaining of the weight of their yoke. Leave them in the enjoyment of liberty, and they know not how to ufe it for their own good.

The diet having come to no refolution about peace or war, and the negotiations with the Turks being infenfibly dropped, the war was continued by virtue of the treaty of alliance, but in a very feeble manner. The army was not commanded by the King, but by Jablonowfki, the hero who was beft able to fupply his place: but the troops were few in number, and ill paid. As he could attempt nothing by open force, he laid a fcheme to furprize Kaminieck. His meafures were well formed; but the Turks, who were attentive to the leaft motion of their enemies, rendered them abortive.

The fucceffes of the league were always appropriated to the fortunate Leopold. But the maxim

(a) Zalufki, tom. ii. p. 1131.

2   of

of ancient Rome, that the beſt time of making up matters with an enemy is after a victory, was not the rule of his conduct. The Turks came to ſue for peace at Vienna, as well as at Warſaw; but he rejected their propoſals. Europe abounded at that time with Generals, particularly France and the Empire. Prince Lewis of Baden carried the Imperial ſtandards into Servia and Bulgaria, where, after having defeated the Turks in three engagements, he took from them the important towns of Niſſa and Widin.

The Infidels had the good fortune to eſcape being moleſted this year by the Venetians. Moroſini was preparing to attack them, but was prevented by a long fit of illneſs; and the republic, which had lately elected him Doge, would truſt the command of its forces with him only. The abilities of the new Prince were equally great in the army and in the ſenate; nor did he at all fear the menace which had been made to one of his predeceſſors, by Mahomet II. who having puſhed his conqueſts to the very gates of Venice, and hearing of the ceremony of the Doge's eſpouſing the Adriatic Sea, ſaid, *that he would ſoon ſend him to the bottom of the ſea to conſummate his marriage:* Moroſini, though enfeebled by ſickneſs, was ſtill dreaded by the Turks.

The Muſcovites were too much agitated with inteſtine commotions (of which the Regent and Galliczin were the authors and the victims) to march out of their own country, and therefore gave no aſſiſtance to the league. This circumſtance was a freſh mortification to the King of Poland, who was expoſed to everlaſting incurſions from the Tartars. A calamity of a heavier nature conſpired alſo to increaſe his affliction; one of the ten miraculous plagues, which deſolated Egypt in the days of Moſes, being renewed in Poland. The whole country was covered, a foot thick, with clouds of locuſts
that

that were brought by the wind from Afia. Their colour was a deep black, and their fize fuch as caufed aftonifhment at Paris, and in other parts of Europe, where they were fent in boxes as objects of curiofity, while Poland was devoured by them. The grafs, corn, fruit, and even the bark of the trees was eat up by thefe voracious infects, which continued plundering for two months from their arrival, till they were killed by the coming on of the froft. Their carcafes made fome amends, though but fmall, by manuring the ground againft the fucceeding year, which proved to be very fruitful.

The prefent year begun and ended in forrow; but the King had a larger fhare of it than his fubjects. A diet in which all his views proved abortive; the mifcarriage of his attempt upon Kaminieck; the dearth that defolated the kingdom; the jealoufies of oppofite factions; the diffenfions that reigned among all the orders of the ftate; all thefe circumftances filled his mind with melancholy. His own fufpicions greatly added to the weight, and pufhed him on to an act of power, which in other countries would have paffed for an undoubted right of the crown. The Grand-Chancellor, Wielopolfki was lately dead, after many fecret conferences with a faction that oppofed the court. A rumour had got abroad that the Sapieha's were contriving to dethrone their benefactor; and that the Primate Radziowfki was an accomplice in the fcheme, as well as Wielopolfki, though both related to the King. It was not faid upon whofe head they defigned to fet the crown; but the perfons, who value themfelves upon prying into every thing, were pofitive that the Sapieha's did not intend to let it go out of their own family. There was already fomething royal in the ftate they affumed; having always a numerous guard, and a retinue that filled
the

the largest ftreets in the city. Even of the perfons, who did not fuppofe them to be either ambitious or ungrateful enough to aim at the crown of Poland, there were few who did not believe that they intended to feparate from it the Grand Duchy of Lithuania, which they already governed with almoft fovereign authority.

The King depended upon unravelling the myftery, by means of the papers which the Chancellor left behind him; and fent Prince Czartorifki to fearch them. The widow refufed to admit him into her palace, and invoked the affiftance of the laws and the grandees of the ftate. The Palatine of Siradia writ and fpoke in her defence; the number of opponents encreafed daily; and the King, being ftopped by the public clamour, got nothing but hatred by his attempt. If he had fucceeded in getting poffeffion of the papers, he would have difcovered nothing, becaufe the Chancellor, finding himfelf near his end, had burnt all that could betray the fecret.

After all, whether the confpiracy was real, is a point about which the memoirs of that time differ greatly: and an hiftorian is bound to relate precifely what he knows, inftead of conjecturing what he knows not. However this be, as every particular order is confidered in Poland as an inftrument of tyranny, the King was accufed of aiming at abfolute power. Some indications of this paffion had indeed efcaped him; but if he was ferioufly bent upon it, is it credible that he would have called together the diet fo often? He could not be ignorant, that when a nation is affembled, it is always fuperior to its chief. But he preferred the interefts of the republic before his own authority; for there was no reign in which the nation was fo frequently affembled, not only in the ordinary *Comitia*, which return every two years, but alfo upon extraordinary occafions, when the law does not require it. This was the cafe in the pre-

F f

fent year, in which a diet was opened on the 18th of January.

The principal fubject of its deliberations was the feparate peace which the Turks ftill continued to offer to Poland : " Reflect, faid they, who were for " it, to the King, upon your fruitlefs efforts againft " Kaminieck, upon your ruinous expeditions into " Moldavia, upon the impoffibility of raifing frefh " fupplies, upon the feven years war which has ex- " haufted Poland, in order to exalt the houfe of " Auftria. Alliances, after all, are binding only " to a certain degree ; and it would be madnefs to " imitate the Saguntines who facrificed themfelves " to their friendfhip for the Romans. The Em- " peror himfelf violates his engagements to the " league, by furnifhing it with fewer troops, fince " he has taken up arms againft France : nor is it " our fault, if he will make peace, neither when he " conquers, nor when he is conquered. Let him " therefore carry on the war with his own forces, or " furnifh us with the means of continuing it *(a)*".

The kingdom of Poland was actually unable to pay its troops. Innocent XI. was dead ; and it was uncertain, whether his fucceffor Alexander VIII. would follow his example in employing the revenues of the church to humble the Ottoman power.

The King, who felt the force of thefe reafons for making peace, was in a very perplexing fituation ; but the Emperor kept him fteady to the league, by giving him great hopes, which might perhaps be fulfilled in the end. The French faction, which talked of nothing but peace, and was encreafing every moment, feemed likely to get it refolved on. This faction was fecretly animated by three French-men ; the Marquis de Bethune, the Abbe de Gra-

(a) Zalufki, tom. ii. p. 1187,

vel,

2

vel, and Caillet de Teil, a Counſellor of the parliament.

The houſe of deputies, being gained over by
Leopold and John, was for war ; and exclaimed
violently againſt the three French Miniſters, but
particulary againſt Gravel. Though he had already
been deſired to leave the kingdom, he reſolved to
ſtay there. The republic ſent him an order to depart,
which he paid no regard to. The King ſignified to
him, by the Grand-Treaſurer, that if he did not
go, he ſhould be tried for his diſobedience ; but he
eluded the menace by taking refuge in a religious
houſe. The diet ſuppoſing him gone, reſumed its
deliberations, and conſented at laſt to the continuation of the war *(a)*. It ſeldom happens that the
nation aſſembles, without giving birth to ſome new
conſtitution. The *Beds of Juſtice (b)* in Poland
have no relation to public affairs. It was ordered,
that, in every diet, the King ſhould, on certain
days, aſſume the office of Judge, and try private
cauſes, by the ſtrict letter of the law. Such are
the *Beds of Juſtice*, or, according to the Poliſh ex-
preſſion, the *comitial judgments* in that kingdom.
Before the time of Stephen Battori, when fixed tribunals were eſtabliſhed, the Kings of Poland travelled into every province to diſtribute juſtice to their
ſubjects. Henry de Valois ſoon grew tired of this
cuſtom : *Upon my ſoul*, ſays he, *theſe Poles have already made me a Judge and a Counſellor: I ſuppoſe
that they will ſoon be for having me plead at the bar.*
He had forgot that the firſt Kings the world ever
ſaw were Judges.

It is uſual to end the diet with a *farewell-baran-
gue* to the King, which is always more or leſs filled
with hyperbole. The great qualities which the

(a) Zaluſki, tom. ii. p. 1162 and 1163.
(b) A *Bed of Juſtice* in France, is when the King comes to
the parliament, and takes his ſeat upon the throne. *Richelet.*

King

King was really poſſeſſed of, ſaved the orator many
a lie ; but he advanced ſeveral falſhoods with regard
to the preſent tranquility of the republic, which he
attributed the honour of to the King. Inſtead of
tranquillity, the factions ran as high as ever ; and
even before the diet broke up, the army entered into a confederacy, and declared to the Generals that
it would not march, till more than twenty millions,
that were in arrear for pay, were diſcharged. The
republic thought herſelf happy, that the ſoldiers
were ſo moderate in the fury of their revolt, as not
to threaten military execution (a).

   This confederacy, occaſioned by want of money,
which is a common evil in a ſtate that has no
commerce, put an end to the whole plan of the
campaign. It was thought ſufficient to keep the
troops upon the frontier, in order to hinder the incurſions of the Tartars, whoſe ravages, however,
were not entirely prevented by this means. They
advanced to the very gates of Lublin, in little Poland ; and had it not been for a ſpy, the King himſelf had been in danger of being taken priſoner (b).
Theſe repeated incurſions were the ſad effects of the
preſent critical ſituation. When troops are ill paid,
and ill clothed, they forget their valour and their
duty. The officers, convinced of the juſtice of
their complaints, were afraid to exert their authority,
and made uſe of perſuaſion only. The Biſhops too
interpoſed, in quality of Senators ; and Olſowſki,
Biſhop of Culm, choſe for the ſubject of his diſcourſe the diſcontent that prevailed in the nation
againſt the Muſcovites ; who, as members of the
league, were obliged to act againſt the common
enemy, when Poland could not ; and yet their ſwords
continued in the ſcabbard. Olſowſki therefore
addreſſed the army, in the ſame terms, that Marius

(a) Zaluſki, tom. ii. p. 118.   (b) Ibid. p. 1167.

did

did his foldiers when they wanted water: *There is* water in the enemy's camp, and you are Romans. " There is money among the Mufcovites, and you are Poles". But this fally of the Bifhop's eloquence did not, nor was it likely that it fhould, produce any effect. Marius was encamped clofe to the enemy: but the Poles were at a great diftance from the Mufcovites, and neither marching againft them, nor againft the Turks.

What kept the Mufcovites unactive, was the report of this feparate peace which was upon the carpet in Poland; and made them afraid of being left as a prey to the Turks and Tartars. The young Czar Peter, who was at this time alone upon a throne which his elder brother did not deferve to fhare, knew that a Chiaoux *(a)* from the Grand-Seignior, and an Envoy from Tartary were at Warfaw; where one of the grandees of his court, was appointed to watch the motions of the republic.

From the time of its firft origin, in 1683. the Chriftian league had never acted with fo little vigour. The Poles, for want of money, did nothing: the Mufcovites, out of policy, kept at home: the Venetians made fome efforts in the Archipelago, but they were too feeble to be much dreaded: Morofini, whofe prefence at Venice was more neceffary than ever, fince his being elected Doge, no longer led the way to victory: and the empire was obliged to make head againft Lewis XIV.

The Turks, being lefs preffed on all fides, and animated by France, to the great fcandal of Rome and the league, took the field very early. They were commanded by *Muftapha Cuprogli*, fon and grandfon of a Grand-Vifir, and lately advanced himfelf to that high office: he breathed nothing but

(a) An officer of the Porte, whofe rank is equal to that of an Ufher, or Exempt of the guards in France. Such are the Ambaffadors which the Grand-Seignior fends to other Princes.

war,

Y. 1690. war, and loudly condemned all proposals of peace.
He begun his miniftry with reforming the abuses
which had been introduced by a bad adminiftration
of feven years, and with reftoring order in the
finances.   At the opening of the campaign, religion
and good morals equally employed his attention.
The mofques of Conftantinople and the pavilions of
the camp all refounded with prayers : and a crowd
of boys who followed the army, and were at once
the occafion of infamous debauchery and unbounded
expence, were fent away, and forbid to appear again,
upon pain of death.   All that now remained was
to revive the courage of the troops, and the Vifir
undertook this office, by pointing out to them the
road to victory with the fabre of his father Cuprogli (a).

The Duke of Lorrain, who of all the Emperor's
Generals, fince Montecuculi, had fhewn the greateft
talents, had lately ended his days.   He had gained
indeed great glory, but lived without dominions :
he flattered himfelf with the hopes of recovering
them, in 1676, at the head of fixty thoufand men;
and the motto upon his ftandards was, *Aut nunc,
aut nunquam, Now or never*; but the latter part of
the alternative was his fate.   He was more fortunate
in acting for the houfe of Auftria, whofe territories he
defended, without recovering his own; a circumftance which he regretted even at his death, and expreffed in the following letter to Leopold.   " In
" obedience to your Sacred Majefty's commands, I
" left Infpruck to come to Vienna; but I am ftop-
" ped here by the will of a fuperior Mafter, to
" whom I muft give an account of a life which I
" have entirely dedicated to your fervice.   Remem-
" ber that I leave behind me a wife to whom you
" are nearly related, children who inherit nothing

(d) Cantemir, tom. ii. p. 182.

                                          " from

" from me but my fword, and fubjects who groan
" under oppreffion." The Emperor was convinced in this very campaign, how difficult it was to
fupply the place of the General whofe death he lamented.

The Vifir Cuprogli, after gaining a complete
victory over the Imperialifts, raifed the blockade of
three places in upper Hungary, took four in lower
Hungary, reduced Albania and Bulgaria, recovered all Servia, and even Belgrade itfelf, in fpite of a
garrifon of fix thoufand men, who were all put to
the fword; and while the torrent was rolling on, fo
as even to threaten Vienna, Tekeli, who was ftill
fupported by the Porte, beat General *Heufler*, and
got himfelf declared Prince of Tranfylvania, after
the death of Michael Abaffi.

The approach of winter gave time to the Princes
of the Chriftian league, to form new plans and recover their ftrength. The King of Poland was ftill
hefitating between Leopold and Lewis XIV. His
reputation in Europe was as great as theirs, but
his power much lefs, and therefore he endeavoured
to keep terms with them both. His inclinations
were for France; but his intereft again determined
him to fide with the houfe of Auftria. France indeed did not fail to make him tempting offers; but
the houfe of Auftria, by being fo near his dominions, was in a condition to fulfill the promifes it
gave, whenever it was difpofed to keep its word.
The King, at this very juncture, had a family-concern to fettle with that court. He wanted to marry
his fon, Prince James; and there was no fit match
for him in Poland, fince that kingdom had loft its
richeft heirefs. France indeed might have offered a
Princefs of the blood; but it was refolved to have
the daughter of a Sovereign: and Leopold, who
at that time difpofed of the empire and all its Princes,
propofed a daughter of the Elector Palatine. She

was

Y. 1691. was fifter to that very Charles of Newburg, of whom Prince James had fo much caufe to complain, and whom he wanted to have met fword in hand ; but Princes forget equally affronts and obligations, when it is their intereft to do fo. By this marriage, the houfe of Sobiefki became allied to all the crowns of Europe, and Prince James was brother-in-law to the Emperor. This was the firft inftance of the Emperor's having dealt fincerely with the King of Poland ; and even in this he confulted rather his own ends than thofe of his ally, whom he fixed more firmly than ever in his intereft by this new connexion.

The Marquis de Bethune had done his utmoft to make the defign mifcarry ; and it was therefore ftipulated that he fhould leave Poland. It was alfo agreed that Charles of Newburg fhould conduct his fifter to the frontiers of the republic, by way of making fome fatisfaction to Prince James for what had paffed at Berlin ; and that the latter fhould refign his pretenfions to the eftates of the houfe of Radziwil (a).

The young couple had their firft interview at Olenifc, where the Princefs came in an Hungarian drefs, and affumed the Polifh habit. The Prince, when he took her hand, was prefented alfo with the order of the Golden Fleece, which was brought by the Count de Holftein. From Olenifc, the nuptial proceffion advanced towards Warfaw, and was met at fome diftance from the city by the Cardinal Primate, accompanied by the great officers of the crown. The Grand-Marfhal, to pay his court to his mafter's fon, carried his ftaff erected before him : but upon the Primate's faying, *You forget then that this honour is due to the King only* ; the ftaff was lowered (b). This mortifying circumftance, which made the Prince recollect, that in Poland the fon of

(a) Zalufki, tom. ii. p. 1166.   (b) Zalufki, Ibid. p. 1218.

a King

a King is only a private subject, interrupted in some measure the joy of the solemnity ; and yet it was only a prelude to all the vexations that followed. It is certain that the King was highly to blame in making this match, without communicating his design either to the Senate or the nobles ; for the Princes of Poland are forbid to marry without the consent of the republic. The King on some occasions had a mind to act the Monarch ; which, instead of facilitating his son's accession to the throne, removed him to a greater distance from it. But it would be anticipating events to relate here what happened in the sequel.

The French party was provoked at a marriage which strengthened the connexion between Vienna and Warsaw, and omitted no expedient to make it useless to the house of Austria. Leopold, when he signed the articles, gave a fresh promise to the King of Poland of a body of troops, and engaged to put him in possession of Moldavia and Walachia, provided that, in return, he would act with vigour against the Turks ; a diversion which was always of great use to Leopold. The Marquis de Bethune was industrious in raising doubts, and these not ill founded, about the value of promises so often made and so often broke. He addressed memorials to the Palatines, and to all who had any influence in the government, in which he censured severely the politics of the house of Austria, in contriving to reap the whole benefit of the war ; and pointed out the certain advantages that would follow from a separate peace with the Turks. He made use also of another argument, which he had more than once found to be very efficacious, and this was gold.

These insinuations, which begun to take effect with the republic, came to the knowledge of the Count de Thun, the Austrian Ambassador ; and induced him to follicit warmly the dismission of the
.Marquis

Y. 1691. Marquis de Bethune. In a letter to the Palatine of Wilna, he said, that France wanted to make a King who should be at her devotion, and this even in the life-time of the reigning Prince; and that Bethune, without regarding the honour he had of being related to the King, was the contriver of this conspiracy against him and the republic. Bethune, provoked at this aspersion, and still more at some expressions that were injurious to Lewis XIV. challenged the Ambassador to fight him. The King, who was personally interested in the quarrel, sent to the Ambassador to demand what proof he could bring in support of so heavy a charge. The Ambassador answered that he was accountable only to his master: *But as for the challenge*, added he, *though the public character which I bear might well excuse me, yet I accept it, though at the risque of incurring the Emperor's displeasure.* The King, being disappointed of the information he sought, and scorning to harbour suspicions, interposed to prevent the duel; and the two Ministers gave a promise in writing not to attack each other, as long as they should continue in Poland *(a)*.

In the midst of these squabbles, the Tartars made an irruption into the Palatinate of Russia, where they burnt fifty villages belonging to the King, but spared the possessions of private persons: a circumstance which gave occasion to say, that the irruption was owing to the intrigues of France, in order to force the King to a peace.

In the mean time, Thun informed the Emperor of what had passed between Bethune and himself; and his complaint was aggravated by another event. A courier, whom he had dispatched to Vienna, being plundered and tied to a tree in the Polish territories, this act of violence was attributed to the

(a) Id. ibid. p. 1220 and 1221.

French

French party, and Leopold demanded satisfaction for it: otherwise, he threatened to suppress the post, which was more advantageous to Poland than to the empire. Bethune's behaviour was still more provoking to him, than the plundering of the courier. After reviving the former complaints against him, of " his favouring the revolt of the Hungarians, and his " perpetual industry in sowing discord between the " two courts, he expressed his astonishment at hear- " ing he was still in Poland, when he ought to " have quitted the kingdom in February last, by " virtue of the marriage articles. I thought pro- " per (said the Emperor) to connive at this delay, " out of respect to the Queen, to whom he has " the honour of being related: but my patience is " at length exhausted; and if the man who has " been audacious enough to insult an Imperial Mi- " nister, does not immediately leave Poland, I will " recall my Ambassador." The Count de Konig- sek, who writ the dispatch, added of his own head, that the Queen of Poland was mistaken, if she flattered herself with the hopes of receiving any advantage from the court of France, which had long ago been exasperated by the Christian league, and lately by the marriage of Prince James; that the only course for her and her family to take, was to join heartily with the court of Vienna; and that it was her interest thoroughly to convince the King of the utility of this measure.

The King, who was too far engaged with the Emperor to look back, was contriving how to pacify him by the removal of the French Ambassa- dor. Lewis XIV. extricated him out of the diffi- culty, by appointing the Marquis de Bethune to be his Ambassador at the court of Sweden, where he died in a few months, without having rose so high as might have been expected from his birth, his alliance with the King of Poland, the employments

be

he had held, and the talents he possessed. During the short time of his residence at the court of Sweden, he had acquired such an ascendant in the cabinet, that the King forbad his Ministers to go to any entertainment that was given by any of the foreign Ambassadors ; a prohibition intended for the French Minister chiefly, though extending to all the rest. The Hungarians, at the beginning of their revolt, had taken such a fancy to him, that they had some design of offering him their crown, if France had thought proper to undertake the support of such a revolution. To the Poles he was always singularly agreeable ; but he had a sort of national pleasantry which sometimes created him enemies. As he was one day speaking of Prince James, whose aspect had a meanness in it, which he did not derive from the King, *He carries*, said he, *a bill of exclusion from the throne in his very face.* The King, who himself loved a jest, was not so much offended at this saying, as it might be expected he would ; and it was with regret, that he sacrificed Bethune to the Emperor.

The Emperor being thus appeased, and the French faction humbled, the marriage-rejoycings were resumed with great splendor, when all was again disturbed by the disagreement that arose in the royal family. The Queen, who still ruled in her husband's heart, had a mind to make the Princess of Poland sensible of her power : the latter was not so tractable as the former expected : Prince James took part in the dissatisfaction of his young wife ; and was, besides this, highly mortified at a thing which concerned his own person.

His brother, Prince Alexander, was now no longer a child, and begun to fix his eyes upon the splendor of the throne. The charms that accompany the first bloom of youth, an open countenance, an agreeable figure, a graceful air, and gentle manners,

had

had gained him the heart of his mother; and she omitted no expedient to make him still more agreeable to the King. Even the nation was already prepossessed in his favour; and it is the nation that makes the King. It was a saying current in the kingdom, that the youngest was *the son of the King*, and the eldest, *the son of the Grand-Marshal*. Besides, as the letter *I* had been found in the collection of the Polish prophecies to point out King *John*; the letter *A* was now discovered to begin the name of his successor *(a)*.

Prince Alexander was therefore considered as a rival by Prince James, whose jealousy rose to a higher pitch than ever, when the King left Warsaw on the 13th of June, and took with him this favourite son to present him to the army, and form him for military glory. And yet, the elder could not complain of being slighted by his august father. The King had invited him to accompany him with the Princess of Poland, who was to stay with the Queen in the Palatinate of Russia, till the expedition was ended. But Prince James, who was dissatisfied with every thing in his present fit of ill humour, answered that he would not expose his wife to the harsh treatment of the Queen; and that as

(a) When the throne was vacant, the Queen Dowager's party did not fail to make the most of the letter *A*, in favour of Prince Alexander. The Prince of Conti's faction was embarassed with this same *A*, and had nothing to say, but that, if the French Prince was not an Alexander in name, he was however an Alexander in valour. Neither of these two got the crown, but *Augustus*, Elector of Saxony; and if the prophecy had gone no farther than the letter *A*, it would have had an air of truth. But it added a terrifying menace, *mor etur brevi*, he shall die in a short time; now Augustus reigned thirty six years; which is as much as could naturally be expected for a King elected at the age of twenty seven. The Poles, notwithstanding this, still insist upon the truth of the prophecy, as they do upon the truth of all those that relate to their future Kings.

to

to himself, having no settled revenue, he could not bear the expence of the campaign. He thought proper to conceal the true reason : and the King, who might have laid his commands upon him, left him to his own inclinations, and departed without him.

The next day, the Prince was still more uneasy ; and having advised with the Austrian Ambassador, gave notice to the Grand-Chancellor that he would leave the kingdom, if Prince Alexander continued his journey ; nor will Poland, added he, disapprove of my retiring, when I shall inform the public in a manifesto, that the King intends the throne for a younger son, in prejudice of his elder. It is possible, that the Queen might even at that time have formed this project, as it appeared she afterwards did ; but the King certainly never thought of it ; and had he been at all prejudiced in favour of his younger sons, at an age when the dispositions of the mind do not yet unfold themselves, it is probable he would have leaned towards Prince Constantine, the youngest, who was his very picture. But Prince James's passion would suffer him to attend to nothing.

The King ordered him to be told, that he might set out, with a father's curse attending him, whenever he pleased ; but that he must never more expect to see his Sovereign and his father. This menace had no effect upon the Prince, who answered, that he was going to retire to the Netherlands, of which Spain had offered him the government. The King was highly exasperated, and had thoughts of punishing him : his punishment was already begun ; for the courtiers durst not visit him, and even his friends forsook him. The Jesuit Vota and the Venetian Resident, both of them eloquent and insinuating, endeavoured in a private conference to convince him of the weakness of his jealousy against

a brother

a brother, whose tender age entitled him to a few
empty caresses; of the injustice of his suspicions with
regard to the succession to the crown; and of the
enormity and the danger of rebelling against his father and his King. They prevailed upon him to
ask pardon, and told him that he would be very happy, if he could obtain it. The Prince therefore
went to the army to throw himself at the King's
feet. The father soon forgave him, and permitted
him to share the laurels which he expected to gather this campaign. It was an affecting sight to
see the hero between his two sons, one restored to
favour, and already inured to arms: the other always beloved, and going to learn the way to conquest: and all three marching against the enemies
of their country. The Queen and the Princess of
Poland staid behind upon the frontiers, and concealed their mutual aversion (a).

It was resolved, in the council of war held by
the Poles, to enter Walachia, as the siege of Kaminieck still appeared impracticable with their present forces; to make themselves masters by the
way, of Sorock, a Turkish fortress upon the Niester;
and to hasten the junction of the Cossacks. The
thing that retarded them was, their having neither
clothes nor money; but the King supplied them
with both, at his own expence; left a body of troops
to be a check upon the garrison of Kaminieck; passed the Niester in the end of August; and halted at
Snyatin, a trading town upon the left bank of the
Pruth. This was the place appointed for his receiving a reinforcement from Leopold; but Leopold
had acquired a privilege of minding only his own
interests, and was besides full of employment with
the Turks and Lewis XIV.

(a) Zaluski, tom. i. p. 1222 and 1223.

The

The King of Poland's still continuing faithful to his ally, after the breach of so many promises, must be accounted for by supposing, that he looked upon the Emperor's behaviour only as a political delay, in order to keep him steady to the league, and not as a direct intention to violate his engagements. He might believe, that the Emperor waited only for the expulsion of the Turks out of Hungary, to fulfil his promises. Upon any other footing, his constancy would be an inexplicable ænigma. There are indeed writers, so zealous for his glory, as to pretend, that, without regarding his own interests, he continued stedfast in the league, and made the necessary diversions, meerly to keep the faith of treaties, and to promote the common good of Christendom. But the designs of sovereigns are not dictated by such generous views ; and besides, their personal virtues should be made coincident with the happiness of their subjects: whereas Poland suffered immensely by the length of this war.

The army, however, marched on with that resolution which the presence of a great General always inspires, and with more joy than their leader was capable of tasting. The discord which he saw encreasing between his two sons, disturbed him as much as the perfidious conduct of the Emperor. Prince Alexander, who was eager after knowledge, and pried curiously into every thing, was perpetually mixing with the troops, visiting the posts, caressing the officers, going into the tents of the soldiers, pitying their hardships, examining into their wants, and making them presents. Prince James treated this behaviour as an ambitious affectation of popularity, as an artifice to seduce the multitude, and as treason against his elder brother. They looked at each

each other with jealous eyes, burst out into offensive words, and sometimes forgot that they were brothers, even before their father, who seemed to foresee that their rivalship would one day occasion the crown's going out of his family. *It will be easier for me*, said he, *to get the better of the enemy I am going in quest of, than of my own sons.*

As the army marched on, intelligence was brought that the Hospodar of Moldovia waited for them near Pererita, with twenty thousand Tartats. This would have been of small consequence ; but it was added, that thirty thousand Turks were advancing through the Budziac; and this was a much greater number than was necessary to dispute the conquest of Moldavia and Walachia. The Tartars soon made their appearance, and the Poles followed them for some days ; but famine attended their steps; and they were forced to cross the Pruth, and march towards the Turks in quest of subsistence. The Turks were in no hurry to meet them, their design being to continue inactive till the advanced season should force the Poles to return home, and not to mind a few places which they might possibly make themselves masters of. In effect, *Sorock* and *Nerzecum* were all the fruit of the campaign, and the Turks never drew their sabres. The vast quantity of snow, which fell uncommonly early, froze the soldiers, broke up the roads, embarassed the artillery and the waggons, and fatigued both men and horses. When the Polish army arrived upon the frontiers of the kingdom, they looked as if they came from a defeat (a). This was the fourth time that the King failed in his attempts upon Moldavia and Walachia; and the Emperor Leopold wanted but little of being equally, or more unfortunate, in Hungary, than the King of Poland.

(a) Zaluski, tom. ii. p. 1236.

G g   Soliman

Soliman III. was lately dead, after having reigned four years, and obtained victories which he did not deserve. He was succeeded by his brother, Achmet II. a Prince equally void of abilities. But Muftapha Cuprogli continued in the poft of Vifir, and was encamped at Salankemen upon the banks of the Danube. Prince Lewis of Baden, the Imperial General, marched to give him battle, not thinking him fo ftrong, or fo well encamped; but he was no fooner arrived, than he had nothing left him but to retreat. He was attacked by the Turks with fo much courage and conduct, that his deftruction feemed inevitable. The field of battle was already covered with expiring Chriftians; but the Fortune of Leopold decreed, that a fhot fhould take off the Vifir, when he had had but little enjoyment of his high ftation; and he died at a time when his glory was at the higheft, and his life moft neceffary. The Aga of the Janizaries was capable of fupplying his place; but another fhot laid him dead alfo, and the infidels, ftruck with confternation, gave up the victory; which, however, was attended with no advantage to the Imperialifts, but the taking of *Lippa*, an unhappy town, perpetually taken and retaken, and equally illtreated by friends and foes. The very favages in their forefts enjoy greater happinefs.

The other powers of the league had ftill lefs fuccefs. The Venetians, being no longer commanded by Morofini, could fcarce maintain their ground in the Archipelago. The Czar Peter's attention was taken up with civil commotions in his own dominions, and he thought rather of fecuring his own throne, than fhaking that of Conftantinople.

This campaign was the laft that the King of Poland ever made. It was not his advanced age that made it neceffary for him to retire; (for he was only

only fixty-one) but forty years fpent in war, during which he had never fpared his own perfon, ten in the great offices of the republic, eighteen upon a throne which required conftant action; all thefe labours had wore out his body, and his mind felt the effects of it. He refigned the command of the army to the Grand-General Jablonowfki, in order to apply himfelf wholly to the internal adminiftration of the kingdom; and even this was above his ftrength. He was in that ambiguous fituation, of being too far gone to govern himfelf, and not far enough to be wholly governed by others.

The protection of the Queen enabled two Jews to get poffeffion of his confidence; one of them, the phyfician, *Jonas*, had the care of his body; the other, who was a farmer of the revenue, of his finances; and they both underftood perfectly how to fupport each other, by affifting the Jews their brethren. The farmer, named *Bethfal*, took a leafe of the King's eftates, at a rent much exceeding their real value; and by this means, gratified the ruling paffion of the King, who confidered wealth as the fureft expedient of fecuring the crown in his family. But the Jew, while he gave with one hand, knew well that he fhould receive much more with the other. He fold all his mafter's favours to the higheft bidder; and farmed out the cuftoms again at moft exorbitant intereft. The Queen was acquainted with this fcandalous traffick; but it was long a fecret to the King, becaufe he was a King, and in a weak ftate of health.

Two prints were handed about in Warfaw; one of which reprefented perfons of different nations counting out money: the Jew Bethfal, drawn to the life, was examining whether the ducats were good; and his mafter, who, if he had not had a crown upon his head, might have been taken for

G g 2   a banker

a banker or scrivener, was putting some of them in a corner of his garment. He had long been accused of avarice : but to judge of the justice of the charge, a distinction must be made between a King who is master of all the public revenues, and a King, to whom the state assigns only a certain income for his subsistence. The former, since he may call for what sums he pleases, is inexcusable in being avaricious ; but the latter is obliged to be frugal. The other print drew tears at the fate of heroes. A Prince, exhausted and meager, was represented sitting in the lap of a young woman, and sucking the breast of an old one. The number of crowns which the sick man had upon his head weighed him down, and contributed to his weakness as much as the disorder he laboured under. Most of his crowns were plain and without flowers, and seemed to be in as bad a state as he that wore them. The young woman, upon whose knees he sat, was meant for the Princess Royal, who endeavoured, by her complaisance, to gain a share in the government with the Queen.

The King bore up against all his afflictions, and endeavoured to conceal his state of decay. He came frequently to the Senate, but seldom staid till the breaking up of the assembly. The only amusement he had left, was that of hunting, though he could not sit long on horseback, but was soon obliged to get into a carriage, where he said that he felt himself less a man than usual ; and reflected with grief upon the opinion which prevailed in the nation, that his mind was grown as weak as his body.

The whole body of the republic was not long without feeling the effects of the languid state of its head. No business was dispatched in the Chancery : confusion was introduced into the administration : the coin, which was already debased by the neigh-

neighbourhood of the Elector of Brandenburg, Y. 1691.
grew ftill worfe, and ruined the little trade that
kept Poland alive. Contributions were ordered to
be levied, but no money came in: the Grand-
Treafurer declared that the treafury was exhaufted:
the army was not paid: there were fcarce ten thoufand men fit for fervice; even thefe were fo many malcontents, who oppreffed the poor peafants;
and Jablonowfki, with fo fmall a force, could undertake nothing. At this juncture, a Tartarian
Envoy came to make the King frefh offers of peace,
from the Sultan Achmet, upon terms with which
he ought to have been contented: viz. the reftitution
of all that Poland had loft, upon the fole condition of feparating itfelf from the league. The King
was indiffolubly attached to that confederacy by
his project upon Moldavia and Walachia, and waited
for the recovery of his health; fo that no refolution
was taken, either to continue the war, or to make
peace. Every one thought only of his own intereft; and all that had power, employed it folely to
raife themfelves upon the ruins of the public.

End of the EIGHTH BOOK.

THE

HISTORY

OF

JOHN SOBIESKI

KING OF POLAND,

BOOK IX.

Y. 1693. AS a remedy for so many evils, recourse was had to the assembling of diets; but the dissolution of these diets encreased the disorder. It was thought, however, that that which met in 1693 would have better success, when a Bishop re-kindled that fire in every breast, which seemed to be just extinguished.

It is a custom in Poland to spare the lands of the church and the nobility, in the appointment of winter-quarters. Sapieha, Grand-General of Lithuania, not knowing how to provide otherwise for his army, thought that all customs and privileges ought to give way to the supreme law of the public good; and therefore assigned quarters to his troops upon these privileged lands, and demanded contribu-

contributions in proportion. The nobility submitted without any complaint; but Constantine Brzatowski, Bishop of Wilna, a man who had a greater regard for the Bulls of Rome than the interest of his country, exclaimed loudly against this violation of the immunities of the church, and called Sapieha an atheist. He accused of meanness and prevarication some of his brethren, who submitted to the exigencies of the time; nor would he even suffer the soldiers to pass over his Episcopal domain. Though Poland is much more extensive than France, it has only seventeen Bishops, who have all coadjutors under them, and two or three Bishops *in partibus (a)*, who take care of the dioceses, while the titular Bishops, by virtue of their senatorial capacity, are wholly employed in affairs of state. Their estates, like their dioceses, are of immense extent, and it cannot be but such great immunities must be a burden to the rest of the nation.

If the Bishop of Wilna had been contented with making his complaint, he would probably have been heard in the first diet, and some accommodation would have been found out; but he armed himself with the thunders of the church, which, at that time, were more dreaded in Poland than they are at present; and after three canonical admonitions, he let them loose upon the head of the criminal. The anathema was expressed in the strongest terms, and ran in this form :

Whereas Casimir Sapieha, Grand-General of Li-
thuania, renouncing his baptismal vow, to obey the

(a) A Bishop *in partibus infidelium*, or, as he is most commonly called, *in partibus*, is one who takes his title from a place which was anciently a Bishop's see, but is now in the possession of infidels, such as Athens, Corinth, Apamea, &c. By this means, having no diocese of his own, he is at leisure to perform the Episcopal functions for such as are too idle, too infirm, or too much engaged in politics, to do them in person.

instigation

inftigation of the devil, has violated the privileges of the church ; it is our duty to cut off this rotten member with the fword of excommunication, left he should infect the body of the faithful. By virtue therefore of the power we have received from God, of loofing and unloofing in heaven and on earth, we do, in the name of the bleffed Trinity, of St. Peter, and all the faints, eject him from the bofom of the church, deprive him of the participation of the facraments, and feparate him from the fociety of Chriftians : and we deliver up him, and all his adherents, to the power of Satan, and to eternal fire (a).

The perfon thus delivered over to the devil was the head of the Lithuanian nobility, a Palatine, Senator, and Grand-General. The nobles, the Palatines, the Senators, and the Generals, all confidered themfelves as wounded through his fides. The perfons excommunicated as his adherents were the officers of the army, and all whom he employed to execute his orders. The indignation was univerfal, and the Bifhop was on the point of being anathematized by the republic. But the King, who wanted to refume part of the great power which he had conferred upon the Sapiehas, took the Bifhop's part ; and a King never declares for any caufe whatfoever, without drawing after him, all who fear his refentment, or hope for his favour. The Bifhop, who was at firft deferted by every one, now found himfelf powerfully fupported, and efpecially by his own order.

The firft ftep was the publication of apologies on each fide, which are both the fore-runners and the caufes of a warm contention to fucceed. The defenders of the excommunication called to their affiftance the decifions of three councils, and feveral Popes, in favour of the immunities of the church ;

(a) Zalufki, tom. ii. p. 1359.

Y. 1691.

nor did they forget the famous bull of Paul V. intitled, *in Cœnâ Domini*, which excommunicates whoever presumes to meddle with any ecclesiastical possessions, without the consent of the see of Rome, and insults all the rights of sovereigns. They quoted also the decrees of several Kings of Poland, who had protected these immunities: among whom were Jagellon, Lewis, Casimir III. Boleslas, and Wenceslas, whose virtues could not fail to be highly extolled upon this occasion: and as the warmth of disputation generally overshoots its mark, the Bishop of Wilna and his adherents did not scruple to maintain, that the church of Poland was indebted, for all its possessions, to the liberality of the Bishops of Rome.

Sapieha's apologists answered, that the Popes could not possibly give away what did not belong to them; that the church in general derived its possessions from either Princes or people; that the church of Poland in particular had received her's, partly from her Kings, and partly from the republic; that wealth, given and protected by the state, ought to support its burdens; that Popes and councils, whose commissions respect only an inheritance in heaven, have no authority over worldly goods; that, if the republic had thought proper, upon certain occasions, to exempt the portion belonging to the church from the common burdens, yet it still retained a right, by virtue of its legislative authority, to revoke this privilege in times of apparent exigence; and in short, that Sapieha was authorized by the republic, to treat the lands of the church in the same manner with those of the nobility *(a)*; from whence, it was concluded, that the excommunication was null and void.

(a) Zaluski, tom. ii. pages 1425, & seq.

This

This opinion was held by all the secular clergy, even of the diocese of Wilna, who refused to publish the sentence of excommunication, and exclude Sapieha from their churches.

The Cardinal Primate inclined also the same way; and writ to Sapieha not to be alarmed at this burst of thunder, which could only stun the ears, without at all hurting the soul, when it lighted upon the heads of innocent persons; and that in a short time every mark of it would be entirely effaced. He writ also to the Bishop of Wilna, giving him to understand, " that he had been led astray by an " excess of zeal for the interests of the church; that " a prudent Prelate could not hold up the thunder- " bolt too long to view, before he hurled it; that " he had gone beyond his power, in consulting " himself only; that he ought to have asked the " consent of the whole body of Bishops, and much " more that of the republic, since an affront to " the person of a General is an affront to the state, " from which he derives his power; and lastly, " that the only way of retrieving his error, was " to acknowledge the invalidity of his sentence."

The Bishop was in too great a heat to listen to moderate counsels, especially being animated by the court; and every new step that he took was a fresh mark of his rigour. He excommunicated all Regulars, and Seculars, all Canons, and Parish-Priests, who refused to read the anathema against the Grand-General, and laid all their churches under an interdict; that is to say, he forbade the clergy, upon pain of eternal damnation, to say mass, perform the service of the church, or administer any sacrament.

Sapieha, in the mean time, had never felt so strong an inclination to frequent churches and sacraments, as since he was excommunicated; and both parties employed their proper weapons; the Bishop,

Y. 1693.

Bifhop, his fpiritual fword; the General, military execution : in proportion as the Bifhop laid a greater burden upon confciences, the General increafed his exactions, upon the lands of the church, and particularly upon thofe of the Bifhop, beyond all due bounds. Now it was that he really made a bad ufe of his power; for whoever was not of his party, was fure to have foldiers quartered upon him, and to be ruined by mercilefs extortioners.

The Primate, in order to attack the evil in its fource, fummoned the Bifhop before him. The Bifhop refufed to appear; and the Primate, having decreed the excommunication to be null and void, paffed a fentence of fufpenfion upon the ex-communicator; which in effect was adding fewel to the flame.

Santa-Croce, the Apoftolic Nuncio, infifted upon it, that the fee of Rome only had a right to try Bifhops. The authority of Nuncios had long been eftablifhed in Poland, and fubfifted at this time in all its vigour. The multitude highly revered thefe Papal Minifters, who omitted no opportunity to extend their power, having ufurped, in times of confufion, many prerogatives, befides the right which they claimed, of trying all ecclefiaftical cau-fes. Thefe prerogatives they retained till the year 1728. The laft century was not the time for churchmen to lofe ground : Santa-Croce's object was to gain it, and he annulled the fentence.

The Primate pretended that this was an en-croachment upon his jurifdiction, both as Primate of the kingdom, and Legate, by office, of the Holy See; and he writ to the Pope to engage him to recall, and punifh his Nuncio.

Sapieha, in the midft of thefe contefts, carried his head much higher than ever. The three other Generals of the republic, Jablonowfki, Potofki, and Slufka, demanded fatisfaction at Rome, for

the

the insult offered to their collegue ; and their claim was supported by some, but disputed by others, in the Senate and Equestrian Order. There were some Senators, who, without having recourse to any ecclesiastical tribunal, were for imitating the conduct of the Venetians, when the Doge and the Senate were excommunicated, and the whole state laid under an interdict by Paul V. in 1606. The Senators forbade the publication of the sentence through the whole extent of their territories, alledging, that they were inspired by God to hang every one that should disobey their orders. It was too late indeed for the Polish Senate to hinder the publication of the sentence, but it was in their power to punish whoever should act in consequence of it. The expedient was rejected, and served only to increase the confusion. Thus were the Poles engaged in quarrels about an excommunication, while the Tartars were ravaging the frontiers of the kingdom (*a*).

The King, when he was in his vigour, would have prevented, or extinguished this flame ; but being now governed by the advice of those who had the art to lay hold of his conscience, by seconding his inclinations to humble the family of Sapieha, he helped to make it burn the fiercer. He ordered Sapieha to come and give an account of his proceedings : the General answered, that he waited for the Pope's decision ; and if Rome did not do him justice, he would appeal next to the republic.

The Pope, being in a great strait between the King and the republic, the Primate and the Nuncio, the excommunicating Bishop and the excommunicated General, was unwilling to disoblige any of the parties. He therefore neither recalled his

_____

(*a*) Zaluski, tom. ii. pages 1229, and 1451.

Nuncio, nor condemned the Primate, or the Bifhop, nor abfolved the Grand-General from the cenfure; but fufpended the effect of the excommunication for a year, on account of the war, and the important part which the Grand-General of Lithuania had to act in the prefent juncture. This was behaving like a prince, not like a Pope; but the expedient, however judicious, was difrelifhed on all fides, and particularly by Sapieha, who, inftead of a fufpenfion of punifhment, expected a fpeedy reparation.

Such was the confufed ftate of affairs, when the King, who lay fick at Zolkiew, iffued out his univerfals. The fubftance of them is worth recording, as they furnifhed occafion for breaking the only fpring in the machine of government, which could have reftored order to the ftate, and becaufe they fhew the difference of ftile between a King, whofe will is fubject to the law, and a King who knows no other law but his will.

" John the Third, to the diet appointed to
" meet at Warfaw on the 22d of this inftant De-
" cember, greeting.

" Whereas it hath pleafed the Divine Provi-
" dence, which raifed us to the government of this
" free people, and in whofe hands are health and
" ficknefs, to vifit us with a fit of illnefs, as we
" were fetting out upon our journey to affift at the
" diet; we receive this vifitation with all due fub-
" miffion, hoping, however, that it will pleafe
" God to mitigate the violence of our prefent pains,
" and to reftore us to our country. We even in-
" tended to begin our journey, notwithftanding
" our weaknefs, if the united advice of our phyfici-
" ans, and the Senators here prefent, together with
" the danger our life was in, had not abfolutely
" prevented us. We therefore make known to
" your dilections, by this authentic document,
" what

A. 1693. " what is our prefent ftate, and how impoffible it
" is for us to be prefent at the opening of the
" diet; and we conjure you, by your regard both
" for your country and our own perfon, to grant
" us fuch a delay as may be fufficient for the re-
" covery of our health, engaging to you our royal
" promife, to appear at the diet as foon as our
" ftrength will permit, which we wifh to recover
" folely for your good.   Being therefore defirous to
" notify to you this our will, we commiffion the
" Cardinal, Archbifhop of Gnefna, Primate of the
" kingdom, and of the great duchy of Lithuania,
" to publifh and promulgate thefe our prefent uni-
" verfals.

" Given at Zolkiew, this 14th day of Decem-
" ber 1693, in the twentieth year of our reign."

It is obvious, from the tenor of this inftrument,
that it was pofterior to another which fixed the
opening of the diet at Warfaw, where the two
eftates of the realm were expecting the arrival of
their King.   It appears alfo, that thefe fecond univerfals, occafioned by the King's illnefs, were addreffed to the Primate, in order to be communicated to the republic; a method, which, though
unufual, would have been thought of no confequence in times of harmony and concord.

It is neceffary to recollect, upon all occafions,
that a fingle Deputy has it in his power to ftop the
proceedings of a diet; and all thofe from Lithuania, being devoted to Sapieha, breathed nothing
but difcord.   The Primate, forefeeing the ftorm,
excufed himfelf from being prefent at the affembly,
upon a pretence of indifpofition; and to fupply
this deficiency, he writ a circular letter to the Senators and Deputies, notifying to them the univerfals which deferred the opening of the diet.   He
addreffed them by the name of *brethren*, a title
which he had hitherto refufed to give them; efpecially

cially the Deputies; but his letter was not the better Y. 1693.
received on this account. The Deputies asserted,
that the Primate, having no authority but in an
interregnum, had nothing to do with the publication of universals; and that it would, in effect, be
acknowledging a fourth order in the republic.
" Besides, added they, as the King has already
" fixed the opening of the diet, it is not in his
" power to alter the time; nor can the day be
" changed, without the concurrence of all the
" orders of the state."

It was in vain for the servants of the crown to
represent, that the King, being sick at Zolkiew,
and unattended by the officers of his chancery,
might well make a mistake in the form of the universals; that his commissioning the Primate to
promulge them, implied a delegation of his own
authority to that Prelate; that it was wrong, for a
mere error in form, upon an extraordinary occasion,
to disturb so good a Prince, and endanger the republic, whose safety depended upon the health of
the King, and the good success of the diet; and
lastly, that the King's proposal was not only just in
itself, but had actually been put in practice in the
reign of Uladislas VII. who put off the meeting
of a diet, which ended very happily.

The Deputies from Lithuania were deaf to all
these representations, and resolved not to hear the
universals read. The Primate had shifted off the
business of publishing them upon the Chancellor,
who came to the church of St. John, attended by
all the orders. There was no mass of the Holy
Ghost, nor any of the ceremonies usual at the
opening of diets. The Polish Deputies ranged
themselves on one side, and the Lithuanians on the
other. All that the Chancellor could do, was to
procure a moment's silence, while he notified the
King's sickness, authenticated by legal proof; but
when

Y. 1693. when he attempted to read the univerſals, his voice was drowned by the confuſed noiſe of a hundred others. He therefore quitted the aſſembly, telling them, that they would find the inſtrument fixed up at the gate of the caſtle of Warſaw: *We will alſo fix up our proteſts at the ſame place,* ſaid the Lithuanians. In ſhort, no diet was held; and never was a diet more neceſſary (a).

The King could not help reflecting, that the Biſhop of Wilna was the firſt author of all this diſturbance, and repented that he had approved his rigid conduct. He repreſented to him by letter, in the ſtile of a friend rather than a maſter, that peace is of all things the moſt valuable; that it is the glory of the Epiſcopal character to conciliate, not to divide; and that he was bound in duty to remove the cauſe of contention, by expreſſing his ſorrow to the General of Lithuania for having occaſioned it. The Prelate was a man of unexceptionable morals, and an honeſt heart; his mind was but narrow, and conſidering, as he did, his bulls of excommunication as a ſacred bulwark, he grew more and more perſuaded that he was the inſtrument of heaven, and that it was better to obey God than the King. Being naturally of a contentious turn, he peſtered the public with his conſcience and his clamours, and declared himſelf ready to die a martyr for the immunities of the church; nor was there any way to reclaim a man, who conſidered himſelf as a ſecond St. Thomas a Becket. Even perſons of ſcrupulous piety blamed his obſtinacy; but his own adherents, in the midſt of this ſcene of confuſion, extolled his firmneſs to the ſkies; and the calamities of the ſtate increaſed every day.

Y. 1694. While the affairs of the kingdom were thus running to ruin, the King was more ſucceſsful in ma-

(b) Zaluſki, tom. ii. pages 1304, and 1305.

naging

naging thofe of his own family. The Elector of Bavaria had lately loft his wife, and was appointed Governor of the Spanifh Netherlands. The child that the Electrefs left him, was confidered as prefumptive heir to Charles II. The unhappy mother, who was daughter to the Emperor Leopold, loft her own life to preferve that of her fon. The Elector, now a widower, was already a great match, but a much greater on account of the expectations he might found upon this fon. Thefe expectations were laid open in a plan, communicated to the Elector by the King of Poland, upon the fubject of the fucceffion to the crown of Spain. It contains the firft origin of one of the moft important affairs that ever involved Europe in war and defolation, and is conceived in thefe terms.

1. " As Charles II. King of Spain has no chil-
" dren, the Elector fhould think of the fucceffion
" to that crown for his fon.

2. " He has two rivals to cope with, the Empe-
" ror and the King of France; and being not
" ftrong enough to oppofe them, he fhould call in
" the affiftance of one of them againft the other.

3. " The Emperor, who lays claim to the whole
" fucceffion, will certainly give him no affiftance;
" nor could he, if he were fo difpofed, either by
" fea or land. By land, France would interrupt
" his paffage; and by fea, he has neither fhips
" nor ports.

4. " The Elector muft therefore connect him-
" felf with France, by making a treaty of partition
" with that crown, and give up fome, that he may
" gain the reft.

5. " Neither the Englifh, nor the Dutch, nor
" the whole league of Augfburg fhould deter the
" Elector from taking this ftep; for though France
" be furrounded with enemies, fhe is not yet fub-
" dued;

H h

Y. 1684. " dued; and besides, it is very uncertain how long
" the league of Augsburg will subsist,
    6. " France is at present attacked on all sides,
" and therefore this is the proper time to treat
" with her; for she would expect more advantage-
" ous terms if a peace should be made. There is
" also another reason for hastening the treaty of
" partition. The child's life is uncertain; and if
" he should die, the Elector has no farther claim;
" whereas it may be stipulated at present, that
" whatever shall be given up to the Elector by the
" treaty of partition, shall be irrevocably his, even
" in case of the child's decease (a)."

This plan is visibly formed upon the supposition
of two events, which were destined to be the occasion of much bloodshed; the death of Charles II.
without issue, and that of the Electoral Prince;
events which were very possible, because misfortunes happen to men much sooner than blessings.
What yet remains undiscovered, is, how the King
of Poland could be so much interested in the Elector of Bavaria's fortune: a circumstance that is
amply accounted for, by observing that he intended
to give him his only daughter, Theresa Cunegunda Sobieska.

The Queen, who was always a Frenchwoman,
in her heart, had at least as large a share in this
negotiation as the King. She saw that it was a
means of fixing the Elector firmly in the interests
of France: a connection, which he would probably have avoided, could he have seen into futurity.
Be this as it will, the marriage was concluded; and
when the Princess took leave of Poland, to go to
her husband in the Netherlands, she was presented
by her father with a farewell-poem, in the form of
an epithalamium. The piece was very indifferent,

(a) Zaluski, tom. ii. p. 1367.

but

but this was more the fault of the age, than of the Royal bard ; for the æra of good poetry is not even yet arrived in Poland.

This marriage was the laſt thing that gave the King any pleaſure ; and yet it was very near being broke off. The Electors's Envoy at Warſaw requir-ed a fortune of five hundred thouſand Imperials ; a ſum, which many a merchant at London, or farmer of the revenue at Paris, can give his daughter, but was thought exorbitant by the King of Poland. The Queen removed the difficulty, by becoming bound, unknown to her huſband, for part of the money ; but when the time of payment came, ſhe found herſelf at a loſs ; for, though the King admitted her into his heart and his cabinet, ſhe was excluded from his purſe. In this diſtreſs, ſhe loaded ten Swediſh ſhips with corn from Poland, and ſent them to France, where bread began to be very dear ; and was thus indebted to trade for being able to fulfill her engagements (a).

The perſon, who ſuggeſted to her this expedient, was the famous *Melchior de Polignac*, Abbot of Bon-port, lately arrived from France with the character of Ambaſſador extraordinary ; and who afterwards diſtinguiſhed himſelf greatly in the ſame capacity, upon other occaſions, as well as in the church, the college of Cardinals, and the republic of letters. It was not long before he was equally admired and dreaded in Poland. The graces of his perſon, the elegance of his wit, the politeneſs of his manners, the brightneſs of his genius, the charms of his elo-quence, and the ſubtilty more than the depth of his politics, gave him ſuch influence, that inſtead of a foreign Ambaſſador, one would have taken him for the firſt Miniſter of Poland. Before his arrival, the Germans were uppermoſt at court ; but

(a) Zaluſki, tom. ii. p. 1407.

France

Y, 1694. France soon gained the ascendant. He made one at all cabinet councils; and while the King was obliged to be taking care of his health, he was often in private with the Queen. The women and the courtiers diverted themselves with this intimacy, without reflecting that the Queen had renounced the foibles of a woman to adopt the passions of a man. This was the topic of Sapieha's declamations, who still continued at enmity with the court, on account of the old grudge of Wilna.

The substance of the manifesto which he published at this juncture was, " that the business of the " kingdom was no longer settled either in the Senate " or the diets, but in the King's, or rather in the " Queen's, cabinet, which was become the grave " of the laws and liberty of Poland: that a scheme " was there concerted to oppress the first nobles of " the state, who might see, by his example, what " they had to fear for themselves: that the French " Ambassador had all the craft of Mazarin, and " all the inflexible cruelty of Richelieu; that he " gave the court a relish for the haughtiness of " his master and the despotism of his country, and " that it was time for all true Poles to watch over " the safety of the republic (a).

In times of disturbance, there is nothing which is not capable of giving an alarm. The King assembled the Senate, but there was no unanimity of sentiment; and the disputes ran so high, as to renew what happened more than once in the councils of state at Rome and Athens (b). Potofki, the great Huntsman of the crown, struck a Senator who was

(a) Zalufki, tom. ii. p. 1364.
(b) When Themistocles said to Euribyades, *strike, but hear me,* the latter had his hand lifted up over him. We may call the manners of those times rude, but they were tender of human blood; and the sword was never drawn but against an enemy.

standing

ſtanding by the King's ſide; and no method was taken to avenge this inſult upon the majeſty of the King and the dignity of the Senate.

Provincial diets were aſſembled, but the members came to them ſword in hand. The Biſhop of Sa-mogitia, who was one of thoſe that eſpouſed the Biſhop of Wilna's cauſe, was taken by the throat; and blood was ſpilt between thoſe that attacked him ſo roughly, and thoſe that ran to his defence.

The confuſion of the Dietines was no favourable omen that reaſon would preſide in the ſubſequent diet; and accordingly, ſenſeleſs fury prevailed. The firſt point entered upon, was how to reconcile Sa-pieha and the Biſhop of Wilna. The Apoſtolic Nuncio had been already prevailed on to ſubmit, and expreſs his ſorrow at having encroached upon the Primate's juriſdiction, in favour of the Biſhop's ſevere proceedings. But the Biſhop continued in-flexible, and it ſeemed as if he took a pleaſure in brandiſhing the torch of diſcord over the aſſembly of the nation. By this means, the firſt meeting was ſpent in mutual clamours. The ſucceeding night, the Caſtellan of Lencici's (a) ſon, having had a warm diſpute at table about public affairs with an officer of the court, followed him thither, and found him in the Queen's apartments. From abu-ſive words, he inſtantly proceeded to threats, and even a blow. The officer laid his hand upon his ſword, and three others were immediately drawn againſt him; for the Caſtellan's ſon had brought with him two of the Primate's domeſtics. An of-ficer of the guard ſtept between, and was run through the body. The Queen hearing a noiſe, opened her door, and was preſented with the ſight of a ſtream of blood, and the officer falling to the ground. The Gladiators were all arreſted, except the moſt

(a) A town of Poland, the metropolis of the Palatinate of the ſame name, ſituated upon the river Bzura.

guilty

guilty of all, out of regard to the Caftellan his father, who ought to have been punifhed for not teaching his fon better manners; and though this violation of the Queen's apartment was confidered as an act of High-Treafon, it remained unpunifhed; becaufe, in the prefent ftate of confufion, authority was unfupported by power (a).

The diet refumed its fittings, but it was only to vent the animofity that the members had in their hearts. The Poles and Lithuanians feemed no longer to have the fame laws and the fame King; nor was the difcord confined to the mafters, but fpread among the fervants. There is an abufe which the republic connives at, perhaps for political reafons, and in order to encourage a martial fpirit among all degrees of men. While the diets are fitting, the fervants of the great Lords, who are very numerous, and moft of them Gentlemen, get together, form themfelves into two armies, a Polifh and a Lithuanian, under two Marfhals, (diftinguifhed by their exploits, fuch as they are) march into the fields with kettle-drums and trumpets, attack each other with fticks and ftones, purfue the vanquifhed party, befiege them in the neighbouring houfes, and afterwards return into the city like regular troops. This war, though carried on without fire-arms or fwords, is generally attended with bloodfhed, but with more than ufual on the prefent occafion.

While the armies were engaged as ufual, two Lithuanian officers, at the head of a hundred and fifty horfe, fell unexpectedly upon the Poles with fabres and piftols, and killed and wounded many. The match being now unequal, the Poles retreated, and the night was fpent in endeavouring to prevent a greater effufion of blood. The mediators hoped they had fucceeded; but the next morning the

(a) Zalufki, tom. ii. p. 1515.

bleeding

bleeding bodies were brought before the castle where the diet was assembled, and the sight roused afresh the fury of the Polish servants. The two Lithuanian officers, who were the authors of the carnage, were imprudent enough to appear at the gate of the castle. The Poles fell upon them, and it was with great difficulty that they were saved by the guards; but their servants were upon the point of being torn in pieces, and rushed into the castle where they were pursued to the chamber of Deputies. The Lithuanian Deputies were themselves insulted; and instantly left their seats, crying out, that since they could not be safe in the very sanctuary of the republic, they quitted the diet, and protested against all its proceedings: a step, which of course put an end to the session.

During the whole time that this frenzy lasted, a Lithuanian could not appear in the streets without danger: it was much safer to be a Turk or a Tartar. Prince Alexander was suspected of having raised this tumult, by distributing secret bribes: but whatever might be its origin, it could not be quieted without troops, and the interposition of the royal authority (a).

In the midst of these intestine broils, it was impossible for the Poles to carry the war abroad; and accordingly they staid at home, forgetting the views of their King, and their engagements with the league. In the mean time, the Imperialists besieged Belgrade, but were forced to raise the siege. The Turks did not pursue them; but the Tartars were ordered to go and ravage Hungary, in order to deprive them of the means of subsisting. The old proverb, *that a flying enemy should be supplied with a bridge of gold*, was found to be a true one upon this occasion. The German General, *Hofkirchen*,

(a) Zaluski, tom. ii. p. 1523.

surround-

Y. 1694. ſurrounded the Tartars that came to ſtarve him, ſo
as to leave them no way to eſcape. In this ſituation, they for the firſt time quitted their horſes to
fight on foot, and force their way ſword in hand.
The expedient was ſuggeſted to them by their Sul-
tain Selim-Gerai, but it coſt them very dear : however, the Tartars, at this time, ſhewed more ſpirit
than the Poles.

Y. 1695.   The republic ſeemed to be haſtening with all expedition to her ruin. Her counſels were brought
to no maturity; the Lithuanians being for one
thing, and the Poles for another; and theſe two
principal parties were ſubdivided into different
branches, engaged in perpetual conteſts with each
other. The Senate conſidered the Equeſtrian Order
as no better than a factious crew ; and the Equeſtrian Order liſtened to the Senate as an aſſembly of
mere idle declaimers. The King was treated with
no ſort of reſpect ; and his diſpleaſure was ſo little
dreaded, that the Grand-Marſhal divorced his
niece, to make room for another wife, and refuſed
to pay back her fortune. There was no union any
where except among the four Generals ; but the two
armies grew daily weaker, becauſe no ſtate can acquire ſtrength but in times of domeſtic tranquillity.

If, in the midſt of theſe civil convulſions, the
Turks had appeared in arms, Poland muſt have ſub-
mitted agan to that yoke from which the King had
delivered it. Jablonowſki was juſtly commended,
for leaving the ſquabbles of the capital, to go and
repreſs the incurſions of the Tartars ; and though
he could not hinder them from ſetting fire to the
ſuburbs of Leopol, he at leaſt preſerved the town.
The King was highly chagrined, that he could not,
as uſual, carry terror into the enemy's country, inſtead of ſuffering their ravages at home. He would
have found an enemy worthy of him, in the Sul-
                                             tan.

tan Muftapha II. Achmet was lately dead, and his
lofs was as little regretted as that of his brother
Soliman. Muftapha, their nephew, fon to Mahomet IV. was deftined to make the empire amends
for the incapacity of his two uncles. He poffeffed
a folid judgment, applied himfelf clofely to bufinefs, was moderate in his pleafures, neither covetous
nor profufe in his expences, an excellent horfeman,
fkilled in the ufe of arms, a lover of glory, and
endued with ardent courage. Such were his perfonal qualities; and he declared, upon afcending
the throne, that he would not bear the name of
Emperor in vain, and would always command his
armies in perfon. He begun the campaign early in
the year; and in order to know what opinion the
army entertained of him and his Generals, he often difguifed himfelf like a common foldier; an
eafy way of coming at truth, but the generality of
Sovereigns like better to be flattered to their faces.
The Sultan heard fome complaints againft his government, and endeavoured to correct his faults;
he learnt alfo that the Vifir had kept back the
fums that were neceffary to put the artillery in a
good condition, while at the fame time there was a
large allowance for this article in his accounts. He
ordered that Minifter to be ftrangled, and his body
to be expofed to view three days before the whole
camp; a fight, which ftruck terror into all, who
had not fo good a claim as the Vifir to be indulg-
ed in robbing the public. The Turks are a people of fierce manners, but they have a fincere regard for juftice. Having given this ftriking leffon, the Sultan paffed the Danube, took and de-
molifhed the towns of *Lippa* and *Titul*, and marched to give battle to General *Veterani*, who convinced him by experience, that the intrepidity of a commander is not fufficient to enfure victory, when his
foldiers are difheartened. The Janizaries were broke,
and

Y. 1695. and took to flight, with several Bashaws at their head : the first that came in the Sultan's way was named *Sebabyn* or *Faulcon*: Go, says he, *thou art but a Crane that drawest other Cranes after thee. I'll set thee a different example.* The Sultan had a drawn scymetar in his hand: the runaways faced about, and returned to the charge: Veterani was wounded, the Imperialists were worsted and retreated (*a*). Under a great Prince, all the springs of government get strength together; and Mustapha was scarce seated on the throne, before he had thought of every thing. The Turkish marine was fallen to absolute ruin. The Venetians, pursuing their successes, had taken the isle of Chio, and from thence gave law to the sea. Their fleet was astonished as at a prodigy, to see a Turkish squadron of such strength, that they durst not stand a battle. The island was again reduced under the Ottoman yoke; and the Sultan, victorious by sea and land, returned to triumph in his capital (*b*).

The immutability of the Ottoman power is an object that may well occasion some surprize; for, from the battle of Vienna to the present time, it has lost nothing but a few conquered cities in Hungary. In order to overturn that Colossus, it must be attacked by a single Christian power of equal strength; but it is better perhaps to let it stand, since providence permits it; besides, it is sparing the blood of Christians as well as Infidels. When they are told of the danger they would be in, if all the Christian Princes should unite against them, they answer, that their Emperor is like a Lion, who never fears the barking of little dogs; and they appeal to the time of the Crusades.

When intelligence of the Sultan's success was brought to Warsaw, it raised the most dismal ap-

(*a*) Cantemir, tom. ii. p. 237.   (*b*) Ibid. p. 239.

prehenfions of his future attempts. He had in effect formed a defign to chaftife the republic in fuch
a manner as never to fear it any more, efpecially
now it was deprived of the protection of its hero,
who grew daily more incapable of defending it.

It was impoffible for the republic to fubfift long
in its prefent violent ftate. The King, who was
more concerned at it than at his own diforder, was
inceffantly exhorting the grandees to peace. He reminded them of all that he had done for the wel-
fare of Poland, of his labours and his victories, of
the wealth he had conferred upon them, of the oath
they had taken to promote the public good, and
of the love they owed their country, which is the
moft facred of all obligations.

The Senate, being delivered from the clamours
of the Equeftrian Order, by the diffolution of the
diet, hoped to carry on its deliberations with more
tranquillity; but the Lithuanian Senators, out of
hatred to the Bifhop of Wilna, propofed the exclufion of all Bifhops from the Senate. But this propofal was a direct violation of the conftitution, and
too unjuft to be maintained; they therefore defifted
from it, and the Bifhops took their feats as ufual.

The firft refolution they agreed in, was to imitate
the conduct of the Roman Senate in times of great
danger. An order was iffued to all the Palatinates
to take care that the republic received no detriment,
ne quid detrimenti refpublica capiat. After this order, which was rather calculated to afcertain the
greatnefs of the danger than to prevent its arrival,
they proceeded to propofe different expedients.

Some were for affembling the Pofpolite *(a)* to
oppofe the enemy abroad, while the Senate fhould
endeavour to reftore peace at home.

(a) The letters that are fent round to affemble this body of
troops, are called *Litteræ eflium.*

Others

Others voted for a diet on horſeback, called *Co-mitia paludata*, which conſiſts of the Senate and the body of Deputies aſſembled under arms in the open field. Its operations are much more deciſive than thoſe of an ordinary diet, called *Comitia togata*; becauſe, in a diviſion of opinions, the ſabre deter-mines the debate *(a)*.

While the Senate was thus deliberating, without coming to any concluſion, the Equeſtrian Order were thinking of a *Rokoſz*, a word of dreadful meaning, which denotes the utmoſt diſorder ima-ginable. All the nobles, by virtue of the *Rokoſz*, are obliged to take up arms in defence, as they ſay, of their country; but the confederacy is in fact al-ways formed againſt the King and the Senate. They ſwear *in caput & animam*, by their lives and ſouls: an oath of bloody import.

The republic was terrified at her own ſituation, and continued in a ſtate of ſuſpence, without re-ſolving on any thing. It was in vain to look up to the King; for he was no longer poſſeſſed of that vigour and prudence, which had ſo often preſerved her from ruin. That ſhe did not periſh in this juncture, was wholly owing to her laws. A ſtate, which is governed by their authority, may indeed feel convulſions; but it is like the trembling of the earth between chains of mountains, which hinder its frame from being diſſolved.

But whatever became of the nation, the Senate reſolved to ſhew its authority in a matter that could not but pleaſe the multitude. The Jew, Bethſal, made himſelf daily more odious: a hundred at-tempts were made to aſſaſſinate him; but his pru-dence always prevented the effects of the public hatred. He had in his pay a guard of thirty Poliſh nobles, who were intereſted to preſerve the life of a man who kept them from want. He was, upon the

the whole, a fort of prime Minifter rather than a farmer of the revenue. The Jews confidered themfelves as living under the protection of a fecond Mordecai in the reign of Ahafuerus ; but the Poles looked upon him as a public peft. Thofe, who had purchafed of him the favours of the court, were the firft to complain of, and accufe, him. He was condemned to death, notwithftanding the efforts of the King, who had but juft intereft enough to fave his life ; which he dragged along in mifery the reft of his days, and at laft died infolvent. The phyfician Jonas narrowly efcaped being facrificed, on account of his connections with Bethfal ; but it was thought too hard to deprive the King of a phyfician in whom he placed great confidence.

It feemed as if fortune took a pleafure in trying his patience to the utmoft ; for to the vexations he underwent at home, there were added others abroad. Bruffels was bombarded by the French ; and his daughter, the Electrefs of Bavaria, who was big with child and feparated from her hufband, was then in the town. The Queen of Poland told Polignac, that the King of France acquired great honour by bombarding women ; and that, if he was fo much bent upon burning towns, Amfterdam might fatisfy him. The Abbot, with all his eloquence, was much at a lofs for an excufe.

The time drew near, when the King of Poland was to end his reign, his life, and his fufferings. It was now four years fince he had given up the command of the army ; he had lately even quitted the frontier, where his prefence kept the enemy in awe, and fixed his refidence at Warfaw, on account of the ruined ftate of his health. He laboured, at the fame time, under the effects of his old wounds, the gout, the gravel, many fymptoms of a dropfy, and a great difficulty of breathing ; and it was uncertain by which he would fall. He daily loft
some

some portion of that ætherial fire which animates the human frame; nor could the furs, in which he lay wrapped upon a couch, restore to him either motion or spirits.

The Turks and Tartars had some knowledge of his condition; but they considered him as a Lion, to whom the other animals shew respect, even when he is asleep. They attempted nothing of importance, at a time when they might have done what they pleased: only a few Tartars made their incursions, which were restrained by the Grand-General Jablonowski.

A circumstance still more extraordinary is, that the King's illness contributed also to save the nation from its own madness. Being just upon the point of losing him, its attention was more taken up with the thoughts of a future leader, than with the divisions that had disturbed its peace for the three last years. They who carried their views beyond their own country, were divided between the Electors of Bavaria and Saxony, and the Prince of Conti: they, who were for chusing at home, mentioned Jablonowski or Konski: the Partizans of the present Royal Family, talked of Prince James, or Prince Alexander. The Queen was accused of designing to share her crown and her bed with the Grand-General Jablonowski, to the prejudice of her own issue; and in case she could not succeed, of procuring the crown for Prince Alexander, preferably to her elder son. In the latter case, as well as in the former, she would have gratified her affections and her ambition together; since Prince Alexander's youth, and the tender attachment he had for his mother, seemed to ensure her of governing long in his name.

Thus were they contending for the spoils of a King who was still alive, till the time came, when money, intrigue, or force should decide to whom
they

they were to belong. There were certainly many unhappy perfons in the kingdom during the time that the King's illnefs made him drop the reins of government; but he himfelf was perhaps the moft unhappy of all.

He was convinced by experience of that melancholy truth which he had told his wife, before he mounted the throne, that he fhould be a mark for the malice of men to aim at, even of fuch as would have moft reafon to be his friends. In fact, as faft as he conferred favours, the number of ungrateful perfons feemed to multiply. He had loaded the Sapiehas with power, wealth and honours; and the Sapiehas had oppofed his meafures upon many occafions, and were even fufpected of having confpired to deprive him of the crown. He had made Wielopolfki, Grand-Chancellor of the crown; and Wielopolfki, though his brother-in-law, had entered into a fufpicious correfpondence with the Sapiehas. He had raifed Radziowfki to the fummit of grandeur; and Radziowfki, though his coufin-german, was at this time concerting meafures for proclaiming the Prince of Conti, and excluding his benefactor's family. The Chriftian league ftill held together, and he was no longer its hero. After fo many ufelefs attempts upon Moldavia and Walachia, he left Kaminieck in the hands of the Infidels. The time was juft approaching, when the confederates were to reap the fruits of the league. Prince Eugene, who took the place of Prince Lewis of Baden, of the Duke of Lorrain, and what is ftill more, of the King of Poland, was preparing to put a glorious end to this long war; and the Turks, being at length irrecoverably beat in a decifive battle at *Zenta*, upon the Teyfs, were going to yield up the Morea to the Venetians, Tranfylvania to the Emperor, Azoph to the Mufcovites, and Kaminieck to the Poles. But the veil of futurity as yet

concealed

concealed all thefe advantages ; and the King, in
the few eafy moments that his acute pains left him,
had a profpect of nothing but misfortunes : his
kingdom difturbed by factions within, and attacked
by enemies without ; the crown, which he had gained by merit, and worn with glory, juft going to become a prey to factions ; uncertain, whether it would
continue in his family ; and that family, by feparating into different interefts, compleating the anxieties
of his mind.

In this fituation, he gave up every thing to fortune ; and, next to the confolations of religion, had
recourfe to letters and philofophy for mitigating the
evils he felt. Polignac and Vota, who never quitted him and well knew his tafte, were admirably
qualified to ferve him in this capacity. But the
Abbot was as much fuperior to the Jefuit, as the
manners of the world are more pleafing than the
education of the fchools and the cloifter. The
King often turned the converfation upon France,
where he had formerly travelled ; and commended
the politenefs, the gaiety, and the bravery of the
French nobles ; but blamed that flexibility of manners which receives the impreffions of evil as well
as good ; which treats vice with refpect, provided it
be not ridiculous ; and that too great pleafantry of
temper, which makes them capable of laughing
when their country has caufe to weep. He could
not excufe them for quitting old names that were
made famous by their anceftors, to take new ones
from their eftates ; a fource of confufion which
leaves no mark of diftinction between upftarts who
buy, and the old family that fells. Polignac alfo
in his turn cenfured the Polifh Lords, but with the
referve that becomes a ftranger, whofe bufinefs it is
to gain the affections of the nation he has to do
with. The Queen, who was more than ever engaged in bufinefs, was charmed that the King had
                                                              found

found two men that he liked, to divert his leisure and mitigate his pains. The Cardinal of Arquien, who had acquired neither genius, nor knowledge, by being invested with the Roman Purple, served as a foil in the conversation by the thoughtless simplicity of his sayings, and the stories he told of his former military life.

In the mean time, the accounts that were given at Warsaw of the King's condition, were widely different from one another. The courtiers, who are never believed whether they represent things in a favourable or unfavourable light, asserted that his abilities were not at all impaired. They who had reasons to wish for a change, represented him as a mere empty shadow both of a King and a man. The real truth was, that his ideas of the great machine of government were not so clear as usual, but he still retained a strong sense of his personal and domestic misfortunes, nor was he insensible of those of the republic.

During this whole winter of 1696, weekly reports of his death were spread over Europe and Asia. At the approach of spring, the increasing warmth of the sun seemed to revive in him a few sparks of life, and he went to his fine gardens at Villanow to breath a purer air; but he was too far gone to enjoy it. The physicians prescribed the use of foreign baths; but a King of Poland cannot leave his dominions, without the consent of the republic. The Senate met on the second of June, and gave him leave to seek a cure wherever he thought proper; but a series of unexpected accidents prevented his making use of that permission. His Jewish physician gave him mercury, perhaps in too great a quantity: the King felt its violent effects, and cried out, *Is there no one that will revenge my death?* The Jew trembled at these words, not only upon his own account, but upon that of

his

his brethren, well knowing how eagerly, every pretence to worry them is laid hold of; for the prophecy must be fulfilled at all events.

The King, when he recovered a little from his pain, and saw his bed surrounded by Bishops, who might make a bad use of what he had said, blamed his own hastiness, and attributed his death to the violence of the disorder, and the necessary imperfection of the art of physic. He even affected to speak kindly of the Jews, and of the assistance they had frequently given him (a).

The Queen, who was uneasy both at the present and the future, thought that no time should be lost to prevail upon him to make his will. The Treasure he had amassed was laid up in the castles of Warsaw, Mariemburg, and Zolkiew; and it was of great consequence to the Queen, that he should dispose of it. She wished also that he would recommend Prince Alexander to the republic to fill the vacant throne, without relinquishing her own desire of filling it with Jablonowski, if fortune should favour her scheme.

The person that she employed to negotiate the affair of the will, was a Bishop who was entirely at her devotion. Details of this sort may perhaps be unimportant in themselves; but nothing that relates to the last moments of great men, can deserve that title. The Prelate was greatly embarrassed with the word *Will*, as if it were impossible for a man of courage to face death, which only transmits him to a better life. He therefore armed himself with certain texts of Scripture (as he knew that the King had a taste for erudition) which seemed to give hopes of his recovery, as it was a means of making his subjects happy. The King replied to this argument, by quoting other texts, which seem to imply that God does not always consult the happiness

(a) Zaluski, tom. iii. p. 5.

4   or

or misery of men, in disposing of the life of Kings : But then, added the Bishop, we will pray so earnestly for your health—and I am now going to my diocese to give orders for public prayers—*I should like the prayers better*, says the King, *if they were put up without orders. Take my advice, and stay at court; you will have time enough to grow weary of your residence at Ploczko.* " That, replied the Bishop, is what I never am; because when I have discharged my pastoral functions, I spend the rest of my time very agreeably with St. Ambrose, St. Chrysostom, Isocrates and Plato; but reflecting lately that all these great men are dead, I made my will."——*Your will*, cried the King, bursting into a laugh, and repeating this line of Juvenal!

——*O medici, mediam pertundite venam.*

" Physicians, open the vein in his forehead to restore him to his senses—He fancies that the living cannot settle their affairs without the consent of the dead."

The Bishop now drew nearer to his point, and endeavoured to convince him that it would be for the benefit of his family, and perhaps of the whole kingdom, to commit his last orders to writing. At this, the King grew serious, and said, " What mischief can I possibly prevent by this means? Do you not see that there is no such thing as integrity left; that a spirit of madness has seized the Polish nation; and can I flatter myself with the hopes of restoring order by my last will? The misery of Royalty is, that we are not obeyed, while we are alive; and can it be expected that we should be obeyed, after we are dead?

To understand what he added with regard to his family, it must be observed, that in Poland the laws

are

are more favourable to executors than to heirs. The former are always chosen among the great, and often abuse their power to keep the estate to themselves. For this reason the King added : " I " commend him, who, in his life-time, does good " to his relations and friends : but how can he be " sure, that what he leaves at his death, will come " to them ? What is become of the testamentary " regulations of the Kings my predecessors ? In a " nation where *gold* governs, it is *silver* that sits " upon the bench : and you would still have me " make a will ! Let me hear no more of it *(a)*".

At this moment the Queen came in, and read the refusal in the Bishop's countenance. She immediately composed her own, and hoped to find a more favourable opportunity ; but that opportunity never came.

On the 17th of June, being Trinity-Sunday, the King took a walk in his garden at Villanow. He even dined with some appetite, and shewed other symptoms of being better ; but death was busy within him all the while. A few hours after, he was seized with a fit of an apoplexy, in the midst of the Royal Family, and fell motionless upon the floor. In about an hour, he recovered his senses ; and regretting, as it were, being waked out of this sleep of death, in which he was insensible of the miseries of life, he said, in a language that was familiar to him, *stava bena*, I was well. Every face, but his own, was froze with terror. He bore his sufferings with the firmness of a Soldier, a Philosopher, and a Christian ; and employed his last moments in endeavouring to convince his children of the necessity of their living in the closest union. He conjured the Queen to have no other interest in view but theirs, if she desired to preserve the crown in her family ; recommending it to them all to fol-

(a) Zaluski, tom. iii. p. 7.

low

low the advice of Polignac, who had merited, he said, their confidence and his.　He exhorted alſo the Senators, who were preſent, to preſerve mutual concord, for the good of the republic ; whoſe wel-fare would be an objeȼt of his wiſhes, even in the preſence of the great ſource of all Power, before whom he ſhould ſo ſoon appear ; and he died, like Auguſtus, on the ſame day of the year that he was raiſed to the throne ; in the ſixty-ſixth year of his age, and the twenty-third of his reign *(a)*.

Were I to write his Elogium, I ſhould tranſcribe the oration, which the *Staroſt of Odolanowſki*, now *King Staniſlas of Poland*, then but nineteen years old, made at his funeral before the houſe of Deputies ; and by tranſcribing it, I ſhould do honour both to the early eloquence of the young orator, and to the me-mory of the Prince whom he praiſed.　The Staroſt ſhewed only the bright ſide of his hero's charaȼter ; but an hiſtorian is bound alſo to point out his faults.

What happened, even before his aſhes were cold, may ſerve to convince Kings that poſterity will judge them without mercy.　The Poles forgot that they had loſt a hero, and remembered only that he had broke his word with the republic.　He had engaged by his *Paȼta Conventa*, to raiſe two forts, where-ever it ſhould be thought neceſſary, and they ſaw only one ; to found an academy for the education of three hundred gentlemen, and he had not done it ; to ſatisfy the Eleȼtor of Brandenburg for his

(a) Moreri, in his Diȼtionary, and Maſſuet, the author of the revolutions of Poland, make him to be ſeventy-two, when he died. This Chronological miſtake is not indeed of ſuch dangerous conſe-quence as the many hiſtorical lies, which change white into black, and black into white.　I take notice, however, of this trivial fault, with a view of teaching thoſe who undertake to write hiſtory, that the firſt buſineſs of an hiſtorian is to doubt.　If Moreri and Maſſuet had read Zaluſki, tom. ii. p. 1169, and Lengnich, p. 269, they would have known Sobieſki's age.

Y. 1696. claims upon the town of Elbing, and had neglected to do it; and it was feared that this omission would one day occasion a war that might be fatal to Poland. He had promised particularly to retake Kaminieck, and had miscarried in his attempts. It is indeed extremely difficult for human prudence to find its way through the labyrinth of events. Notwithstanding his many victories over the Turks, Sobieski could never wrest out of their hands that important fortress; and his successor recovered it at the peace of Carlowitz, in 1699, without striking a blow.

His memory was also reproached with the acquisitions he had made in Poland; though the law expressly forbids the King to encrease his possessions; with his fondness for the Queen, whom he had permitted to meddle with affairs of state, to the detriment of the public; with his endeavours to secure the crown to Prince James, without waiting for the suffrages of the nation; with the extortions of Bethsal the Jew; with the adulteration of the coin; with the useless wars he had been engaged in since the beginning of the Christian league, which had cost Poland at least two hundred thousand men, and more millions of money than would have sufficed to make the kingdom rich.

Instead of lamenting the King's death, the only thing thought of was disputing about his wealth.

The Queen claimed it as her right: Prince James designed to seize it by open force: the Grand Marshal and part of the Senate pretended that it belonged to the republic. After all, this mighty treasure, which occasioned so much noise, and was amassed at the head of a kingdom and an army, would have been thought but a moderate fortune for a Commissary-General of stores in the country where it was carried. It amounted to between five and six millions,

lions, which the Abbé de Polignac, in concert with the Queen, had the address to get conveyed into France, that Prince James might not make use of it to gain the crown, which Lewis XIV. wanted to place upon the head of the Prince of Conti ; but public fame represented it as a much greater sum.

The King of Poland loved money, nor did he deny the charge ; but they who imputed it to him as a crime, should also have owned, that he knew how to lay it out for the advantage of Poland. During the whole time that he commanded in the Ukraine, when he was only Grand-General, his money was of more service to him than his troops, against those prodigious armies of Tartars and Cossacks, which overran the territories of the republic ; and it was a common thing with the Poles, to talk publickly of the *new year's-gifts of the Tartars*. We have seen that in the great expedition of Vienna, he opened his treasures ; and it was well known, that he used them to procure creatures in all the courts of Europe. In the field, his spies extolled his liberality, and no one was better served. His maxim was, never to lay out his money uselesly ; for this reason it was, that so many worthless grandees accused him of avarice. It is true, that towards the end of his life, his frugality grew still more remarkable : he saw the unfavourable disposition of the Poles towards his children, and had a mind to console them for the loss of the crown, by leaving them wealth enough, if they should miss it : a fault which is very excusable, when we reflect that he was a father.

The misfortunes that befel his family are a lesson to the children of Kings, that, for want of mutual concord, they may lose all the advantages of their birth. Prince James, before he had lost all hope of succeeding his father, was pursued sword in hand in a provincial diet, ; and instead of a throne, met with a prifon at Leipfick ; from which he was at length releafed, in order to go and live in Silefia, a fubject to the Houfe of Auftria. Prince Conftantine, having made his efcape out of the fame prifon, went and married in Poland, like a private gentleman. His wife was a German Baronefs, one of the maids of honour to the Princefs of Newburg : a match to which he was prompted by love, and attempted to get rid of afterwards, when it was too late. Prince Alexander went to refide at Rome, where the Pope refufed to fee him, on account of the honours he claimed ; nor did he receive them at laft but upon his death-bed, and in the habit of a Capuchin : having taken the vows of that order in his laft agony, as a means to enfure, as he imagined, his falvation. The Queen, their mother, fpent alfo many years among the Princes of the church ; but was at laft tired of that fituation, and came to die in her own country, in the caftle of Blois, which Lewis XIV. gave her for her laft afylum.

The name of Sobiefki is extinct, but the family ftill fubfifts in the female line, and his pofterity is well known in Europe. The prefent Elector of Bavaria, far more happy than the Emperor his father, in governing only his hereditary dominions ; the young hero whom England difowns, and whom France would be glad to place upon the throne of his anceftors ; and another Prince, whom the bare name of Turenne would fufficiently endear to France ; are all three great-grandfons of the famous Sobiefki, and all three are worthy of their great anceftor.

Thofe who hated, and thofe who envied the King of Poland, gave him, even before his death, the name of *Vefpafian.* If he had one of that Emperor's faults, the love of money, he was alfo poffeffed of his virtues. Like him, he was raifed to

the

the throne by his military services. The charms
of his wit, the readiness with which he spoke several languages, his acquaintance with polite litera-
ture, the agreeableness of his conversation, the
gentleness of his manners, his sincerity in friendship,
his conjugal tenderness, and paternal affection; all
these qualities, which would have made him an
amiable man in private life, would not have been
sufficient for his exalted station. Endued with great
strength of body and activity of mind, deeply read
in the laws of his country, acquainted with the
interest of foreign nations, and versed in the theory
of war, equally eloquent in the diet, and enterprizing in the field, he convinced his countrymen, before he was raised to the throne, of his capacity to
govern and defend them. He possessed, in an eminent degree, most of the virtues that become a
royal station. He did justice to his enemies, as
well as to his friends; and always behaved to the
latter, in the same manner as when he wanted their
assistance to gain the crown. The warmth of his
temper made him soon take fire; but his heart was
void of malice. His cruelty to the Turks, after
a victory, must be attributed to a remnant of the
crusading spirit, which upon these occasions, and
these only, soured the natural humanity of his temper, which was not sufficiently matured by philosophy. He was often affronted in such a state as
Poland, where liberty is always upon the watch
against the hand that governs; and yet he never
lifted up that hand but against those who offended
their country. His zeal for religion was free from
the acrimony of an intolerating spirit; Greeks,
Protestants, Jews, and some remains of the Socinians, lived in peace under his government; and
this was no small matter, at a time, when other
Catholic powers were banishing or massacring their
subjects, in order to convert them. The dignity
of

Y. 1696. of a King did not obliterate from his mind the principles of a citizen, and he assembled the nation much oftener than any of his predecessors. He spent his reign in the Senate, in the midst of diets, and in the fatigues of war; he never thought that the Palace of a King should be appropriated to magnificence and luxury; but made himself thoroughly acquainted with men and things. In concerting the plan of his campaigns, he listened to every one, but was determined by himself alone; and knowing how necessary the presence of a King is, for the purposes of discipline, celerity, and even victory, he always headed his troops in person, till the badness of his health prevented him. His country always admired, and would perhaps have loved him, if a free people were not always jealous of their liberty; perhaps too, if he had been less fond of the Queen. He had the singular glory of humbling the Ottoman power, which for a long time had humbled the Princes of Christendom. All Europe sought his alliance; and Poland acquired an importance under his government, which it has but ill preserved. Charles XII. the Alexander of the north, lamented his death in these emphatical terms: *So great a King ought never to have died*; but history is more severe than Princes.

The truly great King of Poland will be he, who, leaving the Turks and Tartars in peace, and turning his attention towards a fertile soil, fine rivers, and the Baltic and Black Seas, shall introduce shipping, manufactures, commerce, wealth and inhabitants into this great kingdom; who shall abolish the Tribunitian power of the *liberum veto*, to govern the nation by a plurality of suffrages; who shall teach the nobles, that the peasants who supply them with food, and are descended from the Sarmatians their common ancestors, are men; and who, in imitation of a greater King of France than either

Clovis

Clovis or Charlemagne, shall extirpate that civil Y. 1696.
pest of servitude, which destroys emulation, industry, arts, sciences, honour, and prosperity. Then
may every Pole join in saying:

Namque erit ille mibi semper Deus.

ENd of the NINTH and last Book.

INDEX.

INDEX.

A.

INDEX.

Escapes

. I N D E X.

Advan-

Dif-

INDEX.

Gravel

INDEX.

Mag-

INDEX.

K k 4

Particu-

Michael

His

Attends

Soon

Returns

INDEX.

INDEX.

Takes

I N D E X.

W.

.INDEX.

W.

F I N I S.